Br

"This lush urban fanta
Sunspears, and Shadc
delight of dark chocola
book."

—Ann Aguirre, national bestselling author of *Blue Diablo*

"In *Bitter Night,* Diana Pharaoh Francis has created a dark, unique, and electrifying world in the urban fantasy genre. . . . Max is a Shadowblade warrior to die for."

—Faith Hunter, author of *Skinwalker*

. . . And for the Novels of Diana Pharaoh Francis

"An original world, real people, and high-stakes intrigue and adventure. Great fun!"

—*New York Times* bestselling author Patricia Briggs

"Francis grabbed me with her very first sentence and didn't let go."

—Lynn Flewelling, author of the Nightrunner series

"Diana Pharaoh Francis caught me with a compelling story, intrigued me with the magic . . . and swept me away with her masterful feel for the natural world."

—Carol Berg, author of *Breath and Bone*

"Well-plotted and exhibiting superior characterization."

—*Booklist*

"As tasty as toasted almonds."

—Speculative Romance Online Magazine

"One of fantasy's most promising new voices."

—David B. Coe, award-winning author of *The Horsemen's Gambit*

BITTER NIGHT

A HORNGATE WITCHES BOOK

Diana Pharaoh Francis

Pocket Books
New York London Toronto Sydney

Pocket Books
A Division of Simon & Schuster, Inc.
1230 Avenue of the Americas
New York, NY 10020

First Pocket Books paperback edition November 2009

Designed by Jacquelynne Hudson
Cover illustration by Chad Michael Ward

Manufactured in the United States of America

10 9 8 7 6 5 4 3 2 1

ISBN 978-1-4165-9814-5
ISBN 978-1-4165-9819-0 (ebook)

To Tony, Q-ball and Syd.

Acknowledgments

As usual, I have a lot of people to thank for helping me create *Bitter Night*. So many, in fact, that I may have inadvertently forgotten someone. If so, I apologize and please know it was not intentional.

To start with, I want to thank Lucienne Diver and Jennifer Heddle for believing in this book and giving me the chance to tell this story. Without them, you wouldn't be reading this book right now.

Next, I want to thank those of you who helped me in my research. First off, thank you, Traci Castleberry. She kindly went and took pictures of locations in San Diego and also gave me a great deal of information about the place. Thanks also to Maryelizabeth Hart, Anne Ugaretechea and Jessica DeMilo. Thanks also to Fighter Guy for his usual amazing help with fighting and guns.

Next, I have to thank those of you who read this book in draft and gave me brilliant feedback to improve it: Missy Sawmiller, Megan Schaffer, Christy Keyes and Kenna. But most of all Ilona Andrews, whose feedback gave me the tools to dig much deeper into my characters and make this book so much better.

I want to thank also those people who read my blog

and answer my desperate calls for information. You have been invaluable, and not only for information, but also for encouragement and support. Writing is a lonely business and you have made it far less so.

As always, my family has been incredibly giving and supportive and amazingly patient with me and I thank them with all my heart.

Finally, thank you, my readers. Thank you to all who picked up this book and gave it a chance. I really hope you enjoy it and I would love to hear from you. Please visit my website and leave a comment on the blog or send me an email: www.dianapfrancis.com.

BITTER NIGHT

MAX'S PHONE RANG. IT WAS SET TO A HIGH-pitched tone that most humans couldn't hear. But being human hadn't been Max's problem since 1979. She eyed the cell, then reluctantly picked it up out of the console. The caller ID said it was Giselle. Instantly Max's body seized tight. All the Zen detachment she'd scraped together on the long drive from the covenstead in Montana shattered apart as craptastic reality returned in a shitflood.

She drew a deep breath. Her lungs felt like rocks. She exhaled slowly before flipping open her phone. "Yeah?"

"Where are you?"

Max grimaced. Just the sound of the witch's voice ignited familiar hate in her gut. It was like a bottomless volcano. She swallowed the heat down, tasting its bitterness with determined satisfaction. She banked it like a campfire. It belonged to her—the only thing that did, and the witch-bitch could never take it away. "Coming into Barstow. Why?"

"I want you to go check out a nasty little murder near Julian. It tastes of both the Uncanny and the Divine."

"Don't you think that's a little stupid? You can't just go fucking around in another witch's territory. It could mean war if I get caught. Are you ready for that?"

Giselle didn't hesitate. "It's a risk I have to take. The vision was—"

She broke off and Max wondered what it was she'd stopped herself from saying.

"It was too powerful to ignore," Giselle continued. "I have to know what's going on there. Just look around and get out." She gave a pained sigh. "And, Max, I shouldn't have to tell you this, but do not *accidentally on purpose* let anyone see you."

"Why would I do that?" Max replied all too innocently. "I couldn't anyhow. You tied me up in compulsion spells. They would never let me do anything you didn't want me to do, right?" Except there were ways around the spells. And Max had made herself an expert at them. "Besides, you know how I feel about you. Your wish is my fondest command."

Silence. "Then I wish you wouldn't be such a pain in my ass all the time. Stop trying to sabotage everything I do. This is important, Max. Don't screw it up."

The tense uneasiness in Giselle's voice triggered a cascade of alarms inside Max. It was like a switch was flipped inside her as her compulsion spells took over. Her anger cooled instantly and every one of her magically heightened senses strained to hard alertness. She sat up in her seat. If one thing was true about Giselle, it was that the witch-bitch didn't get nervous. As far as Max knew, she didn't have the gene. Just what had been in that vision? What sort of apocalypse was going down in Julian?

There wasn't any point in asking. Giselle would already have told her if she was going to say anything.

"Anything else I need to know?" Max asked, turning businesslike as she allowed the predator inside her to take over. Cold detachment slid over her like armor, and her mind focused into sharp, clear lines. It wasn't that she couldn't feel. She just didn't want her emotions to interfere with what she might have to do. She gave a slight shake of her head. No, it was that her spells wouldn't *allow* her feelings to get in the way, which only made doing what she had to do that much worse. Better to become ice and deal with the thaw later. Much later.

"There's an orchard north of town," Giselle said, interrupting her thoughts. "That's where it's going to happen."

"Going to?"

"In a couple of hours, give or take. It's fixed, you can't stop it. I'll see you in San Diego tomorrow." Giselle stopped, but didn't hang up. Then: "Max—be careful. This might be ugly."

The phone went dead. Max looked at it a moment, hesitating, then speed-dialed a number. Oz answered in one ring.

"Max? What's wrong?"

"Does something have to be wrong for me to call you?" she asked, then winced. *Ask a stupid question . . .*

"I've been with Giselle almost as long as you have. In all that time, you've never called me except when the shit's in the fire. So what is it?"

Max lowered her phone to her lap, thinking. Oz said her name impatiently. She stared down the freeway.

Should she say anything? But the undiluted worry in Giselle's voice prodded her. She lifted the phone back to her ear. "I've got a feeling something bad's coming, and I can't shake it. Just make sure you and your Sun-spears stick tight to Giselle. Have my Blades do the same."

She could almost hear his grin. "If I didn't know better, I'd think you actually cared about her."

"Don't make me kick your ass. I told you, if anybody gets to kill Giselle, it's going to be me. In the meantime, keep her in one piece until I get there."

"When is that?"

"By morning, if nothing goes wrong. I've got a stop to make first."

Max didn't give him the chance to answer or ask questions. She snapped her phone shut and dropped it back onto the console before swerving off onto the shoulder and grinding to a dusty halt in the desert darkness.

According to her atlas, Julian was about a hundred and fifty miles away in the mountains. The drive would take her almost three hours, but it didn't matter when she got there. The murder was fixed. She closed her eyes, leaning her head back on the headrest, rubbing her fingers over the spot between her eyebrows. It wasn't her job to help people. She was no one's knight in shining armor. She was a killer, Giselle's favorite weapon. Besides, even if she could get to Julian in time, nothing said that anyone there was worth saving. She swallowed hard. Giselle had said the murder tasted of the Uncanny and the Divine. So that meant that whoever was mixed up in this likely deserved it.

Her stomach didn't believe it. She reached for the steering wheel again. Her stomach didn't get a vote. Besides, she hadn't eaten for hours. She was just hungry.

Max pulled back onto Highway 15 and hit the gas. It was nearing ten o'clock, and behind her lights beaded in the darkness coming down the hill from Las Vegas. In Victorville she pulled off and stopped at a McDonald's.

In the parking lot, she considered going through the drive-through, but her bladder had other ideas. She glanced through the dark-tinted windshield, considering. It was a night short of the full moon and not a cloud in the sky. Grabbing her leather jacket from the backseat, she pulled it on and zipped it up to hide the .45 in the holster against her left ribs and the knife sheaths on her forearms. She had a .380 strapped to her right ankle and another double-bladed combat knife in the small of her back.

She yanked her Big Sky Brewing Company hat down low over her sunglasses and short silver-blond hair and pulled up the collar high on her coat.

Pocketing her keys, she opened the door of the Chevy Tahoe. Instantly she felt the burn as the brilliant moonlight bubbled her skin. The reflected sunlight seared the backs of her hands, a seam on her neck, and the unshadowed portion of her face. There was a faint sizzle and the nauseating smell of burning hair. She grimaced and strode quickly to the door, heading straight for the bathroom. There was no one in the dining area to notice the blisters, or that as she walked between the tables, her skin smoothed back into flawless marble. She ignored the unrelenting itchiness that followed after, a side effect of her healing spells.

Inside the bathroom she peed and splashed her face. The compulsion spells that required her to protect and obey Giselle sent pulsing aches down Max's spine to her heels. They read her worry and wanted her to hustle off to the witch's side to protect her. They didn't care much about what Max's orders were, only that Giselle be kept safe. *She's got plenty of protection,* Max told herself. *Oz and his Sunspears and all of my Shadowblades are with her. My absence won't do any harm.*

She returned to the dining room and ordered forty double cheeseburgers and a large Coke. Todd, the pimple-faced cashier, lifted his brows.

"You gonna eat all those yourself?"

Max laid a fifty and a twenty on the counter, her brows flicking up. "Do I look that hungry?"

"Naw. You don't look like you eat much."

His glance was admiring. Max could imagine what he saw. A pretty girl a few years older than him, looking sly and tough and wild like a biker chick or a metal band's roadie. She was taboo and exotic—every high school boy's wet dream. If only he knew what she really was—how many people she'd killed. He'd start running for the hills and wouldn't stop until he hit Canada, and maybe not even then. She did her best to look sweet and harmless.

"So you going to a party or somethin'? I get off soon. Maybe you want to go together?" he asked hopefully.

Her gaze ran over him. He was maybe seventeen and cute beneath the ugly uniform and acne. His face was still curved with baby fat, but in a few years he was going to be a lady-killer. She felt her face hardening. In a few years, he'd be a tempting target for a witch. He blanched at the sudden violence in her expression and took a step back. She heard his heart start to race and smelled the sour scent of fear. In a minute he'd pee his pants.

Fuck. She grabbed her change and the Coke cup and went to fill it. She leaned her hip against a bolted-down chair and studied the floor until her burgers were ready. *No danger here. No danger here.* She repeated it to herself, hoping Todd would feel it and believe. When he plopped the two grocery-size sacks on the counter, she grabbed them without a word and strode out the door.

In a few minutes she was back on the freeway. With effort she put Todd from her mind and began eating. The burgers were hot, greasy, and tasty. She gobbled one after another. The magic in her body sped up her metabolism so that she required around twenty to thirty thousand calories on a normal day. That was if nothing tried to kill her, if she didn't have to pick up a car and throw it, if she didn't have to run fifty miles in a couple of hours . . . in short, if she didn't have to use the spells that made her what she now was—a Shadowblade.

In forging a coven, a witch created warriors to serve and protect her. Some took their power from the sun, the dark poisoning them. Some took their power from shadows, the sun—even reflected from the moon—burning their flesh. Sunspears and Shadowblades. Max was Giselle's Shadowblade Prime—leader of the thirteen Blades in her crew. Oz was her Sunspear counterpart.

She sighed, finishing the last of the burgers and fiddling with the stereo. Guns N' Roses's "Mr. Brownstone" began pumping through the speakers. Max turned it up so that she couldn't hear anything else. She had a bad feeling that in the next few days, she was going to need a whole lot of calories. This trip was going to be nothing but trouble.

SHE PULLED INTO JULIAN JUST BEFORE 2 A.M. IT NESTLED in the desert mountains northeast of San Diego. It was small and dusty—there hadn't been a lot of rain this year. The moon had gone down and Max had the windows open. In the distance she could smell the salt brine blowing up from the Pacific Ocean. Overlaying it were the scents of pine, juniper, and oak, along with the hot tang of apples and grapes from nearby orchards. Signs all over the small town invited visitors to come to Harvest Days and the Grape Stomp Fiesta.

Max had turned off her stereo and lights as she came to the city limits and began driving slowly through town. She sifted through the air and eventually found a hint of what she was looking for—the earthy, metallic flavor of the Uncanny, and the creamy, caustic flavor of the Divine. It's not that the two couldn't be found together—she was Uncanny and Giselle was Divine. The basic division between the two was that Uncanny beings lacked the ability to cast spells or share their magic in any way. The Divine could. The obvious conclusion was that a witch was here with her Shadowblades and whatever other pets she might have in tow. And they had killed someone. *Why?* was the question. And what did it have to do with Giselle?

She followed the trail to the other side of town. When she turned north on Farmer Road, the smell of magic billowed suddenly and her hackles rose, cold sliding like oil down her spine. Giselle was right. Something big had happened here—maybe was still happening.

It was time to get out and and go on foot. Max slowed and eased off onto a dirt lane, rolling across an irrigation creek and parking behind a mounding blackberry tangle on the fringe of an apple orchard. She killed the motor and donned her hat again before quietly lifting herself out the window. She reached for and grabbed her cell phone, thumbing it off before tucking it into a roomy thigh pocket on her black fatigues. Next she opened the back door and popped up the bench seat. Beneath it was a small armory of weapons and ammo that included guns and steel knives, flash bombs and grenades, bags of herbs and salt, knives of rowan, hazel, willow, and silver, and a collection of charms. Max ignored most of it, opting for the pistol-grip sawed-off shotgun. It was lousy for distances, but most fights were up close and personal, and it would make enemies of most stripes—magical or human—think twice. She loaded it and shoved a handful of shells into her front pocket before pushing the seat back down and shutting the door.

She turned, letting her senses unravel across the night like a gossamer spiderweb, collecting every last scent, sound, taste, and texture. Nightbirds sang and an owl hooted. She heard the yip of coyotes and the deep bark of angry dogs. A horse whinnied and a calf bawled. Somewhere close, something scritched in the dirt. She cataloged the sounds, sifting through them for anything that didn't belong. But there was nothing. Max swiveled her head, sniffing. The stench of magic overwhelmed almost everything, even the tang of the orchard and the wet, green smell of the irrigation ditch.

Magic slid over her skin like a sticky web, stinging and caressing at once. It was like a runway beacon pointing the way. She slung her shotgun over her shoulder, her right hand wrapping the grip and holding it ready before her. Just in case. She glanced around one more time, then slid like a shadow under the orchard canopy, following the magic.

She broke into a ground-eating jog, zigzagging between the squat trees. Adrenaline pumped through her. Her arms flexed and her stomach tightened, her muscles rolling beneath her skin. She loved this feeling. She felt powerful—like she could pick up the world on her back, like there was nothing she couldn't do. As much as she hated to admit it—and she'd die before she ever told Giselle—being a Shadowblade was better than any other high she could imagine. It was better than being the soft, weak human girl she'd been. Now she was fast, strong, and capable. She didn't wander through her life scared of anything—not roller coasters, not jumping out of airplanes, not the big bad monster in the closet or under the bed. She'd met monsters; she'd killed them. If she could have this feeling of being the hunter and never having to cower helpless—if she could have that without Giselle and without the horrors that went with serving the witch-bitch, then Max would never want anything else. It would be every Christmas and birthday present wrapped into one.

She covered the sloping ground quickly, pausing here and there to test the air and listen. About a mile along, she picked up the first scent of blood. She stopped and dropped to a crouch beside a knobby tree trunk. The coppery flavor marked the blood as human, and there was a lot of it. Enough to cut through the stench of magic. There was Uncanny blood, too. The smell tingled at the back of her throat, tasting hot and corrosive. She didn't recognize it. She scowled, something angry rising hot and hard in her. Suddenly she started running. Someone might be alive. Giselle could be wrong.

A mile farther in, she topped a rise. Between the trees she could glimpse a set of buildings on a hill beyond the orchard. Even from here she could see the lavender witchlight flickering through the trees. The smell of blood was stronger, and there was something else—something wet, cold, and bleak, like winter wind over a frozen lake. It was Divine.

Max crept closer, clinging close to the tree row. She paused every hundred yards to scan the trees and listen, but there was nothing. Everything was silent except for dogs barking some distance away. The din was unrelenting. Dogs knew the stench of magic when they smelled it.

She knew when she stepped into the chaos zone. They used to be called faery circles, but faeries weren't the only cause. The zones were places where magic had exploded out of control. Maybe a spell ruptured, maybe a circle couldn't contain the conjuring, or a ritual had gone haywire. It wouldn't be safe until the magic dissipated, which could be a few seconds or a few centuries.

Max strode inside without hesitation. The protection

spells Giselle had carved into her bones and flesh protected her from most malevolent magics. A little wild magic just cleared her sinuses.

Inside, there were no natural sounds: no nightbirds, no crickets, no mosquitoes, nothing. The barks of the dogs snuffed out like blown birthday candles. Currents of thorny magic twisted in the warm, still air. She jerked as a high shrieking sound wrapped her skull and sent darts of pain down her nerves. She shook her head, crouching low as she jogged forward. When she came to the treeline, she dropped and crawled beneath a John Deere tractor, concealing herself in the shadows of a massive tire.

A nimbus of lavender witchlight surrounded a two-story, red-steel-roofed farmhouse. A white, crushed-gravel drive led down to the road beween lofty, smooth-skinned English walnut trees. It circled the house, corralling a close-clipped lawn dotted with bushes and flowers and a large gazebo covered by climbing roses and grapevines. Behind it was a barn-style garage with a matching red-steel roof that looked big enough to hold six cars. On the other side of the house was a pool. Max could smell the chlorine. A brass-and-iron sign above the steps leading up to the rustic veranda said JULIAN SPRINGS ORCHARDS.

From her vantage point, Max could see four human bodies sprawled on the white gravel. One woman, three men. Trails of blood on the ground indicated they'd been dragged there. There was nothing to say who had done it, nor was there any evidence of ritual in the killing.

A sudden squabbling gabbled up loudly from the other side of the house. Growls and whimpers were followed by a snarling and loud cursing. Max couldn't make out the words. She was pretty sure they weren't speaking any language she knew. Then suddenly the shrieking sound erupted again. It bored into Max's eardrums, made hypersensitive by Giselle's spells. Max pressed her palms against her ears until it stopped.

As soon as the noise died, she crawled out from under the tractor and ran down the low hill to the driveway. She carried the shotgun in front of her, her finger resting lightly on the trigger. She stopped at the first body. She wanted to be clinical and detached. She didn't want to care for strangers who'd never even had a chance. She didn't know them and she sure as hell couldn't help them. But as she surveyed their wounds, anger and horror crashed together like locomotives inside her chest. Max gasped, hot tears burning in her eyes as an unexpected need to find them vengeance swamped her. She knuckled her eyes and examined the bodies, not letting herself look away.

The first corpse had been a young man, maybe in his early twenties. His chest had been ripped open. His ribs were a mangled mess, and his entrails were gone. There was a smell of shit and urine and rotting meat. His legs had been gnawed on and one of his arms was missing. His eyes were open and staring, his mouth wide-open, his tongue protruding. Around his neck he wore a gold chain with a peace sign pendant.

The other three victims were in much the same condition, although the woman had been chewed on more than the other two. Her legs were twisted and splintered, and most of the flesh had been chewed off them. Both her arms were gone.

Max's fury flamed as she looked at the woman. She was wearing shreds of a pink nightgown, like she'd been snuggled in bed when she was attacked. She was hardly a woman—maybe just into college. On her wrist was a butterfly-tattoo bracelet in blues and purples.

The anger twisted and dug hard claws into Max. She drew a sharp breath. They were all so innocent and so horribly ruined. It made her want to kill someone—find them vengeance. Her mouth drew into a tense line. At least these four had been permitted to die. It could have been worse. She tried to take comfort in the thought, but it was elusive. She wiped more tears from her cheeks and ordered herself to be done with crying over crap she couldn't change.

She stood slowly, her jaw hardening. Someone *was* going to pay, she promised herself.

She let the predator in her rise, animal instincts flattening human concerns. Her head dropped and turned as she searched the yard eagerly. It was time to hunt. She jogged to a corner of the house. Bushes provided her with cover as she edged into the backyard. There was no one here. She loped across the lawn, hunching down and staying close to the house. At the other corner she stopped and peered around.

A small swarm of wizened redcaps were milling around the edge of a charm circle, its boundary glowing lavender witchlight to match the nimbus above the house. There were thirteen of the creatures, or had been. Three lay dead. The remaining ones were growling and yipping at one another, pushing and shoving and tearing with their hooked claws and orange teeth. One was chewing on a human arm like it was a turkey leg.

Others were garlanded with the intestines of the four murdered people on the driveway.

It took all that Max had not to blow the little beasts away with her shotgun. She wanted to—oh, how she wanted to make them suffer. Her hands clenched. But more was going on here than a simple murder, and it would be beyond stupid to rush in without knowing what. She gritted her teeth, her lips pulling back in a snarl, and scanned the scene again.

Inside the charm circle lay something human-size, though Max couldn't make out what it was through the gyrating little bodies. The one thing she knew for sure was that the vicious little redcaps were Uncanny, and whatever was inside that circle was Divine.

She needed to get closer. She inched back out of the bushes, then skimmed back around the garage. She skirted the hedge dividing the orchard from the back of the yard, stooping to keep out of sight. The hedge intersected the weathered wood fence that hid the large swimming pool. Max vaulted silently over the five-foot fence, landing in a crouch amid the thickly perfumed camellias and geraniums on the other side.

The pool was a rectangle of inky black surrounded by a wide patio-walkway. Nothing moved here. Max picked her way out onto the sidewalk. She hurried up to the opposite end, careful not to knock into any of the tables or chairs littering the poolside. The charm circle was opposite the gate. Slowly she eased up the latch at the top, letting the gate drift open a bare inch.

The redcaps and their prey were only thirty feet away beneath the spreading branches of an oak tree. Now Max could see inside the circle. On the ground, huddled in on herself, was a bony, old woman. No, not a woman. A Hag. Her thin, angular face was almost cobalt, her long hair white as the grass that grows in darkness. She was dressed in rags, her long, thin limbs poking out at sharp angles. She was weeping black tears, and a sound like several mouths whispering came from her lips as she watched the snarling redcaps.

Max frowned, racking her memory. What did she know about Hags? There were a number of them, from all over the world. With her blue face and white hair, this one had to be . . . Max mentally flipped through the pages of the many books she'd studied on faery lore. Yes. Cailleach Bheur—a Blue Hag from the Scottish highlands. But what did the redcaps want with her? Her Divine blood would do nothing to feed them, and redcaps were walking stomachs.

One of the little beasts shouted and tossed a powdery handful of something at the Hag. It enveloped her in a cloud and she began to shriek again. Max pressed herself back against the fence, covering her ears as best she could as the scream went on and on. It cut into her bones like the ache of winter. Blood seeped from her nose and she pinched it. She was running out of time. They were going to smell her soon.

Suddenly the cry cut off. Max lowered her hands, firming her grip on the shotgun as she peered out through gap in the gate. The Hag lay flat on the ground. She was breathing, but barely. Her skin was raw and looked like she'd been flayed. The redcap who'd thrown the powder was muttering vehemently at the Hag, shaking his steel pike at her. She did not respond.

Max scowled. The biggest rule in warfare is, don't

get involved before you know which side is which. But sometimes you just didn't have time to twiddle your thumbs and wait for the answers to appear. One thing she knew for sure was that the redcaps had murdered the people lying out on the driveway. As far as she was concerned, that was enough reason to return the favor, no matter what her orders were. As she watched, the redcap leader dug in his pouch for more of the powder. Max didn't think. She pushed the gate open, holding her breath as it made a faint creak. None of the redcaps noticed. She eased out, sliding into the shadow of a walnut tree. Leaning around, she sighted in on the leader.

As she leaned around the tree, there was a sudden popping of small-caliber weapons. Max jerked back and the redcaps screeched and scattered—those who were left standing. The noise thundered in Max's sensitive ears. She winced. She'd got so caught up in her hatred that she'd stupidly forgotten to look for anyone else. Selange—the witch who owned this territory—would have sent her own recon team once she got a reading that something was going down.

A pale-skinned Shadowblade with fiery orange hair to her shoulders emerged from around the pool enclosure, her gun held before her. She didn't notice Max as she ran forward and dug to a stop at the edge of the charm circle.

Several more Blades streamed out of the darkness. One of them was clearly the Prime. He radiated authority, and Max could feel the others cowing, turning toward him like flowers to sunlight. He wasn't physically imposing, topping out at around six feet tall, with short black hair and dark Mediterranean skin the color of bitter tea. His muscular frame was lean and compact, but compared to the two Incredible Hulks on either side of him, he was a pygmy.

All the same, Max couldn't drag her eyes away from him. It wasn't that he was handsome—though he was. No, something about *him* was mesmerizing. Every lithe movement spoke of confidence and barely restrained raw power. He radiated grace and an aloof magnetism that triggered something primal in Max. He was her equal in ways that most men—most Shadowblades—could never be. But there was more to her sudden lust than just that tangible power. For one thing, she hadn't gotten laid in close to six months. And for another, the bastard was her type. In fact, he was the dictionary illustration of it—dark, lean, and dangerous. His thin face was chiseled and bleak, and his hooded, dark eyes swam with deadly purpose. He was the bad boy every girl dreamed of.

Max grimaced. He was also the enemy. If he caught her trespassing on his witch's territory, one of them would die. She didn't think the odds were in her favor.

"Mercury and Attila, go round up the rest of the redcaps. You have fifteen minutes," he ordered in a soft, almost conversational voice. The two hulks obeyed instantly, peeling away and trotting off with a stealthy grace that belied their bulk.

Max smirked. Mercury? Attila? They sounded like rottweilers. But a lot of witches thought of their warrior creations that way and gave them what they thought were power names.

The Prime lifted his head, turning to scan the house

and the yard with slow precision. Max pressed against the tree, hiding the telltale paleness of her face against the bark and hoping the stench of blood and magic would continue to disguise her smell. When he didn't spot her, she eased around to watch again and froze as he stopped in midturn. He seemed to be looking right into her eyes, and the weight of it slammed Max like a Peterbilt truck. She suppressed the urge to leap to her feet. If he'd really seen her, he'd already be at her throat. Instead his attention slid away to the three dead redcaps and the five his Blades had shot, then to the Hag.

Max let go a silent breath.

"You going to paint a picture, Alexander?" the flame-haired woman asked snidely.

Max saw something ripple through the Prime. He didn't acknowledge the question. She scowled. If one of her Blades had questioned her that way in the field, she'd have dropped her like a stone and the bitch wouldn't have got up again. Not that it happened often. Apparently Alexander had more patience for fools than she did.

"Thor, move the bodies into the house, then rig the gas line. We will burn all the evidence. Tell the others to bring up the trucks. The Hag and the redcaps come with us. Selange will want them."

The others hurried off, leaving Alexander and the orange-haired bitch.

"This is stupid," she pushed. "We should just leave before the cops show up."

"Selange would disagree" was his indifferent reply. And then seemingly tangentially: "Marcus is not strong enough to take me. Do not put all your money on a losing horse, Brynna. You could get hurt."

He said it idly, as if he didn't really care, as if he weren't thinking about her at all. He was pacing back and forth over the ground, following a trail that Max couldn't see. She eased herself to her feet for a better look.

Brynna laughed, a shrill sound. Max stared in disbelief. Brynna was clearly no match for Alexander in strength, cunning, or power. She was one of those women who depended on their big eyes and curvy bodies to pry them out of whatever trouble their mouths, got them into—even as a Shadowblade. And she was digging herself a deep hole. Alexander clearly had no interest in the bitch and she was too stupid to see it.

"You don't get it, do you?" Brynna pushed. "Marcus is everything you're not. He's young and strong and he knows how to make Selange purr. She wants him. Not you. You're way past your expiration date, and pretty soon she's going to toss you out with the rest of the trash."

"I know well enough that Marcus is not like me."

Max grinned. It wasn't a compliment. Her gaze ran irresistably over Alexander again. Shit. She really had to get laid. The trouble was, she didn't like messing around in her own backyard. She liked to get far enough away from Horngate that her one-night stands didn't come back to haunt her. But since Giselle liked to keep her on a short leash, Max tended to have long dry spells.

"You should be careful of Marcus. He is reckless. He will get you killed. As for Selange . . . who she sleeps with is her business. Does not seem to leave a lot of room for you, though. Are you going to sit by the bed like a hungry dog and beg for scraps?"

Alexander's tone had not changed. He still sounded absent. He crouched and touched something on the ground, then lifted his fingers to taste. Brynna was spitting nails. But before she could say anything else, he stood up again. He sauntered over to her, his attention honing in so that he seemed to see nothing else. Max watched in delight as Brynna realized the shit was about to hit the fan. The flame-haired moron stepped back, the gun in her hand twitching like she desperately wanted to shove it in his gut. Alexander slid a gentle hand around the back of her neck, his thumb pressing against her throat as he leaned close. She shrank in on herself, her mouth twisting with fear.

"You should watch your mouth. I am losing patience with you. Straighten up or I will kill you," he said softly.

"Selange would have your balls in a jar," Brynna choked. She was shivering, the smell of her fear sharp.

Alexander smiled dangerously. His unruffled calm had turned menacing and angry—a volcano burned inside him. Max wondered if he ever lost control entirely. "Perhaps. Perhaps not. But that would do little to help you, would it?"

His thumb gouged deep into her neck, and Brynna wheezed as he picked her up off the ground with one hand. Her feet twitched and then stilled. Fighting back would surely make her punishment worse, if not fatal. Max watched the lesson with approval. The word of a Prime was law, to be obeyed instantly. Disobedient Shadowblades got people killed. It couldn't be tolerated.

"I am done with your bitching and backstabbing. The next time I have to talk to you about it, I will not be talking, do you understand?"

Brynna gave a minuscule nod of her head, all she could manage. Alexander let go. She dropped to the ground and staggered, gasping. He looked at her a moment, as if waiting for her to start mouthing off, but apparently she wasn't as stupid as Max thought because she didn't say a word. Alexander nodded, his expression smoothing into the sort of surface calm that hides shark-infested waters beneath it.

"Stay here and watch the Hag. Careful of the redcaps. The five we shot will start waking before long." With that, he walked away around the side of the house.

Max smiled as Brynna's face silently contorted. Would the woman throw herself on the ground and have a really good tantrum? But disappointingly, she managed to suck it up and keep her mouth shut. The redhead sent a venomous glare after Alexander, then skirted around the spell circle to look over the redcaps. None were moving yet, but they would. Bullets were a human solution. They slowed down most magical critters, but they didn't usually kill them.

Brynna kicked one with a booted foot, then turned and wandered over to look at the Hag. Max shook her head. She really was a moron. Redcaps were vicious and smart. As soon as they woke, they'd be on her. She should've taken up a stance with her back to the house where she could watch the redcaps, the Hag, and the yard at the same time without fearing someone creeping up behind her. Like Max was about to do.

She didn't let herself think about why she wasn't

safely retreating and getting the hell out of Julian. Instead she leaped across the few yards separating her from Brynna and clubbed the other woman in the head with the shotgun. Brynna crumpled bonelessly to the ground. Max grappled her collar and dragged her into the pool enclosure. It took her ten seconds to strip away the other woman's guns and drop them in the water before hurrying back to the charm circle.

The Hag breathed in short, sharp gasps that jerked her body. She was covered in the powder the redcap had thrown over her, and her skin looked like someone had drenched her in acid. The black tears on her blue skin made her look demonic.

"Mother of winter, can you hear me?" Max whispered, keeping one eye on the redcaps while she glanced around for the return of Alexander and his Blades.

The Hag made no response. She was close to death. Max grimaced, then stood, walking around to see what Alexander had found so interesting on the ground. She stopped first by the three redcaps who'd been dead before she arrived. They were stiff and desiccated. Their lips were pulled grotesquely from their pointed, orange teeth and their hats had crumbled to dust.

The lawn around the mummified trio was gouged up. Max followed their track back along the side of the house and found an incomplete salt circle. She squatted down, leaning her elbows on her knees. It looked as if the redcaps had tried to seal the Hag inside the circle but she'd fought her way out. That accounted for the wild magic over the house and the chaos zone. Blood was splattered about, belonging to both the Hag and the redcaps. Max frowned, swiping a hand over her mouth. What was the Hag doing *here*?

Her gaze snagged on a little grotto. It was a small pool surrounded by pungent rosemary, climbing roses, and gardenias. Lily pads floated on the water. Of course. Julian Springs Orchards. The spring. This was the Hag's home. The redcaps had lured her out of the water and captured her. Straightening up, Max looked again at the incomplete salt circle. Except it wasn't a circle. It was a barrier curving around the front of the grotto to keep the Hag from returning to safety in the spring.

A rumble of voices from inside the house spurred Max to return to the charm circle. She set her shotgun on the ground and slid one of her forearm knives free, then hesitated a fraction of a moment. Up until this moment she could justify what she was doing as reconnaissance. Giselle would want to know the redcaps had been hunting the Hag. Now that Max knew what had happened, she should walk away. Those were her orders. Even contemplating breaking them made agony blossom in her gut as the magic that demanded she obey Giselle clawed at her. She drew a steadying breath, firming her grip on the knife.

She *wasn't* going to leave the Hag. She'd fought a good fight and she was helpless. She deserved a chance to escape. Alexander's witch would imprison her and either enslave her or find a way to steal her magic. The image of the four tortured bodies on the other side of the house rose in Max's mind's eye. The sudden rage that erupted in her gut came without warning. Her fingers shook with the force of it. No one else was going to suffer tonight. Not if she could help it. She hauled back her anger and pushed it deep into the hollow place inside. Emotions only got in the way. She focused instead on confusing her compulsion spells. It wasn't hard; she had plenty of practice.

It's for the good of Giselle, she told the magic firmly. And that was true, as far as it went. It was definitely better for Giselle if a rival witch didn't get ahold of the Hag. Max didn't let herself think about what could go wrong—like getting caught. The agony flower inside her began to wilt, and she smiled with fierce triumph. There were always shades of gray in the interpretation of her orders. She'd learned she could make decisions for the *good* of Giselle that she knew damned well the witch-bitch wouldn't like. The compulsion spells didn't care how the witch felt, just that she was protected and served. Magic didn't understand nuance.

Max didn't wait any longer. She slashed downward through the lavender witchlight and into the salt circle. Power walloped her, throwing her backward. She landed hard, her head snapping against the ground, the air exploding from her lungs. Instantly she flung herself up onto her feet, gasping for breath. Her hand was scorched red and her arm ached fiercely. She didn't know where her knife was. She shook her hand as if that would cool it and returned to the edge of the circle.

The witchlight was gone. On the ground was a ring of gray ash. Max scuffed a gap in it with her foot and went to kneel beside the Hag.

"Mother of winter, we must move you."

The Hag opened her eyes. They were pale blue and cold, like glacier ice. Her lips peeled back from her stalactite teeth and she spat something in a language Max didn't know.

"I don't understand you. They're coming back for you. Can you walk?"

Max offered the Hag her hand. The Hag twitched, her mouth twisting as she tried to move. She slumped, her eyes drifting closed, her breath rattling in her throat. Cold radiated from her. Max's breath plumed in the air.

"What can I do?" Asking was risky. It implied a promise. Much could be made of that.

The eyes lifted slowly. "Feed."

Max jerked back, then caught herself. *What the hell am I doing?* She should just kill the Hag and put her out of her misery. Cutting her heart out would do it. Max's stomach churned. No. Not tonight. There had been enough deaths here. It wasn't often that she could save lives. And she could spare the blood.

She didn't let herself think about the stupidity of creating a blood bond with the Hag. She slid her other knife out of its sheath and slashed her wrist in one sharp motion. She cut deeply. Her healing spells would kick in too quickly otherwise.

She held her arm out and let the blood run into the Hag's lipless mouth. Her blue tongue, pointed like a lizard's tail, swept out and licked the drops from the air. The change was almost instantaneous. Her eyes burned neon and her body spasmed. She clutched at Max's arm with her knotted fingers, pulling it down to her mouth with iron strength. The black, pointed nails drilled into Max's skin.

Instinctively Max yanked back, but the Hag was too strong. Her mouth fastened on the wound as she licked

Max's flesh. Cold followed. It crept up Max's arm with searing intensity, numbing her skin and turning it white. Max groped for her knife, knowing the Hag could drain her in a matter of minutes.

Instead of the knife, her fingers found the shotgun. She scrabbled for it even as the Hag let go. Max clutched her arm against her stomach, shivering. With her other hand she hefted the shotgun. The Hag sat up. With her long tongue, she licked the trickles of blood from her chin and cheeks.

"Can you move?" Max asked through stiff lips. "We've got to get out of here."

The Hag twisted her head, tilting it as she examined Max. Her eyes still glowed brilliantly, and Max recoiled from the power swelling in them.

"What do you want?" the Hag whispered in a voice that sounded like gravel in a blender.

"To get out of here alive. Which we won't do if we don't get a move on."

"No. What do you *want*?"

Max struggled to her feet, swaying. "Come on. They'll be coming soon." How long had it been? Eight minutes? Ten? She could hear the rumble of diesel engines and a faint crunch of gravel. The trucks were on the long, shaded drive.

The Hag stood jerkily, like she'd been pulled up with strings. She was almost a foot taller than Max, maybe six and a half feet. Her skeletal hands hung at her sides, the fingertips curled loosely.

Max stepped back, firming her grip on the shotgun. "I want to get going. Understand?"

The Hag shook her head, the long, ropy strands of her

white hair moving as if alive. "You burn," she said. A bony finger prodded the air near Max's belly button. "Rage." She drew the word out as if savoring it. "What do you want?"

"Don't move."

Max whirled around, swinging up her shotgun. For a split second, she met Alexander's piercing gaze as he sighted down his .45. Then with a motion too fast to comprehend, a flash of blue struck Alexander, wrapping him in a cocoon of blue witchlight.

"Stillness," said the Hag.

It was, Max realized, a command. Alexander didn't move, didn't even blink. He was frozen. Slowly she lowered the nose of her shotgun and glanced sidelong at the Hag, who held a staff in her skeletal hand. It was made of black wood sheathed in ice. Spiky holly leaves twined around its length, and the top was carved in the shape of a crow.

The Hag looked at Max again. She tilted her head, pointing with her staff. "There will be war. It stands already on the threshold. Many, many will die. The world will be remade. Soon you will stand at a crossroads. You can choose fire"—the staff prodded Max in the stomach—"or you can choose blood." The staff touched her wrist where the slash had already closed. "Be warned, either path will have a cost. Lives will be saved and lives will be lost."

The Hag bent close so that her nose nearly touched Max's. Max fought to stand still, though every instinct told her to run like hell.

"You gave blood. There is a debt owed. I give you this." The Hag reached into a tattered pocket and withdrew a silvery white lump. She set it in Max's hand. It burned with cold, but did not melt. A hailstone. "When the time is right, swallow it. Know what you want. You will have it."

With that, the Hag skimmed over the grass to the pool in the grotto. In her wake, frost glittered on the grass and cold wind gusted, despite the August heat. She did not turn as she stepped into the water. In a blink she sank and was gone. The wind died.

Max pocketed the hailstone without looking at it again. Her mind reeled; she didn't know what to think, and she didn't have time to sort it out. She faced Alexander. The blue light that held him was dimming. A few more seconds, a half a minute maybe, and he'd be free. It didn't matter if she got away before that. He'd seen her. They both would be at tomorrow night's Conclave—every witch was required to bring her Shadowblade Prime. Now or then, there would be a showdown.

She raised the nose of the shotgun, pointing it at him as she thumbed the hammer back. At this range, the blast would take his head off. No one else would know she'd ever been here. She stared at him, her eyes locking with his, her finger hovering over the trigger. Her compulsion spells raked steel thorns through her, pushing her to kill him. She still hesitated. There was something about the way he looked at her—as if he recognized her. Maybe not *who* she was, but *what* she was. She felt like he could see all the way inside her, and the feeling was both deeply unsettling and strangely welcome. No one got close to her. After Giselle had turned her, she'd wrapped herself in emotional Kevlar, and that was the way she wanted it. When her body felt the need to be touched, she found strangers in bars and enjoyed a roll in the hay and then was on her way—no ties. She held everyone at arm's length, even her Shadowblades, whom she'd come to care for despite herself. But Alexander's gaze cut through to the core of her. Without even speaking a word to each other, she knew that he already understood her better than anybody else in her life. It was a gift she hadn't known she wanted, and she couldn't just blow it away.

Abruptly she lifted the gun and rested the barrel on her shoulder, easing the hammer back down.

"My name is Max," she said, not sure he could actually hear her. "I'll see you at the Conclave."

With that, she ran past him, heading for her Tahoe. Tomorrow night was soon enough for them to try to kill each other.

2

THE HAG'S MAGIC HELD ALEXANDER HELPLESS. He could not move, not even to breathe. Even his heart stopped. He was frozen like a mosquito in amber. All he could do was watch and listen and wish to hell he understood what was happening. Nothing tonight made any sense. Redcaps didn't hunt Hags, and what were they doing in Southern California? Both belonged to the Scottish highlands, and as far as he knew, traveling across continents was not something they made a habit of. And if that wasn't enough, now another witch was involved.

The strange Shadowblade woman was clearly a Prime. There was no mistaking that aura of volcanic power and authority. Even shaking with blood loss, she moved with the total confidence of a predator who knew her capabilities and was willing to take them to their limits. Alexander could feel her strength—a heady blend of molten iron and bottled lightning. He had not encountered the likes of her in many years—maybe not ever. Which made her a riddle. Any Prime as powerful as she was had to be bound to an extraordinary witch, someone the equal of Selange. That worried him. He did not know any who would fit the bill. Such a witch would be old and established with a large coven and he would have heard of her. Or him.

His compulsion spells woke, sliding over him like razor wire. There was danger for Selange here and he was helpless against it.

He watched the Hag give the Prime something, then the Hag sped out of sight and the Prime turned to look at Alexander. She wore a black hat pulled low over her eyes. A fringe of blond hair escaped from beneath it. Her face was angular, beautiful in the relentless, bold way that eagles are beautiful. Or cobras. She was shorter than him by four or five inches, but that made her no less dangerous. She raised her eyes and the nose of her shotgun at the same time. Everything in Alexander seized as electric fire seared his muscles. He was hypnotized by her gaze. Even if he could have, he would not have looked away. All thoughts of Selange faded, and he was sliding deep into something he did not know how to resist. He was not sure he wanted to.

A long moment passed and he was aware that the Hag's magic was weakening. He could tell she saw it, too. Any moment she would pull the trigger. But then shockingly she lifted the shotgun away, resting the barrel on her shoulder. Her brows rose in a challenge, her jaw jutting with defiance. "My name is Max. I'll see you at the Conclave."

Then she disappeared, running past him. He caught a whiff of her—a sharp tang of citrus, a hint of something earthy, a zest of sweet venom overlaid by the thick taste of greasy hamburgers.

He could not let her get away. He did not want to. He struggled against his bonds. Ten seconds. Twenty. He broke free and sprinted after her, crashing into Thor as he came around the corner.

"What the hell?" Thor demanded, shoving him away.

Alexander caught himself on a garden bench, spinning to scan the treeline. "We had company." He shook his head. "She will have a car somewhere. We will not catch her now."

He scowled, turning back to Thor. The big blond looked like a street thug from Cow Town, USA. He wore a short-sleeved, black T-shirt with BRMC scrawled across the front in white block letters, worn black jeans that had long since faded to gray, and battered cowboy boots. Blood smeared his hands, forearms, and cheek. He wore a straw cowboy hat cocked back on his head, a bowie knife on his left hip, and his .44 revolver on his right, strapped down and slung low like he was about to step onto the set of a spaghetti western. His eyes were as cold as the ocean depths as he waited for orders.

"Is the house wired?" Alexander asked.

Thor nodded.

"Then go find Brynna. See if she is still alive. Have the others collect the redcaps. I want to be on the road within the next five minutes."

Thor loped away without another word, leaving Alexander alone on the lawn. He jogged up the berm past a tractor and stopped under the eaves of the orchard. Deep footprints trailed away in the soft loam, spread widely apart. Max had been running full tilt. As he expected, she was beyond reach. But not for long. Selange was hosting a Midsummer Conclave tomorrow night. Every witch who held a covenstead west of the Rockies would be there, and every one would be bringing his or her Prime. His fingers flexed on the hilt of his gun, and he slowly slid it back into its holster on his hip.

He rubbed a hand over his goatee as he looked into the trees. This was not over. He would see her at the Conclave, and it would be ugly. Selange did not tolerate trespassers in her territory, and she would want to know what interest Max's witch had in the Hag and the redcaps. He grimaced. By any accounting, Max should have killed him. It was stupid not to. She could have escaped with no one knowing she had ever been here. What had stopped her?

But he remembered the devouring pull of her eyes and knew why she had not, just as he knew that when they met at the Conclave, there would be no room for mercy or any of the silent things that swam between them. They would be at war.

"TELL ME AGAIN WHAT THE HAG SAID. LEAVE NOTHING out," Selange ordered, the words curling with a faint French accent. She had been in America for more than a hundred years and still the accent clung to her like the sultry perfume that she wore. She sat primly behind her delicate desk, her silky legs crossed demurely together. She was small, only five feet tall and not quite a hundred pounds. She was also one of the most powerful witches in North America. She did not ask him to sit or offer him refreshment. A reprimand—for so many things.

Alexander examined her with slow deliberation. Her hair was cut in a sleek black cap that curled under at the shoulders, her bangs a straight line across her forehead. Her face was rounded, her eyes brown and lined with thick, dark liner, her mouth a red slash across her pale face. She wore a high-necked, sleeveless mandarin sheath in dark blue. On her feet were four-inch stiletto heels. She was sitting with her hands together, staring intently at Alexander.

He was surprised at just how little he felt for her. For many years he had adored her with single-minded devotion, captivated by her beauty, power, and exotic charm. There was *nothing* he would not have done for her. She had wrapped him in spells that made him strong, fast, and deadly—he had been a god among men. She taught him how to read and write, how to speak and dress, and then she had given him the world. There had been nothing he did not want to try and nowhere he did not want to go. He had been like a child ransacking the proverbial candy store. His new life had been as glorious as touching the sun, and he had no words for his gratitude—then or now—for the gift she had given him. The price was worth it. He had embraced becoming one of Selange's Shadowblades and never once looked back.

But over the years things had changed for him. He no longer burned with unquenchable desire for Selange. His passion had begun dwindling long ago, and then nearly forty years ago she had dealt those softer feelings a final death. Not that he hated her. He did not know if his compulsion spells would allow it. But neither did he blindly believe in her the way he had when he was first made a Shadowblade. As brilliant and brave as she still was, she was also vain, spiteful, selfish, and ambitious. He did not know if there was anything she would not do to gain power. Certainly she had crossed lines that sickened him—so much so that after the last time, he had threatened to walk out into the sun if she forced him to participate again. It was no idle threat. Even his compulsion spells could not stop him. Hence the need for her to groom another Prime. She did not tolerate rebellion. But it would be a long time before Marcus could best him. Until then, Selange needed Alexander.

"The Hag asked what the Shadowblade wanted," he said, answering her question for the third time, not letting any hint of impatience color his voice, much as he wanted to get this over with. "Then the Hag said there was a war coming. Soon. She said it stands on the threshold. She said that the Shadowblade would have to choose—fire or blood, and that either choice would have a grave cost. Lives would be lost. Then the Hag gave the Shadowblade something. She told her when the time is right, to swallow it and know what she wants. Then she will have it."

Alexander told Selange everything but Max's name, and the way she had chosen not to shoot him at the end. Selange would read more into it than there was. Collusion, because he had let Max get away. It did not matter that he had had no choice—now that he had defied her once, she did not trust him anymore.

Selange's wine red fingernails clicked against the desk. "The Hag must have given her a hailstone," she thought aloud. And then to Alexander: "And the Hag's staff? She didn't have it until after the Shadowblade let her feed?"

"That is correct."

Selange's fingernails tapped harder, then stilled. "Very well. I will send the Sunspears back to the orchard this morning to see if they can recover the Hag."

Alexander studied her. Something was going on here she was not telling him. She fairly quivered with suppressed *something*—excitement? Anger? Her nostrils flared slightly, and in the quiet he could hear her heart speeding. She sat back, her eyes narrowing. She had made him to be a bloodhound, a lion, a bloodthirsty dragon. But she did not like it when he turned his magical gifts on her.

"Is that wise?" he asked. "The police will be investigating."

"It is my command," she said flatly. "I've no further need of you until the Conclave tonight. You may go."

Dismissed, Alexander retreated, his jaw knotting. He wanted to ask more questions—as her Shadowblade Prime, he needed all the information he could get to protect her. But she would not answer. She had told him all she was going to.

Just as he opened the door, a chime sounded. It echoed, growing louder. Selange rose to her feet, excitement firing her expression.

"Alexander, come with me."

With that she strode rapidly out through a long gallery of pink-veined marble. He followed a step behind, an uncontrollable chill rolling down his spine. The curved ceiling was made entirely of glass. All that separated him from the sun were the blackout shutters. If they should accidentally be opened, he had nowhere to hide.

The long tunnel emptied into a spacious waiting

room shaped like an octagon and full of comfortable white couches and chairs. Like the gallery's ceiling, this room's glass walls were sealed by blackout shutters with the exception of a broad set of double doors on the far wall. They were made of oak bound in iron and carved with mystic symbols. To one side was a heavy oak desk, behind which sat Selange's secretary. Kev was a Tatane faery from the Easter Islands. He was dark skinned with full lips and green eyes, his hair curling close against his head. He looked perfectly human except for the faint flecks of gold burnishing his skin and dancing in his eyes. Until he spoke. Then you could see that his tongue and the interior of his mouth were as dark as his skin. Besides being a secretary and faery, he was also a shape-shifter and Selange's familiar. One of them.

He stood with boneless grace as they entered. "They are here," he announced in a low voice that made Alexander's hand tighten into a fist.

He did not know what it was about Kev that set him on edge. The Tatane had been with Selange nearly as long as Alexander, and he had never done anything to hurt her. But there was a promise lurking in the corners of his glance and in the grooves of his voice, a pledge of danger and betrayal. Alexander had to check himself when Kev stepped in front of the desk to block Selange's path.

A sudden change swept the faery, a hardness, as if he had turned to stone. His skin looked as gray as the Moai statues of his Easter Island homeland. The gold in his eyes spiraled slowly, his eyelids drifting half-shut. A prickle chased across Alexander's scalp.

"Know that you stand at a threshold," Kev intoned, his voice dropping. "Cross, and you cannot again close the door. There is both peril and promise on the other side. Turn back now without either consequence or prize."

Selange hesitated. "Can you see an outcome?"

Kev's head tilted. "I see only the threshold. I feel only the possibilities. It is for you to take the final step and know what could and will be. Or turn around and leave the threshold unbroken."

The hardness melted away and his skin once again turned warm brown. Kev blinked and stepped back, waiting. Selange did not move.

"Who has come?" Alexander asked.

Selange started, coming out of her reverie. She smoothed her dress, lifting her chin and taking a breath, her red lips curving in a false smile.

"Guests. They are expected. Let us not keep them waiting."

With that she walked deliberately past Kev and pulled open the carved doors. Alexander hurried to join her.

They stepped into a round, windowless room forty-five feet in diameter. The vaulted ceiling was well over two stories above. Inlaid in the wood floor was the *anneau* floor, composed of a circle surrounding a pentagram with a triangle in its center. At the very center was a silver disk the size of a Frisbee. The walls were bare and the wood of the floor was scuffed and scarred. But Alexander's entire attention was fixed on the creature standing inside the glowing lines of the triangle. He drew his gun from its holster on his hip and started to step in front of Selange to shield her, but she stopped him, resting trembling fingertips on his arm.

"He is safe enough inside the wards." Her voice was firm, belying her nerves.

Alexander held back, but remained tensed and bristling.

The angel was nearly seven feet tall. He wore ragged blue jeans, and his feet were bare, as was his chest. Sprouting from his back was a pair of wings, the feathers black and iridescent. Glimmers of blue and orange flickered along the bottom edges of his primary feathers. Where his wing tips brushed the floor, charred scores appeared, matching those on his pant legs where he had not been careful enough. The smell of Divine magic rolled off him, mixed with the stench of burning feathers. His eyes were red and his white hair was cropped short, his face and body chiseled like one of Michelangelo's statues. He appeared to be about twenty, though he was undoubtedly many thousands of years old.

"I offer greetings, Lady Selange," he said with a mocking bow. He was careful not to step on any part of the glowing triangle.

"I hear your greeting," Selange answered cautiously, not offering any welcome that might obligate her. "Do you bring a message from your mistress?"

"She offers this proposal." He pulled a scroll out of the air, holding it up.

"What does it say?"

His brows rose tauntingly. "I am not privy to her private correspondence."

"Very well." Selange muttered something and gestured. The star lit with witchlight. More words, another gesture, and the light of the triangle faded. "If you would, place the message within the star and return to the triangle."

He turned the scroll in his fingers, then sauntered forward and bent to set it down. He then retreated. Selange reactivated the triangle, but made no effort to release the star and retrieve the message. The angel said nothing, merely standing with his thumbs hooked in the belt loops of his jeans, his gaze fixed on her with a malice so cold it seemed to chill the air. There was a coiled stillness about him, a crouching wildness, like the first flickers of a wildfire.

If Selange's wards did not hold, Alexander was not sure he could protect her. He edged forward again. The angel's red eyes shifted, skewering him. Heat blossomed in Alexander's skull. The angel smiled in a not unfriendly way, then dropped his eyes. Alexander blinked, drawing a quiet breath, his legs shaking. He knew angels had dreadful power, though he'd never before encountered one. They did not often walk the earth. His eyes narrowed. Just who was powerful enough to hold his leash? Who was powerful enough to use him as a mere messenger? And more important, what the hell kind of trouble had Selange got into?

"Is there anything more?" Selange asked in a strained voice.

"My mistress wishes to demonstrate her commitment and fidelity. She offers you a gift of her good intentions."

Selange flinched. "Your mistress is kind. Please convey my regards."

Again, she was careful not to obligate herself, but Alexander could hear the nervousness in her voice. It shocked him. He had been with her more than a century. She was not easily cowed.

"You do not ask about the gift. Curious." The angel

crossed his arms, his wings flaring slightly. Droplets of flame spattered the floor and began to burn.

"I would never presume so much."

"Ah. Then it will be a surprise. Look for it to begin before moonrise tomorrow. I will return for your answer to my mistress very soon."

With that, the angel leaped into the air, his wings snapping wide and sweeping downward with a violent motion as he arrowed upward. Flame erupted, boiling up and filling the triangular space. A brilliant yellow light flared near the ceiling. Alexander jerked around, shutting his eyes. There was a concussion and the walls and floor trembled. The light winked out.

He looked up. Splotches spattered his vision. The bastard had vanished, and the floor inside the triangle was black, but the wards had held. Before he could say anything, Selange cut off all questions.

"Leave me now." She raised her hands and flicked her fingers. Dismissal.

Alexander did not move. "What is going on?" he demanded.

"I told you to leave," Selange said. Her face was screwed tight in an expression of hatred and maybe fear.

"Not until you tell me what is going on. I cannot protect you if I do not understand the threat."

She did not answer, walking slowly around the edge of the circle, eyeing the message scroll. The star was still lit, which meant she suspected a malevolent spell was attached to the message. She stopped and looked at him finally, her scarlet mouth twisting with cruel humor. "Protect me? From him? From his mistress and her *gifts*? Do you think you can?" Her gaze fell back on the scroll. She pinched her upper lip between her fingers. "There's nothing for you to do. Leave me."

Alexander couldn't stop himself. "And Marcus? Is this the reason you groom him for Prime? You think he will do better than I who have served you for a century? Do you think he can take on the angel and win?"

Selange whirled and marched purposefully toward him, her legs stiff, her heels clicking hard on the floor. Alexander did not give ground. She stopped with her hands on her hips, her eyes stony. Magic made her hair rise and shift on an invisible current. It rippled across her skin like webs of blue lightning. His mouth went dry. She had the power to kill him. It would take some work—she had made him powerful. But his compulsion spells would not allow him to hurt her. Nor would they allow him to back down now. She was in danger.

"I *groom* Marcus for the same reason I *groom* Lance to replace Arthur as Sunspear Prime," she said, prodding him hard in the chest with her finger. "I do it because I am going to need an army of Primes for what is coming."

He latched onto that small sliver of information. "What is coming?"

She turned, looking back at the scroll. Her lips trembled. "The end of the world. The birth of a whole new order. Now go. Send me Kev."

Her voice brooked no more argument. Alexander stepped out of the room, shutting the doors behind him. Kev sat at his desk.

"She wants you," Alexander told the Tatane faery, and then strode out into the gallery.

He felt as if a trap were closing around him, and the need to claw himself free was overwhelming. Except he could not see the trap nor the invisible enemy that breathed hot across his skin. The end of the world? What did that mean? And how was he going to protect Selange from it?

SELANGE SENT FOR HIM AT DUSK. SHE HAD CHANGED clothing, wearing a fitted black skirt to her knees and a high-necked, long-sleeved jacket with a teardrop cutout that was deeply revealing. A ruby pendant rested between her breasts. Anyone else might not have noticed the slightly gaunt look of her face, the haggard slope of her shoulders, or the slight tremble in her hands. But Alexander had known her for more than a century, and he could read her well enough to know when she had tested her magical limits. On opening a message? Or had it been the contents that had thrown her?

"You are well?" he asked, though he knew it would annoy her, and more than a little because it would.

She waved the question away, sitting on the corner of her desk. "I have sent my Sunspears after the Hag. It is my hope they can recover her staff. It was the goal of the redcaps."

"What would they want with it?" he asked, and was surprised when she answered.

Her lips tightened. "Someone sent them to get it. They would not—or could not—say who that was."

He could guess. Redcaps, like angels, could only be controlled by someone with a lot of power—much more than a mere witch, even one as strong as Selange. And at least one of them had taken a special interest in her. He felt like the ground was shifting beneath him and he was sliding off the edge of the world. He was entirely in the dark about who or what might be behind it. Damn Selange for her secrets! She knew what was happening, and she had known for a while, and yet she had not said a word to him. How was he supposed to keep her safe?

She began to speak again, shocking him. How afraid did she have to be to give up information she considered no one else's business? That sent a chill of fear burrowing deep inside Alexander. She was truly afraid, and that meant things were much worse than he imagined. And he imagined pretty well.

"After I questioned the redcaps, I spent some time researching today. Some legends say that the staff of a Blue Hag can control the destiny of humans. It can also control weather and even the shape of the land. Any of those things would be a power worth having, especially now. And unlike her hailstones, her staff can be used by anyone who has possession of it. I want her staff. This is the time of the year when she's weakest, and it is possible I can succeed where the redcaps failed."

She rolled the ruby pendant between her thumb and forefinger thoughtfully, as if considering saying more. Alexander kept his mouth clamped tight. One word from him and she might shut down.

"I believe the Hag gave the intruder Prime a hailstone in return for her sacrifice in feeding the Hag fresh blood. I want it. Toward that end, I will issue a challenge at Conclave. The Prime trespassed in my territory, and it is my right. Instead of the usual contest of arms, I will choose one of endurance. The winning witch will take possession of the losing Shadowblade."

She rested the tips of her fingers together, her lips pursing. "I can be very creative with pain. I do not think this Prime will last long beneath my ministrations. But no matter how long she holds on, you must hold out longer. Do not fail me, Alexander."

"And if she has given the hailstone to her witch?"

"She will still be useful to me. I will make her tell us her witch's weaknesses, and you will hunt her down and retrieve the hailstone." Selange's lips clamped together a moment, her eyes flattening. "This is no mean magic, Alexander. The Cailleach Bheur are old creatures and their magic is very powerful. With the hailstone and staff, I may be able to keep us free of entanglements."

"Entanglements?" Alexander repeated warily, holding himself tightly reined. He wanted straight answers. He wanted to know just what exactly the angel's message had contained and who had sent it.

"If you prefer, you can call it. . . indentured servitude," Selange clarified softly. Then she stood. "Come now. We don't want to be late."

3

Max drove into San Diego before sunrise, but she did not try to find the warehouse where Giselle was waiting with her mobile village of light and dark sealed RVs, cars, and tractor trailers. The witch had come fully prepared for things to go south. Even at a Conclave where everyone was supposed to be on their best behavior, trouble could swiftly erupt. And it often did. If any of Giselle's people were injured, if they had to run, they had everything on hand they'd need—a doctor and two nurses, a hospital truck, a fully stocked restaurant truck, and motels on wheels.

Max pulled off into a strip mall housing Mysterious Galaxy Books, a Starbucks, a chiropractor, and a McDonald's. The sky was already starting to turn pink. Her stomach growled as she pushed open the door of the Tahoe, and she eyed the Starbucks longingly, then gave a reluctant shake of her head. Even a flicker of sun and she'd be charcoal. Maybe she should have gone to the warehouse. But she needed to think before she came face-to-face with Giselle. The cold of the hailstone burned through her pocket into her thigh. *Freedom*.

Mechanically, she went to the rear of her vehicle and popped open the door. Filling the cargo area was a light-sealed steel box about four feet deep, five feet wide and a little over four feet tall. Inside was a memory foam cushion, a stash of powerbars, beef jerky, Gatorade and water, an iPod, a couple of pillows, a copy of a David Sedaris book, and a change of clothes. The back panel slid up about eighteen inches, and Max wedged herself underneath, pulling shut the Tahoe's rear door with her foot as she did. Then she let the box door slide down and flipped the latches that kept anyone from the outside from opening it.

She squirmed around in the narrow space, ripping open a powerbar and devouring it before guzzling an orange Gatorade. Three more bars quickly followed. Once the edge was off her hunger, she dug in her pocket for her cell phone. She hadn't turned it on since Julian. She stared at it a moment, then hit the power button and punched in Giselle's speed dial.

The witch picked up on the first ring. "Where are you? What happened?" she demanded.

"San Diego somewhere. I was seen."

Giselle's silence was livid. "Are you all right?"

The question was sharp. Max's mouth twisted. It wasn't personal. Giselle didn't want her prizewinning pit bull getting hurt right before the Conclave.

"Fine."

"What happened there?"

Max sketched out the events of the night, leaving out the part where she fed the Hag and where she didn't kill Alexander and get away clean.

For long moments, Giselle said nothing. Then: "I'll

have Oz send someone to pick you up. Where are you?"

Max was tempted to just let them find her by the tracking GPS in her phone and Tahoe, but she swallowed her defiance. There wasn't anything to win at the moment, and her compulsion spells spiked her hard, demanding she return to Giselle's side as quickly as possible. "Off the 805 on Claremont. A strip mall."

Before Giselle could say anything else, Max flipped her phone shut. She drew a breath, smelling the lovely greasy smells of McDonald's sausage-and-egg McMuffins overlaid with coffee from Starbucks. Her mouth watered. She tore open another powerbar and chewed it mechanically.

It took her another ten minutes to will herself to pull the hailstone from her pocket. It lumped there, a seed of winter in the increasing heat, unmelting and unchanging. At last Max drew it out, turning it in her fingers. It did not look like much of anything. A lump of white ice. But it smelled of Divine magic. Max closed her hand on it, slumping down so she could lean her head against the wall of the box.

Tears leaked from the corners of her eyes and trickled down her cheeks. It couldn't be real. This *chance*. This hope. To finally get back at Giselle and be free.

When the time is right, swallow it. Know what you want. You will have it. She sucked in a breath and it sounded like a sob. Her hands fisted on her bent knees as she knocked her head back against the steel wall of the box.

Max's mind ranged helplessly back over that night. Thirty years ago and she remembered it with crystal clarity. It was a warm Thursday night in September and she was writing a paper for her wildlife-biology class. Her friend and roommate Giselle teased her away from her homework. *Just for a few hours. You're almost done anyway. I'm bored*. What followed was a bountiful mix of drinks—Thursdays were two for one at Mr. B's, a local bar. Harvey Wallbanger. Tequila Sunrise. Singapore Sling. Colorado Bulldog. Long Island Iced Tea. And dancing. Wild and fierce. Then came the questions. Hypotheticals. Ridiculous. Make-believe. *What if you didn't have to die? What if you didn't have to grow old and saggy and blotchy? What if you never got weak or sick? What if you could climb like a cat? What if you could run fast as a wolf? What if you could smell and hear like a bat? Would you want to? Would you say yes? Would you?*

Sure.

And then . . .

Max woke up months later, no longer human.

She was in a strange bed in a windowless room and she couldn't remember anything about how she got there. The lights were too bright and her body was wasted. Giselle was there. Smiling. So pleased. Bouncing like an eight-year-old girl on her birthday. She made no sense. *Did you know you have witch blood? Not much. But some. I thought so. It made it harder than I thought. Took longer. But I gave you all I promised and more.*

And more.

Shackles of magic. A body and mind that weren't *right*. Weren't human. She'd been made a Shadowblade—a witch's warrior powered by the elemental magic of the dark. She could never stand in the light of the sun again—even moonlight would hurt her. She tried to run away, but that meant pain. But she tried. Nearly four months the first time, ten the second, an entire year the third. Each time she crawled back, her body ravaged by the fight, reeled in by an invisible tether. Each time Giselle took her back to her altar of pain. To punish, to enhance, to wind the bindings tighter. When Max was weak, when she'd gone past the limits of herself, she could no longer resist. It made it too easy for Giselle. She stopped running.

Giselle was puzzled by Max's anger and betrayal. *But you said yes. I asked.*

Max swiped away her tears, her mouth twisting bitterly. "I said yes to the impossible—a faery tale. Not slavery," she muttered to herself in the hot silence of the steel box.

But since becoming a Shadowblade, she'd made herself an expert in faery tales, poring over them, learning all she could. Because as it turned out, they were all too real. And the fact was, faery tales were full of naïve idiots doing stupid things because they didn't know better. In faery tales, being stupid was a crime with a lifetime sentence.

She opened her hand, turning the hailstone in her fingers. She knew exactly what she wanted. She wanted to break the magical ties that bound her to Giselle's will. And then she wanted to kill the witch. Slowly and painfully. Max wanted Giselle to suffer the way she had suffered over the years, knowing there would be no mercy. Eye for an eye. Justice.

Could it happen? Was this chunk of ice enough to win her freedom after thirty years? She swallowed, ravenous hope clawing through her. With rigid fingers she shoved the hailstone back into her front pocket.

She couldn't think about it. Doing so made her compulsion spells claw at her. It felt as if her flesh were being flayed from her bones. Max closed her eyes and tried to let herself drift into sleep, but the spells weren't fooled. Then, too, the fire of unexpected hope was like a fist punching a dead heart to life. She didn't know when she'd be able to sleep again.

Less than an hour had gone by when she heard a key fitting into the driver's door.

"It's me, Lise," came the careless voice of Oz's second-in-command. The Tahoe shivered slightly as she got in. "You've got Giselle climbing the walls. Should be a good show when we get back. I've got popcorn in the microwave and front-row seats. Try not to disappoint, won't you?"

The smell of coffee curled through the cracks of the box, making Max's mouth water. Trust Lise to taunt her with it. "Sometimes you're a real bitch," she said, eyeing a Gatorade with loathing.

"Mostly I'm a real bitch," Lise replied with perfect equanimity as she turned the engine over and backed the Tahoe out. "Gotta be what you're good at, right? Just like you're a hard-ass with authority issues and a knack for scaring the shit out of people."

Max grinned. "I don't scare you. Rabid bears with grenades don't scare you."

"On the contrary. I've had to change my panties more than once after seeing you in action. I'm just glad you're on our side."

They took a sharp corner and Max braced herself against the steel. On *our* side. That was the hard part about killing Giselle—what would happen to everyone else who lived in Horngate? It was easy to say they'd all get along fine—join other covensteads or live free like most everybody else, but the truth was that joining a covenstead was no easy task, and most wouldn't know what to do with themselves without a witch to serve. That was the part Max wasn't sure she could live with, and it made her want to kill Giselle even more, if that was possible. The witch had done this to her. She'd chained Max with magic, then reinforced it with razor-wire bindings of loyalty and friendship.

Horngate was small, made up only of the twenty-two coven witches and their families, the Sunspears and Shadowblades, and a handful of others. It was situated in the unforgiving mountains west of Missoula, Montana, and spread across ten square miles of Rocky Mountain forest, though Giselle's territory ran south to Pocatello, east to Ennis, north to the Highline, and west to Kellogg, Idaho. As an elemental witch, Giselle drew magic from the powerful geological forces at work below the stone skin of the mountains. Most of the minor witches who served in the coven were also elementals, though a few practiced Glyph magic, which used symbols such as numbers, words, pictures, gestures, and so forth to generate and harness magic. There were no flesh mages in Horngate—they didn't have much to work with in Montana. The populace was too sparse.

The main hall of the covenstead was an underground fortress where Giselle lived with her Sunspears and Shadowblades. Most everyone else had built cabins in the surrounding mountains, close enough to be summoned quickly, far enough to gain a little privacy. Most of the witches and their families worked in the Keep or in the massive greenhouses that provided a steady income to Horngate. Through the year, they grew every manner of vegetable and fruit and sold them throughout the Pacific Northwest. Thanks to magic, the greenhouses were lush and productive, their produce in heavy demand. That business provided a stable income—enough so that the IRS didn't look at them twice. A few witches and family members worked in Missoula or Hamilton. Two were surgeons, five more were nurses, one was a farrier, one was a machinist, and two were teachers. But the bulk of Horngate's wealth came from magical services that Giselle sold at exorbitant prices. There was never a shortage of willing buyers.

To Max, Horngate was a sanctuary—a wild, fierce Eden for predators like her. She didn't know when, but it had become the place she thought of as home. If she destroyed Giselle, she'd destroy Horngate. If she didn't kill Giselle, if she only broke the bindings that held her prisoner, it wouldn't be enough. Giselle would hunt her to the end of the world. Max closed her eyes. She'd be forced to kill the hunters who came for her—Lise and Oz and the rest. Her hate flared white-hot and her earlier sense of hopefulness wilted. Her fingers curled into claws. *Damn the witch-bitch!*

The increasingly strong smell of the ocean and diesel fumes told Max they were driving into the warehouse district along the docks. The Tahoe turned this way and that, bumped over some railroad tracks and along a rutted road, then stopped. Max heard the sound of a metal door rolling up, and then they rolled forward. The door rumbled closed with a clang, and Lise drove a little farther, then put the Tahoe in park and shut it off. Max was already unlatching her light-sealed box. She slid the door up just as Lise popped the hatch.

Max wriggled out and levered herself upright. Lise was already walking away, heading for the kitchen tractor trailer affectionately dubbed the Garbage Pit. Max stretched, cracking her back. "Save me some coffee."

Lise waved dismissively. "Like you need the caffeine."

Max stretched, wishing she could follow. Her body had already burned through the powerbars and Gatorade, and the smells of garlic and fresh bread wafting through the air made her stomach cramp. Instead she glanced around the warehouse, taking its measure with a quick examination. It was windowless and sealed against light and dark. Witchlights illuminated the interior—even the darkness of a warehouse did bad things to Sunspears. The hospital semi was parked next to the far wall, and beside it, Giselle's RV. The Garbage Pit was slotted in next to it, and another couple of smaller RVs and a half dozen cars and trucks were parked haphazardly about on the concrete. It was a gypsy village, ready to roll at a moment's notice.

"Max. I want you. Now."

Giselle stood in the doorway of her RV, her voice echoing off the corrugated-steel walls of the warehouse. She didn't look like much. But then neither did black-widow spiders. She was beautiful and delicate like those spindly museum chairs that are useless for sitting and porcelain cups that break the moment anyone picks one up. She had straight chestnut hair hanging to her waist and was wearing blousy cotton pants with a halter top. She looked as weak and helpless as a baby lamb. Max snorted. A lamb with a streak of Jack the Ripper running through her.

The witch turned and went inside. Max followed her up the narrow steps. Inside, the RV was like a small, luxurious apartment. The cabinets were cherrywood and the floors covered in thick wool rugs. A small kitchen was on the left and a sitting room on the right. The walls were slid out to make it spacious. Giselle sat in a red leather chair with wooden-clawed feet. She curled her feet up under her, weaving her tanned fingers primly together. Max remained standing.

Giselle wasted no time. "Tell me again."

Max repeated her report, ignoring the cold of the hailstone radiating down her thigh from her pocket. She should have hidden it in the Tahoe, but she couldn't bring herself to be separated from it.

"How did you get caught?" Giselle's voice was accusing. She glared at Max, her hair lifting and curling on invisible currents. Max eyed it with a smirk of victory. Sure, it was childish, but she took what she could get, and needling Giselle always made her day. The witch noticed Max's look, and her hair smoothed into a starched silk curtain.

"When I broke the charm circle on the Hag, the magic burst attracted some attention. I took a hit and couldn't get under cover fast enough." Max shrugged. "I figured you'd prefer that to the Hag falling into the wrong hands, right?"

Giselle leveled a suspicious look at her. "You were thinking of what *I* wanted?"

"Yeah, well, she didn't seem to be all that happy being trapped and tortured."

Giselle sighed. "Thirty years and you still can't get past it," she muttered, recognizing the dig for what it was.

Anger rippled hot through Max. "You've got to be fucking kidding me. Which did you want me to get past? Being turned into a mutant freak by my best friend? Being enslaved by her? Or maybe all those hours of torture on your altar while you chained me tighter? Oh, yeah, I can see where you would think I could just forget all about that. After all, it's only blood under the bridge, right? Hardly worth thinking about."

"Max, I need you. I don't think anyone has ever made a stronger Shadowblade than you. Whether you know it or not, you're very precious. If you wouldn't resist my magic so strongly, I wouldn't have to drive you out of your head with pain before I can start working on you."

"Must be all my fault then," Max said acidly.

"You know, it's not like you didn't benefit from becoming a Shadowblade. You're stronger, faster, you'll never grow old, you don't get sick, and you're hard to kill. And I pay you very well. Most people would kill to be you."

Max felt her face contort. She willed her muscles to relax, feeling her usual mask sliding back into place. She took a breath. One more.

"Don't act like you've done me any favors. You screwed me over and you still are. Not giving me a choice is called rape and slavery."

There was a pause. Giselle lifted her chin, meeting Max's hot gaze squarely. "I couldn't have bound you if you hadn't agreed."

"I never agreed to this." An old argument. Max was tired of it. "Are we done here? I'm hungry."

"Not yet. What is your impression of what happened in Julian?"

Max forced herself to shift gears away from her anger. It served no purpose at the moment. "Someone sent the redcaps after the Hag, and I don't think it was the territory witch—her Blades were on cleanup. Whoever was behind it has to have balls of brass if half the rumors about Selange are true."

"They are," Giselle confirmed, her gaze narrowing hard on Max, who pretended not to know what she was thinking. Which was, what sort of payback for Max's trespassing was Selange going to demand tonight at the Conclave?

"Then our fearless invaders took a big chance. But why would anyone want the Hag? If the redcaps hadn't been stopped, they'd have killed her."

"Most likely they didn't care about her; they just wanted her staff. It has a great deal of power and anyone can use it. Legend is that it controls the destiny of humans—at least any humans near enough to get caught up in its spell. Which means either it's a powerful weapon for killing, or it can be used to control the population. Think about it. A flesh witch gets ahold of that and suddenly has an unlimited source of power. All she has to do is stir up the local humans and magic pours into her." Giselle paused. "Selange is a flesh mage. Now that she knows the Hag is there, she won't be able to resist that staff."

Flesh mages siphoned their magic from ordinary humans, who vented it like steam off a sauna. It came from their passions, their hatreds, their battles, and their burned-out hopes. Every emotion and interaction a human experienced created magic, and a flesh witch collected it like a big vacuum cleaner. And if that wasn't enough, or if they needed a really big spike of magic, they turned to sex rites and blood sacrifice. Thank whatever beings looked out over the universe that Giselle was not a flesh mage. Max couldn't draw a lot of lines as a Shadowblade, but she didn't hunt down helpless people and turn them into sacrifices so that some witch-bitch could generate a few more watts of magic.

She thought of Alexander. Did he?

"Go eat," Giselle said. "Stock up. Selange is going to issue a challenge—she likes unarmed combat to the death. Are you ready?"

Max shrugged, her grin pure malice. "If I win, I win; if I don't, I'm dead and you lose your favorite chew toy. Either way, I can't lose."

Giselle's mouth tightened and Max couldn't tell if she was biting back a smile or grimace. "Some might say dying is a loss. Your uniform for tonight is in your bunk. We leave as soon as it's dark enough."

MAX WANTED A SHOWER, BUT FOOD WAS MORE IMPORtant. The spells that made her a Shadowblade would start feeding on her body if she wasn't careful. The powerbars in the Tahoe had helped to replace what the Hag had taken from her, but she needed to calorie load and quick.

The Garbage Pit was putting off a mouthwatering mosh of smells. Max went around to the back of the semi where a set of stairs led up into the interior of the trailer. At the cab end was the kitchen, and lining the walls on either side were stainless-steel tables bolted to the walls and chairs bolted to the tables. The floor was matching stainless steel, as was most of the kitchen.

Low, haunting music played through the speakers. Except for Magpie, the cook, no one else was there.

Magpie glanced up, her eyes a shade or two darker than Max's, with two streaks of pearly white interrupting the blue-black ponytail that fell to the middle of her back. She was a witch of the outer circle, which meant she had some power, but not a lot, and not nearly enough to hold her own coven. She was also a damned good cook, and that's all Max needed to know.

"Sit," Magpie ordered, walking over to her with a jug of milk and an empty glass. "What are you hungry for?"

"Whatever you've got. You know what I like."

Magpie nodded and gave a half smile. Her teeth were white against her tanned skin. "I've got a couple of pans of enchiladas on the warmer. You can start with those."

"Sounds good." Max's stomach growled and she laughed. "Better hurry."

Magpie patted her shoulder and hurried back into the kitchen. Max drank a couple of glasses of milk in quick succession, then turned the glass between her fingers broodingly. She wanted to touch the hailstone, but didn't want to call attention to it.

Footsteps on the stairs made her twist around. The first person into the Garbage Pit was Oz. He stood about six foot three with sandy brown hair, blue eyes, broad shoulders that looked like they could hold up a tank, and about a dozen dimples. He didn't look like a Sunspear Prime, but just as with Alexander, power surrounded him like a cloud of hot lightning, and hiding behind those smiling eyes was an unrelenting violence. He was *scary*. When he walked into a room, anyone with sense started thinking about finding the exits.

Behind him came Niko, Max's second-in-command. He was about the same height as Max and looked to be as broad as he was tall—all of it was muscle. His eyes, like his fists, were stone. He always wore the latest New York fashion, which made him the object of much teasing among his fellow Shadowblades, all of which he took with good-natured humor. Still, Max knew she could count on him to have her back, no matter how bad things got. He didn't know how to back down or back off, and he could inflict more damage than a platoon of marines.

After him trailed Akemi. She was Chinese, with a broad forehead and rounded chin. She was the only Shadowblade in Max's crew who was actually shorter than her. More than a few idiots had mistaken her size for weakness. She'd set them straight—and dead. No one handled knives better than she did. She was also clearheaded, smart, and careful. Max had never seen her lose her cool. She smiled fleetingly as she entered, her eyes dropping. Dangerous as she was, she was also ridiculously shy. She was exactly what Max would expect the daughter of a geisha and a terminator to be.

Oz slid into the seat opposite Max. "Want company?"

"Do I have a choice?"

He smiled broadly, taking a drink from the milk jug. "Nope."

"What happened to you last night?" Niko asked. He sat at the table across the aisle, kicking his feet out and slouching down, tapping his fingers on the table in a drumbeat.

Akemi sat across from him, her hands folding together on the table, her back straight. She watched Max from beneath lowered lids.

"Trouble, of course," Max said, rubbing her forehead.

This was the hardest part of the role she played for Giselle. She liked Oz. She liked Niko and Akemi, though Akemi continually treated Max as some sort of half-god. The problem was that she *did* like them and she didn't want to. She didn't want to care. She didn't want Giselle to have any hostages against her good behavior. But she'd lost the knack for keeping them at arm's length. It had been easier in that first fifteen years. She had spent so much time running or laid out on Giselle's altar that she hadn't had a chance to get to know the other Shadowblades or Sunspears before they got killed in the line of witchy duty. Once she'd stopped running, she'd learned all she could about combat, strategy, tactics, and most especially about the world of magic—she had a mission. She wasn't going to die doing Giselle's dirty work until she could kill the witch-bitch herself.

That's when the rest of the Shadowblades and even a lot of the Sunspears started looking up to her, asking her for help, for advice. For years Max had been Prime in name only and finally had to take on the role for real or watch her friends die from sheer ignorance and inexperience. But the job came with confessions of fear and misdeeds, longings and hopes, grudges and frustrations. It brought them closer to her. Every day it grew worse. Attachments of the heart, drilled in with titanium screws she didn't know how to dislodge. Worse, she wasn't sure she wanted to anymore. Beneath the table, her fingers brushed across her pocket, feeling the cold of the hailstone. Maybe she didn't have to. Maybe there was a way out without destroying everything she'd come to care about. *There had to be a way.*

She gave them the bare bones of her night's activities. As she finished, Magpie delivered a plate of enchiladas and Max dug in.

"This could get ugly. Selange isn't going to take this sitting down." Oz pointed out the obvious while stealing one of the folded tortillas on the edge of Max's plate.

Max pointed her fork at him. "Touch my food again and I'll eat your hand."

He smirked. "Might be worth it. I always wanted to know what it would be like to have your mouth on me."

Akemi made a squeaking sound of disbelief and Niko snorted.

Max set her fork down carefully, pressing her hands flat on either side of her plate. She stared at her plate for a moment. Then she looked up at Oz. He looked wary, knowing he'd tested a line. Another day she'd have tossed back a razor remark or broken his jaw for him. But today . . . today she'd been given the first real hope for freedom.

A daring she hadn't felt for years swelled in her chest. It was heady. Oz flinched as Max pushed herself upright. She leaned over the table, stopping mere centimeters from him.

"All right then," she said, then closed the distance, pressing her lips to his.

Oz went rigid, then kissed her back. Their tongues touched tentatively, and Max tipped her head. He reached up, holding her face with his fingertips as if afraid she'd break, or maybe he was afraid she'd bite him. He tasted of milk and mints, and his tongue was deft and light. A sense of dizzy wonder rushed through Max. Like she was back in college with a future full of possibilities.

She pulled away slowly. Her brows rose. "Satisfied?"

Oz touched his fingers to his lips. His eyes were wide, his cheeks flushed. He shook his head. "Hardly."

She shrugged and sat back down, returning to her food. "I was afraid of that. I'm a bad kisser."

"That's not what I meant," he protested.

"But you weren't satisfied. How disappointing for you."

Niko chortled. Akemi was simply staring, her mouth open.

"You're just screwing with me now," Oz said.

Max shook her head. "And risk being judged unsatisfactory again? Oh, no. My ego isn't that strong. I'll leave screwing you to others."

His hand flashed out and grasped hers. He pulled it to his lips, waiting until she met his gaze. "One day, you're going to take me seriously."

She smiled, tugging her hand back. "I always take you seriously, Oz."

Magpie brought out more food, and the rest of the meal passed in pleasant ribbing. Max was more comfortable than she had ever been, and Akemi even loosened up enough to tease Niko about his love of designer clothing.

"It's a little silly in our line of work, don't you think?" she said softly, cutting her steak into precise cubes.

Niko smoothed a hand over his dark blue polo shirt. "What else am I going to spend my money on? And don't I look great in Dolce and Gabbana? It's made of bamboo. Looks like silk, washes like cotton. Blood comes right out of it. Women love me in it."

Akemi rolled her eyes and Max chuckled. "You're the

most fashionable man in Montana. The grizzlies and elk have never been so impressed. Besides, wouldn't you rather women love you *out* of it?"

Before he could answer, Max's phone chirped its high-pitched ring. Oz's followed in quick succession. His played the Miss Gulch theme from *The Wizard of Oz*. Max grinned at him, flipping open her phone. It was a text message.

Trouble. Come now.

Before she could think about what kind of trouble, Max had leaped over the table and down the stairs to the floor of the warehouse, Oz hot on her heels. Max flung open the door of Giselle's RV and climbed the stairs in two lunging steps.

Giselle flung her phone against the wall as they entered. She turned, her expression taut. "Alton is on his way."

"You told him where we are?" Oz asked in a flat voice that did little to hide his fury. Away from the covenstead their wards were not nearly as strong, making them far more vulnerable. Secrecy protected them from attacks, and Giselle had thrown it away.

"He's Horngate's oldest ally," she said. "And he can't reach Old Home. There's not been a word since last night."

Old Home was Alton's covenstead, a postage-stamp-size territory in the lush old-growth forests of northern Idaho.

"Did he scry?" Max asked with a frown. There should be no good reason a covenstead didn't answer.

Giselle shook her head. "He's too worked up. He's asking for our help." She looked at Oz. "Go guide him in. He can bring in his Spear Prime, but no one else. He also removes his personal wards."

Oz nodded. "I'll have my Spears close the perimeter. No one else will come through after him."

"Good. Go now."

He departed and Max eyed Giselle. With a mental twist, she forced aside her antipathy for the witch, focusing instead on the threat. "You really think this is an attack? You and Alton have been allies for a decade."

The witch shook her head. "I don't know what to think. But something *is* wrong. I can feel it. I can't treat him like an enemy—what if Old Home is in trouble? But we're vulnerable here, and he's the only one I might tell where we are, and only for something as dire as this. If he or somebody wanted to attack me, there would be no better way and no better time. I can't ignore the possibility. All the same, Max, he is an ally. Be as careful as you can without being too obvious."

"You're warded?" Max asked.

"I am, though if he's come for war, he'll be prepared and my personal wards won't stand."

"Then I'm about to be as obvious as a sword up his ass," Max said. "If he's innocent, then he'll just have to suck it up and get over it. Don't come out until I say so."

With that she exited the RV. Niko and Akemi were waiting outside.

"Alton's coming in with his Sunspear Prime," Max told them. "He says Old Home's gone silent and he wants help. It might be a trap. Roust the Blades. I want four snipers trained on the two of them from the moment they enter. You two join Oz in guarding them, and everybody else will shield Giselle. Questions?"

The two shook their heads and hurried away. Max went to her Tahoe and flipped up the cargo box beneath the backseat. She once again pulled out her shotgun. Flash-bombs would blind her Shadowblades and do nothing against Alton's Sunspear Prime. Grenades were too indiscriminate. Instead she loaded her .45 with shot shells. The steel pellets inside spread on penetration, and most of the steel remained inside the flesh. Both Uncanny and Divine beings were susceptible to the power of cold iron—which is what steel was mostly made out of. Hollowpoints would blow apart their heads or pulp their insides and tear a hole the size of a bowling ball on the way out, but at short range, the shot shells had enough stopping power to drop both Alton and his Spear Prime and still leave them alive to answer questions.

She frowned. Alton was a mediocre territory witch, relying on Giselle's strength to protect his covenstead. His coven was small, with only himself and six other witches. But he was as ambitious as any witch and tended to brag loudly and strut around to hide the fact that he didn't have a lot hanging between his legs. He was, in a word, a weasel. Max didn't like him. She snorted. She didn't like witches. But Alton was barely one of those. His Sunspears and Shadowblades were equally unimpressive. She could break Dorian, his Sunspear Prime, in half with one hand.

Ten minutes later Oz returned with Alton and Dorian in tow. Niko and Akemi waited just inside the small side door as it opened. They stood well out of the way of the wedge of sunlight that fell inside, then closed ranks on either side of the witch and his Sunspear Prime as the door swung shut. Oz and the two Blades held their guns ready, though politely aimed at their visitors' feet rather than at their chests.

Max stood in front of Giselle with six of her Shadowblades ranged in a circle around the witch, all of them armed to the teeth. Alton and Dorian both got the message.

"What is this, Giselle?" Alton demanded as he stopped. "Is this the way you greet your friends?"

He was a slender man dressed in tailored clothing that no doubt cost more than Max's Tahoe. He wore a ruby stud in one ear and a silver cuff bracelet on his left arm. His eyes were ringed in dark makeup, which, combined with his heavy brow and lantern jaw, gave him a look of brooding anger—sort of like a pissy housecat, Max thought. He also looked twitchy and worried. But what caught Max's attention was that he looked younger than the last time she'd seen him four months ago. The lines around his eyes and mouth had smoothed, and he walked more vigorously, his eyes bright with energy. Her shoulders tensed. Only magic could make a witch younger, and plenty of it. More than Alton had, or why would he have let himself age in the first place?

"Keep him there," she barked, and Niko, Oz, and Akemi leaped back and spun around to face the witch and his Sunspear Prime, their guns rising to heart height.

"Max?" Giselle said softly.

"He's lost a good ten years," Max said softly. "You can talk to him from here."

"I demand an apology," Alton called out, his voice rising. "I am here to call on our friendship and alliance and you point guns at me? This is intolerable!"

"All the same, Alton, the precautions are necessary. You are looking *very well,*" Giselle said. "I've never seen you look so young."

He stiffened, his chin jutting stubbornly. "I would speak with you in private."

"Say what you have to say or get out," Max said, her words hard as bullets.

"Put a leash on your dog, Giselle. She's crossed the line."

"I would, Alton, but Max is protecting me. Even if I order her away, she will not go. Her compulsion spells won't let her. Tell me about Old Home."

His face twisted, though with frustration or fear, Max couldn't tell. Maybe it was both.

"I have not been able to reach them since last night. The phones are down and no one responds to my computer messages."

"Did you scry?"

He dragged in a harsh breath, the muscles in his jaws knotting as he clenched his teeth. Red seeped into his cheeks like war paint. Max watched his hands. If he made even the slightest twitch like he was going to fling a hex, she'd drop him like a rabid dog.

"I could not settle myself enough. I have come to ask you to scry for me. You see far better than I do, anyway."

"Of course I will help. But it must wait until after the Conclave is over," Giselle said.

"No! That is too late. What if they need me?" he said hoarsely.

"There is nothing you can do from here. A few hours will make no difference."

He swayed forward. "Please! I left Caro there."

Max bit down hard on her lower lip. Caro was Alton's fourteen-year-old daughter. Behind her she heard Giselle draw a sharp breath. But her response was adamant.

"I'm sorry, Alton. I can't spend that much energy before the Conclave."

"You promised me help when I need it!"

"And I will give it. After the Conclave. Maybe you should go back to Old Home. You will almost be there by the time I can scry."

"I can't," he said, his teeth clamped together. "I must attend the Conclave."

Witches did not meet often, and usually people died when they did. Only at Conclaves was there a mutual peace, and this was the first in almost nine years. Max didn't know the purpose of this one, but only territory witches were invited, and to miss was to put up a neon sign saying you were too weak to sit at the grown-up table. Alton's cotton-glove ego couldn't handle that. He'd rather see Old Home swallowed by hell first.

A sly, menacing look slid over his expression. "That's what you want, isn't it? I go home and don't attend the Conclave." He paused a moment, his mind tumbling with the possibility. Suddenly he shouted. "Bitch! What have you done to Old Home?"

Silence echoed in response. Then Giselle said coldly, "Get him out of here."

Max heard her turn and step up into the RV. The door shut firmly. For a moment no one moved. Alton's mouth hung open in shock, and Dorian's brows furrowed as his gaze ran back and forth, figuring out just how deep was the shit he was standing in.

"You heard her. Time to go," Max said, striding forward.

"I refuse. Put your hands on me and I will fry you," Alton told Oz, who had begun to reach for him.

Dorian stepped in front of Oz, bristling. He was smaller than Oz by a couple of inches, and not as muscular. His weapons had been stripped before entering the warehouse, and now he held his fists like a boxer. Dumbshit. Oz had a gun and he didn't have any stupid ideas about playing fair. He'd put a hole in Dorian's head without batting an eyelash.

Suddenly Dorian turned and hoisted Alton over his shoulder in one smooth movement before jogging for the door. Maybe he wasn't as dumb as he looked.

"Put me down, Dorian, damn you! Giselle! This is the end for us! Our alliance is over! I will make you regret this!" Alton was still shrieking as Dorian carried him out into the sunlight. Oz followed.

As the warehouse door shut, Giselle's RV door opened. "Max, come inside."

Max did as ordered, setting her shotgun on the kitchen counter as she entered. Giselle was standing in the little hallway leading to her bedroom. She had her hands pressed flat against the wall on either side of her and she was shaking. Her face was gray-white.

"I'm sending Oz to Old Home. He'll take a mix of Sunspears and Shadowblades," she said abruptly.

Max shook her head. "That leaves you too vulnerable. We should wait until we get back to Horngate and then send out a team."

"No. This is an order, not a request. I want them on the road within the hour." Giselle started to turn away.

"Why? You generally aren't stupid, and this ranks right up there with canned cheese and clothes for cats. Better make a good case for it or Oz's compulsion spells will keep him right here where he belongs." Max couldn't help her smirk. Giselle's spells forced her Sunspears and Shadowblades to protect her at all costs. If it came down to a choice between obeying her orders and keeping her alive, the spells won every time. At Giselle's wince of annoyance, Max's smile widened into a grin. "Sucks, doesn't it?"

Her smile vanished as magic enveloped the witch in a crackling nimbus. Giselle crossed the kitchen in two strides and slapped Max across the face. The blow itself was nothing, but the magic was another thing entirely. It crashed over Max in a wave of black energy. It was like standing inside a nuclear reactor. Liquid heat filled her, cutting channels through her flesh and bones. Swords with electric blades stabbed her over and over. Max sank to her knees, gasping. She didn't fight, not that she could. She breathed, counting to four with each inhalation and exhalation. Her vision swam. She clung to consciousness, her fingers gouging streaks in the linoleum floor. Her body convulsed and her legs and arms twitched uncontrollably. The magic swelled until it felt like her skin would split.

Minutes passed as Max struggled in silence. She *would not* let her moans of pain escape. Her bladder clenched and her face screwed tight as she clamped down on the urge to pee. It wouldn't be the first time she'd ended up at Giselle's feet in a pool of her own piss, but she had no intention of doing it today. Finally the magic began to subside. Max felt certain spells inside her coming alive and beginning to gather it up to use for food. Brilliantly, Giselle had made Max's punishment as strengthening as it had been debilitating. Slowly Max pushed herself up, holding onto the counter as she swayed, her head spinning.

Giselle sat stiffly in her chair, her hair pushed back behind her ears, her hands clamped together. Her face was expressionless as she watched Max recover.

"Well, that cleared the sinuses," Max said in a raspy voice. Fueled by the residual magic, her healing spells were writhing inside her like a giant ball of spiders, fixing whatever Giselle had broken. "Feel better?"

"You need to take this seriously," Giselle said, her lips a gash across the lower half of her face.

Max frowned, studying her. Giselle looked haunted and worn. Her makeup barely disguised the shadows around her eyes and did nothing to cover the hollowness of her cheeks. Max straightened, her head ducking slightly, her knees flexing, as the predator in her took over from what was left of the human girl. "I'm listening. Tell me a bedtime story." She yawned and patted her mouth, unable to resist needling the witch.

"Is it so bad, being a Shadowblade?" Giselle asked, then flittered her fingers in the air. Her voice shifted, becoming crisp. "Never mind. You've made yourself clear on that often enough. I have some things you need to know. It's time." She paused and licked her lips, the corners of her mouth twitching in something like a nervous smile before flattening out again. She watched her fingers as she spoke.

"I have never spoken of this to anyone before. It is far too dangerous. But I have to trust you." She gave a wry shrug and glanced at Max from beneath her brows as if looking for a reaction.

Max's mouth fell open. She stared stupidly. "Are you kidding me? I spend most waking moments thinking of ways to kill you." She was so used to the rake of pain that accompanied her words that it was hardly noticeable. But then Giselle had made certain she had a high tolerance for pain. Practice makes perfect and all that crap.

Giselle snorted. "That's not exactly a state secret. But what I'm about to tell you might make you reconsider, if only for the sake of Horngate. My mother was a seer. A truly rare ability. One day she had a vision of the future. It was so powerful it nearly killed her. Then it wouldn't leave her. It came to her again and again. It tormented her. It became all she could see. She became a shadow of herself; her body could hardly handle the sendings." Giselle's face twisted and she stared hard at the cabinets above Max's head. Her voice roughened. "Then she was murdered. The entire coven was butchered. The blood was terrible." She swallowed and brushed at her eyes. "I was with my father when it happened. When we returned—" She broke off, her fingers pressing against her lips.

"We ran. Every time we thought we were safe, someone found us. They wanted no traces left of my mother's vision. But eventually we managed to find a haven. And then I started preparing for what is coming."

"And what's that?" Max couldn't help imagining the small, sunny child that Giselle must have been, arriving home to find a bloodbath, and no one left alive. Then being hunted, always hiding, always looking over her shoulder, always fearing what might be waiting around the corner. A grudging sympathy wriggled to life inside her.

Giselle scrubbed her hands across her face, rubbing circles on her temples as she drew a deep breath. Her hands fell to her sides. "My mother's vision said exactly what the Hag said. There is a war coming. It is already begun. It is going to get very ugly."

"A war for what? About what?"

"Magic—the very existence of it. Once it was everywhere—like the wind and rain. But then humans came along and started finding ways to kill it. Bit by bit it has disappeared. Many Uncanny and Divine creatures have died off or hidden themselves deep underground or inside magical pocket realms. The way things are going, all magic is going to disappear forever. The Guardians have decided that they will not allow this."

"The Guardians? As in mythical gods?" Max asked in disbelief. They were like bogeyman stories or Loch Ness monsters—constantly seen but never existed.

"They are not mythical, and no one is all that sure they are gods, either. But they are enormously powerful, and the Uncanny and Divine—every one of us—serve them. Refusal is . . . not allowed."

"What would they do to you?" Then it clicked. "Is that what you think happened to Old Home? Alton refused to serve and they destroyed his coven?"

Giselle's shoulders shifted in not quite a shrug. "It's possible. Maybe he just didn't act quickly enough. The Guardians are impatient. They don't tolerate disobedience or failure."

"Sounds like a witch I know."

"To prevent the destruction of all magic," Giselle continued, ignoring Max's barb, "the Guardians will raise armies. They will unleash a maelstrom of magic so that the earth itself strikes against humanity. They mean to slaughter most of the people and let magic return to the world. They have already begun. Hurricanes, fires, volcanoes, floods, droughts, earthquakes—have you noticed how many disasters have been happening recently? These aren't random or global warming. They are the first feints of battle. They mark the wrenching open of doors to all the places where the creatures of magic have gone to hide from human encroachment. All the creatures of the Uncanny and Divine are being summoned to fight, and the witches will be their generals. They will not allow anyone to sit safe on the sidelines. The devastation will be unimaginable. All we can do is try to stay alive and protect what we can. That's why I built Horngate. That's why I made you. I cannot do this alone. I need your help to keep our people safe."

"Why me?" The question had itched at Max since she'd first awakened on Giselle's altar. Of everyone to choose from, why her? Why not some other sacrificial lamb?

Giselle smiled, leaning her head back. "I had a vision of you, years before we met. It was only a flash, but you *glowed*. I can't explain it, but I knew you were going to be important in this struggle."

"Lucky me. Did you ever think to just ask instead of getting me drunk and tricking me?" The sting of Max's usual venom was dulled. Even to her the words sounded like reflex. Somehow she believed Giselle's story. The witch had never lied to her. Even in the bar that night, peppering Max with questions, she'd never actually said anything that wasn't true.

But Max didn't know if any of it changed anything. Her hate still burned. Hate and betrayal and fury at herself for being so stupid. Could she put aside all the hours and days of torture on Giselle's altar? Could she forget, even for a while, the endless agony, her mind made half insane by the horror of what was being done to her? And not just once or even twice, but over and over and over. It happened every time Giselle added a new spell. Every time Max's bonds started to loosen. The few drops of witch blood in her veins lent power to her furious resistance, and those bonds loosened regularly. How could she just let it go like it didn't matter?

"I couldn't risk that you would say no. I needed you to say yes—otherwise I could not have bound you. I hoped our friendship would mean something, that you would know I did not do this lightly. I hoped you would be pleased with the changes in you. If you think about it, you will agree that this life suits you. Do you think you could go back to an ordinary, human life now that you know what else is out there?"

"It should have been my choice," Max said adamantly.

"Perhaps. I have often wondered what you would be capable of if you were willing. Even as bitter and resistant as you are, there is no better Shadowblade. But you can't change what you are. Even if I wanted to, I can't unwind the magic that has made you. You are a Shadowblade and you always will be. So now, knowing what is coming, you have a choice to make. This business with the redcaps and the Hag and the ominous silence at Old Home—it all stinks of the Guardians. If so, they'll be knocking on our door soon."

"What exactly are you asking?" Max's stomach

churned. It felt as if the world were turning inside out—which, if she believed Giselle, was exactly what was about to happen. Did she believe? Honestly? *Yes, dammit.* But what was she willing to do about it?

"I am asking for your help. I am asking you to stop fighting me and start helping me."

Max tensed. Though she already knew the answer, she had to ask, "If I do? What will you give me in return?"

Giselle shook her head. "You want me to say I will free you. When it's all over. But I don't know if it will ever be over, and I won't lie to you and say it will be. I don't think I can ever let you go."

Max's teeth bared in a snarl. "You ask too fucking much. You always have."

"I know. Will you consider it?"

"Go to hell."

Max slammed out of the RV. The steel walls of the warehouse closed in on her. Her throat closed. She could hardly breathe. She shivered. She reached for her anger, wanting its comforting heat. But it was cold and bitter, like ash. She thought of the Hag's promise: *Know what you want. You will have it.*

She wanted her freedom; she wanted revenge.

But she couldn't have either.

Will you consider it?

Thirty years ago Giselle had bound her in magical chains, and today the witch-bitch had bound her again, this time in chains of duty and friendship. Not for Giselle. But for Oz. For Niko and Akemi and Magpie and Lise and everyone else who called Horngate home. Including Max. She had no choice.

Horngate needed Giselle, and the witch-bitch needed Max—the best of her—heart, mind, and soul.

A sound tore from Max's throat and her hands curled, her fingernails cutting deeply into her palms. Hot tears burned her eyes and a hollow space opened in her chest. Giving up her battle against Giselle tasted too much like consent—like she approved of what Giselle had done to her. Like she accepted and condoned it.

Her stomach heaved violently and she swallowed, swinging around and punching her fist into the side of the RV. A hand snatched her arm before she could connect. She stopped, tracing the arm to the shoulder and face. Niko. He looked worried, but he didn't let go.

She wrenched away. "What the fuck do you want?"

"You do realize that the protections on the RV haven't changed. Hitting it will only powder your bones. It won't even scratch the paint."

"Yeah, well, maybe it would make me feel better."

"Because a shattered hand makes everything better," he mocked.

"I could always hit you, though your head is hard as a rock."

"True. Now, not to be insulting, but you could really use a shower. Even Akemi thinks so."

He glanced over to where the Chinese woman stood with her arms crossed. She flashed a look of annoyance at him. "When you find your clothes in the burn barrel, you'll know how they got there," Akemi said.

Niko blanched. "That's just mean." Suddenly he grinned. "Look at that, Max. It's like seeing a baby take her first step, ain't it?"

"Pook gai," Akemi shot back, color flushing her round cheeks.

"Whoa!" Niko said, glancing at Max. "Did you hear that? I think she swore at me. Wow. That's two steps. I'm so proud."

"Niko, shut up before she cuts your tongue out," Max said, humor eating away the hot edge of her fury. "I'm going to shower. Do try to play nice." With that she stomped away, heading for her bunk.

4

MAX STEPPED INSIDE HER CRAMPED, LIGHT-sealed room in the bus. She wore a T-shirt and her underwear, her wet hair slicked back against her head. Her room was really nothing more than a cubicle paneled with fake wood with a narrow, folding bunk along the outside wall. Strapped to its underside was a collection of weapons and ammo. A small nightstand was beside it, and above it, a footwide closet. There was a mirror on the wall facing the bed, and nothing else.

On her nightstand was a note. She picked it up. It was a Taco Bell receipt. Scrawled across the back was one line: *Keep yourself and Giselle safe.* Oz hadn't signed it. So. Giselle had convinced him to go. He'd folded fast. Max wondered what Giselle had told him. Much to Max's relief, there was no mention of their kiss. Hopefully he hadn't taken it seriously.

She wadded the note and flung it against the wall, glaring balefully at the clothing laid out on the bed like a deflated corpse. The skintight, forest green suit consisted of leather pants and an almost-whole vest without any shirt. With a jerk of her arm she swept it onto the floor and lay down on her bed, setting the alarm for eight o'clock. She didn't fall asleep immediately.

Her mind roved over what Giselle had told her as she stared at the ceiling. The Guardians were real beings. Fuck. And Giselle was afraid of them. Which made Max want to curl up in a ball and hide under a mountain. Giselle was made of stone and ice. Max sighed, frowning. She didn't know a lot about Guardians. A lot of the legends claimed that they had created most of the Uncanny and Divine races, then abandoned earth for other dimensions. Which was a good thing because what little Max did know about the Guardians wasn't good. They were cruel, petty, and terribly powerful. Some said they'd set off Mount Vesuvius to teach one merchant about too much pride. Then, too, they were credited with the disappearance of Atlantis, the creation of the Sahara Desert, the black plague, and a billion other things large and small. Even if only a fraction of those stories were true, humanity was way the hell up shit creek.

She fell asleep, and though she dreamed, when the alarm went off, she couldn't remember any of them. They left behind a bad taste in her mouth and a residue of unease on her skin.

She swung off the bunk and grimaced as she reached for her night's uniform. She shimmied into the pants, then began wrestling with the vest. It was like putting on a straitjacket. Finally she got it on right and fiddled with the laces until they were tight enough so that it wouldn't fall off and would still be loose enough to let her breathe. By the time she was done, she was cursing Giselle in a low, unrelenting string.

She looked down at herself, tugging on the front of the vest, then over her shoulder at the small mirror on the wall. The lacings revealed wide strips of pale skin down her stomach and back, and two more beneath her arms. Her breasts bulged, halfway to falling out of the plunging neckline. What was annoying was the fact that the pants were too tight to let her do a good spin kick, and the vest offered precious little protection from pretty much anything stronger than a cool breeze. Not to mention that it would be incredibly inconvenient if her breasts flopped loose in the middle of a fight. On the other hand, it was pretty obvious that she wasn't concealing much of anything, least of all weapons. Which of course was the point.

The trouble with Conclaves was that no one was allowed to go in armed. Not that every Shadowblade wasn't a walking weapon and every single witch as deadly as a taipan snake and ten times as vicious. But that didn't mean Max was going to the Conclave unprepared for this whole thing to go south and in a hurry. Not after Giselle's warning.

Max packed a small backpack with her usual black jeans and long-sleeved T-shirt, a hat, her .45, and a half dozen clips loaded with shot shells, and another half dozen clips with hollowpoints. She threw in her knives, a garrote necklace, a handful of powerbars, and a body bag that was charmed against light. She'd put her hiking boots in later. She wasn't allowed to wear shoes to the Conclave either—that had everything to do with magic and nothing to do with weapons—even the witches went barefoot. She planned to stash the pack near the Conclave site. If and when the shit hit the fan, she wanted to be ready for it.

Now all she had to do was hide the hailstone. It was safer here than with her. She examined her small room, then opened the closet cabinet. She had a jacket hanging inside and a stash of books, powerbars, two bottles of Gatorade, a gallon jug of water, and a few other odds and ends.

Max reached up and pushed the short clothes bar out of its cradle. It was aluminum and hollow and offered the only possible hiding place. She tore the sleeve off one of her T-shirts and wrapped it around the glittering hailstone before shoving the package inside the bar. She settled it back in its cradle and hung her jacket back up. The hailstone wouldn't roll around and rattle and entice the curious. Besides, no one who wanted to live would come sniffing around, and she didn't have a roommate—privilege of being Prime.

She shut the closet and slung her backpack over one shoulder before stepping out of her room and closing the door firmly behind her. The back of the forty-five-foot RV was lined on either side with small compartments much like her own, except each of the others held two of the foldaway bunks. The hallway was narrow—barely two feet wide. There were no slideouts in the rear in order to keep the coach light-tight. In the front was the usual galley kitchen and a slide-out that provided a small lounge. The table and two small couches on either side plus the swiveling driver and passenger seats provided all the furniture.

Max grabbed a cherry Gatorade from the refrigerator

and guzzled it, tossing the empty bottle into the trash and heading out the door. A quick scan of the warehouse floor told her that Oz had taken one of the RVs and three cars. Niko and Akemi leaned against her pickup, and Tyler sat smoking a cigarette on the hood of her Tahoe. One of her Shadowblades, Tyler was tall and lanky with long, wispy blond hair, hazel eyes, and a close-trimmed mustache and beard. He was loose-jointed like a ballet dancer and rarely spoke unless he had something worthwhile to say. All three of them looked at Max as she came out.

"Who do we have left?" she asked Niko as she tossed her pack onto the passenger seat of her Tahoe.

"Us three, and Oz left four Spears. They are still on patrol."

"Go get 'em," Max ordered, and went to Giselle's RV. She hammered the door with her fist, then vaulted up inside without waiting for a reply.

Giselle sat in lotus position in her chair, her eyes closed, the fingertips of both hands pressed carefully against her face. She looked very witchy, wearing a sleeveless maroon silk blouse and matching pants, both batiked with a complex pattern that Max assumed had magical properties. Cuffs of silver chased with gold and copper circled her biceps and ankles. They were set with disks of black-veined turquoise and jellow jasper, the stones gleaming with subdued spell fire. A matching, wide, flat collar circled her neck, and twisted wire earrings holding round beads of turquoise and jasper dangled nearly to her shoulders. Her feet were bare but for three toe rings on each. On the right was a copper band set with an oval sunstone, a plain gold band, and one of iron set with amber all the way around. On the left was a silver band set with pearls, a platinum band set with black opal, and a thin band made of jet sandwiched between bloodstone. Each bit of stone and metal enhanced Giselle's magic.

She opened her eyes slowly and lowered her hands. "You know I could have been in the middle of a spell. If I had been, breaking my concentration would have been fatal to both of us."

Max shrugged. "And that's bad because . . . ? Besides, you'd be stupid to waste your strength now right before the Conclave. You aren't that dumb, but if you were, you'd use a proper spell web to contain yourself, and you'd be the only one dead."

Giselle sighed, unfolding her legs. "You really know how to give me a headache. Your attitude hasn't improved. Does that mean you are going to keep fighting me?"

"It means I still want you dead."

"Color me stunned. Should I call CNN?"

Max's mouth twitched. "Sun's almost down. Are you ready?"

"What have you planned?"

"I'll scramble the nest out of here and start them north. They'll find a shopping center somewhere up on 15 where they can wait for us to catch up. Just in case we need the hospital truck."

"Sounds good."

"I can't tell you how thrilled I am to hear you say so. Now, you'll ride with Akemi. Niko, Tyler, and I will shadow you in the cars. I'll drop the Tahoe and stash my gear as near to the Sagrado as I can before meeting you at the parking lot. You'd better pray there's no trouble. There's too few of us to handle a major attack."

"It's Conclave. The law calls for peace from dusk to dawn."

"You witch-bitches only obey the laws you can't get away with breaking," Max said.

Giselle shrugged. "No one can get away with it at a Conclave."

"Famous last words. You'll excuse me if I plan for the worst."

"That's what makes you the best."

"Fuck you. I'll stir the hive. You've got five minutes."

Max didn't wait for Giselle to reply. She stepped down out of the RV and shut the door hard behind her. Strengthening spells on it kept it from warping in its frame. It wasn't the first door Max had slammed.

She turned just as enthusiastic clapping broke out, and someone with a death wish gave a low catcall.

"Shut up, Lise."

"You are so smokin' hot," Lise replied with a leer. She and the three other Sunspears had joined Niko, Akemi, and Tyler at the cars. "Can I borrow that outfit when you're done? You can still be in it if you want." Her eyebrows waggled suggestively. "I'd never kick you out of my bed."

Max's teeth bared. "That's because you're a female tomcat. And you're welcome to it if I don't burn it first." She glanced around the group. "You Sunspears will ride with the nest. Tyler is going to take Lise's car, and Niko, you're in Kamikani's El Camino."

Kamikani was Hawaiian, with smooth skin the color

of aged mahogany and long, curly black hair. He wore a white T-shirt with the arms torn off and a pair of faded blue jeans with ragged white holes in the knees. He was only a couple of inches taller than Niko, and not quite as broad-chested. His 1969 El Camino was his pride and joy. He'd restored it himself and guarded it with his life. But at Max's order, he swallowed and handed Niko his keys.

"Don't scratch her," Kamikani said in his quiet, musical voice. "I will hurt you."

"Max isn't Prime because she avoids trouble," Niko said cheerfully. "Don't worry. I'll help you fix the car if anything happens. Or throw a hell of a funeral."

Kamakani shook his head. "Damned haole."

"That's me." Niko stretched out his arm. "White as alabaster. Beautiful as Michelangelo's David, aren't I?"

"Women don't like corpses," Kamikani said, shoving the arm away. "Or statues."

"I manage all right," Niko said smugly, twirling the keys around his finger. "I don't need a pretty car to get them to look at me."

"Baby, neither does he," Lise said. "He's gorgeous, he cooks like a pro, *and* he surfs. And just look at those eyes. . . . If I liked men, I'd fuck him every chance I got."

Kamikani flushed.

Niko feigned hurt. "But not me? No wonder you like girls. Help me out, Max. You like men. Which of us would you curl up next to on a cold night?"

Max eyed him balefully. "I'm too much for either of you two pretty boys to handle. I'd snap you in half. Now, Sunspears—keep your weapons ready and the safeties off. Wear your radios and keep your cells handy. If we need you, you'll have to come out and play in the dark. Hopefully not so long that it kills you."

Unlike Shadowblades, who either melted into a pool of liquid carrion or exploded in flame under enemy sunlight, Sunspears could function for a while when exposed to darkness—and it didn't matter what kind—a cave was just as bad as the night. They could last up to a few hours, depending on how much moonlight there was, how much sunlight they'd been exposed to recently, and how old they were. But eventually all of them would gradually freeze dry and crumble to dust. All of Giselle's Spears carried flash bombs as part of their emergency gear, and all their bunks were wired with LED lights backed up by magic in case the batteries failed.

"Akemi, you have Giselle. There's a place to hide the Tahoe up the canyon. I'll hike back and meet you. Once you park, there's no leaving until it's over, so you'll have to sit and wait in case things go well. If they don't, you'll likely be on your own. Don't let them catch you. They'll kill you for sure, and painfully."

The other woman was still a moment, then her neck stiffened and she nodded. Good. Max had been training her for six years. Akemi was better than she knew.

Max grabbed a map from her glove box and spread it out on her hood, pointing at the area. "The Conclave is right around here." She pointed to a spot east of Balboa Park. "It doesn't show up on any maps, and there is only one road in. It leads into a box canyon and ends in a gravel parking lot.

"The canyon is one of several others surrounding a broad, lone butte. It's got a lot of tree cover—it may be the only place in San Diego with a plentiful supply of water, thanks to witchcraft. At the top is the Conclave site—the Sagrado. Niko and Tyler, I want you to wait out here on the public roads." Max tapped an area between Pershing Drive and Fern Street. "Most of these other streets are residential, and they dead-end above the canyons—stay out of there. If anyone sees you cruising around, they'll think you're casing the McMansions and call the police. Niko, I want you here at Thirtieth and Palm. It's commercial and no one will look twice at you. Tyler, I want you down here at Juniper and Fern. Do not go to sleep or get distracted. Both are a good mile or more away from the Conclave, and if there's trouble, you'll need to haul ass.

"The road into the canyon runs down along the ridge at the edge of the golf course, here." Max stroked her finger along the green blotch on the map. "It feeds out into Elm Street, though none of you will be able to access it. The veil is thinned tonight for Conclave, but you still need a witch to get through."

"How are you going to do it alone, then?" Tyler asked.

Max glanced at him. He was smart, which most of the time was a good thing. But she didn't really want him to know how she was going to get through the veil.

"I've got a talent for that sort of thing," Max replied with a finality that slammed the brakes on following that question any further. "Niko, if we come your way, we'll be on foot with wolves chewing our heels. Be ready for it. Tyler, if we come to you, it will be a car chase. Any other questions? Everybody know what they have to do?"

"Why don't I wait up on Elm? It's only five blocks down," Tyler said, pointing on the map.

"Because if things go the way I think they will, we're not coming out Elm Street," Max said. "We'll be climbing out on foot somewhere along here or here." She stabbed the map impatiently, then forced herself to reel in her anger. It was a good question, and Tyler had never been to a Conclave. None of them had. It was like jumping into a pit of lit dynamite. It wasn't so much a matter of *if* it would go off, as *when*. "If we make it back to the Tahoe, I'm more likely to four-wheel it across the golf course to Pershing or Florida Drive, than try for Elm Street. No sense making an easy target out of ourselves by going where we're expected."

There were sober nods of understanding and agreement.

Just then Giselle stepped out of her RV. Max waved at everyone to load up. She stepped up on the running board of the Garbage Pit. It would lead the others out. Magpie rolled the window down.

"Head up 15 and find some place reasonably inconspicuous to spend the night. If you don't hear from us by the time the sun's been up a couple hours, hit the road and keep going. You won't be safe until you hit Horngate."

Magpie nodded. Then suddenly she twitched oddly like someone had shaken her. Her eyelids dropped low and her body went rigid, her head snapping back against the headrest. Her eyes sprang wide and went entirely white. Her lips opened and her voice was guttural when she spoke. "No safety there, not for anyone. Not until you return. Only you can make it safe."

Before Max could react, Magpie slumped. She pushed her hair from her face with trembling fingers. Her eyes had turned black again.

"What was that? What did you mean?" Max demanded. Her fingers tightened on the side-mirror frame, crushing the fragile metal.

"What did I say?" the other woman asked, then waved her hand sharply. "No, don't tell me. It wasn't for me or I would remember. It was meant just for you. But, Max, I warn you—the things that I say are *true*. Ignore it and you'll probably regret it."

With that, Magpie rolled up her window and turned up her radio. Max stepped down, scowling. *There will be war. It stands already on the threshold.* And Old Home wasn't answering its phones, and in Julian redcaps had gone hunting a Blue Hag. The Guardians were real and ready to destroy the human race. And now a mystical warning from Magpie. Max tapped her fingers against her thighs. Danger was gathering, coiling in tight knots of unbearable, unstoppable power. Max could feel it like a swelling thunderstorm. When it burst free, there would be death, and a lot of it. She was certain of it.

Only you can make it safe.

A chill unfurled slowly down her spine and ran all the way to her heels. Goose pimples rippled across her skin. How the fuck was she supposed to do that?

She shook her head, clamping her teeth together. That was a problem for tomorrow. Today she had to get through Conclave and keep Giselle alive. Otherwise tomorrow didn't matter a rat's ass.

Max finished checking the other rigs, then went to the warehouse entrance and rolled up the two main doors. She motioned Magpie to move out first. The cook didn't look at Max as she rolled past. The other

RVs and the hospital truck followed, spewing clouds of diesel exhaust.

When they were through, Max slid into her Tahoe. As she pulled out onto Commercial Street, heading north for the Conclave, she thought again of the hailstone and wondered if she shouldn't have made her wish before it was too late to do so.

5

TRAFFIC, AS USUAL, EVEN AFTER DARK, WAS HEAVY. It was eighty thirty. In Montana, it wouldn't have been full night for another hour and a half. There were, Max decided, one or two good things about San Diego. She would have liked to swim in the ocean, but this wasn't a vacation.

Glancing in her mirrors, she saw that Akemi was riding her bumper with Tyler on the left and Niko behind him. Max turned off on Twenty-seventh Street, then wove aimlessly about, making right and left turns with no reason or rhyme. A little after nine, Max pulled off Dale onto Elm. Akemi followed, while Niko and Tyler turned in the other direction. Max speed-dialed Akemi.

"Cut your lights and pull up behind me. Tuck against my bumper and don't back off until we cross the veil. Once inside, drive as slow as you can. I'll catch up with you before you reach the parking area."

She snapped her phone shut on Akemi's quiet affirmative. A moment later, the red crew cab jolted Max's bumper. At Granada Avenue, Elm came to a dead end. Ahead was a garden fronted by a pair of crepe myrtles, a cluster of oaks and eucalyptus, an enormous prickly pear cactus, and a low screen of bushes and palms. Between the two myrtles at the curb was a yellow sign with a double-ended arrow helpfully pointing out the dead end and directing traffic to turn. Below it was a red, diamond-shaped sign that said nothing at all. It had nothing to do with guiding traffic. It was there to thin the veil for the Conclave.

Both Granada and Elm were eerily quiet. The repulsion spells that kept curious people from investigating past the dead end had been expanded, gently pushing traffic well away from the entrance to the Conclave road. Those same spells had pushed away the residents as well. Max nodded. She'd timed it so they'd likely be one of the last to arrive and no one would see the extra car crossing.

Max lifted her foot off the brake and onto the gas. The two vehicles crept forward and up over the crumbling curb. Max drove between the myrtles and through the sign. For a moment there was a grinding sound as the signpost pushed back. Then suddenly it folded gently to the ground. Max drove over it and past a small PROTECTED HABITAT sign.

Just beyond, the air turned thick as syrup and everything outside the Tahoe runneled together like melting wax. Forces moved against Max. They bumbled, large and blind. They bulled into her chest and head and nuzzled against her with all the grace of an angry elephant.

The pressure ground against her, loosened a moment, then clamped hard. The breath exploded from her lungs. She gagged and coughed, still pressing firmly on the gas. The Tahoe rolled relentlessly forward, the engine revving loudly. The magic of the veil held it to a slow crawl. Inside the Tahoe, the air around Max hardened until she felt as if she were caught in a block of glass.

She couldn't breathe; she couldn't move. Aching pain swelled in her muscles. Her body convulsed, her teeth grinding together. Her fingers clenched on the steering wheel. The resin cracked under her grip.

Almost there . . .

She tipped her head back against the headrest, every muscle rigid. She coaxed herself, *C'mon . . . Anytime now.*

Then suddenly she felt a *give*.

The spells that Giselle had carved deep into her flesh and bone more than twenty years before shivered and woke. A tornado of sparks roared through her. Max gasped, feeling tendrils of magic uncoil from beneath her skin. They plunged through the veil like sturdy roots. Instantly the pressure began to subside. She drew a deep breath, blinking away the muzzy film gauzing her eyes. She swiped at the trickle beneath her nose and frowned at the blood on the back of her hand.

Fucking hell. If the veil hadn't been thinned, she'd have probably gone unconscious. The lock-spell was supposed to work better than that. *And when had it ever?* She jeered at herself silently, licking her blood from her skin.

She eased the Tahoe onto the gravel road just ahead, checking her rearview to see how Akemi and Giselle fared. They were right behind her. Giselle had opened a slit in the veil to allow them to pass through. Max's lock-spell should have done something similar for her. But it wasn't that easy. It never activated until she was at least half-dead. Which, according to Giselle, was because of Max's bad attitude. "It's your witchblood. It gives your stubbornness muscle. You can *will* the spells stronger if you want, and you can *will* them not to work. Look at the healing spells. They work instantly because you are so completely determined to stay alive to kill me. All you have to do to make the other spells work just as well is accept being a Shadowblade—accept that this is your life now and you can never go back."

All she had to do . . . Max shook her head sharply. "Bet that's what Mengele said to his victims, too," she muttered aloud, then grimaced. Wasn't talking to yourself a sure sign of insanity? But then, she didn't really have anyone else she wanted to talk to about Giselle.

Abruptly she pressed down on the gas. The Tahoe fishtailed and gravel shot into the air. Max eased up slightly, straightening up and steering the Tahoe down the steep road. Trees crowded close—mostly juniper and scrub oak with scraggly bushes in between.

She reached the turnoff for the box canyon where the parking was and the trail up to the Conclave began. The road was made of stone, each square of gray rock etched with centuries-old magical symbols. The forest that rose up around her now was a bizarre mix of trees that had no business growing in San Diego.

The turnout that Max had been looking for was just where she remembered from her only other visit to the Sagrado. It was a shadowed cleft in the canyon wall bracketed by two juts of rock dotted with clumps of dried grass and scavenger bushes. Max backed in, maneuvering until the Tahoe was well under the trees. She got out, pulling her backpack with her and leaving her cell phone on the console. There were no signals inside the veil. She hid her keys in the crook of a knobby oak and launched herself up the canyon wall. The moon was hidden by a bank of clouds that hunched low in the east, making it easier for Max to see. She reached the top of the ridge and found a deer track through the trees. She sprinted along it.

Near the Conclave butte, the path veered around the edge of a rocky ravine. Tall pines grew up out of a thicket of scrub. She edged down, rocks sliding beneath her feet. At the bottom of the ravine, she chose a pine that couldn't be seen from above. From her backpack she pulled a spool of fluorocarbon fishing line. She unwound several feet and tossed the spool high over a branch. It looped over and fell back to the ground. Max slipped off her backpack and knotted the end of the line around the top loop and snapped the spool off the other end before tucking it back inside the pack. She stepped out of her hiking boots and shoved them inside, then quickly drew the pack up until it was snug against the limb. Anyone looking would have a hard time seeing either the line or the pack. She tied off the other end around the trunk of the tree, then climbed back out of the ravine.

At the top, she stopped to sniff the air. The cocktail stench of the city had faded only slightly inside the veil, making it nearly impossible to smell danger. Not that she needed to. She could feel it swallowing her. Its teeth slid along her skin, its breath licked her like flames. Swiftly she began to run again, this time angling back just east of where she'd concealed her Tahoe.

She made good time, and Akemi had driven very slowly. Max crouched in the trees as the Chevy truck wound nearer to her. When it curved around the bend, Max streaked across the ground and vaulted into the open rear window of the crew cab.

"Any trouble?" Giselle asked.

Max raked her fingers through her short cap of blond hair, pulling out a twig and a couple of pine needles. "No."

"But you think there will be."

"You don't?"

Giselle said nothing for a long moment, and Max didn't think she was going to answer. Then the witch said, "I trust your instincts."

Max felt herself recoil. She didn't want Giselle to trust her. She wanted the witch-bitch to fear her. She wanted her to always be looking over her shoulder, wondering when Max would finally break her chains and rip her head off.

"You trust my instincts, but still we're going to walk into the fire." Magic itched at her, raking steel claws down her nerves. Her compulsion spells prodded at her to carry Giselle off somewhere safe. Max fought to keep from leaping over the seat and grabbing the wheel.

"There is no choice."

"How am I supposed to keep you in one piece if you just bumble stupidly into trouble?"

"You will do what you do best, same as always," Giselle said with a dismissive wave of her fingers. Then her voice hardened. "If the war my mother foresaw has finally begun, then we have to know what the rest of the covens are going to do. It's the only way Horngate will survive." She turned her head, her delicate profile coldly austere. "Understand, Max. I'll do whatever it takes to keep Horngate safe. That means I sometimes have to risk myself. This isn't the first time, and it won't be the last. So shut up for once and do as you're told."

"Yeah, well, next time you decide to throw yourself under a bus, do me a favor and loosen up the compulsion spells so I don't have to die with you."

"But I don't plan to die. You *will* protect me. I have total faith in you."

"Bite me," Max said, her fingers curling into claws, her stomach clenching tight. The pain of the compulsion spells was harder to ignore than ordinary, physical pain, and it hurt far worse. Probably because she'd got so good at managing agony, Giselle had felt compelled to up the ante so that Max couldn't ignore it.

But she could manage this, too.

She drew a breath and forced her muscles to relax. For years she'd endured pain and torture that no ordinary human could ever have survived. Time after time, she'd lain on Giselle's altar while the witch pushed her to the brink of death and insanity, until Max inevitably broke and Giselle was free to etch her spells into Max's flesh, bone, and soul. Each time Giselle was driven to greater effort. Each time it took longer and more pain for Max to break. She'd learned to embrace the agony, to savor its mouth-full-of-salt corrosion and welcome its hot, caustic touch seeping through her entrails and burning through her heart. She began to draw a perverse strength from it. The pain reminded her of who she was. And so long as she remained so, she could still get revenge on Giselle. For that nebulous promise, Max could suffer anything. Even if sometimes *anything* was more horrifying and painful than she could imagine. And Max had a hell of an imagination. But then, so did Giselle.

Now she let the pain ripple through her. A tremor ran down her neck to her heels as her body perverted the hurt to certain pleasure. Max smiled, triumph burning hot in her gut. Each time she accepted the pain, she grew stronger, and Giselle had to work harder to break her.

Max straightened up, looking through the windshield. Ahead was a lush blackberry-bramble wall. Like all the other plants that shouldn't have existed inside the veil, it was fed by springs induced to the surface by magic. The road disappeared through a notch wide enough for only a single vehicle. There were no guards that Max could see.

Akemi drove through slowly. The parking lot was full of expensive cars, including a half dozen limos. Shadowblades stood about like stiff soldiers, mostly watching each other suspiciously, though a few talked together and a handful played cards on the hood of a Jaguar. They all turned to watch Akemi's truck enter.

"Pull around and back into that spot over there," Max said. It wasn't really a space. The back bumper of a yellow Hummer hung well into it. Akemi would have to shove her truck into the bramble. Which meant that anyone attacking her would likely come from the front or over the Hummer. It also gave her a straight run at the entrance or thorny back exit.

The bramble gave way grudgingly, scraping the side of the truck viciously. Akemi gunned the engine, her knobby off-road tires gripping the ground hard. The truck lunged backward until the bed was overhung with brambles and the hood was half-covered.

Akemi glanced in the rearview mirror at Max. "You owe me a paint job."

"I'm good for it," Max said, her mouth stretching in a pirate's grin.

She crawled over to the other door and let herself out and walked to the front of the truck. The other Shadowblades continued to watch the newcomers. Max recognized one or two and nodded at them. Her scalp prickled. All around her swelled the scent of magic. It was almost smothering in its intensity.

"I thought there would be someone guarding the entrance," Akemi said in a quiet voice.

"There is," Giselle said. "Just hope you don't ever see them. It will be the last thing you do. You won't get out the entrance until the Conclave releases and I come back for you. If something happens, try going over the bramble wall. You might have a chance, then."

"Nothing like that guarded the place last time," Max said.

"Last time the Guardians didn't call us here. The Sagrado belongs to no witch. It lies inside Selange's territory, but it belongs to the Guardians. They have rules and they send minions to enforce them. Tonight—who knows what creatures stand watch. Be warned. Whatever they are, they will offer no mercy if you attempt to leave before the Conclave ends. It is the law."

Akemi had gone pale at the the word *Guardians*. She swallowed and nodded.

"We're going to be late. Max, let's go." Giselle strode toward the entrance. Max overtook her and walked in front of her.

"There's no danger here," Giselle said. "The Guardians won't permit it."

"What if they can't stop it?" Max muttered, and prowled ahead.

"They are the reason we are here tonight. They will not permit any of us to come to harm."

Max stopped, pivoting to stare into Giselle's green eyes. "And what if they want to hurt you?"

Giselle's brow pinched. "Why would they?"

"Hell if I know. You know more about them than I do. But given what's happened in the past couple of days, I don't trust anybody tonight."

"Very well," Giselle said.

As if Max needed her permission.

They walked back out of the parking area. The feeling of the magic swelled, sliding over Max's skin like razor-edged gossamer. She heard breathing—deep, slow, rasping sounds like the grinding of rocks beneath a glacier. In the grass beside the blackberry-bramble wall was a matted spot the size of Akemi's truck. There was a snorting sound and the grass fluttered on an invisible wind. Something was sitting there.

Above there was a flapping sound. Max's head jerked up. She saw nothing but the stirring of wind across the leaves. A smell like rotting vegetation and carrion drifted sluggishly through the air. A sudden sweep of motion burst past Max's head, lifting her hair. There was a low, laughing sound, feminine and hungry.

Max swung around, tracing the invisible flight of the creature through its smell and the curling of the air behind it.

"Forget it. They aren't going to bother us. We need to get up to the Conclave," Giselle said.

Though Max wasn't convinced, there was little

point picking a fight with invisible monsters. Instead she turned back up the mossy path and broke into a slow jog. Behind her, Giselle followed suit. The trail wound back and forth in wide switchbacks, climbing steeply up the butte through the thick trees and underbrush. Max let her instincts take over. Her senses reached out like floodwaters, pushing into every nook and crevice and tracing every edge of the night. Her ears snared every sound, her nose sifted myriad scents, and her skin logged every shifting caress of the air. She sank down into the sensations, her body coiled to strike.

Halfway up the butte she stopped short. Giselle came up to stand beside her. Max turned her head to the side, her eyes closed. She'd never smelled magic quite like it. It smelled of glacier ice and mountain rain with an acid quality that warned of fire, stone, and steel. It crossed the path and circled to the left and the right around the shoulders of the slope.

"What is it?" Giselle asked.

"Magic—but not Uncanny or Divine. It's a boundary and very powerful. It wasn't here before."

"It's one of the Conclave spell circles. There are three. As the last witch crosses, each will close and keep anybody else out."

"And everybody in," Max murmured. Would her lock-spell be strong enough to get her out if necessary?

Giselle took Max's hand. The witch's fingers were warm and strong and fine-boned. She stepped forward, pulling Max with her. The two passed through a paper-thin thickening of the air. It was frigid cold. The chill flashed through Max, crystallizing in her throat. Then they were through. She drew a breath of the warm night air, shaking off Giselle's hand.

Movement caught her attention. She spun. White vines of mist rose out of the ground and twisted into the air, curling and coiling together in a ghostly filigree filled with demonic faces. As they watched, the weaving grew into a dense barrier. It sounded dry, like the rubbing of a snake's body against itself. The wall marched toward them, swallowing the downhill ground.

"Keep moving. You don't want to let it touch you," Giselle warned, her shoulder rubbing against Max's as she glanced over her shoulder.

The moon had broken free of the clouds and hung shining and brilliant in the sky when they crested the top of the butte. The dapples of moonlight blistered Max's exposed skin, which healed and blistered again as she passed in and out of the shadows. She suppressed the urge to scratch the maddening healing itch. The path curved around to the right and coiled completely around the flat hilltop before straightening to cross a flat greensward of emerald grass. Here the path changed to flat amethyst tiles.

Max strode unflinchingly from the protection of the trees. Her vision clouded as her eyes bubbled. She could hear a faint sizzling sound as her skin cooked. The pain rippled over her and wrapped her in a pulsing cocoon. She shook herself, embracing the hurt. It was hers. It was good.

The greensward swept away on either side of the path, surrounding a great stone hulk of a building that looked like an old mission. The front was cornered by a domed tower on the left and a shorter bell-tower on the right. Max guessed Spanish monks had built it—or witches masquerading as monks.

Flowering jasmine hung on a leafy curtain over the rough-hewn stone, and creeping masses of rosemary humped around the foot of the ancient church, the pungent stems sprinkled with tiny blue flowers. There were no doors or glass in the arched openings that ran down the length of the building. Instead they were filled with the flickering glow of candlelight. The strong odors of herbs and oils drifted through the empty windows, mixing with the heavy scent of the flowers, smog, and swirling magic. The miasma was so strong that Max could hardly detect the odors of the people within. She knew a crowd was inside—easily three or four hundred people.

Max stopped suddenly, her back stiffening. She swiveled her head. They were being watched.

6

Alexander had begun to wonder if Max and her witch were coming to the Conclave after all. Maybe they thought they could run from Selange. He did not know whether to be glad of it or not. He was more than a little intrigued by Max. She had saved the Hag and forged a blood bond with the Divine creature. It bordered on insane, or criminally stupid. So did leaving him alive. He did not think she was either. So why?

The questions itched. He knew he would get his answers eventually. Once he won the night's challenge, Selange would pry the answers out of Max. His jaw hardened. It did not matter if she gave the information freely. Selange would never believe any of it without torture. His witch trusted it better than other means of questioning. After, Max might be useless. Or dead.

He remembered that long hypnotic moment staring into her eyes. He could almost feel himself facing her again and that sensation of falling into an abyss. Heat filled him and, just as swiftly, died beneath a chill that stabbed through him like a spear. He wiped a hard hand over his mouth. He was attracted to her. He could not argue that. She was beautiful, smart, capable, and powerful—everything that made him hungry for a woman. He wanted her and it had been a long time since he had wanted anyone. But the pull was deeper than that—like a riptide dragging him under. It was as if he recognized her—or something in her. Whatever it was spoke to him down deep in his gut. Sort of like getting kicked. The idea of Selange torturing her to death set his teeth on edge, but there was nothing he could do.

Thus when Max and her witch appeared on the amethyst path and the mist rose in a white wall behind them, his feelings were mixed. He watched Max prowl ahead, her head turning from side to side, her stride boldly confident. He watched a moment, then went to inform Selange of their arrival.

He found her in the nave. She stood talking to two witches from Arizona, both with crow-black hair shining blue in the candlelight. Selange tapped her red-tipped nails against her thigh, glancing about impatiently. Alexander slid through the crowd of witches and stopped at Selange's elbow.

"They have arrived."

Her crimson mouth tightened and then curved. "Finally. Go wait with the others. The challenge must wait until the Conclave business is over."

Dismissed, Alexander retreated through a small door at the east end of the Sagrado—it was the Spanish word for "sacred," given to the Conclave site on its founding. Most did not remember that, or care. Alexander liked to know the history of things.

Outside was an outbuilding so overgrown with jasmine that only small red patches of its terra-cotta roof tiles showed through. A fountain made from a single scepter of smoky quartz rose from a mosaic stone circle in a grassy courtyard between the buildings. The quartz glowed from within as water gurgled from the top and splashed down its sides.

Alexander glanced up at the moon and pushed his glasses more firmly up his nose. The reflected sun heated his skin and soon he'd start to blister. He considered the jasmine-covered building. Shadowblades milled inside, some talking and laughing, some playing cards or dice, and more than a few getting belligerent. Alexander didn't hesitate as he passed by the fountain and went to lean in the shadows of one of the basalt monoliths circling the fountain like sentries. It did nothing to hide him from Shadowblade eyes, but it kept the moonlight off him. He touched the reddened skin of his cheek, feeling his healing smoothing away the heat. He crossed his arms, watching the Sagrado . . . waiting for Max.

Nearly twenty minutes had gone by before the door finally opened. She shut it behind her, but did not leave the shelter of the small alcove. Instead she stood a moment, then dropped lazily into a watchful crouch, her elbows propped on her leather-clad knees.

Mosquitoes buzzed and night birds chirped. There was a crackle of a seedpod popping open, and a rustle of a frog through the rosemary. Finally, when it was clear she would wait out the Conclave where she crouched, Alexander pushed himself away from the watch stone.

Her attention riveted on him the moment he stirred. Her expression was impassive, and Alexander did not doubt that she had seen him standing there from the moment she emerged through the door.

He stopped at the bottom of the steps so they were nearly eye to eye. She did not speak. Once again he felt unsettled by her dark-eyed regard. Anger uncurled slowly inside him. At last he was compelled to break the silence.

"You know Selange will challenge your witch because you were in Julian?"

She nodded. "Yes."

Her indifference stirred the flames of his annoyance. He wanted to break her cool mask and see within. "It will not be combat to the death. Selange wants you alive. She wants . . . you."

Her brows flicked up in momentary surprise, then her face smoothed. "Does she now?" Max drawled. She tipped her head. "I noticed she didn't know my name. Why didn't you tell her?"

"Maybe it was self-preservation," he suggested.

She nodded with a dark understanding, and something bleak and violent shifted in her eyes. For a moment her face seemed made of ice and steel.

"Thanks for the heads-up. I suppose the challenge will be endurance?"

"Yes."

She nodded again, scanning the night. "Sorry, then."

"For what?"

She gave him a sideways look, then the corner of her mouth quirked in a half smile. It was cynical and lasted but a moment. "Giselle is a good torturer." She looked back out into the night. "And I am a very good victim."

The last caught Alexander up short. What did she

mean? Much as he did not want to, he could not avoid the obvious conclusion. It made his stomach clench. Selange had plenty of faults, some that made his stomach turn, but she did not routinely torture her own people. What sort of witch was Giselle?

Max smiled again, this time in a bleak, distant way. Alexander had a feeling she was looking inward and wasn't pleased with what she found. He searched for something to say, but words failed him. Strained silence pooled between them. In the end, it was Max who broke it.

"I hope whatever you were up to out there in Julian was worth what we're about to go through."

Alexander replied automatically, unthinkingly, "I would suffer anything for Selange and be glad of it." But it was not true. Long ago he'd drawn a line he would not willingly cross again. But the words were gone and the damage done.

Max's head slowly turned. "Is that what you really believe?"

No. Not anymore. Not for a long time. But loyalty and years of habit would not let him say it. She was his enemy, tonight at least. And he would show her no weakness, no doubt. "Of course."

Her lip curled as if she would like to spit at him. Instead she turned away. Transparent shadows hollowed her cheeks and eyes so that for a moment she looked cadaverous. "You are a waste of skin," she said slowly.

Alexander recoiled from the flat hate in her voice, even as answering anger flowed through him, heating his voice. "I am a Shadowblade and I serve my witch with all my heart and soul," he said. "It is what I am and I make no apologies for it."

"Honor," she scoffed. "And what has she done to deserve your heart and soul? Not to mention your pain and suffering?"

"She has given me a life I could only have dreamed of. She gave me gifts beyond measure."

Max rolled her eyes. "We'll see if you still think so when Giselle has her way with you." Max shook her head. "Like I said, waste of skin. Why don't you go hide in your doghouse until your mistress whistles for you?"

"And do you think yourself better than me?" he lashed back. "I hear you whine like a spoiled child and I see you risk yourself stupidly for a Hag and let yourself be caught on top of that. If any of my Shadowblades behaved like you, I would give them a lesson they would not soon forget."

"So why don't you teach me," Max said, her brows rising, daring him.

"The Conclave rules forbid it. But if you want to die, have the balls to walk into the sun so others do not have to suffer because of you."

She smiled wide. "I just might, once I take care of a couple of things."

It was on the tip of his tongue to ask what, but he bit back the question before it could escape. "You call me a waste of skin, but you are no better. I would hate to have to depend on you for anything."

With that he spun around and walked away. He strode around the Sagrado and out along the perimeter path. Mist roiled outside the edge like an army of mad ghosts. Max's words wormed inside him. His body clenched against the invasion, but there was no stopping it. *Waste of skin.*

He paced. Resentment and anger spurred him hard. It was unlike him. He was always the calm at the center of the storm. But tonight he could not seem to find balance. It was not just Max setting him on edge. It was Selange. She was scared. When she was cornered, she would do anything to survive—to win. All day he had imagined what she would do with the Hag's staff if she found it. She could stir San Diego into bloody riots and drink the magic of the violence and the death. His teeth ground together. She would not hesitate, and the slaughter would be biblical. It would cross the line he had promised he would never cross again. But so what? Would he walk into the sun as he had threatened? He could not fight her; he could not stop her. But suicide was gutless.

A sound that was more a ripple in the air jerked him around. The candles in the Sagrado windows blurred as white mist flowed upward, sealing the Conclave from the inside. Abruptly the murmer of voices within muted. At the same time, the roiling mist beyond the path rose in a murky dome overhead, swallowing the top of the butte entirely.

A bare crunch of gravel and a slither of movement made him tense. Max emerged from around the Sagrado and strode toward him. She was graceful in a martial way, her body more angles than curves, though the outfit she wore was dramatically sexy. She stopped in front of him, her jaw sharp and jutting.

"I probably shouldn't have said that."

"Probably?" He was surprised that he was glad for her company. It was better than his own thoughts.

She rolled her eyes. "I sometimes forget how to shut my mouth. It's genetic. Nothing I can do about it."

"But you still meant it."

She grimaced, one shoulder lifting in a shrug as she folded her arms, her legs bracing wide. She sighed, looking down at her feet, her toes curling. "I didn't choose this life and I sure as hell don't want it. As far as I'm concerned, the only good witch is a dead witch. But that doesn't give me any right to judge you. Maybe your witch is okay." She said it with a look like she had a mouthful of hot peppers.

Alexander ran a hand over his mouth and jaw, not entirely sure how to reply. To say she'd surprised him—again—was an understatement. "Tell me the truth—are you insane?"

She gave him a sideways look as if wondering if he was serious, then pressed a dramatic hand to her forehead, tilting her head back. "Oh, dear—you've guessed my secret." She said it in a bad Scarlett O'Hara accent.

"What secret? You bounce off the walls like a blind crow trapped in a carnival fun house. A mannequin could see you are insane. How the hell did you end up Shadowblade Prime?"

"Because I'm clearly such a bad risk?" She asked with a fleeting self-derogatory smile. "The nutshell version is—bad taste in friends. You?"

"I have not regretted it," Alexander said defensively, and wondered who he was trying to convince.

"That wasn't the question."

"Sure it was."

She grinned. "Fair enough. So does that mean we have a truce?"

"All right. Now what?" He watched her with no clue as to what she might do or say next.

She glanced around, a smile playing around her lips. "Hmmm. I guess coffee's out. No clubbing either. What does one do at a Conclave for fun?"

Alexander found himself smiling back. "We could walk and talk," he said, gesturing toward the path. "We can discuss . . . food." He raised his brows in a question.

"Seems safe enough."

She began to walk and Alexander fell in beside her. But even as he began to tell her about one of his favorite hole-in-the-wall Italian restaurants, his mind wandered back. *Waste of skin.* The words would not leave him alone. He thought of Selange with the staff and his stomach churned.

DAWN WAS JUST TWO HOURS AWAY WHEN A WAVE OF magic rippled outward from the Sagrado as the Conclave ended. It shimmered through the air like a heat mirage, and the mist walls peeled away from the butte, sinking into the ground as they went.

Alexander looked sharply at Max. They had spent the last hours talking about little of any consequence. He had discovered she was mercurial in her moods, that she longed to see the rest of the world, and that she had a dream of going to Machu Picchu and another of learning to skin-dive. He had also pieced together from a few unguarded remarks that her hate for her witch was as real and fierce as her devotion to her coven. He had not decided if she was truly suicidal, but did know she was reckless, and that was just as bad. Maybe worse. And he had discovered he enjoyed her company. She was honest and unexpectedly playful. She liked to laugh, though he thought she probably did not do so often. But with the breaking of the Sagrado wards, that woman disappeared and the Shadowblade Prime returned. He felt the savage violence swallow her as completely as if she had sloughed her thin skin of humanity and let the brutal animal inside emerge. The transformation happened in the space of a heartbeat and was utterly complete. His warm, funny companion of the last hours vanished as if she had never existed, and in her place was a cold, iron-willed predator.

"Time to go face the music," she said through marble lips.

She did not wait for a reply. Alexander followed as she walked away, his own body tensing for battle. At least he would not have to hurt her. He did not want to be responsible for that.

Just before she reached the sweeping, moss-covered front steps, the moon slid from behind the clouds where it had been hiding much of the night. The glare made Alexander glad for his sunglasses. Max hesitated, one foot resting on the bottom step. She glanced up.

"Priceless," she muttered, and trotted up the curve of steps through the empty arch at the top.

Even as she did, Alexander saw the sweep of hot red that washed her exposed skin, followed by a bubbling of white blisters. He stared. The light of the full moon gave him a slight burn, but nothing like that. She reached the shadows beneath the arch and turned to look at him. The blisters filming her eyes cleared and her skin smoothed back to ice white.

"Coming?"

Alexander joined her at the top of the stairs. "I've never seen a Shadowblade burn like that."

She shrugged. "That's me, one of a kind."

She started to turn away and he caught her arm, pulling her around to face him. Though she tensed, she did not jerk away as he expected. "What are you?" he demanded.

"I'm a Blade, same as you."

"Not the same. Even I do not burn that way."

"Even you, huh? Wow. I must be a super-duper special snowflake, then."

His fingers tightened. "Who is your witch? Where did you come from?"

She grabbed his hand and twisted it away. He let her. "None of your business, Slick. Now they are waiting for us to entertain them. Let's get on with it."

They entered a shadowy foyer. Its stone floor was strewn with fresh herbs and flower petals. The scent of them was pungent and cleansing. On the opposite wall was another opening leading into the rectangular nave. Inside, the air was humid with too many bodies. The room swam thick with antagonism.

Alexander and Max strode through the wide door shoulder to shoulder. Inside, the throng of witches waited, standing outside the *anneau* floor made up of the encompassing circle surrounding a five-pointed star, which embraced the triangle, and at the center of it, the eye. The last was a ruby-colored, oval stone set flat into the blond wood.

Half-melted butter-colored candles traced the brilliant hues of the circle, star, and triangle, each shape inlaid into the floor in glimmering precious and semiprecious stones. The walls were swathed in jewel-bright painted silk tapestries. They depicted scenes of erotic couplings and pastoral scenes of Uncanny and Divine creatures juxtaposed with violent images of human battle and depravity. Sinuous wood carvings in shapes of arcane power interspersed the wall hangings and windows. Six-candle chandeliers, made of heavy, black iron, dangled from the high, beamed ceiling.

Above the tall windows was a narrow balcony that ran down both sides of the long walls and across the rear of the Sagrado. Narrow stairs slotted down in the corners. They were filled with a moving line of men and women dressed as scantily as Alexander and Max, many more so. They crouched and stood, predators poised for attack, spectators for the show.

Alexander assessed the gathered witches. They comprised both men and women, some surprisingly old, with silvered hair and lined faces. Some wore dramatic clothing off the pages of a Shakespeare play or a King Arthur tale, while others were dressed in chic high fashion, while still others looked like they were off to do a Cirque du Soleil performance. Each had bare feet and bare heads, as required by the laws of Conclave, and each had that hard, arrogant, unrelenting look that Alexander always associated with territory witches. These were leaders—kings and queens of magical countries, their borders constantly under attack.

His gaze came at last to rest on Selange and Giselle. They stood together. Selange's cheeks were spotted with red, her mouth quivering. She was furious. By contrast, Giselle looked ethereal and calm, as if she already knew the outcome of this challenge and did not fear it. Her glance flicked between Alexander and Max, one brow rising in a silent question to her Prime.

"Welcome back, my friends, to the show that never ends," Max murmured.

"What is that?"

"It's from a song. Pretty much covers the story of my life. But we should get this over with. There's not much night left."

With that she strode forward. Alexander followed. They went around the circle, coming to a halt in front of the two witches.

Selange glanced at Giselle, then raised her voice to the assembly. "I claim the right of challenge. The witch Giselle has invaded my territory. I demand atonement."

"I deny your accusations," Giselle said in ritual answer. "I claim the right of challenge to demonstrate my innocence."

"Then we shall proceed," Selange said smugly. "As the offense is against me, I claim also the terms. If you are innocent, the Guardians will not let you fail."

She spoke the last by rote—quoting witch law. Alexander expected that she had studied the language today.

"So mote it be," Giselle answered without any uneasiness at all.

"These are the terms. Our Primes will stand champion for each of us. They will be bound inside the circle. It will be a test of each of our skill and power in the making and breaking of them. Any attack is permissible, short of killing blows. Whichever of them falls unconscious first will forfeit the challenge. The winning witch shall claim the fallen Shadowblade as her prize, to do with as she chooses. Additionally, the winning witch shall claim a tithe from the other in the form of a treaty that shall include the right of free passage through the other's territory for the span of seven years. Do you agree?"

"I shall look forward to possessing your Prime," Giselle said with a slow look that traced Alexander from head to toe and set his teeth on edge. "Passage into your territory will be quite valuable to me."

Selange's lips thinned. "Do not claim your prizes yet. I may prove more formidable an opponent than you expect."

"You might," Giselle agreed, sounding unconvinced. "Shall we begin? The sun will rise soon. There is not much time."

"This will not take long," Selange said. "Step into the circle."

Alexander stripped off his silk shirt and dropped it on the floor with his sunglasses on top before entering the circle. He took a deep breath, the muscles of his stomach tightening. No matter how short the duration, this was going to be very difficult. Beside him, Max brushed against his arm. He looked at her, oddly wanting to reassure her. But she needed none. Her body was loose and relaxed, her face almost serene. She faced forward, but Alexander wondered if she saw anything at all. Her eyes were shuttered as if she had left her body altogether. Alexander frowned. Was that possible? If so, he could not defeat her. It would be like competing with a corpse.

"Light the circle," Selange said. The gathered witches sifted into a line along the outside of the ring of candles. They stood palm to palm in a chain and began a high-pitched chant. It was a rusty scrape of ice and steel from the base of Alexander's skull to his tailbone.

As the volume increased, magic sluiced into the

hall. These were the most powerful witches in western America. Each had built his or her own covenstead and held the reins of a stable of lesser witches. So it was no wonder that the magic they summoned here was powerful enough to make the containment spells of the Sagrado shudder and the chandeliers sway. Alexander felt the magic ripple through his flesh. It pressed against his ears and sinuses and tugged at his lungs, running through the marrow of his bones like acid.

Suddenly the half-melted candles surrounding the stone circle flickered and flared. Alexander had already closed his eyes so that he would not be blinded. The heat from the flames wafted like a midsummer's breeze. The radiance on the other side of his eyelids dimmed and he slitted them open. The candles had melted into sweet-smelling puddles on the floor, and their flames had sunk down into the circle, lighting the brilliantly colored gemstones like the shattered fragments of a rainbow.

The unearthly voices of the witches rose in a discordant crescendo before abruptly cutting off. The silence resonated with anticipation. Above on the balcony, Alexander could hear the shifting of the watching Shadowblades as they pressed forward to see the show.

"The terms are set," Selange said into the silence. "Do you have any last words before the challenge begins?" She looked at Max.

Max snorted, glancing at her. "Shut up and let's get on with this, bitch."

Alexander recoiled.

Selange's face contorted. "You will pay for that when you are mine," she said softly.

Max's teeth bared in a snarl or a bitter smile—Alexander couldn't tell. "Fuck off."

Selange's mouth snapped shut and she jerked as if slapped. Alexander's first thought was fury. He stepped protectively in front of Selange, turning to face Max. Even as he did, a second, unexpected thought crept through—did she not know that angering Selange would only make this ordeal worse for her?

"Shut your mouth," he said, his voice low. "Or I will shut it for you."

Her lips quirked, her eyes cobra-flat. "You could try. Wanna play?"

There was no emotion in her voice. Was she that good? Or was this suicidal recklessness? She hated serving Giselle—she'd made that clear. Somehow the thought made Alexander feel slightly ill. "Those aren't the rules," he said.

"Fuck the rules. I didn't make them."

"Enough." This time it was Giselle.

Max's attention slid slowly from Alexander back to her witch.

"Remember why you are here."

There was something more behind Giselle's slow, precise words than Alexander could understand. But Max did. She went still, then drew herself up. She gave a regal nod. Slowly the heat in her eyes cooled, and once again she withdrew deep inside herself. Her eyes turned almost vacant as she shut the doors on her mental fortress.

"And you, Alexander. Do you have something more . . . eloquent?" Selange prompted.

He turned and bowed and was surprised to hear Max's muttered, "thought it was damned eloquent, myself."

Selange did not hear, though she scowled, seeing Max's lips move. Alexander spoke quickly. "I live only to serve you, my witch. It is my pride and honor to stand here as your champion."

She smiled at him. "I know you will not fail me," she purred.

But the warm promise in her eyes left him cold. He kept his expression bland.

"Let us begin," Selange said to Giselle.

Selange wasted no time. Her scarlet-tipped fingers flicked. A crimson line opened at Max's breastbone, her skin unzippering as the wound traveled down below her belt. Blood ran from the wound, trickling down her legs to drip onto the floor. Only her tightly laced vest kept her intestines from spilling out of her body. But she made no sound, only wrapping her arms around herself and pushing the wound together to help her body heal.

Then Alexander was struck with such pain that his mind scattered before it like ash. He fell to the floor, writhing and moaning, unable to stop himself.

There was something crawling around inside him.

He screamed, the horror of the realization making him vomit. He felt the creatures wiggling and squirming and . . . chewing.

Agony rippled through him. He bucked against the floor. Pain burned in his back and abdomen and he felt digging and tearing as the things sought a way out. They pushed and nuzzled, gnawed and clawed. He screamed again, his head cracking against the floor. He looked down at himself. His stomach lumped and then his skin split. A bloody, whiskered snout protruded through. A blood-slicked head followed.

It was a sewer rat.

Another squabbled with the first. They fought and pushed through, stretching and tearing open the rent in Alexander's skin. Then another hole opened and another. His stomach and chest felt full of them. They hooked their claws in his flesh and scrabbled for freedom in a frenzy of panic. He felt one crawling up to gnaw and dig at his throat. Another burrowed through his back, sending spasms down his legs.

The agony was awful. But the horror of it was more than he could bear. He screamed and thrashed, rolling and snatching at the rats and yanking them from his flesh. He threw them and they returned, crawling over him, biting him. He dug his fingers into the wounds, trying to drag out more of the creatures. All rationality fled. He began to strike himself, trying to kill the rats within.

He vomited convulsively, choking on bile and screams. A rat squirmed up his throat into his mouth. It was too much.

His body bowed backward with only his head and heels on the floor. Every muscle knotted and strained, and the rat crawled out of the rictus of his mouth. Then blessed darkness swept a protective hand over him and he knew nothing else.

7

ALEXANDER DID NOT KNOW HOW LONG HE HAD been unconscious, but it could not have been long. Adrenaline still raced through his body, and his heart pounded rapid-fire. He still lay inside the circle.

The rats were gone.

Relief as profound as anything he had ever felt filled him. Tears burned in his eyes. He blinked them away, clamping his mouth shut. The memory of the rodents wriggling and clawing through him sent his mind spinning with horror. Blood ran from his nose and mouth, and more leaked from the wounds in his chest and back, and his ears rang oddly.

Over his head and from a distance that seemed very far away, Alexander heard Selange speak.

"You have won the challenge." The cold rage in her voice could have shattered diamonds. "Open the circle."

He had lost. That meant something—something terrible. But his mind was too scattered to allow him to understand. Instead it flittered away, twisting up with the chants of the witches. A flare of light blinded him and he squeezed his eyes together. He heard the quiet sound of Selange's feet as she approached. He struggled to sit up, but pain pulsed down his body like dull-hitting sledgehammers. His muscles felt wasted. He collapsed. Selange set her hand on the crown of his head. Her perfume washed over him, cloying and smothering. He blinked, clearing the blurriness of his vision. Her jaw was shaking.

"You failed," she snarled, her red lips twisting. "I always knew you'd break when I needed you most. Good riddance."

It was not until that moment that he understood what she was doing. Her hand tightened on his scalp as if she clutched a handful of loose yarn. Her nails dug furrows in his forehead. She twisted and yanked as she stood erect. For a split second it seemed as if nothing had happened. Then Alexander felt it. It was like she had pulled a thread to unbind his soul, and it continued to unravel his entire being. He felt himself coming apart, his mind splintering, his skin flaking away. Then fire erupted, scorching him from within. He convulsed, his body bucking and flopping. A cascade of violent seizures racked him. He bit his tongue and lips and cheeks. His head and hands beat wildly against the blond wood floor as he screamed.

It went on for minutes or perhaps hours. Finally his body settled, his fingers and legs twitching. He gasped, tasting blood.

Above him Selange waited. She watched him with angry triumph—he had failed her and she had taken her revenge. Clutched in her hand was a tentacled thing. It looked like a jellyfish made of neon blue witchlight.

Its quivering tentacles hung unevenly, some worming along the ground beside his head as if searching for him. Alexander went still as death. He could not tear his eyes from it. It was a spell—the one that bound him to Selange. Or had.

Horror crashed into him. He could not breathe. It was like watching the display of his own severed leg or arm. Except this wound would not heal. He opened his mouth—to beg, to scream—he did not know. Nothing came out. He tried to breathe, struggling against the sudden ice filling his chest. No! No! Selange was his life! He was nothing without her!

She walked away, her heels clicking sharply. She did not look back.

He closed his eyes, slumping, his mouth opening in a silent howl. *Loss* was too small a word for what he felt. A hungry, black maw of unspeakable grief sucked at him. He wanted to let go and disappear inside. Only the mind-blinding aches of his body kept him anchored to reality.

Hands gripped him under the shoulders and lifted him.

"C'mon. We have to get out of here before we can't anymore."

Max's voice was hoarse. She got him on his feet and pulled his arm over her shoulders, while bracing him around the waist. He sagged, his head lolling forward. He felt blood still seeping from the open holes in his side. His healing spells were sluggish, made more so by Selange removing her binding.

Alexander heard himself moan softly and clamped his mouth shut, trying to pull away from Max. Her arm did not loosen. He staggered and swore softly and let her pull him along. Her breathing was labored and he could smell a stench of burnt hair and flesh. He tried to raise his head, but it was too heavy. Murky darkness filled his head, and the remembered horror of the rats crawling through him made him vomit again.

"Easy," someone else said in a tight voice. It took him a moment to sort out who it was. Giselle. Max's witch—his witch now, too, though that would not last long. Shadowblades did not change covens. They could not be trusted. She would pry out of him everything he had to tell about Selange and then she would kill him.

Again that vast black emptiness opened up and he felt himself starting to slide in. But no. He would not take the easy way out. He had failed. There was a price to pay. He made a furious sound, trying to pull himself back from the precipice.

He lost track of everything but his battle, coming back to himself outside on the amethyst path. He was slumped heavily against Max. She had both arms around him. His cheek was pressed against her collarbone. He could feel her ribs bellowing noisily as she panted.

"Get out of here. Go to Akemi," Max ordered, her voice thin and weary. It sounded like she spoke through clenched teeth.

"Like hell," was Giselle's angry response.

"If you don't, you'll get us all killed," Max ground out. "My compulsion spells are eating me alive and I'm already half-dead. As soon as she can get to the veil to pass her Shadowblades through, Selange will send them after him. She can't afford to let you have him. If you're safe, I might be able to get him out alive. But the longer you stand here being a target for any witch who wants a piece of you, the worse my compulsions get. In a minute I'm going to pass out."

"Then leave him. Keeping him alive isn't worth risking you."

Alexander nearly collapsed at Max's adamant "No." He thought he must be hallucinating.

"I command it."

"Fuck you. He's yours now. I paid dearly for him and I'll not waste my pain." She paused, her teeth grinding. Her body jerked and shook with a palsy. "I'm his Prime and I don't leave any of mine behind," she wheezed.

The silence that followed crackled with nuclear fury. Alexander's astonishment was complete when he heard Giselle's quiet "Very well. I'll go. But if you get yourself killed—"

"Then you're screwed and I win." Max's voice twisted and frayed. Her fingers dug hard into Alexander's flesh as a cascade of shudders ran through her. "Better go or I won't be able to walk out of here."

He heard the slap of feet as Giselle dashed away. Max's chest rose and fell as she drew a deep breath. The tremors eased from her body and her grip firmed.

"C'mon."

Alexander's mind whirled. *His Prime*. She'd defied her witch for him. *Waste of skin*. It made no sense. But it drove him to draw on the last reserves of his strength—he would not let her die for him. He straightened his spine and forced his legs to move. He still leaned heavily on her, but he no longer slumped like a bag of dirty laundry.

Feeling the change, she pushed him into a staggering

jog. When she reached the edge of the perimeter path, she crossed into the undergrowth. Bushes scraped at Alexander's bare chest and arms, and the rocky ground tore at his feet. Twigs and branches snapped and crackled loudly. No one following could miss their trail.

Max held him up as they scrabbled down the short drop to where the path returned from its circuit around the hill. On smooth ground again, she increased their speed to a slow lope. Alexander kicked his feet, but remained clumsy and awkward, doing more to hinder than help. She paid no attention, neither chastising nor encouraging him.

They had gone about three-quarters of the way back to the parking area when she stopped. "This is where we get off."

Alexander was panting and could not speak. His body was still trying to deal with his wounds, and his mind quaked beneath the memory of the rats crawling inside him.

She dragged him off through the trees and brush along the swell of the butte. The ground was steep and uneven. She stumbled and grabbed a branch to keep herself from falling. Her breathing sounded loud and harsh. She did not pause to rest, and Alexander fought with all the strength he had left to keep up.

They came to a sheer-sided ravine that entirely blocked their path. The pines growing up from the bottom filled the cleft in an impenetrable thicket, and a dense screen of scrub bushes shrouded the sides. Max stopped, dropping him awkwardly down on a boulder.

"Wait here."

He raised his head, getting his first good look at her

since the challenge had begun. For a moment all he could do was stare. The leather of her pants up to the middle of her thighs was burned away except where ragged bits clung to the seeping black char of her flesh. A thick hatch of bloody stripes showed through the laced-up gaps of her vest, down her arms, and across her face. He could see white bone through the shredded tops of her feet.

A strange relief slid through him like rusty razors. A part of him had wondered if Selange had taken advantage of the challenge to be rid of him. But seeing the damage to Max, he knew Selange had pulled no punches. Max had simply won.

"I'll be back," she said. "Wait here."

"Where—" He broke off, coughing.

"Just rest."

He struggled to get to his feet. "I'll come with you."

She pushed him back down hard. "I have one rule. Don't get anybody—even your own idiot self—killed. And that means doing what I say when I say. Stay put."

With that, she turned, pushing into the bushes. A moment later he heard the scrabble of rocks and a sliding sound as she went over the edge of the ravine and down into the trees. After a moment of silence, Alexander heard the crunch of twigs and leaves. Silence fell again, broken only by the rustling of the wind and the faint sounds of departing witches.

He sat on the boulder, waiting as ordered. He did not have much choice. He could do nothing else. Besides, she was his Prime. For now, anyhow. He looked down at himself. The rat wounds had closed, but a pressure was growing inside. He was bleeding internally. His stomach felt swollen and hot, and his organs felt as if someone were squeezing them. He could not get a deep breath. Cramps radiated around his abdomen and dug burning fingers up into his chest.

He coughed and spat blood.

What was going to happen now? Would Giselle accept him into her covenstead or would she tear him apart to learn what secrets he knew about Selange? He wondered what Max would have to say about that. She had called him a waste of skin, and then she had claimed him, defying her witch and protecting him with her life. Would Max do all that just to let Giselle kill him? As little as he knew her, he did not think so. Not that she could stop the witch. All the same, it made no sense. He would not have done the same.

Why did that disgust him so?

He strained to hear her or any sounds of pursuit. Max was right. Selange had left the rest of her Shadowblades waiting just outside the veil near the end of Burlingame Drive. It would not take her long to get there once she retrieved her Hummer from the parking lot. She would bring a kill squad in to finish him, and without Giselle to free them from the veil, he and Max would be trapped.

But Max had a plan. He had to trust her.

He spat again, brushing a fly away from the blood drying on his stomach. The minutes ticked past. The pressure in his gut was getting worse. His head was starting to spin and his body throbbed with damage caused by his convulsions. He had definitely pulled muscles and tendons and maybe separated some ribs. He needed sleep and food and a lot of both. He did not think he was going to get either soon.

A crackling from behind his right shoulder made him

drop down beside the boulder, twisting around as he did. He swallowed the cry of pain that followed. His fingers curled around a stone and he hefted it, ready. Adrenaline surged through him, and he forced himself to breathe slowly and steadily, despite the pressure against his lungs.

Then Max appeared out of the trees. She jogged fluidly along the edge of the gully. A backpack was slung over her shoulders and she had changed her clothes. She wore loose black jeans and a close-fitting, long-sleeved, black T-shirt. A baseball cap turned backward covered her short blond hair. Her feet remained bare, her wounds still seeping and raw and black with char. In her right hand she carried a .45.

She had been prepared for trouble. Alexander's eyes narrowed as he let go of the rock he held and pushed himself upright to sit back on the boulder. She was good—savvy and tough. Maybe they would get out of this alive after all.

"Here."

She shoved the gun behind her into her waistband and dug a couple of powerbars from her pack. He tore the first one open and gobbled it in two bites, and quickly did the same with the second.

She crouched beside him, pressing her fingers against his distended belly. Pain flared. A long, twitching shudder rolled through him. His hands clamped into fists.

"Your exterior wounds have stopped bleeding, but you're still leaking inside. It usually helps to cut a hole or two to drain things, but that will have to wait. Probably should have waited on the food. It'll boost your healing, but it's going to make it hurt worse."

She sounded apologetic, surprising him again. Then he caught the meaning of her words.

"Usually?"

She nodded, not looking at him as she stood. "I told you before, I'm a very good victim, and Giselle likes to practice. Let's go."

Alexander gaped. "She . . . You . . . I do not understand."

"You don't have to. Probably better if you don't."

She did not give him the chance to say anything else. She pulled him up, putting her arm around his waist and hurrying him along the top of the ravine, pushing him faster than before. His gut was screaming. The powerbars seemed to have set off a bomb in his stomach. He kept moving, focusing entirely on his feet, letting her guide them. It was the best he could do.

They followed a deer track along a ridge, slowing at last as they came to the edge of a canyon wall, its steep slope pocked with bushes and clumps of grass.

"Careful," she said, and pulled him over the edge.

They skidded downward, using the grass and bushes to slow their descent. They crabbed sideways to keep from sliding straight down, but at the last fifteen feet, Alexander lost his footing and went down hard, dragging Max with him. They slid down on their backs, rocks grating through their clothes and skin.

A cloud of dust puffed up around them, rising on the slow drift of wind. Max looked up at it, then sneezed. "Hurry. They won't miss that."

Her face and hat were dusty, and blood seeped from the scrapes on her left cheek as she reached down to grasp Alexander's hand and haul him to his feet. He staggered and his knees started to buckle. Max caught him around the waist before he hit the ground. Another forty steps and she stopped, turning him around her hip and propping him on the fender of a black SUV.

She dropped her backpack to the ground and braced herself against the rear window a moment, her head dangling as she panted raggedly. She had lost her hat. Alexander could see the strain in her face, the set of her jaw and the thin slash of her mouth. Her arms trembled. Despite her exhaustion, she did not let herself rest long. She left Alexander sitting there, retreating back into the trees, pulling her gun from her waistband as she did. She reached up into the crook of an oak tree and fished out the keys to the car. She limped back, unlocking the doors with the electronic key fob.

She bent and picked up the backpack and tossed it on the front seat before returning to stand over him.

"Are you going to live?"

"I think so." But he doubted it.

"Better be sure. Seems pointless to go through all this for a corpse."

A waste of skin. Why did it bother him so much? "Then I will not die."

"See that you don't," she said.

She gripped him under the arm and levered him up, pushing him to the front of the car. She opened the door and pushed him inside, before going back around to the driver's side. She put her pack in the backseat and slid behind the wheel and buckled her seat belt. She glanced at Alexander, then reached across and did the same for him. He gave her an amused look.

"Bad driver?"

"The ride looks like it's going to be bumpy." She turned to look out the windshield. "Lucky for us, they left it too late."

Alexander twisted his head to follow her gaze. A semicircle of Selange's Shadowblades closed around the front of the car. There were eight of them. The rest must have stayed with Selange.

Mercury and Attila stood ten yards in front of the headlights carrying heavy, double-bladed axes cradled in their hands. As Alexander watched, they prowled slowly forward. The other six were more sensibly armed with shotguns and handguns. Thor had an Uzi. Brynna, in the middle, held her Glock dangling down at her thigh, pointed at the ground. Stupid. She knew better. Alexander had taught her better. But she made a habit out of arrogance. She was entirely opposite to Max, who seemed to be completely competent without any self-importance at all. It had made him underestimate her. If they survived, he would not do so again.

For a moment time seemed to freeze. Alexander looked into each face, reading death there. There would be no concession to the fact that until an hour before, he had been their Prime. It did not matter that he had taught them, guarded them, laughed with them, mourned with them, loved them. These people were his family. A homicidal family.

The moment snapped when Max tapped the barrel of her gun on the steering wheel. He looked at her. Her gaze was calculating and ruthless. Alexander wondered if she knew how to panic, or even worry. Then he remembered the hours during the Conclave before the challenge. She was not as cold as she seemed.

"You do know they're going to kill you, right?" she asked.

"Yes." He forced the word out through a throat tight with loss.

"Then you know what you have to do."

She handed him her gun without waiting for an answer. She did not ask him if he would use it, or if he would kill her and try to escape back to Selange. He took the weapon, his heart thudding. All he had to do was twist his hand and he could kill her.

"It's chambered," she told him, her voice as steady as if she were commenting on the weather. "Bullets are hollowpoints." She stared straight ahead at the closing semicircle of enemy Shadowblades. The corner of her mouth turned up in mocking humor as if she knew what he was thinking. "Don't miss."

"I will not." Or so he hoped. His head was spinning and his eyes had begun to blur.

She flicked a quick glance at him. He could almost read her thoughts. *Was he worth all this blood and pain?* She looked away, clicking the key a notch and pressing a pair of buttons on her door to slide down both front windows. She jerked her head at Brynna to come around, even as she quietly slid in the clutch and put the Tahoe into first gear.

"Look, I don't give a shit about this asshole. What's it going to take for me to get out of here alive?" Max called, infusing her voice with nervousness.

Brynna, arrogant bitch that she was, bought it. She stepped in front of Thor, fouling his sight lines, a triumphant smirk twisting her lips.

As soon as Brynna tangled Thor, Max twisted the key,

let out the clutch, and floored it in one swift, smooth motion. The four wheels of the SUV spun, sending gravel and dirt flying in a cloud. The vehicle fishtailed sideways, then leaped forward as the wheels caught traction. Brynna, Thor, and Attila lunged out of the way on the left. There was a *thump! thump!* as the tires popped over something—or someone. Alexander was leaning out the window and squeezing the trigger. Bullets whined through the air. He heard the popping as they hit the car, the crash of glass shattering, the *boom!* of shotguns, and screams and shouts of fury and pain.

Alexander hardly felt the impact as a lump of lead jolted his shoulder, burrowing deep into his flesh. A streak of fire erupted on his neck and another in his right bicep followed.

He shot swiftly, knowing he hit at least some of his targets. He aimed to kill, a horrifying and inconceivable act of betrayal. But his world had turned inside out and upside down. Though his feelings had not yet caught up to the fact, he no longer belonged to Selange, and these men and women he had called friends and family wanted him dead. He was their enemy, and a dangerous one. What he knew could kill them all.

The Tahoe swerved and fishtailed again. They were past their attackers now. A spray of bullets crashed through the rear window and pelted the back of the seats. Max was in third gear and shifting to fourth. The tires screeched on the road and they sped around a jut of rock and skimmed along the winding road, the dense trees screening them from their pursuers. Alexander slumped against the doorjamb, letting his eyes drift shut, his hand still firm on the gun resting on his thigh.

Max slowed down only slightly when she hit the gravel road leading to the edge of the veil. The jolting of the car made Alexander's wounds flare. He gritted his teeth.

"Are you all right?" Her voice was as calm as previously, though she sounded tired. So. She did have limits after all. It was more comforting than it should have been. He felt as if he'd been mauled by rhinos, and she was acting no worse for wear. It was embarrassing as hell.

"Not particularly," he said slowly, deciding pretense was impossible. The spells protecting him were less potent than hers, or his wounds much worse. His strength had run out. He could not even hold his head up. He had three bullet wounds and his stomach was about to explode. He was having trouble breathing, and his heart was beginning to flutter weakly. Max's gun dropped to the floorboards with a thud.

"You said you wouldn't die," she reminded him. "Did you lie?"

"Not so far."

"I don't like liars."

"I will remember that."

"You do that."

Suddenly the Tahoe veered, diving down a steep incline. It jolted and bounced. Alexander flopped in his seat, unable to swallow his cries of agony. Branches and leaves clawed through the open window, and then the SUV leveled out.

"Hold on, if you can," Max said in a strangled voice. Then nonsensically: "I want it to work. Please work."

A heartbeat later, they slammed into the veil. Magic roiled around them. The engine of the Tahoe revved high as Max floored it. But they hardly moved. For a moment they were caught like a mosquito in amber. Then miraculously, the Tahoe began to roll.

A second later they were clear. The SUV jolted and leaped, even as Max eased up on the gas. Alexander wanted to ask how she had done it—how she had got them through the veil—but he was too weak. Beside him he heard a rattle on the console, then he heard her flip open a cell phone. It beeped twice as she punched a number into the speed dial and hit send. The call was picked up almost immediately. She did not bother with a greeting.

"Things went way fucking south. Is Giselle with you? . . . Good. Get her out of here."

A pause. A man was demanding to know where Max was.

"I've rabbited. Outside the veil. Going across the golf course now."

Her voice had become sluggish and her words were starting to slur. There was a bubbling sound to her breathing. Alexander fought to open his heavy eyes and turn his head.

"Use the . . . GPS. Be . . . quick. I'm almost . . . done," she said haltingly.

Her hand dropped before anyone could reply. The phone skittered over the console onto the floor. The car swerved and straightened, then jolted and coughed as her foot released the clutch. A moment later the motor died.

At last Alexander got his eyes open. He twisted his head to look at her. Max was slumped against the door, her hands loose in her lap. Her eyes were closed. Blood ran from a deep gash in her scalp, matting her hair to her skull. The entire right side of her face was awash in crimson. The smell of blood was thick; he had thought it was his own.

His gaze wandered lower. He sucked in a ragged breath. Sticking out of her upper thigh was a knife. He recognized it; it was Brynna's. She must have grappled onto the door as they made their escape and struck Max through the open window. Alexander had been too busy shooting out the other side to notice. From its angle, he knew the blade had sliced into the femoral artery. Because Brynna had not had a chance to jerk it out, Max had not yet bled to death. Shadowblades were hard to kill, but slashing the femoral artery would take out a healthy Shadowblade before any healing spells could kick in. Max was not healthy.

"Are you going to live?" He had to get her talking. Keep her here with him until help arrived.

Her lashes flickered. Her answer was slow in coming, her words barely audible through her unmoving lips. "Maybe. Maybe not." Then: "Damn. Forgot to . . . tell them . . . not . . . to kill . . . you."

Her body went slack—boneless and far too still.

8

THE SECONDS TICKED BY LIKE MINUTES. GRAY wings fluttered at the edges of Alexander's vision. He blinked, holding hard to consciousness. He could do nothing to help Max. He had no strength to put pressure on her artery, and even if he did, he did not dare touch the knife. If he even jarred it a little bit, he could speed the bleeding out. All he could do was wait for help to arrive and hope she did not die before it did.

Alexander shied away from the possibility. Anger flared. He was not entirely helpless. He could at least protect her. Selange would not give up. Her Shadowblades would be tracking the Tahoe. He shook his head to clear it. Pain lanced along his neck and drilled through his arm. He choked on the pain, swallowing hard. But it helped clear the fog from his head. How long had it taken Brynna to get back to Selange? How long before Max's Shadowblades came to fetch her? Who would arrive first?

With nothing left to do, he fumbled at the door until the lock snicked. He groped for the handle and pulled it open, letting his body fall against the door, his arm dangling on the outside. Slowly it swung open. He followed, his rubber legs sagging. He gripped the door under his arm to keep himself from collapsing to the ground. The pain of his wounds was terrible, but he pushed it away. There was no time for it.

Clumsily he reached for the gun on the floorboards. He popped the clip. He was down to three bullets. They would do little against a mob of Shadowblades. He needed more. He knelt excruciatingly on his seat and reached into the back of the car for Max's backpack. He moved carefully so as not to bump her and loosen the knife. He unzipped the pack and pawed inside, finding what he was looking for in the bottom. He snapped a full clip into the .45 and pushed three more into his front pocket before sitting back down on the seat, his back to Max. He watched their backtrail, straining for any signs of enemies coming through the veil.

Blood continued to run down his neck, shoulder, and arm. His hands had begun to shake and his eyes were fogging again. Not good. He could hear car sounds from the city and the twittering of birds and crickets. In the east, the sky was beginning to lighten. Dawn was still another hour away, but with Max's extreme response to moonlight, Alexander was sure the twilight of dawn would be dangerous for her, probably fatal in her current state. If she lasted that long.

Not more than five minutes later, he heard them coming. He found his feet, slewing drunkenly sideways as he stood up. He shook his head, thankful for the shooting agony that cleared his vision again.

Engines roared as two—no, three—vehicles approached. They came from . . . the west. Slowly Alexander turned to face them. He lifted his arm, bracing it along the top of the open door. The cars bounced over the golf course at high speed. The first was a vintage El Camino. It was well ahead of the others. It was followed by a yellow Mustang and a red Chevy crew cab.

The El Camino plowed to a halt, skidding sideways on the wet grass and tearing dark scars into the turf. The door was open and the blocky, dark-haired driver was sprinting toward the Tahoe before Alexander could blink. The driver bent low, guns in both hands.

Alexander wasn't so far gone that he could not aim. He shot at the other man's feet. "Stop."

The other two vehicles caught up to the first and three more bodies boiled out of them—Max's witch among them—even as the first Shadowblade dropped to a crouch, both guns trained on Alexander.

Before he could shoot, Giselle interrupted, "Drop your gun before Niko drops you."

Relief warred with his instincts that told him that these people were his enemies. Slowly Alexander released the hammer of Max's gun and raised the nose. Instantly Niko was moving again. He glared at Alexander, but made no move to disarm him, and instead went to Max's door.

"Careful!" Alexander cried. "She's got a knife in her leg. Move it and she'll bleed out."

To his surprise, Niko listened. He leaned in the window, assessing the unconscious Max. When he pulled back, his face was grim.

"How is she?" Giselle's face was pale and strained. She ignored Alexander entirely.

"He's right. She's lost a lot of blood," Niko said. "Cuts and scrapes on her head. I can't see what else." He slammed a fist on the roof, leaving a fist-shaped dent.

"We will have company soon," Alexander said, all too aware of the compact Asian woman standing silently behind him, her gun leveled at his back. "Selange will not let me go so easily."

"Don't look like it was easy," the slender, blond Shadowblade said. He stood behind Giselle holding a shotgun across his forearm, the muzzle aimed at Alexander. He did not blink. "What do you want to do?" he asked the witch.

"We have to move her," Giselle said. "We need to get her to the hospital truck and quick, or she'll die."

"Might die anyhow, the way she's cut," the blond said in a soft, deadly voice.

"No. I won't let her get away from me that easily," Giselle said fiercely. Alexander was shocked to see tears running down her cheeks. "Quickly. Tyler and Niko, lift her into the truck. Hurry."

"What about him?" the Asian woman asked.

Giselle's hot stare fastened on Alexander. He looked back patiently, resigned to his death sentence.

"You could have killed her," the witch said in a stone voice. "Instead you guarded her."

"She's my Prime." The words came out before he knew he was going to say them. They felt right.

Giselle jerked back, her mouth falling open.

"We've got to hurry," Niko urged. "She's hardly breathing."

The witch nodded, still staring at Alexander. "Get yourself into a vehicle if you can. We won't wait on you."

Shock ran through Alexander. He did not understand this witch, her Prime, or the game that they played. In the same situation, Selange would have cut her losses and put a bullet in his head and probably in Max's, too.

Giselle was no longer paying any attention to him. She opened the driver's-side door. Niko squeezed through and caught Max, gently pulling her out. Tyler slung his shotgun around so it hung from his back and slid his arms beneath her thighs. Giselle stripped off her own shirt and pressed it around the knife, holding it in place and putting pressure on the wound. Blood dripped across the ground as the three carried Max off toward the truck in a tight knot. The Asian woman climbed inside the backseat to help ease Max across.

It happened so fast that Alexander forgot to move. Tyler stepped away from the truck, his arms, chest, and thighs wet with blood. Niko followed after, and Alexander realized he was going to be left behind if he did not hurry.

Without thinking, he snatched up Max's backpack and pushed himself away from the Tahoe, clutching the .45 against his stomach. He staggered across the smooth, green grass toward the El Camino. He was startled when an iron arm wrapped his waist and nearly lifted him off his feet as Niko propelled him to the car, shoving him inside and slamming the door. A half second later Niko was in the driver's seat, twisting the key.

The engine roared and Niko spun the wheel and stomped on the gas. The El Camino fishtailed and lunged in a tight circle, sending chunks of dirt and grass flying. A few moments later they had overtaken the Chevy truck. It was going slowly.

"She's going to die if we don't get a move on," Niko gritted through his teeth.

"She is tough," Alexander said, though he did not know if Max was nearly tough enough, even with magic enhancements. "And Giselle is helping her."

"She's—" Niko broke off and punched the dash. His hand went through the thin metal. "Fuck."

Behind them, an explosion rocked the early morning. Alexander looked over his shoulder, hissing at the pain. Behind them, orange and yellow tongues of flame leaped into the sky. So much for the Tahoe.

"He'd better have cleaned it out," Niko muttered. "She'll kill him if he blew up her stuff." He paused. "If she lives."

His worry was palpable. And personal. He truly cared about her. Alexander was not immune. He found himself silently urging the red truck to go faster.

"Who are you?" Niko asked as they jolted across a low ditch and up onto Twenty-sixth Street, turning right.

"My name is Alexander. I am—I *was,*" he corrected, "the witch Selange's Prime. This is her territory." Forming the words was difficult. He was still bleeding and the pain in his stomach had not lessened any. He held the gun loosely, unable to firm his grip. His head bobbed and jerked. He could hardly hold it up any longer.

"Max beat you in the challenge tonight."

"Yes."

"So you did that to her?"

Despite Niko's quiet tone, Alexander could hear his rage. He was looking for someone to blame, and someone to hurt in revenge.

"No. The challenge was endurance. The witches tested themselves on us."

"What happened to you?" Niko demanded belligerently.

He was really asking why Alexander was not the one lying in a pool of his own blood, a half step from death. And the truth was, the reason was Max.

"Selange sent her Shadowblades after us."

"You mean *your* Shadowblades."

"Not mine, not anymore," Alexander said firmly. How fast they had turned on him. One moment he was their Prime, the next their prey. It said something about him, and nothing good.

The silence was thick. Alexander knew what Niko was thinking. Had he fought hard against his former brethren? Had he let them do this to Max? But Alexander bore the wounds and Niko could not refute them. And he had kept watch over Max until help arrived. He grimaced. He had done little but watch while her blood leaked out onto the floorboards.

"It should have been me," he said quietly. "It was my fault they came after us."

"You're damned right," Niko said harshly. "If she dies, I'll kill you myself."

"I know."

They drove on through San Diego. Alexander slipped in and out of unconsciousness. Fever rose in him. He began to shiver and sweat. He was hardly aware when they pulled to a stop and Niko leaped from the El Camino. Alexander sat in a stupor, unable to do anything else. The sun was coming. He shuddered from head to foot. He needed to get under cover.

Suddenly the door opened. Hands grabbed him roughly, yanking him upright. The gun was twisted from his hand. They hauled him over the ground and up a ribbed-metal ramp. Walls closed around him and a blessed roof. There was a clanking as doors slammed and a bolt shot home.

Alexander was carried to a metal operating table. He blinked in the bright overhead light and struggled to sit up. An implacable hand on his shoulder held him still.

"Stay put," Niko ordered.

Alexander stopped fighting and twisted onto his side instead. They were in a semitruck trailer. Four stainless-steel hospital beds were lined up in a diagonal row down the middle, and the sides and front were lined with medical equipment and storage lockers. Max was laid out two tables down. Giselle and three others in blue scrubs crowded about her, all of them speaking quickly and urgently as they cut away her clothing and jammed needles into both arms. They hung two IV bags on each of the poles poking up from the top of the table. On the left the bags were full of clear liquid; on the right they were red. Machines were attached to Max and began to beep alarms. The witch and the medical team worked furiously on Max, hunching over her limp body so that Alexander could only glimpse what was happening.

A curly-headed, dark-haired nurse fetched supplies as the doctor ratcheted out orders. Hanging back out of the way of the frantically working medical team were the Asian woman and a grim-faced Tyler. The stench of blood began to overwhelm the antiseptic smell of the trailer, and Alexander swallowed, queasiness making him dizzy.

"Dammit!"

"Pressure—hurry!"

Brynna's knife clanked to the floor, casting a crimson arc of blood into the air.

"Gotta be fast now."

"Suction it. There's too fucking much blood."

"It isn't closing . . . why the hell isn't it closing?"

"She's resisting me. Half-dead and still too damned stubborn," Giselle said with a harsh laugh that sounded like it tore her throat. She bent down close to Max's ear. "Max! I know you can hear me. Let me help you. You're going to die, do you hear? Let me help!" She straightened, twisting to look around. Her hair was matted and stained red as if she had pushed bloody fingers through it. More blood smeared her cheeks and forehead. "Tyler, Niko, and Akemi, talk to her. Tell her to come back."

The three Shadowblades stared a split second in surprise, then surged forward.

"Tell her you're here," Giselle urged. "Put your hands on her. Talk to her. She won't be able to leave you; don't let her go."

Alexander watched as the three Shadowblades stretched out hands to touch her. Their voices hammered against each other, fervent and demanding.

Tense minutes ticked past. The cacophony surrounding Max rose in a crescendo. Wads of red-drenched surgical gauze fell to the floor. Giselle held Max's head between her palms, her fingers curving like talons beneath the unconscious woman's jaw. She chanted, her eyes closed, her lips tight as wire. Alexander gasped, realizing he had been holding his breath. His stomach spasmed, sending tremors through his body. Chills ran over his skin and sank down deep inside. He shivered, his teeth chattering. His body clenched.

"Don't stop—it's working!"

It was the last thing he remembered.

HE CAME AWAKE INSTANTLY, SITTING UP IN THE SAME MOment. Someone had a hold on his shoulders. Alexander did not think. He flipped over into a crouch, gripping the hands and twisting in the same instant. He yanked his attacker up onto the table and ground a knee into her back, thrusting an arm around her neck, his other hand on her jaw. At that moment, his mind caught up with feral instinct.

He looked down, fear curling like burnt paper in his stomach. He held Giselle pinned. All around him he felt predatory silence. His glance flitted from side to side. Niko, Tyler, and Akemi stood ready, bodies taut, faces snarling. They did not dare move in case he broke her neck. But if he did, he would not get out in one piece, or even twenty.

Slowly he released his fingers and pushed himself off her, holding his hands up. Instantly he was grabbed and slammed to the floor, his arms bent up behind his back.

"Let him go."

Her voice was raspy and weak, but it was Max. She was alive.

The others got off him. Alexander started to push himself off the floor when he was grabbed under each arm and hauled erect. They held him like a wishbone they dearly wanted to snap in half.

Giselle had gained her feet again. She rubbed her lower back with a wince. She had changed into scrubs, and blood still matted her hair in places, though the rest of her was clean. "I hope you don't wake up that way with your girlfriends."

Alexander could only stare bemusedly at her, waiting for the punch line. Bruises were already rising on her neck where his arm had pressed, and no doubt more would appear on her back and jaw. She ought to be punishing him. Severely. Max had said the witch was a good torturer, and he knew firsthand how very true that was. So why was she not disciplining him as he deserved? Alexander's eyes narrowed. Maybe she was simply waiting until she had more energy.

She yawned. "The healing help I gave you will have to be enough. I've got to rest. I'll have food sent in for all of you, and then we'll get on the road. We've been here too long already."

With that she withdrew through a panel near the front of the truck. It opened on a light-sealed space. She slid it shut behind her, and the green light above turned to red and a low-pitched chime sounded. A moment later the light turned green again.

"Let him go," Max said again, and the two men holding Alexander slowly released him.

Still reeling from Giselle's gentle reaction, he turned around to examine Max. She was lying flat on her back, her eyes closed. The IVs continued to pour blood and clear sustenance into her veins. He could see no evidence of any injuries. The floor had been cleaned and the sharp stench of antiseptic clogged his nose and made his eyes water. Fans whirred, stirring the air.

He started toward Max's supine body, stopping when Tyler thrust an arm out to block his way.

"Peace, Junior. Keep your distance."

Junior? Alexander could not help his dry chuckle, though he knew there was nothing funny about the situation. Then he started to cough raggedly. Akemi handed him a bottle of apple juice and he drank it gratefully. He eyed the too still Max again, then looked at Tyler.

"She will be all right?"

"*She* can talk for herself," Max said acidly without opening her eyes.

"And?"

"I'm hungry and tired. Can you people not shut up?"

"What about him?" Niko asked.

Max's head tipped to the side and she looked at Alexander. "What about him?"

"What do you want us to do with him?"

"Feed him. Watch him. Put a bullet in his head if he starts any trouble." She closed her eyes again, rolling her head back up to face the ceiling. "Whatever you do, keep it quiet."

As promised, Giselle sent in food. The chime on the door sounded and the light turned from green to red to green. Akemi opened the door, picking up a stack of pizza boxes, followed by a gallon of milk and a six-pack of beer. Last came a stack of paper plates and a roll of paper towels.

She set the food on the nearest gurney and piled several slices of deep-dish pizza on a plate. She carried it to Max, along with a cup of milk. Max groaned and sat up slowly, swinging her legs over the edge of the table. She eyed the milk and then the beer, then grabbed the cup and drank it in one gulp. Next she started devouring the pizza.

"Damn, that's good," she said.

Alexander waited until the others had begun eating and served himself, pouring milk into a paper cup. All of them ate steadily without speaking. Before they had emptied the boxes, the door chimed again. This time the offering was Chinese food. They all piled their plates with lo mein, fried rice, General Tso's, cashew chicken, egg rolls, and barbecued pork.

A half hour later, Alexander was beginning to feel comfortably full. He felt his healing spells drawing on the energy of the food, and though exhaustion still weighted him, he felt no worse than if he had been in a fistfight. The pain in his stomach was completely gone. For the first time he became aware of two bandages pulling at the skin on his chest—one low on his left side, the other higher on his right. His gaze drifted lower. He was still wearing his bloodstained jeans. They were all he had left to call his own.

His food churned uneasily in his gut. He had been alive for more than a hundred years, and it was like he had been born again. He did not like it. He felt too new, too vulnerable, and entirely alone.

He set aside his plate. He had no place in Giselle's coven. He could challenge Max for Prime, but after tonight, he was not sure he could win. And even if he should happen to defeat her, her Shadowblades were clearly too loyal to suffer him to live. That left serving under her, if she could learn to trust him. He dragged his hands through his hair, then shoved them into the front pockets of his jeans. It was impossible. She would be stupid to. She was anything but stupid. And yet—*I don't leave any of mine behind*.

The door chimed yet again, and now Niko fished out two grocery sacks stuffed with pints of Ben & Jerry's ice cream. He pawed through them, grabbing a carton and taking it to Max, along with a spoon. She pulled off the lid and scooped out a spoonful, her eyes closing as she savored it.

"Food of the gods," she murmured, a look of heavenly satisfaction on her face.

"Want some?" Niko asked Alexander, surprising him.

He shook his head, his hunger gone. Tiredness netted him. Without another word, he climbed onto his gurney. He lay on his back, feeling entirely too exposed. His stomach clenched rock hard. He was entirely at their mercy. Even if he escaped, he doubted he could go back to Selange. Did he want to? He thought about it. His initial knee-jerk reaction was yes. But when he considered . . . He realized he felt free in a way he could never remember feeling. It was as if everything he was and had been had burned up in a fire, and he had walked out nameless and without any shackles tying him down. *He was free.*

He recoiled from the thought. He did not want his

freedom. He was a Shadowblade and he needed a coven and a witch to serve. He neither knew any other life nor wanted to. All he could do was wait to see what Giselle would do with him and hope Max had meant what she said.

Mine.

9

MAX HAD NEVER BEFORE IN HER LIFE BEEN QUITE so close to death. Surprisingly—no, shockingly—she found that she did not want to die. Even when the velvet darkness had beckoned so closely, even when it seemed she did not have the strength to climb back up from the abyss, still she couldn't give in to the ease of rest. She felt compelled to return. No, it was more than that. She *wanted* life. She wanted to tease Niko and Oz, drink beer with Tyler, needle Akemi and Lise, walk through the forests at Horngate and swim in the high mountain lakes . . . so many things.

She ate her ice cream slowly, reveling in the sweet richness, her nose wrinkling at the smell of antiseptic cleaner and, beneath it, the tang of blood, sweat, and old fear. She felt shaky, but the food and IVs would fix that soon enough. In another twenty-four hours she'd be completely healed. She glanced at Alexander, lying two tables down. He appeared to be sleeping, though she would be surprised if he was. She frowned. Just what the hell was she going to do with him? What was Giselle planning to do with him?

"What happened?" Niko asked, coming to sit beside her and digging into his own ice cream.

Max gave him a sidelong glance, raising her brows quizzically.

Niko's jaw jutted. "What?

"Getting a little pushy, aren't you?"

He shrugged. "But now I've seen you naked. That makes all the difference, doesn't it?" He paused, humor draining from his face. "Of course, you were almost dead."

"Don't tell me you'd miss me," Max said wryly, digging another spoonful of ice cream from the carton.

His reaction stunned her. "Fuck you," Niko said, throwing his carton. It dented a cabinet and clanged loud in the truck trailer. He jumped to his feet, spinning to face her. "Just fuck you. I don't deserve that. None of us do."

Max looked at him, taken aback. He was quivering with fury. The muscles in his arms and neck corded as if it was taking all his control to hold himself back from hitting her. She set her ice cream down and held up her hands.

"Down, boy. It was a joke. What crawled up your ass and died?"

He sneered, "If it wasn't for us calling you back, you'd have died on the table. Wouldn't she?" he demanded, looking at Tyler and Akemi.

They nodded slowly, faces tight and cold, sharing Niko's anger.

"What do you mean?"

"I mean you were as good as dead. Giselle said you were keeping her from fixing you. She told us to talk to you, call you back. So we did. You want to know why? I'll tell you. All three of us are still alive because of you—because of your training and because you're not a stupid Prime. You always watch out for us. We can trust you. We like you a lot, when you aren't acting like an asshole." Niko's gaze slid to Alexander, who had sat up when the ice cream had hit the cabinet. "We don't fucking want any other Prime. We want *you*. We belong to *you*. Get it?"

Max couldn't find any words. She'd never really thought of what her Blades might think of her. If anything, she'd imagined that they looked at her with a mixture of resentment for beating survival skills into them, flavored with a bizarre gratitude for keeping their skins intact. She'd always thought of herself as infinitely replaceable and preferred it that way. That way she didn't have to worry about them if she got killed.

"Okay. Got it," she said finally.

"And?"

"And what?"

"And turnabout is fair play. If we belong to you, then you belong to us and you've got to start acting like it."

"Okay," she said slowly. "What does that mean?"

"It means we've got a right to watch out for you, too," Tyler said suddenly.

"That's not your job. You exist to protect Giselle."

"We're calling it our job," Akemi said in a quiet, iron-hard voice. "Protecting Giselle means keeping you around. All of our compulsion spells know it. I don't know why you don't."

That floored Max. She looked at each of them, her

mouth gaping. "What do you mean?" Then her stomach clenched and she felt sick. Had Giselle woven an extra compulsion into their spells? "No. You are not responsible for me. I won't be the reason you guys get killed."

"You're the reason we have stayed alive this long," Niko countered. "Get this straight. We want to be responsible for you and we mean to be. The hell with whether you agree or not."

He went and picked up his ice cream, then came and sat back beside her. "So what happened?" he asked conversationally.

Max sat a moment, then shook her head, giving in. For now. "The usual sort of thing. Selange wanted retribution for me being in Julian. I deserved it. I shouldn't have got caught." She did not look at Alexander. "Anyhow, she chose endurance for the challenge, with the loser Blade forfeit to the winning witch. She wanted to know why Giselle sent me to Julian and probably figured she'd be able to torture it out of me."

"But you won."

Max nodded. "But before we could get free of the veil, Selange ported through her Shadowblades and they ambushed us. We got out, but with a couple of souvenirs. That's about it."

"What about him?" Tyler asked, jerking his thumb at Alexander, who was staring annoyingly at Max.

The intensity of his look drilled through her. Like he wanted something from her. She looked away, shrugging. "What about him? He fought hard. He belongs to us now."

"You can't trust him," Niko argued.

She met Alexander's gaze again. "Yeah. I know." Then she shook her head, grogginess making her body feel clumsy and slow. "I need some sleep."

Instantly Niko slid off the table, taking her ice cream. "We'll keep watch."

She didn't have to hear the end of it to understand his meaning—they'd watch Alexander in case he tried anything. He wouldn't. He was too smart for that. But there was no point in telling them so. They weren't going to listen.

Max yawned, her jaw cracking. She lay back down, closing her eyes, her head starting to ache. "Okay. Take turns. We all need to be as sharp as possible. I've got a feeling there's plenty more trouble coming, and until we get back to Horngate, we can't afford to relax even an inch."

"Don't need to be able to scry to know that," Tyler muttered. "Anybody who doesn't know it deserves to be pushing up daisies."

Max smirked, but didn't answer. Instead she tried to think and plan. But fractures of exhaustion opened up ribbons of darkness in her mind, and soon she found herself sinking into velvet sleep.

When she woke again, dark was falling. Though the doors remained closed on the truck trailer, she felt the surge of night deep inside the marrow of her bones. Sometime in the day the trucks had moved—she'd been aware of the rumbling and movement.

She swung her legs over the edge of the gurney and sat up. Akemi paced along the wall, while Niko and Tyler slept in the aisles on either side of Max's perch. The moment she moved, they rolled to their feet. Alexander sat up slowly, running his fingers through his short hair, making it stand on end.

Max began to stretch and then caught herself. With a grimace she pulled the IVs from the backs of her hands and tossed them aside, then slid down to the floor. Her skin felt tight and hot and her body felt achy, as if she had a fever. She braced back against the table, waiting for her body to settle and her muscles to firm. She was sore, but that soreness was fast evaporating. Watery strength flowed sluggishly through her. She straightened, shaking herself and rolling her shoulders to loosen them.

"I need a shower," she announced, then made for the door. She stopped before opening it and looked back. Akemi was right behind her. "Find him some clothes," she told Tyler and Niko, jerking her chin at Alexander. "Then set up a watch outside."

Max didn't wait for a reply, stepping through the door into the light-sealed throughway and closing the panel behind her. When it snicked shut, a light inside switched from red to blue, and she slid open the outer panel, stepping out into a closet-size room. It contained a couple of fold-down bunks like the ones in the RV, a cabinet full of food, and another of weapons and emergency supplies.

Lise was sitting on the bunk with a shotgun across her knees. Strapped to her hips were two Glocks. She was ambidextrous and could hit two apples at the same time out of a tree at fifty yards without any trouble. She stood up when Max came through, propping the barrel of the gun against her shoulder and giving Max a quick once-over.

"Shit. They said you were alive, but I wasn't sure anyone could survive that." Lise tipped her head to the side. "If you didn't want me to borrow the clothes, you could have just said so."

Max grinned. "Sorry. Maybe next time. Where's Giselle?"

"In the RV."

"Where are we parked?"

"Unocal 76 truck stop in Ontario, just off the 15 and the 10."

"Good. That puts us out of Selange's territory. She won't have an easy time finding us with the wards active. I've got time to shower." Max turned to Akemi, who'd followed her. "Go check on Giselle, then grab some food and rotate out with Niko and Tyler so that you all eat before trouble hits again."

"What about the *pook gai*?" Akemi asked, her eyes flat as a snake's.

Clearly she didn't welcome Alexander in the fold. "Put clothes on him and feed him. We may need him."

The smaller woman curled her lip silently. "He has no loyalty."

"Would you rather he had let them kill me?"

Akemi's mouth tightened and her eyes widened. She gave an adamant shake of her head. Then, as if the words were dragged out of her: "He was their Prime. *You* would *never* turn on us."

Her total faith in Max made her knees sag. "You don't know that. Besides, it's survival. He doesn't have much choice."

"I do know and he does."

There was no arguing with such a black-and-white

view of things. Max drew a breath and let it go, envying Akemi's certainty of right and wrong and good and bad. She wished she could be so sure. But her world was gray on gray. "Regardless, Giselle claimed him. He's ours." *I don't leave any of mine behind.* She'd meant it. "Now I'm going to shower," she said. She felt sticky and itchy and she reeked of the antiseptic they'd used to clean her up.

She ignored Lise's casual salute and opened the door. They were parked in the back of the truck stop not far from the freeway. She could hear the passing engines of the freeway growing louder, then fading behind her. All around her trucks idled while inside their drivers slept in air-conditioned comfort. The smell of diesel exhaust and fry grease smothered the night, along with stale urine, old coffee, and the grime of the parking lot.

Giselle's RV was parked next to the hospital truck, and beyond it was the Garbage Pit and the sleeper RV. Max strode down and hoisted herself up inside. She could feel the stiffness in her body starting to relax and iron out. She went to her bunk and stripped off her borrowed scrubs. She wasn't wearing any underwear. They'd probably had to cut it off. She fished in her dresser for fresh clothes and grabbed her shower bag and towel from her closet.

She used all the hot water for her shower and finished with an icy spray. She dried and dressed quickly, her stomach growling insistently. Back in her bunk, she noticed her backpack on her bed with her cell phone lying on top. Someone had cleaned the blood off it and charged it. Her keys were there, too. Max tucked them both in her front pocket. She'd have to look for a new car to replace the Tahoe. She was going to miss the equipment and weapons from under the backseat. She doubted there had been time to rescue them.

She slid on her black nylon shoulder holster and pulled her .45 out of the backpack. It had also been cleaned, oiled, and loaded. She checked to make sure a bullet was chambered, then slid it into the holster. There were four more clips tucked inside the two mag pouches along the right shoulder strap. She slid her knife sheaths onto her forearms and over them a black sweat jacket, zipping it up enough to cover the harness. She grabbed a black Montana Griz baseball cap and yanked it down over her swiftly drying hair.

Around her right ankle she fastened her .380 and shoved a spare combat knife into her rear waistband, then drew on her socks and boots, bouncing lightly on the balls of her feet. The shower had washed away a great deal of her fatigue. She felt pretty good, considering she'd been half a breath away from dead twelve hours ago.

Last of all, she took the hailstone from its hiding place. It chilled her hand as she cupped it in her palm. She still didn't know what to do with it. Finally she reached for the leather medicine pouch that hung on a hook in the back of her closet. A shaman friend had given it to her several years before. Opening it would likely break its spells, but it was a good way to carry the hailstone. Max pried open the top and slipped the stone inside before tightening the strings and sliding it around her neck. The cold of the stone radiated through the leather, cooling a spot between her breasts.

She grabbed her wallet and slipped it into her back pocket and settled her sunglasses on her nose. She paused outside to scan the parked lines of trucks. A man peed on a tire three trucks down, and two women argued somewhere out of sight. Several dogs yapped, and a couple of trucks pulled out while three more pulled in. Max squatted, scanning beneath the bellies of the rigs, looking for odd-shaped shadows or furtive movements. There was nothing. She straightened, dusting her hand off on her pants.

She found Niko prowling behind Giselle's RV.

"You look like roadkill," he said, glancing at her and then away, his eyes moving ceaselessly as he scanned for trouble.

"Where is Alexander?"

"In the Garbage Pit with Tyler. Akemi is on patrol. She ate first," he assured before Max could ask.

"All right. I'm going to see Giselle, then eat."

"You need food more," he said with a scowl.

"Next you'll be telling me to eat my veggies and cut my meat small," Max retorted. "I've got to see my witch. Compulsion spells, you know?"

"Never bothered you much before."

"True. Maybe it's a sign of how depleted I am," she suggested mockingly. "Or maybe I've been born-again, eager to serve and to please."

Niko snorted. "Right."

"You didn't used to get so mouthy," Max said, her glance narrowing on him.

"You didn't used to come that close to dying."

"You'd be surprised," she murmured, thinking of the times she'd lain on Giselle's altar. But if she was honest, she'd never come quite this close to never waking up. "You're getting soft."

He spat on the ground. "Hurry up before you waste away to nothing."

"Careful. I may have to knock that chip off your shoulder."

"Whenever you want to try."

Max smiled started to walk away.

"Oh, tell Kamikani I'm sorry about his El Camino. Tell him I'll help him fix it."

She looked over her shoulder, brows raised in a question.

He shrugged. "There's a hole in his dash that looks like a fist. And a bunch of blood on the passenger seat."

Max nodded. "I'll tell him."

She headed again for Giselle's RV. As usual, she didn't knock, but opened the door and climbed inside without any ceremony. Inside Kamikani leaned on the edge of the table, facing the door. As the door had opened, he'd leveled his gun. When he saw Max, he lowered it, flicking a look behind him at Derek, another Sunspear, who stood in the hallway leading to Giselle's bedroom. He, too, lowered his gun.

"How is she?" Max asked softly, closing the door behind her.

"Still asleep," Derek said. "I'm supposed to wake her when you show up."

"Better do it then."

He turned and disappeared into the back. Max eyed Kamikani. "I hear there's some damage to your baby."

The corner of his mouth twitched, though whether it was anger or humor, Max couldn't tell. The rest of his expression remained impassive as stone. "Yeah."

"Niko says he'll make it right."

"It's righteous. I'd have done the same if it was me."

"Has anyone heard from Oz?" Max asked.

"He called from just south of Salt Lake a few hours ago."

"They're hauling ass," Max said, unsurprised. None of them took chances with speeding unless it was an emergency. They didn't want to call attention to themselves or risk getting hauled off to jail. It was too easy to get caught out in the light or the dark and die. But with Old Home not answering calls, speed was of the essence.

"He figured they'd make Horngate before dawn, and Old Home by midafternoon."

"Good. I'll check in with him later."

Max shifted to face the hallway as Giselle slouched into the small living room. She looked skeletal, her skin pasty, her eyes bruised. Her hands shook and her hair looked dull. Her gaze fastened on Max, running from head to toe. At last she jerked her head in a satisfied nod.

"Out," she ordered, her glance flicking to the two Sunspears. "Wait outside."

Max stepped out of the way as they wordlessly obeyed, fastening the door behind them. The RV was spelled to prevent any sound from escaping.

Giselle eased into one of her lounge chairs, dragging her fingers through her hair. She made no effort at small talk.

"Selange will be coming for us. We have to get on the road as soon as possible."

It was a bad idea. With Giselle so depleted, Max understrength, and a handful of Sunspears and Shadowblades, they were extremely vulnerable. It would be much better to wait until tomorrow night when Max was up at full strength. But a moving target was harder to hit than a sitting duck. "I need to eat first."

Giselle nodded. "How are you?"

"About eighty percent. With food and no battles, I'll be a hundred percent by morning."

Giselle's eyes closed and she took a ragged breath, letting it out. "Thank the Spirits for small favors. I thought you were dead. You *wouldn't* come back for me. If not for Akemi, Niko, and Tyler—" She broke off, staring at Max accusingly. "Don't do that again."

Max gave a sardonic smile. "Yes, ma'am. Whatever you want. Your wish is my command."

"I mean it. I told you we can't lose you. You should have listened to me. You should have left Alexander like I told you to."

"I don't leave mine behind," Max said quietly, folding her arms and leaning her hip against the counter.

"Dammit, he's *not* yours. You can't trust him."

"He's mine because you made him so. I know I can't trust him, but he did fight off his own Shadowblades for me, and once we were across the veil, he could have just taken off running. He had a decent chance of getting away from both you and Selange."

"No, he didn't. He could hardly stand. Don't think you owe him," Giselle said coldly. "He's not like you. He's only looking out for himself."

"And I'm not?"

Giselle laughed harshly. "You don't even know how. Last night is proof enough of that." Before Max could answer, Giselle raised her hands. "Enough. What do you plan to do with him? I can't bind him, not here, and even if I could, I can't afford to waste my strength on him."

"Then we take him with us. I'll keep an eye on him. Now, if that's all, I need food and we need to hit the road."

"Fine. But if you let him hurt you, I'll make you regret it."

"Whatever."

Giselle's fingers curled like claws on the arms of her chair. After a moment she grimaced. "There's no talking to you."

With that the witch stood and did her best to storm down the hall. Max ignored her, opening the door and motioning the two Sunspears back in. They looked a little gray from exposure. She glanced at the windows and windshield, noting that the blackout shades were down. They'd do well enough in the RV for now.

"I'll send food," she said, then closed the door behind her.

For a moment she stood in the darkness, her face tipped to the sky. The moon had not yet risen, and the power of the dark flowed into her like water over parched earth. She shivered with the hot surge of it, then started for the Garbage Pit, smelling garlic and beef and a myriad of other mouthwatering scents.

The steps in back were lowered, the door above firmly latched. Max climbed up and pushed inside. Alexander and Tyler sat opposite each other, with Tyler facing the door. Food was piled on the table between them. Or rather, stacks of empty plates. Alexander had turned to look at her and now wiped his mouth with a napkin, his gaze running over her assessingly. Max felt herself flush, her gaze settling on his mouth. Holy mother of crap, she needed to get laid.

"Go help Akemi and Niko," she said to Tyler, motioning with her head. "We're going to take off soon."

He stood with a dancer's grace and headed for the door. He paused beside her, bending close so that his breath brushed the nape of her neck. "Do take care of my Prime. Anything happens to you again, I'll take it personally." A moment later he left.

Max shook her head and went to take his seat across from Alexander. Last night had given her Shadowblades ideas about her that she wasn't sure she liked at all. Before she sat, she grabbed up some empty plates and carried them to the back. Magpie eyed her over the counter, but said nothing, her hands moving steadily as she chopped walnuts. Max stopped, remembering the other woman's warning before they left the warehouse: *No safety there, not for anyone. Not until you return. Only you can make it safe*. Max's stomach clenched. *I warn you—the things that I say are true. Ignore it and you'll probably regret it*. Horngate was in danger. The problem was, she had no idea what Magpie's warning meant.

Her fingers tightened and the plates in her hand cracked loudly in the quiet of the trailer. It was too quiet. Max couldn't remember the last time there hadn't been music playing. She clenched her jaw and set the broken dishes down with a bit of a clatter and went back to scoop up more.

This time Magpie glared at her. "Sit down before you break them all," she ordered in a voice as sharp as barbed wire.

Max had sense enough not to argue. She returned to the table and sat down opposite Alexander.

"You all right?"

She just nodded. He was sitting back in his chair, his hands clasped in his lap, watching her. His brow was crimped, as if she presented a difficult puzzle for him to solve. He was wearing a faded blue-denim shirt over a white, V-necked undershirt and a pair of Levi's. They belonged to Oz and didn't look like they were Alexander's style at all. Which was probably good because if he looked any better, she'd start tearing off his clothes and— She slammed the doors on that thought.

She didn't ask him how he was feeling. She was sick to death of hearing the question aimed at her.

Magpie set a jug of milk and a glass on the table with a thunk, then scooped the remaining dirty dishes into a bus tub and marched away. A moment later she returned with a big dish of bread pudding drizzled in bourbon sauce and piled with whipped cream. Max stared at it a moment, then began resignedly to eat. Despite her growling stomach, she wasn't hungry. She ate because she needed the calories and because Magpie would fillet her if she didn't.

Suddenly Alexander stood. He sniffed the air and then went to the door and opened it. Max set her fork aside, every instinct on alert. She stood, reaching for her gun at the same time.

"Do you smell it?" he asked.

Max cocked her head and sniffed, closing her eyes. She sorted through the scents her sensitive nose picked up, searching. Diesel, garlic, sweat, asphalt . . . she sifted deeper. A taste of the ocean, a hint of eucalyptus . . . There. Smoke. Not just smoke. Something else with it—no, intertwined with it. Divine.

Her eyes opened. Alexander met her gaze broodingly like he knew something about it. A chill rose up her back. *She could not trust him*. "Something you need to tell me?"

"We've had a dry summer and fire isn't unusual this time of year. But the other—" He shrugged. "I don't know."

She stared a long moment. Was he lying? She was sure he was—about something. The question was—what? Did this have something to do with Selange? There was no telling. But it was too coincidental not to wonder.

"It's a fire. Unless you're going to go put it out, sit and eat before the food gets cold," Magpie ordered in a surly voice from behind.

"You're a nag," Max said, returning to her seat. She watched the deft movements of the cook for a long moment. Magpie's warning still prodded at her. But the fire was far to the south. Neither they nor Horngate were in danger from it. Though Max trusted her instincts that screamed it was a threat, she could do nothing about it at the moment. "Kamikani and Derek need some food, by the way," she told Magpie at last. "Better take Giselle something, too. She looked like she wanted to bite something."

"Or someone?" Alexander asked shrewdly. "You maybe?"

"You could have said so when Tyler was here," Magpie said, snatching up a tray and beginning to pile it with food.

"We'll help," Max said, standing up again. She really didn't want to upset Magpie, who was known to get payback by tampering with the food. Nothing like burned lasagna or supersalty meat loaf to bring about a quick apology.

When they returned, Max dug into a bowl of fettuccine Alfredo.

"What are you planning to do with me?" Alexander asked suddenly. He'd sat down opposite her again and was watching her eat.

"I don't know. What should I do with you?"

"You cannot trust me."

The corners of Max's mouth quirked as she wound noodles around her fork. "Can't I? Gee golly willikers, Homer. That never would have occurred to me. Thanks for the heads-up."

He smiled, a lean, wide expression that made Max swallow hard. *So fine,* she told herself sternly. *He's very pretty. Admire him all you want. Drool all you want. But he's as dangerous as a bouncing betty land mine and more likely to tear you to bits. You. Will. Not. Touch.*

"I merely wanted to point out that I realize it would be stupid for you to trust me."

"And everybody knows I couldn't possibly be stupid," Max said sardonically. Then, "Do you have to talk that way? Like you're wearing a tux and tails and have a stick up your ass?"

He looked faintly affronted. "I was not aware."

"There you go again." She waved her hand. "Never mind. Look, I don't know what I'm going to do with you, Slick. You did protect me and you didn't have to. You could have tried to win your way back into Selange's good graces by giving me up. I owe you for that."

"You do not owe me. You carried me out of the Conclave and defied your witch doing it. You nearly got killed for your trouble. Besides, I doubt Selange would have taken me back," he added softly.

"You don't play poker, do you? You're not supposed to give everything away. Besides, you were her Prime. She wouldn't want to lose you."

"Maybe," he said, looking down. "But you heard what she said. I failed her. There is no greater crime." He hesitated, his hands clenching on the table. "Those rats . . . They were— It was—" He broke off, his face turning pale, his breathing ragged.

"I know," Max said sympathetically. Alexander hadn't been the first time Giselle had tried that particular attack, and Max remembered the horror of it all too well. "You break faster when they go after your mind rather than just your body. That's how Giselle got to you. Next time try not to care."

His glance was sharp, delving. Damn. She *did* play poker. She changed the subject. "Anyway, Giselle will decide what she wants to do with you. It's not up to me. You don't have to kiss my ass."

He shook his head. "I think she will listen to you. And I would like the chance to earn your trust," he said. And then, "Kissing your ass would only be a bonus."

Max's brows shot up in surprise. "Are you flirting with

me?" *Please no.* Because if he started that, she might not be able to resist, and she didn't need that kind of trouble. Plus she had rules. She did not mess in her own backyard, which meant—the kiss with Oz notwithstanding—she did not screw the men of her covenstead, no matter how much she might want to.

That slow smile came again like he knew the effect he was having on her deprived libido. Max's stomach tightened. Holy crap. "Is that against the rules?"

"You bet your ass it is," she snapped, pushing aside her empty bowl. "So what difference does it make if I trust you?"

He frowned. "You are my Prime now. You said so yourself. I am useless if you cannot trust me."

"True. Except you're not bound to Giselle yet. You could just . . . leave."

His mouth fell open, then closed in a firm line. "Just leave?"

She shrugged. "Why not?"

"And do what? What witch would have me?"

"Why would you want one? You could be free."

He was quiet for more than a minute. "I told you. I am Shadowblade. I am made to serve. I neither know nor want anything else."

"One doesn't make the other necessary," she argued. "Not if you're unbound."

Alexander was looking at her oddly, his gaze searing. Max flushed and ducked her head. She'd said too much, and freedom wasn't his dream.

"That is why," he blurted. "That is why you helped the Hag. I could not figure it out. It seemed so—"

"Stupid?" Max filled in helpfully.

He only nodded.

She shrugged. "You're right. It was. I could have died. As it was, you caught me. But then, I'd call serving a witch stupid if you didn't have to, so it's a case of the pot calling the kettle black."

He winced and she remembered what she'd called him. *Waste of skin*. He remembered, too. She could see it on his face. She'd apologized for it once. She didn't do it again.

Impatience suddenly swept over her. Her expression hardened and so did her voice. "All right. Here's the way it is. If you do anything to risk or hurt my people, I'll slit your throat. Clear enough? As for what I'll do with you—that really does depend entirely on Giselle."

"She ordered you to leave me behind," he pointed out, untroubled by her threat. "You did not. You defied her and she let you. I think a lot more depends on you than you are willing to say."

"Giselle can make me do anything she wants," Max said. "If she cares to take the trouble. Where do you think she learned that rat trick? Don't think I can—or will—save you. It's a fool's bet."

"You have already said I am a fool."

"I hope to hell you're smarter than that."

He leaned forward, speaking earnestly. "You are my Prime. You take the job very seriously. I have seen the way your Blades are with you. They would follow you into the bowels of hell if you asked, and even if you did not. If Giselle ordered them to kill you, I think she would have a revolt on her hands. There is a reason for that. You would give your life for them—you would give a lot more than that. I think," he said slowly, sitting back in his chair, his fingers tapping slowly on the table, "you are a decent bet."

She shook her head. "That's the thing about gambling. The house always wins. Don't be a sucker. Get the hell out of here while you can."

10

MAX STUFFED HERSELF UNTIL HER STOMACH felt like it would explode and then she ate more. She didn't know if it was in preparation to answer the foreboding that collected like the smoke from the distant fires, or if it was to try to smother her conflicted feelings—for her Shadowblades, for Alexander, for Giselle. Worst of all Giselle. Now that she knew what the witch was up to with Horngate, fighting her seemed selfish. More than that—it seemed wrong. And yet agreeing to permanent slavery seemed wrong, too.

She finished eating and bused her table and thanked Magpie. "We'll be rolling as soon as we can," she said. The other woman nodded shortly, but made no comment as she continued to knead a mass of dough. Her silence was welcome. Max found herself falling into a dangerous, angry mood, and the slightest spark would set her off. Even Alexander seemed to know it. Like Magpie, he said nothing to her as she motioned him to follow her out of the Garbage Pit.

Outside Max felt claustrophobic. She needed open air, trees, and tall mountains. That made her pause. When had that happened? When had Giselle's mountains become more of a home to her than the grass prairies and cornfields of her birth? She'd grown up in the sticky humidity of the Midwest, where the land rippled beneath a sea of grass, corn, and soybeans, all fading into nothingness, unbounded by any impertinent mountains. There the rivers ran brown over mud beds, and seeds sprang to vigorous life wherever they happened to drop. It was a verdant place, a welcoming place, a refuge. Montana, on the other hand, was austere and unforgiving. Its mountains were sharp and forbidding, its forests full of teeth and claws. Winters were bleak and frigid, and life did not easily take hold there. Still, she longed to be back, climbing the sheer sides of the peaks, losing herself in the rich silence of the trees and the cutting winds and the brilliant skies. Perhaps it was that the place better matched what she'd become. Hers was a life of blood, battle, and death.

"Are you all right?"

Max started and twisted her head to look at Alexander. "Not you, too. Do I look broken?" Immediately she wished she hadn't asked. She wasn't sure she'd like the answer.

"No. But you do not seem yourself."

"What the fuck do you know about me?" she snapped back and then spun and walked away. It was time to get on the road.

Her phone buzzed in her pocket. She checked the screen on the front. Oz. Finally. She flipped it open.

"What's going on? Where are you?"

"In Dubois, about to head up over Monida Pass. Wanted to check in with you. Word is we nearly lost you."

There was a warm edge to his voice that reminded her of her Midwest home. She felt herself recoil. "I'm fine, if that's what you're asking," she said, more coldly than she meant to.

Silence. "Glad to hear it. What about Giselle?"

"She's tired."

"When are you getting on the road?"

"Soon as I finish with you." Max scraped her foot against the pavement, impatient for the call to be over.

"All right. I'll let you know what we find at Old Home." Oz stopped, as if trying to figure out how best to proceed through a battle zone. A short sigh. "Keep yourself safe."

"Yeah. You, too," she said, then snapped her phone shut and shoved it in her pocket.

She glanced at Alexander, who remained silent. It annoyed her that he was in Oz's clothing. She felt like both men were hovering over her like vultures, waiting for something. What it was, she did not know.

A sudden disturbance rippled through the air. Max stopped dead, then whirled and sprinted for Giselle's RV. Alexander raced after her.

A flash of witchlight lit the night. It was brilliant white, fading to yellow, then orange. The ground rumbled and the parked semis shuddered and groaned as a thundering force wave blew by like a hurricane wind. Blinded, Max stuttered and slowed. Alexander shouldered into her. She shoved him away, her head up as she smelled the night. Uncanny and Divine magic uncurled like tentacles in the air. She tasted salt brine and char and smelled seaweed and burnt feathers. She raced forward.

Giselle's RV looked like it was encased in gray shadow. Its protective wards were gone, accounting for the explosive flash. Max could hardly believe her eyes. Beside it stood an angel. He was nearly seven feet tall with ebon wings rimmed in fire and eyes as red as garnets. He wore ratty jeans and his sculpted chest was bare. She barreled forward, spinning with her back to the RV, facing the intruder.

She didn't bother to make conversation. She hitched forward, sweeping her leg at the angel's knees. The sudden force of it shattered one of his knees with an audible crunch. He should have dropped. Instead he swept a wing between them like a shield. Flames flared bright along the feathers. Max had a blade in her hand and crouched, ready to attack. Giselle stopped her.

"Max, wait."

Max stopped. Stillness settled around them, like the quiet just before a nuclear explosion. Max could hear the soft crackle of the flames burning along the angel's black feathers and smell the stench of burning tar as the flames scorched the asphalt. He stared at her with his red eyes, his expression eerily blank. Max smiled, silently daring him to try something.

"What do you want?" Giselle demanded.

"My mistress sends a message for you" came the angel's baritone voice.

"Does she? Is she declaring war?"

"No."

"Then why do you attack?"

"A mere accident, witch. You have my apologies."

He didn't sound remotely apologetic.

"Who is your mistress?" Giselle demanded, not

sounding like she believed him any more than Max did.

"This scroll shall explain."

The bleached-blond angel was holding out a rolled-up parchment. Bone knobs wrapped in red and purple threads protruded from the ends. The knobs were carved in the concentric shapes of the circle, star, and triangle, with a single point in the middle, like an *anneau* floor. The threads wrapped the scroll in a complex weaving. Before Giselle could even think of taking it, Max leaped in front of her.

"Hands to yourself, asshole," Max said, her knife raised between them.

A noose of Giselle's remaining Sunspears and Shadowblades closed around them, and the angel's wings flared warningly, sparks drifting down to ignite tiny fires on the pavement.

"I should warn you about my fire. One does not usually survive its touch." He spoke to Max, still holding out the scroll.

"Try to touch my witch and I'll rip your damned wings off," she answered.

"Bravely said. But my fire would eat your flesh and turn your bones to ash."

"Not before I kill you."

"For a witch?" the angel said contemptuously. "I had heard you were not so loyal."

"Maybe it's my compulsion spells. Or it could be I just don't like you," Max retorted.

He grinned, an expression of genuine humor. It took Max aback. He was ethereally beautiful, as all angels were supposed to be, but the smile changed his entire face and made him look almost human. Almost. His head tipped to the side as he studied her with his bloody eyes. She firmed her grip on her knife.

"Slavery does not suit you," he said softly.

For a moment Max couldn't speak. Her mouth was unaccountably dry. "Slavery doesn't suit *anyone,*" she said finally. "But what do you know of it?"

This time his smile was as bitter as lye. "More than you think. My mistress sends a message. Will you accept it?" He looked past Max to where Giselle still stood on the steps of the RV.

"I'll take it," Max said. "Give it to me."

"That might prove . . . fatal," the angel said with a slight frown. "It is protected from all but the witch's touch."

He didn't say Giselle's name, as if it weren't worth knowing. Max shrugged. "Then I guess you'll be taking it back."

"Max," Giselle said warningly.

"No," Max said flatly. "Shut the fuck up and let me do what you made me to do."

To her surprise, Giselle said nothing. The angel's frown deepened. Max wanted to laugh at his confusion. She didn't really understand herself either. For thirty years she'd wanted Giselle dead at any cost. A day ago she would have talked her compulsion spells into letting the witch take the scroll, hoping it would blow her head off. But today Max was different. More was at stake. Things weren't about just Giselle and Max anymore. This was about Horngate and the men and women that looked to Max to protect them. She wasn't alone. She hadn't been for a while, but today Max actually realized it. And like it or not, Giselle and her magic were the life-blood of Horngate. Without her, nothing Max could do would keep its denizens safe, no matter what Magpie's vision said.

"Either give it to me or hit the road," she told the angel, holding out her empty hand.

For a moment he did not move. Something moved deep in his eyes. Then he pulled the scroll back and reached down and plucked a small feather from the underside of his wing. Blue flame flickered along its edges, then sank inside. The iridescent black bled to blue, and heat rippled visibly from it. The angel slid it along the covering of the scroll and melted away the net of thread. Power exploded from his hands, billowing outward. It thrust against Max and rocked the RV from side to side. She stood firm, feeling Giselle clutch her shoulders.

The threads dropped away, sticky and black. The angel closed his fist around the feather, and when he opened his hand again, it was gone. He held the scroll out again, this time offering it to Max. She didn't hesitate. It felt hot in her hands as if it had been pulled from an oven. She turned it over in her hand and looked at the angel again.

"Is that going to cost you?"

He shrugged, his mouth twisting, his nostrils flaring. "Everything costs. I can afford the price," he said disdainfully.

"Yeah, but you didn't have to."

"My mistress gave me a task. I may complete it as I see fit."

Exactly as Max had always done, and in the process she'd made a point of provoking Giselle any way she possibly could as often as she could. For that, Max had always been willing to pay. Slowly she slid her knife back into its sheath. A gesture of peace.

"Do not think you can trust me. We are not enemies now, but we may be when next we meet," he said, watching her deliberate movements.

"I'll worry about it if the time comes," Max said. "For now we are . . . not. I owe you my thanks. You could have let me suffer the consequences of that spell. So thank you. I owe you."

Max heard Giselle's loud gasp. The witch's fingers clawed deep into Max's shoulder. The angel's eyes widened and he stiffened. "Do you know what you have done?"

Max nodded. "I know the rules of the game."

Giving him thanks gave him a hold on her; it opened a dangerous door between them. That was bad enough. But putting herself in his debt gave him a real link to her. If he chose to call it . . . With his magic—and angels were powerful creatures of the Divine—she'd be his puppet, dancing as he pulled the strings. It could give his mistress a door into Horngate. All in all, it was a damned stupid thing to do, but all the same, it was the way the game was played—at least, if you played by the rules. She'd made a sacrifice for the Hag, and the Hag had gifted her the hailstone. The angel had sacrificed as well. Who knew what his mistress would do to him for breaking the binding spell on the scroll? Whatever it was, Max was sure it would be unpleasant. That much she could read in the set of his jaw and the strain around his eyes. So she owed him. And when you owed, you paid. She didn't have much, but she still had her pride and her integrity and her good word.

"I must go. I will return soon for your answer," the angel said to Giselle, never looking away from Max. His chiseled, white brow was furrowed.

"One thing," Max said, stopping him. "The fires I smell—they are yours." It wasn't a question.

"Yes."

"Why?"

"They are a gift. And perhaps a threat. For others it is a promise," he said cryptically. "We will see each other again. Farewell."

With that he leaped upward. Above the RV, his wings spread wide. They beat powerfully and he rose into the sky, winging westward.

Giselle's hand dropped from Max's shoulder. "Max, inside with me," she ordered icily, and stepped up inside her RV.

Max looked at the gathered Sunspears and Shadowblades. "Get the rigs ready to move." They started to disperse, all but Alexander, who didn't budge. Tyler grabbed him by the arm to haul him off. Max held up a restraining hand. "Have you got something to say?"

"Do you know what you've done?" Alexander asked, repeating the angel words. "You'll never be rid of him. He'll never let you free."

"Is that all?" Max said coldly. Her mind was twisting tight and she felt herself withdrawing inside the emotional shields she'd long ago built for herself. She didn't regret her decision, but Alexander was right. She'd opened Pandora's box, and there was no closing it now.

Alexander started to say something else, then shook

his head and held up his hands in surrender. He turned and went with Tyler.

Max drew a deep breath, steadying herself. Then she followed Giselle inside, shutting the door carefully and handing her the scroll.

"What in the hell did you do?" Giselle demanded as soon as Max was inside. "What were you thinking? He owns you now. I can't do anything to help you. When he decides to use you, I won't be able to stop him."

"Oh, damn. How will I ever cope?" Max asked sardonically. "Being a slave will be such a change."

"I told you how important you were to me, to Horngate," Giselle cried. "Then you go and put yourself under his power. You're useless now. Useless! I can't trust you at all. I'll never know if you are his puppet. You almost got yourself killed for that worthless Alexander, and now this!"

"You know I won't betray Horngate," Max said softly. "That's the one thing in the world you and I agree on. We both want to keep it safe."

"How will you stop yourself if he tells you to?"

"Same way I stop myself when you start pushing me around too much." Max leaned on the edge of the kitchen counter and folded her arms.

That caught Giselle up short. She slowly sank into a chair, her hands knotting around the scroll. She seemed wholly unaware that she was even holding it.

"Can you?" she asked finally.

"You know me. What do you think?"

"If anyone could, it would be you. But you have no idea the power angels have. And his mistress— You've done some stupid things, Max, but this one is imbecilic.

Why? Why now? Old Home may have been attacked, and Horngate may be next. Selange will be on the warpath after us, and you decide *now* is a good time to put yourself into the debt of an angel? Have you gone insane?"

"I owed him."

"I need you. Horngate needs you. That should take precedence over whatever you think you owe him. What did he do for you anyhow? Save you from a bomb he planted himself? It's ridiculous. If you hadn't insisted on taking the scroll, we wouldn't be in this mess."

"And if it had blown your arm off or killed you—where would Horngate be then?" Max shook her head, biting hard on her lower lip, tasting blood. She stared down at her feet, reaching for calm. Quietly she began again. "Let me spell it out for you. For those of us who don't have much freedom to make our own choices, it costs us dearly to break the rules." She looked up at Giselle without lifting her head. "You know all about that. So, yes, he brought that spell and it was trap. But he didn't make it and he didn't send it. His bitch mistress did. And he chose to help me when he didn't have to. You can bet your life that his mistress will punish him, and we both know how creative you witches can be about that. So while it might seem to you to be unnecessarily risky to acknowledge his gift, the truth is that for me and for him, what he did was huge and it deserves a return on investment. It's the only thing of value creatures like him and me have left to give."

Giselle shook her head. "It was a mistake and it could cost Horngate everything," she insisted.

Max shrugged tiredly. It was pointless to talk about it

anymore. It was done. "Are you going to read that thing and find out what I bought for us?"

The witch rigidly unrolled the scroll. Her hands were shaking. Max's gaze narrowed. Foreboding uncurled along the marrow of her bones. She watched Giselle read. A minute ticked past, then another and another. The color drained from Giselle's face. She reached the end and her hands clenched convulsively on the parchment. When she looked at Max, her eyes were like black holes.

"The angel's mistress is Hekau."

She announced it like Max should know who it was. "Who?"

"Hekau. She's a Guardian."

Max stared. "As in *the* Guardians?" Giselle nodded. "What does she want?"

Giselle pressed a hand over her mouth as if to stop an angry scream from escaping. Or maybe it was to hide the tremble of her lips. A moment later her hand dropped to her lap, her face going still as a frozen lake. In a monotone she said, "She summons me to serve—me and all of Horngate. To fight under her banner in the coming war—she is calling it the War of Retribution. If I refuse, Horngate will be destroyed. Like Old Home."

Max could only stare. It was exactly as Giselle had warned from her vision. It was so exactly the same that she couldn't help but doubt that the witch was telling the truth. Max's expression must have told the tale.

"Are you going to tell me I'm lying?" Giselle asked, rubbing her brow tiredly. "That all of this is just an elaborate manipulation to get you to cooperate and obey me?"

Max bit the tip of her tongue. This was it. She'd already decided. Horngate meant too much to her. But she hated to give Giselle the satisfaction. And one day she *would* be free, come hell or high water. She swallowed. There was no other choice. Giselle hadn't sent herself an angel love-gram. It was time to plan and act.

"What do you want to do?" she asked at last.

Giselle stared a moment, then closed her eyes, her shoulders slumping with palpable relief. A second later she straightened, her expression turning determined. "You have to get the Hag."

That was not what Max had expected. "What?"

"I think . . . If I refuse to go to war, I'm sure that Hekau will use angelfire to strike at Horngate—to make an example out of me. That must be what happened at Old Home. But why didn't Alton tell me?" Giselle frowned, perplexed, then shook her head. "The angel was a warning—to tell us what Hekau could do to us. The Bitterroots hardly need more than a spark to turn into a conflagration, and angelfire has to be put out with magic. Once it's burning wild, I won't have the magic to put it out, not even with the rest of the coven helping. Horngate will be burned to ash.

"But with the Hag, we might have a chance. She commands water and winter. Between us, I think we could smother angelfire. If you can convince her to come to Horngate and help us, it could buy us some time to figure out a way to get out of going to war."

"Me? How am I going to convince her?"

"You said it yourself. You saved her; she owes you. If you hadn't broken the spell circle, she'd be a prisoner of Selange."

Except that the Hag had paid for her freedom and the breakfast of Max's blood with the hailstone. But Max wasn't going to tell Giselle that. The stone was hers. Nor did Max remind her that the angel now had a similar hold on her. Not that she needed to. The bitter set of Giselle's mouth said that she already recognized the irony.

"I've still got half the night. I'll take Akemi's truck. I'd better take Alexander with me, too."

"Alexander?" Giselle asked sharply. "Why?"

"I don't want to send him to Horngate with all of this hanging over our heads. He's too dangerous. He could bring Selange down on you."

"I don't like it. He could just as easily stick a knife in your back."

"Maybe. But that will still keep him from calling Selange down on your doorstep. And with you so short-handed and your wards gone on the RV, I don't want to take the chance that he'll come after you. He could very well succeed. He was Prime, which means he's very good."

Giselle tapped her fingers on her knee. "Fine. Get going and take him with you. But be careful."

"I always am."

"Liar."

The worry in Giselle's voice was palpable. Max hesitated. "I'll be as careful as I can."

"Hurry back. We won't have much time before the angel comes back demanding an answer. I can't just say no."

"I want you out of here now. Don't take I-15. Go up I-5 through Oregon, then up through Washington and

Idaho. Keep moving. Don't stop except to fuel up and switch out drivers," Max ordered.

"I will."

"Then I'm on my way."

Max turned and reached for the door, but was arrested by Giselle's quiet words.

"I know that today is Tris's birthday. I'm sorry you missed it."

Max couldn't hide the pain that twisted her face. With her back to Giselle, the other woman didn't see it. "It's not like I can do anything but watch like a stalker," she said, her hand squeezing the door handle until the metal crushed in her grip.

"Still, she's your sister."

"No, she's not. Not anymore. Not for thirty years."

Tears slipped down Max's face as she pushed open the door and pressed it firmly shut behind her. Tris was forty-three years old today. She was married with two kids. Max's brother was only thirty-three. She had never really known him. He'd been born right before she left for college. Now he was divorced and remarried, with two stepsons and a daughter from his first marriage. Both of Max's parents were still alive, too. Her father was diabetic, but he managed it well, and her mother was spry and healthy. Every year between Christmas and New Year's, Max made a pilgrimage to see them. They never saw her. And half a year later, she returned for Tris's birthday. She couldn't stop herself.

She sucked in an aching breath and squeezed her eyes shut, willing away the tears and the memories. There was no time. She had to get Akemi's truck loaded, collect Alexander, and get the rest of them on the road.

Twenty minutes later, she and Alexander sped silently down the freeway, on their way back to Julian after watching their companions start west on I-10. Max had added her own weaponry that Tyler had rescued from the Tahoe to Akemi's stash beneath the backseat of the crew cab, as well as a duffel of spare clothing and a cooler of food in the light-sealed emergency-refuge box in the back of the truck. She'd ransacked Oz's bunk for more clothes for Alexander and snared a pair of hiking boots for him from Tyler.

Now they drove in silence. Alexander asked no questions about where they were going or why, though if he had two brain cells to rub together, he'd have figured it out the moment they headed south. Time was of the essence. Silence settled thick in the cab of the truck, pressing down like a thousand feet of ocean water.

Max drove on autopilot. She felt raw, her emotions running too close to the surface. She thought of the angel. What would he want from her? She knew it was stupid to even imagine she could trust him, and she didn't. Still, they were the same. Slaves to witches, even if his was a witch dosing on magical steroids.

"Fuck," she said aloud, dragging one hand through her hair.

"What is it?" Alexander asked quickly.

She gave him a sideways glance. "Nothing," she replied shortly, then reached for the stereo, turning on the CD player. Instantly the cab of the truck filled with a slow, mournful jazz song. Max's lip curled and she turned it off. She and Akemi did not share tastes in music.

Her fingers flexed on the steering wheel. Alexander said nothing so loudly it made her jaw hurt. Suddenly they came up on the Pala Road exit. Max veered off, barely slowing as she spun the truck around east on Pala Road, running the stop sign in the process. She followed the curves past farmland and through the town of Pala, then through more farmland until they reached mountains. She rolled her window down, tasting smoke. An Uncanny wind was blowing and smoke choked the moon and stars. The fire had to be huge. What had the angel said? *A gift, a threat, and a promise*. But for whom? Giselle? Other witches?

Suddenly she hit the brakes and pulled over, gravel and dust spinning into the air. She turned to face Alexander.

"It's time to fish or cut bait. You can get out right here and go back to Selange or go wherever the hell you want. I don't give a shit. Or if you want, you can stay with me and join my Shadowblades. But if you do decide to stay, then I have to be able to trust you like one of my own. I'll need your word."

In the world of witches, too many times a man's word was a flimsy thing. Still, it was all Max owned, and it was all she could ask of Alexander. He didn't even own the clothes on his back.

"Well? I don't have time to waste. What's it going to be?"

11

ALEXANDER SAT STUNNED. SHE HAD SUGGESTED before that he could just leave, and he had not taken her seriously. How could he? He was a wealth of information for Giselle. Not just about Selange, but many things he had learned in the last hundred years. Letting him go was— He almost laughed. *Stupid*. He kept using that word when it came to Max, but she was not stupid. Nor was this some sort of test. If there was one thing he had learned in the last thirty hours, it was that she did not have the patience to lie. This was a real offer.

"I told you, Selange will not want me back, except to make sure I keep my mouth shut. And I am made to serve a coven," he said, playing for time as he tried to sort out his thoughts. What did he want to do? He could go back to Selange. Telling her about the angel's visit to Giselle might buy him some goodwill, though not much. Better if he brought back Max like a trophy to lay at her feet. He looked at her. He was not going to do that.

"That answer doesn't inspire a lot of confidence, Slick.

If the only reason you want to stay is because you've got nowhere else to go, then I don't want you."

"I do not even know you. You hate your witch and you are reckless beyond measure. Why should I stay?"

"You don't have to convince me. I couldn't agree more. So take a walk. Now. Get out."

She watched him, her eyes implacable. And the one thing that Alexander knew for sure in that moment was that he did not want to leave. He thought of Giselle's tears when she realized the extent of Max's injuries, and he remembered the fierce loyalty of her Shadowblades as they fought for her life. Then there was Max's promise to the angel—*I owe you.* He wondered what Giselle had said about that. Yet, despite the danger such a promise presented, she had not punished Max or killed her, as any other witch would have done.

What it all came down to was that the people surrounding Max were tainted with her sense of what was right. They fought for her and for each other, because they cared about each other, and because Max gave them all everything she had and expected the same from them. None wanted to come up short. Alexander found that he was no different.

He met Max's hard gaze. Her eyes were shuttered. Even as he watched, he could see her withdrawing inside of herself to that place she had gone during the Conclave challenge. It was so deep and so armored that it was almost like she was not there at all. Something in him twisted sharply. He did not want to let her go there. It was a cold, bleak place, but more than that, when she was there, she became more reckless. She needed him—for tonight at least—to watch her back, and whether she knew it or not, to pull her back from the edge of reason.

"I want to stay with you." He stressed the last word slightly.

Max scowled. Something hot and angry rippled over her expression and vanished. The seconds ticked past. Alexander waited. Would she kick him out anyway?

She sat rigid, staring out over the hood of the truck. Her throat jerked as she swallowed hard. She gave a little shake of her head, then put the truck in gear and pulled back onto the road. She never said a word.

Alexander chewed the inside of his cheek, tasting blood. He watched the mountains speed by, smoke lying in their folds like clouds. If he was really committed to Max . . . and Giselle . . . then he had to go all the way. No secrets.

"The angel visited Selange just before the Conclave," he said abruptly into the silence. "He gave her a similar scroll. I do not know what it said, but Selange was not pleased to receive it. She was worried. She sent Sunspears to find the Hag and her staff. And she made the challenge to get your hailstone. She said that with the Hag, the staff, and the hailstone, she might be able to avoid 'indentured servitude.' Her words."

When Max did not reply, he glanced at her to gauge her reaction. Her mouth had twisted down and her hands whitened on the steering wheel. "All right," she said flatly. "Anything else I should know?"

"This fire was supposed to be a gift for Selange. My guess is it will allow her to expand her territory by getting rid of the witches south and east of her territory. There has long been friction there. It will also give her an influx of power as she collects the magic from the panic and deaths. And one thing more. The angel said he would come for Selange's answer on the new moon."

"Anything else?"

"No."

"Why would Selange get a gift and Giselle a threat?" Max wondered aloud. "It doesn't make sense. And if they really did burn out Old Home—" She broke off like she had said too much.

"Old Home?" he asked.

She hesitated. "Old Home is an ally of Horngate. Just before the Conclave, it went silent. Alton, Old Home's witch, was in a panic. Giselle believes it might have been destroyed because of what was in the scroll. She thinks Alton got one, too."

Max knew more, he could tell. She spoke carefully as if paring down the facts. "Did all the scrolls say the same thing?" he wondered aloud. "And can whoever sent them be trusted?"

She glanced at him sharply and opened her mouth, then shut it and stared back out at the road. They made the rest of the journey in silence, the smoke thickening the closer they came to Julian. Without asking, Alexander knew that must be where they were going. Either Giselle wanted the Hag and her staff for her own use, or she did not want to let Selange have her. But Selange had sent her Sunspears to Julian the morning before the Conclave.

"Do you think she is still there?" he asked, more to break the silence than to hear the answer.

Max made no effort to pretend she did not know what he was talking about. "The Hag? Maybe. Probably. I'd bet on her."

"Selange will not give up. My— Her Shadowblades will be on the hunt if her Sunspears failed to capture the Hag."

"Then we'll have to be careful."

She said nothing more.

By the time they reached Julian, the smoke was so thick they could no longer see more than twenty yards in front of the truck. Ash floated thickly in the air. It was as if a volcano had erupted, or hell had opened a door into Southern California. An unnatural wind gusted, buffeting the truck. It smelled of the Divine.

Max drove through town, pulling off in a dirt lane and parking behind a mass of tangled blackberries on the edge of an irrigation ditch. She got out, opening the rear door and flipping up the seat. She pulled out a second .45 in a hip holster and belted it on, fastening it to her thigh with a Velcro strap, then reached for the pistol-grip shotgun she had been carrying that first night. Alexander came around the front of the truck.

"Take your pick," Max told him, slinging a bandolier filled with flashbombs and iron-shapnel grenades over her shoulder before stepping out of the way.

Alexander hesitated a bare instant. She was not playing games; she had taken him at his word and chosen to trust him to watch her back. He could not imagine doing the same in her position. He would not have turned his back on her, much less given her a weapon.

He took out a MAC-10 and looped the strap over his shoulder, then grabbed a .45 and buckled it around his hips. He tucked a combat knife into his waistband at the small of his back and slid a folding knife into his borrowed boot. He straightened and turned. Max was already moving toward the trees. He hurried to catch up with her.

The smoke and magic in the air overwhelmed all other scents. Ash and dirt whirled on the wind, clogging Alexander's nose and eyes. Max seemed hardly to notice. She flowed over the ground like a shadow. Her head swiveled back and forth, but never in Alexander's direction, as if she trusted him to guard and defend her flank. He wondered what she would do if he decided to attack her after all. It was an idle thought. He had made his choice. But that did not diminish the miracle of the trust she placed in him.

He stayed twenty feet behind her, ranging back and forth, camouflaging himself in the shadows of the trees and the writhing curls of smoke unwinding along the ground. The wild magic of the chaos zone had vanished, leaving only small, lingering pockets of malevolence and dreams. Alexander skirted them easily. They could not harm him, but they were distracting.

He could not afford distraction. If Max was right and the Hag had not yet been found, his Shadowblades would have returned to continue the search. The same ones that had tried to kill him the previous night.

He knew without a doubt that had Max lost the challenge, her Shadowblades would never have gone hunting her, except as a rescue mission. They would have died before hurting her. Compared to her, he was a failure as a Prime. The knowledge irritated him. What could he have done better?

The ground was soft and his boots left deep tracks in the loam. But Alexander was not worried about what might be tracking them. The real danger was ahead.

Max held up a warning hand and Alexander dropped into a crouch, straining to hear. The only sound was the sough of the wind in the trees and the drone of helicopters and airplanes to the south. At last Max started to move again. Alexander closed the distance between them by half. Selange's Shadowblades were here somewhere. He could feel it.

They finally emerged from the skirts of the apple orchard. Before them was a tractor and beyond it the ashen remains of the house. Little was left besides a black hole in the ground and some debris that had been blown clear when Thor had detonated the house. Beyond was the pool enclosure, and to the far right of it, the small grotto that was home to the Hag. Max squatted at the front of the tractor. Alexander followed suit.

"If they are not here, then they have found her," he said. "Selange would not have given up." The wind shredded the words, but Max nodded once to let him know she had heard.

They sat watching for fifteen minutes. Max never even turned her head, much less fidgeted. At last she glanced up. The moon was nothing more than a smudge of light behind the smoke. There was only a few hours of darkness left. She looked at him over her shoulder.

"Scout the perimeter. I'm going to find the Hag."

She turned and trotted away, her shotgun ready in her hand. Alexander caught himself before he could follow, though every instinct told him she should not go alone. Instead he did as ordered and went the other way.

There was little enough cover left. The house was gone, and with it the bushes and trees that had grown in its shadow. The lack forced Alexander to take a longer, more circuitous route than he wished, knowing that Max had taken a direct line to the grotto.

He came around the back side of the pool enclosure and leaped over the fence. He dropped down in the bushes, painfully aware of the crackling shuffle of the leaves as he landed. He froze, listening. He heard nothing. Slowly he eased out of the garden bed and out along the sidewalk. He padded across to the other side and crouched again by the brick barbecue.

The hairs on his neck rose. The wind gusted. Now he could smell them. So close. Alexander slid to the fence and peered over. Max stood between the grotto and the remains of the house. Five Shadowblades surrounded her, each of them pointing a gun.

"Move and you die, bitch," Brynna said. "I thought I killed you." She took a step closer. "Never mind. I'll make sure you die this time. I owe you for that knock on the head." Eagerness sharpened the viciousness in her voice.

"Selange wants her," Thor said in his Texan drawl.

"*I* want her," Brynna pouted. "Selange doesn't even have to know. All she really wants is the Hag and her staff anyway."

Alexander did not wait to hear more. Max's face told him all he needed to know. She was not going down without a fight. He backed away from the fence and ran to the other end of the pool enclosure, just around the corner from the Hag's grotto. He vaulted the clapboard fence. His feet touched down at the same moment he pulled his combat knife from his waistband. There was no time for finesse. He was running full tilt as he leaped over the grotto pool. A rock humped up behind Max. Alexander dug to a halt behind it even as he snatched

Max's hair in his fist and yanked her back. She tried to catch herself, but the rock confused her feet. She sagged against Alexander's chest. He held her in place with an iron arm, the point of his knife—her knife—jabbing sharply into her neck.

"Do not move," he warned. He looked at his stunned Shadowblades, giving a predatory smile. "Nobody's killing this bitch but Selange."

With that, he pulled back and clubbed the hilt of the knife against the side of Max's head. He felt her skull give and she slid boneless from his arms. He let her fall, never taking his eyes off the surrounding Shadowblades. Would they try to kill him? He was not sure, but Cleo looked faintly abashed, and Thor's face could not seem to decide between a smile and a scowl.

"What the hell do you think you're doing?" Brynna demanded. "You are no longer Selange's Prime. In fact, you're not one of us at all. Take him," she ordered, gesturing at Thor.

"But I am one of you," Alexander said, sliding his knife back into his waistband. He spoke more to the others than to Brynna; she was not going to listen to anything he had to say.

"I have been with Selange more than a hundred years. She made me. I am hers forever. I certainly do not belong to some child-witch who has barely come into her powers. Did you think Selange truly cut me loose?" He shook his head, sneering. "Surely you know how devious she is. It was all show to get me inside her enemy's coven and bring back this trash." He nudged Max with his boot, glancing back up at his audience. Were they buying it?

"Someone had better bind her before she wakes. Make it solid." He looked mockingly at Brynna. "If that is all right with you, Brynna, since you seem to be handing out orders tonight. Did Selange make you Prime instead of Marcus?"

She flushed. "He put me in charge tonight. He had other things to do." She spun around and looked at the others. "Tie her up. Tie them both up. We'll let Selange decide if he's telling the truth."

They used riot cuffs on Alexander's and Max's wrists and ankles, then ringed each of them from head to toe with a series of heavy-duty cable ties spaced every two to three inches. Taking charge of Alexander, Brynna tightened the ties so they gouged deep into his flesh. Trussed this way, neither prisoner could leverage enough strength to break free. Bound like mummies, neither could they walk.

Thor put Alexander over his shoulder and Cleo hoisted up Max, who remained unconscious.

"Dump them in the van and keep an eye on them," Brynna ordered. "The rest of you, look for the Hag. We leave in an hour. If you don't find her this time, there's going to be payback. I'm not taking the blame for failing, I promise."

Alexander snorted. If she kept that up, she'd soon find herself with a bullet in her brain.

Just beside the driveway, a firebreak road looped out around the property, tracing the edge of the orchard. Two gray box vans were parked there. Thor yanked open the rear doors of the first one. There was a bench seat behind the driver's seat, and the rest of the back was open. Thor slid Alexander inside, more gently than expected. Cleo tossed Max in beside him. Her head thudded loudly on the floorboards.

The minutes ticked by slowly. Neither Cleo nor Thor spoke as they stood watch. About a half hour later, Max woke. She did not move nor open her eyes, but Alexander heard the shift in her breathing and felt a purposeful tension hum through her body. He waited for her to speak, to condemn his betrayal. She said nothing. She did not have to; he knew. *Waste of skin*.

THE RETURN TO SELANGE'S COVENSTEAD WAS A SILENT, tense affair. Neither the Hag nor her staff had been found. Brynna was both furious and edgy. She'd spent a few minutes arguing on her cell phone and now sat fuming in the passenger seat, frequently glancing back at the bound prisoners as if they might be her salvation.

Alexander knew what he had to do. He had no alternatives. He glanced at Max. With luck he could keep her alive, but she would never forgive or trust him again.

They pulled into the underground garage of Aulne Rouge just before dawn. The heavy steel doors rolled closed with a loud rumble after the two vans rolled through. They parked and got out. Thor pushed open the rear doors, yanking Alexander out by his feet and flopping him over his shoulder. Cleo followed suit with Max.

"Selange is going to be happy to see you two," Brynna gloated as she bent over Max, whose eyes had finally opened. Brynna ran her fingers over Max's cheek, then bent closer. "She'll peel your skin off you and rip your bones out while you watch. You'll scream until your throat is shredded and you'll shit your pants. You'll beg for her to stop and she won't. I can't wait to see it."

A slow smile unfurled on Max's lips. "That bedtime story might terrify you, Kitten, but it sounds like Disneyland to me."

Brynna sneered and pulled back. "We'll see about that."

But Alexander could almost feel the rats still squirming in his gut. He remembered what Max had told him—*I'm a very good victim, and Giselle likes to practice*.

They were taken to cells located a level below Selange's chambers. Each was a cage of iron bars wrapped in steel mesh. An outer frame of woven bone, wire, salt, and wood was layered with imprisoning spells. They were designed to hold the most powerful Uncanny and Divine creatures, though Alexander had doubts that they could have held the messenger angel.

Thor wordlessly laid Alexander down on the floor inside his cell and locked the outer doors. Cleo carried Max inside and dropped her with a sodden thud, then kicked her in the stomach with her booted foot. Brynna brought in a green-and-white-striped rope and hooked it through a loop welded to a crossbar on top of the cell. She tied a hangman's noose and dropped it gleefully around Max's neck, then pulled the rope until Max was balancing precariously on her tiptoes in the center of the cell, gasping for breath. Brynna tied the rope off.

"That will keep you thinking," she said viciously, then locked the cell doors.

Next she went to a thermostat on the wall and pushed the temperature button. Heat began to pour through the ducts. Brynna kept pushing until the thermostat read 101 degrees. Then she went to a sink on the wall and turned the cold-water spigot on.

"When your mouth is so dry that you can't swallow anymore, when your body stops sweating because it can't afford to lose the fluid, when you're so hungry that you start cannibalizing yourself to keep from dying—I want you to think of me and remember that I am responsible for your own private Disneyland. Enjoy it, bitch."

Alexander snarled silently. He should have killed her when he had had the chance.

Brynna left, leaving the two prisoners alone. Except they were not, Alexander knew. The room was fully wired for sound and video. Somewhere, Selange was watching.

He rolled over and managed to squirm upright, leaning back against the bars so that he could watch Max. She did not look at him. Her chin was held high by the rope and she could hardly keep her balance.

Hours passed. Sweat dripped from the both of them and water continued to run tantalizingly in the sink. The heater ran continuously. Alexander's eyes were parched and his lips cracked. His tongue clung to the roof of his mouth. He watched Max with furrowed brows. Her injuries the previous night had nearly killed her. How long would it take her to break?

She tipped back and forth here and there, but mostly remained straight, showing no outward signs of strain. He could not tear his eyes away from her. He could feel the raw power of her—it was like standing naked in front of a hurricane. She held inside herself a violence, a wild recklessness, of the sort that could erase a town or tear apart a forest. Instead of weakening her, captivity seemed to peel away everything else but her essential force. She was terrifying and enthralling. He could imagine why a man might stand up against a killer storm just to feel the full breadth of its power as it swallowed him.

It was close to sundown when Selange finally deigned to visit them. Max had begun to pant and her skin was dry. Her body was shutting down to protect itself. She looked gaunt, but her presence filled the chamber.

The door opened and Selange entered. She wore spike-heeled boots over red velvet jeans and a loose white blouse. She stopped outside Max's cell, examining her from head to foot. Then she came to look at Alexander.

"What exactly are you up to, Alexander?"

He had thought of what he needed to say all day. "You gave me a task. I completed it. I brought her to you," he said hoarsely.

"You failed the challenge," she said, her nose rising, her lip curling. "You screamed like a child. You made me look weak in front of the entire Conclave."

"Let them think you are weak," he said dismissively. "They will learn better soon enough. I may have failed the challenge, but I have not failed you. I have lured her back to you, and I bring news besides."

"News?"

"Your angel delivered a scroll to the witch Giselle last night."

Selange frowned, her gaze narrowing. One finger rubbed back and forth along her upper lip. "Anything else?"

He shook his head. "I beg you to forgive me. You know I am bound to you by chains of loyalty and love. I wish only to serve you once again."

"Marcus is my Prime now."

"He is inexperienced and I am stronger. You need me. You need all the strength you can get."

She gave him a measuring look, her eyes cold. Then nodded. "You were not strong enough last night. But you have done well, bringing her to me. I will give you a test of loyalty. If you pass, then you may return to serve me. But be warned, I will not tolerate any more whining from you. If I let you come back, then you will do what I say when I say it, no matter how much you don't like it. Do you understand?"

"Of course. I will do anything you want. Whatever it takes. I want to come home."

"Fine. Tonight is your test. Without the Hag's staff, I have to find another weapon. I have to summon and bind to me something equally powerful. For that, I will need blood magic."

She paused as if waiting for a reply. Alexander had none. Selange was a flesh mage; she drew her power from people. They gave off so much magic in their daily lives—in their passions and wars, in their joys and their despairs. Magic poured off them in waves, and flesh mages such as Selange collected it for their own spells. But sacrifices gave off a much greater power.

"Who?" he asked, hoping she would believe the rasp of his voice was from his parched throat rather than sick horror.

She smiled at his discomfort. "Children. I must have at least thirteen of them, but twenty-one would be better. They must be innocent—unmolested and drug-free. None may be older than six. You and Marcus will take the Shadowblades tonight and find me what I need. I will conduct the spell at sundown in three days."

"So soon? Can you be ready that quickly?" Alexander asked, his stomach churning. Selange was not given to taking such desperate risks. He wished to hell he knew what the message in the scroll had been.

"There is no choice."

With that she returned to Max's cell, opened it, and went inside. "I can feel it on you. Where is it?" She did not seem to expect an answer. She held a flat hand out just inches from Max, stroking from side to side. Her fingers hovered between Max's breasts. She shook her head. "So easy? I thought you would be a harder nut to crack."

She slid a small knife from a sheath in her sleeve and sawed a slit in Max's shirt.

Max tried to twist away. "Fucking bitch," she whispered.

Selange ignored her, sliding her fingers into the tear. She grasped a pouch and pulled it out, sawing through the strings to free it.

She smiled, gripping the pouch until her knuckles turned white. "This will help. With this and a champion of my own, I think the Guardians cannot force me to do anything."

"Guardians?" Alexander repeated harshly in surprise, then coughed raggedly. But their involvement made sense. No witch could control an angel. But witches served the Guardians. What was Selange doing? Why would she choose to defy them? There was no power on earth that could protect her from them.

Selange ignored him. "I'll be back to question you later," she said to Max. "Try to be more polite when I do." She gave Max a shove, knocking her off her delicate balance.

Max swung from her neck, twisting and wiggling until at last her toes scraped the floor again and she came to a teetering halt. She gasped wrenchingly, her face scarlet. "I'm going to kill you," she whispered at Selange, who was locking the cell.

"You're not going to have the chance. As for this—" The witch held up the pouch containing the hailstone. "You should have used it when you had the chance. Now I will use it to become stronger than any Guardian."

"She . . . gave . . . it . . . to . . . me," Max wheezed. "Use it . . . and you'll . . . be . . . cursed." She laughed, a coughing, hacking sound that knocked her off her feet again.

Selange watched her, the tip of her tongue running back and forth over her lower lip. Finally she shook herself. "I will take that into consideration. In the meantime, you can stew about just how stupid you were not to take advantage of the hailstone when you had the chance."

The witch went to the wall and pressed her hand against it. A shimmer of pink witchlight flickered over a small square area, then a compartment popped open. The inside was lined with metal and held a wood box. Selange twisted open the lid and put in the pouch, then closed and replaced the box. She shut the door and sealed it with magic.

"It will be safe there until I'm ready for it. Think of it—the means of your salvation only a few feet away and you can't do a thing to get it. I bet that chews you up, doesn't it? But don't worry, I don't plan to give you all that much time to agonize. I will harvest you, too. I will unwind the magic that makes you. The more you suffer, the more you hate, the more you fight—all of that will feed my strength."

With that, Selange opened the door and stepped out. A few minutes later, Thor apeared. He pushed into Alexander's unlocked cell and used a pair of wire cutters to snip the heavy cable ties.

Alexander could not help jerking away when Thor lifted him to his feet. He could not stop the memory of the other man standing in front of Max's Tahoe with an Uzi cradled in his hands. For the first time since that night, he felt fury at Selange's dismissal and his own Shadowblades' betrayal. He felt Thor recoil as his anger swelled into something almost tangible. The air grew thick and heavy. Thor retreated a couple of steps, eyeing Alexander warily. "Selange wants you ready to roll by sundown. She says to put a feed bag on you and let you have your sticks and stones back. Says you're one of us again."

"Never wasn't," Alexander said, glaring. The Texan's gaze dropped almost instantly. Alexander's fists knotted and he strode out of the cell. He halted outside of Max's. She met his gaze for the first time since he had helped capture her. He felt the impact like a blow to his chest. He glanced up at the rope knotted to the metal loop above her. He could loosen it. Over decades, the spells Selange had layered into him had connected, fused together, and evolved, allowing him a certain amount of telekinetic power. Only Selange knew of it, and if he loosened the rope, she would know he had done it. He could not risk it.

He gave Max one more hard look. She was a survivor. She was not going to let Selange kill her easily. With any luck he would be back to free her before dawn.

He spun around and started out of the room, pausing to twist off the faucet and click off the heater. That much he could get away with.

"It would be stupid to let her die before Selange is ready for her," he said aloud. He followed Thor into the hallway and shut the door firmly. He would be back, and whatever it took, he would get Max out. He had to. He would be damned if he did less for her than she had for him.

12

An hour later Alexander found himself back in the gray van. Cleo drove, Brynna sat shotgun, Thor slouched beside Alexander on the right, and on his left hulked Mercury. No one spoke. Alexander clenched and unclenched his fists. Mercury took out a knife and started jabbing it into the upholstery. Thor rolled his thumb over his forefinger in an endless circle. It was the only outward sign of his distress. Brynna tapped her polished nails on the dash. The sound hammered sharp and hard at Alexander's skull.

They were headed for Balboa Park and the zoo. The other two teams of Shadowblades were headed for SeaWorld and the beach. Bile filled Alexander's mouth at the thought of what they had been ordered to do. Even the endlessly ambitious Brynna was troubled. Alexander had always refused to attack innocents when he was bound to Selange, though he was aware she had employed others willing enough to conduct such ugly business on her behalf. Her Tatane familiar topped that list. Jade-eyed Kev was a stone-cold killer.

They reached their destination all too soon. They parked on the west side of the park grounds near the miniature railroad. There were still cars in the parking lot, despite the fact that the railroad and the zoo had closed for the night. Usually families crowded the park on a midsummer's night, picnicking and listening to music and attending the variety of other events. But a thick pall of smoke from the southern fires hung low, and he hoped those families had found other things to do this night.

Thor stepped out onto the pavement. He carried a pellet gun. Lifting it, he shot out the streetlights with casual ease, and sheltering darkness settled over them.

Quickly the other four levered themselves out of the van. Thor climbed back inside to return the pellet gun to its brackets.

"We should split up," Alexander said when no one seemed willing to take charge. Who wanted to be in charge of such a despicable mission as this? "We will be less likely to be noticed."

"No," Brynna said. She pointed a finger at him. "I don't know what the fuck you're up to, Alexander, or what you told Selange, but you are *not* one of us, and I'm not letting you out of my sight."

He shrugged. "Then the rest of you scatter and see what you can find. Take some tape. We do not want screaming." Rolls of duct tape were piled in a sack in the back.

For a long moment, no one moved. Then Brynna snarled and snatched up the bag. She handed a roll of tape to each of them and took one for herself, sliding it up on her arm like an industrial bracelet. "Fine.

Questions? Kids no older than six. Don't worry about mistakes. We'll sort it out later when we're back at the covenstead. If we get a couple that won't work, we'll take care of it later."

Take care of it? Did she mean kill them? Did it matter? For what Selange wanted to do, children would die. Alexander turned the tape in his hands. He had had every intention of following through with this. He planned to go after the children and bide his time until he could disable his companions. Then he would release the children and hightail it back to the covenstead to get Max. He grimaced. Idiot plan. He should have known he could not go through with terrorizing little boys and girls. Not even for what he owed Max. He did not think she would blame him, much as she despised him now.

He eyed his companions. Thor was still in the van. Good. Alexander drew a breath, shaking his head slowly. They were about to find out exactly what made him Prime.

With blinding speed he rammed his fist into Brynna's back, then caught her back-flung head and twisted it sharply on the stalk of her neck. Bones cracked loudly and she made a single gasping sound. A look of absolute shock was on her face as she stared at him, her head turned the wrong way around on her body. Then she slumped. She was dead. Shadowblades were strong, but not invincible—a lesson she frequently forgot.

His attack had taken only a second. Alexander pivoted and flung Brynna's body at Mercury. The other man staggered backward and grappled her aside. Alexander ducked as a shot rang out. A bullet whistled past his head. Another creased his neck. Thor was shooting from the van. Cleo's Glock had hardly cleared the holster on her hip.

Alexander lunged for her. She had a bad habit of planting her feet. It made her slow to move and react. He had spent many hours trying to train her out of it. Now he was grateful. He seized her wrist with both hands. Her gun went off, bucking in her hand. Alexander gripped hard, twisting and bending. Bones snapped. She screamed in agony.

She punched him in the ear with her other hand. Pain exploded through his skull. But his bone-strengthening spells were old and powerful. He shook off the momentary blurriness in his vision and swung her hard around, hurling her toward Thor, who was outside the van now. He was the better shot of the three. He was also smarter and faster. One day he would be a good Prime.

More gunshots. One burrowed into the back of Alexander's thigh. Another pinged from the fender. Alexander yanked the mirror from the door and flung it at Mercury. He followed it, never stopping. He was fast—faster than they knew. He had never showed them all that he could do, nor how viciously he was willing to fight.

He lunged low, shouldering into the blocky man's legs. It was not enough to do any real damage, but it gave Alexander time to reach into Mercury's knees and shatter them with his telekinesis. The joints cracked sickeningly. Mercury made a high-pitched sound and crumpled to the pavement even as three of Thor's bullets pounded Alexander's chest in quick succession. The impact slammed him backward. The pain was fierce and his right arm went numb. But astonishingly, Thor had missed anything vital. Alexander let the momentum of the bullets carry him over. He somersaulted backward onto his feet, snatching for his gun in the small of his back with his left hand as he rolled. A bare second later he was on his feet, breathing raggedly.

"Do you think you can get me before I drill you?" Thor drawled in his Texan twang.

Alexander froze. He might be able to foul Thor's gun with telekinesis, but breaking Mercury's knees had cost him. He had four bullet wounds and was losing blood fast. Between the two, he could not muster the focus he needed.

Cleo had come to her feet, her face twisted in fury. "Kill the bastard," she urged, cradling her mangled hand against her chest. Mercury lay on the ground clutching his knees and swearing.

Thor ignored her. "Brynna said we couldn't trust you. Guess she was right."

"I will not hunt children," Alexander said flatly.

"Then you don't want back into Aulne Rouge. Because that's the price."

Alexander lifted his chin, a muscle in his cheek twitching. He said nothing.

Cleo suddenly swore. "I knew it. This was bullshit all along. I couldn't figure out why you would agree to catching kids, no matter how bad you wanted back in. I figured you had to be up to something. What is it?"

What was he going to do? Cleo and Mercury would not heal quickly—if he could take out Thor, he could deal with the other two. His right arm hung at his side, nearly useless. Blood soaked his shirt and ran down his leg. His healing spells had been so taxed in the last couple of days that they would be slow to close his wounds. Thor was unhurt. Alexander knew he could not defeat him physically. He had to try telekinesis. Max was depending on him, whether she knew it or not. His hand tightened on the grip of his gun dangling at his side.

"Are you going to finish what you started the other night?" he asked, playing for time as he collected his focus. He was only going to have one chance at this. "You were eager enough for my blood. So much for friendship."

"We were never friends," Cleo said sharply.

"I noticed." Alexander paused, then gave an inward shrug. Why not say it? It did not matter if they did not believe him. But saying the words did. "I am sorry. I should have been a better Prime. Had I been— I am beginning to learn what makes a good Prime and I was not. Not like I could have been."

Thor frowned. "What're you talking about? You always did okay by us."

The corner of Alexander's mouth went up, thinking of Max and her Shadowblades. "Not enough to keep you from trying to kill me."

"We had our orders. It wasn't personal," Thor said.

"Maybe it should have been," Alexander said quietly.

"We're wasting time," Cleo said. "My fucking arm is killing me and Mercury is crying like a baby. Put a bullet in his fucking head and let's get outta here."

Thor sucked his teeth and gave a faint shake of his head. "Not so fast. I figure Selange is going to want to have a little talk with him." His head tipped to the side as he scrutinized Alexander. His pale eyes narrowed. "I never would've figured you to turn on Selange. Never heard of a more loyal Prime than you."

"She cut me loose," Alexander said. "I do not owe her anything."

Thor shook his head. "Doesn't make sense. Somebody else maybe, but not you. And why come back with *her*—the other witch's Prime?"

Alexander felt himself smile as if someone else, some alien force, had taken possession of him. Or perhaps it was that for the first time in many years he was letting go of a habitual disguise, a second skin that he could no longer endure. Maybe the real alien was the man he truly was, without disguise.

"She is *my* Prime," he said, elucidating every word carefully so that no one could mistake them.

"*Your* Prime?" scoffed Cleo. "That's a load of crap. You'd never serve any witch but Selange, and you sure as hell wouldn't give up being Prime for some scrawny bitch who wouldn't know how to find her ass with both hands."

"Would I not?" Alexander asked, never looking away from Thor. "Maybe I found a Prime worth serving."

"We're Shadowblades. We serve witches," Thor corrected, staring intently.

Alexander lifted his shoulder in a half shrug.

"Why?" Thor asked. Alexander could hear the belief growing in the other man's voice.

"She defied her witch for me, when she should have left me to die. She should have let her Shadowblades kill me. She offered me freedom. Any one of those would be enough."

Thor didn't immediately answer. Then: "What were you doing in Julian?"

"Same as you. And now I have to get her away from Selange."

"That's it?"

Alexander knew what Thor was asking: was he planning to hurt Selange? Nervous hope unfurled through his tense muscles. Thor would not be asking if he was not considering helping Alexander. "That is all," he promised. "I plan to go free her and get the hell out of Aulne Rouge. I do not want to set eyes on Selange again."

Thor nodded. In a minuscule movement, he let the nose of his gun dip. It looked like an invitation. To murder? Or something else? Alexander took the chance. He whipped up his .45 and shot Thor in the chest twice, then dropped as Cleo whirled and kicked a roundhouse at him. He avoided it, and she swung past, staggering as she struggled to balance. Her useless arm threw her off. He dove at her, slamming into her stomach. He picked her up and plowed her against the side of the van. Glass shattered and steel crumpled. He dropped her and spun to face Mercury. The other man was scrabbling for his gun, pulling himself along on his elbows. Alexander leaped for him and rammed the butt of his gun against the back of the other man's head, dropping him in a heap.

Alexander turned slowly, examining his handiwork. Both Cleo and Mercury were out cold. Thor lay on his back, his gun resting on his stomach, the hammer cocked, his finger on the trigger. He could have shot Alexander at any time. Blood soaked his T-shirt and flecked his square jaw. He held out the gun and Alexander took it

"You should hurry," he rasped. "You don't have much time before they wake up. Better tie us up good or we'll have to warn Selange you're coming."

"Why? Why are you helping me?"

It was Thor's turn to smile. "Not the first time. Wasn't you I was shooting at the other night."

Alexander stared. "I thought you said you had your orders."

"I didn't think much of 'em. I owed you more than that."

"Thanks." Alexander did not know what else to say. He had misjudged the other man and that hurt, even as discovering Thor's loyalty was a balm. Having his Shadowblades turn on him so easily had hurt more than he could let himself acknowledge.

"Best get a move on. These wounds will keep Selange from thinking anyone helped you. But I'm healing fast, and when I do, I'll have to try to stop you."

Alexander nodded and snatched up the duct tape he'd dropped. Efficiently he wrapped the ankles and arms of his three captives, leaving Thor for last. When he was through, he sat back on his heels.

"Not enough," Thor said.

"You used most of the cable ties on me and Max," Alexander said.

"Max? That's your Prime?"

"Yes."

"Not much of a name, is it?"

"Her witch seems less interested in theatrics than Selange," Alexander said drily, wasting time, putting off the inevitable.

Thor sobered. "Do it. Pain is just pain and you need to buy time. Bonus is we won't be hunting children tonight, maybe not tomorrow if you do it good enough. That's worth a lot."

Alexander put his hand over Thor's, gripping it tight. "I owe you."

"Don't do that, son. I don't want your debt. I owed you for shielding us from the worst of Selange for so long, and for keeping our skins intact. Call us even."

"Not the same thing, my friend. That was my job. This is more. *I owe you,*" Alexander repeated, echoing the words Max had said to the angel. The irony was not lost on him. He had never offered his debt before—he had always been too leery of the cost. But her example was inspiring, demanding the best of him. He wanted to give it.

He said nothing more, rolling Thor onto his stomach. Alexander pulled his knife from its sheath, and without letting himself think, he cut deeply into Thor's lower back, severing his spinal cord. He stood and did the same to Cleo and Mercury. It was the sort of wound that would take a day or more for their bodies to repair. Their other wounds would only slow their healing. He lifted each of them into the van, digging through their pockets for their cell phones. He smashed them, then popped the hood of the van and yanked out the spark-plug wires and snapped them in half. He cut the stems off the two front tires. Air hissed out into the night.

Returning to the rear of the van, he pulled down the blackout door separating the back from the front seats. He latched it and did the same with the metal roll-up shutters on each of the windows. If no one found them before dawn, they would not burn to ash. He looked the three of them over once more. Cleo and Mercury were still unconscious. Thor lay unmoving, watching Alexander.

"I meant what I said," Alexander said. "I owe you."

With that, he hit the locks and closed the rear doors. From their arrival to now had taken less than ten minutes. Alexander ran across the parking lot to a row of cars. He found an older Toyota Celica. He broke the window, yanking out the ignition assembly with his fingers and hot-wiring it in a matter of minutes. His right arm was functioning again, though it was a bit clumsy. Blood still leaked from his wounds, but the holes had begun to close.

Swiftly he shoved in the clutch and put the car in gear. It would take him nearly half an hour to get back to Aulne Rouge. If Selange had not changed the wards since the Conclave, he could get inside easily enough—he had built several escape routes in the case of attack. But the real problem was going to be getting Max out of the cage. He was dearly hoping that once he released her bindings, she could manage the rest. After all, she had driven through the Conclave veil without the aid of a witch. If she could do that, maybe she could get through the containment spells on her cell. If not—

If not, Alexander was going to have to make Selange open it. He did not want to bet on his odds of coercing a powerful witch into doing anything she did not want to do. But he would try, because he owed Max. Not for saving him, though he owed her for that, too, but for giving him back his faith and his integrity. It was a debt he doubted he could ever pay.

Aulne Rouge was located east of San Diego just past Granite Hills off Interstate 8. It was carved into the top of a hill, as much aboveground as below. It was surrounded by a narrow band of scrub oak and brush. Beyond that were houses and a couple of small towns. It was close enough to people to fuel Selange's magic, and secluded enough to allow her some privacy. The witches of the coven lived within a ten-mile radius—easy to summon at a moment's notice and far enough away to keep from annoying Selange.

Alexander parked on a dirt road at the rear of the covenstead. He pulled the Celica up beneath the spreading limbs of a gnarled black walnut, hoping the car would go unnoticed. He sat a moment, collecting himself. His wounds still seeped, though they were nearly closed. They burned fiercely. Blood loss made him a little woozy. He needed food and rest, but knew he wasn't going to get them anytime soon.

A wrought-iron and brick wall marched the border of the covenstead. Inside, the grounds were artistically wild and lush. Selange had lured a spring to the surface and used its water to create a green wonderland of verdant trees and twining vines.

He walked along the wall until he found a small gate. Trespassers attempting to use it would be trapped in a painful net of magic until collected by Selange at her leisure. Jumping over was not an option. Those wards did not care who was trying to get in; they would fry him like a bug zapper. Alexander flexed his fingers. He doubted—he hoped—that Selange had not bothered to change the wards after he had failed to beat Max at the Conclave. She had more urgent matters to consider and had surely expected him to be in Giselle's cell. But there was only one way to be sure.

He reached out and grasped the latch. Magic crawled over his hand and up his arm. It was gelid and sticky as it spiderwebbed over his skin. In less than three heartbeats he was enveloped in the spell lattice and unable to move.

He waited.

Magic wormed beneath his skin and wriggled along his bones. Alexander had no idea what it was looking for; he never had. If it sought his bond with Selange, then he had lost his gamble. But more beings than just the members of the covenstead used this gate. And that was what he was banking on.

The seconds ticked past. He held his breath. Then suddenly the magic withdrew, leaving behind a faint itching. Alexander sagged, then collected himself and pulled open the gate. Quickly he slid through, letting it close behind him. Leaving would be easier. Selange did not waste the coven's power on wards to keep anyone inside.

The wild garden provided ample cover. More than once he stopped, feeling as if someone was watching. The feeling rubbed up against him like the hot electricity of an approaching storm. Each time he waited and the feeling passed. He had no idea who the hunter was. All of Selange's Shadowblades were in San Diego.

He kept off the paths as much as possible, pushing through the thick undergrowth. He went slowly, making hardly a sound. The night birds were oblivious, chattering at one another like gossipy old women. Insects buzzed, riding the humid air. The scent of gardenia and orange blossoms mixed with smoke was enough to cover the scent of his blood and sweat. Whoever was hunting him would have to come very close to smell him.

At last he arrived at the entrance to the main compound. A sheer wall of rock thrust out of the ground, sculpted by magic. Set into it was a brown metal door. Anyone else would have seen only rock. Alexander had had Selange cast an illusion on the door. It was a quick escape route in case of attack. On the other side was a hallway that led directly to Alexander's quarters, which lay below Selange's apartments with a perpendicular shaft connecting them. The prison cells were a scant hundred feet away from his rooms on the same level. That way Selange had quick access to her prisoners, and Alexander was close enough to be summoned quickly should the need arise.

This door was not warded. Instead it was locked in a fashion that only Alexander could open. He splayed his hands against it and pushed his senses inside the door, where eight titanium bars radiated out into the stone. There was no door handle or exterior mechanism to open it. Only the coven witches with their magic and Alexander with his telekinesis could retract the bars.

But he was drained. The damage the rats had done to him and the bullet wounds in the escape after the Conclave had taken a heavy toll on his healing spells. The wasting dry heat of Selange's prison cell had only stressed him more. Now he was wounded again. His jaw clenched. Max had been injured far worse than he had, and she had suffered longer in her cell. He needed to get her out.

He pressed hard against the door, letting his forehead rest against the metal. His muscles knotted, as if physical force could help. He squeezed his eyes shut, hardening his focus. The back of his neck prickled as he felt that same watchful hunter creeping near. Instinct told him to find cover. He ignored it. Instead he concentrated on the locking mechanism inside. It was a four-inch wheel fixed in place by a tiny lever. Once he flipped that lever, he merely had to turn the wheel until the hydraulic system caught.

The hunter was drawing closer. Adrenaline exploded in Alexander's body. He held himself tightly in check. Max. He pushed up on the internal lever. It refused to move. Drawing a harsh breath, he pushed again. This time it flicked up sharply. Now he shoved against the wheel. It quivered. He threw himself harder against it and it rotated. He felt the hydraulics catch. He slumped with relief. His head throbbed. Inside the door he felt a vibration then a hum as the bars retracted. They snicked into place and the door popped open a crack. Alexander swung it open and slipped inside.

He did not dare lock it again. He had hardly had the strength to open it, and he still had to release Max. He pushed it closed. A hidden switch farther up the hallway would trip the lock manually, but he and Max might not have the time it took to unlock the door when they made their escape if they were pursued. He would have to chance the outside hunter getting inside.

He strode quickly up the hallway and into his apartment. He snatched a powerbar from the dish of them he kept near the door and ate it in two bites. He took another, cracking open the main door to look out.

He peered out into the hallway. It was deserted. That was not unexpected. All of Selange's Blades were out hunting children. His mouth twisted with disgust. She was doing an evil thing and he could do nothing to stop her.

But he could steal Max away from her.

Alexander ran silently down the hallway. At the corner he paused to glance down the cross-corridor. Far away he heard the sound of voices and the strains of music. Quickly he crossed and kept going. A minute later he stood outside the dungeon. Selange was probably preparing herself to sacrifice the children. She had little reason to be watching Max right now. At least he hoped so. He would find out soon enough if not.

He pushed inside. The room was much cooler now. Alexander went to Max's cell, relief sweeping through him. She was still on her feet. He had not let himself worry about her losing so much strength that she hanged herself. She stared stonily at him as he entered. Her gaze dropped to the blood soaking his shirt and then to his leg, then back up. He did not waste time explaining or making excuses for what he had done. Words would not make her trust him; he was not sure what would. Right now, he had to get her loose of her bonds.

"I can get the rope off and get you out of the cable ties, but I cannot open the cell," he said.

If she was surprised he was there to help, she did not show it. "Hurry the fuck up," she rasped.

Alexander reached for a chair and sat. He pulled his focus in, concentrating on the rope tied above her. His head still ached and his mind felt foggy. He raised his hands and pressed his palms against his temples. Slowly he forced out every other thought but the green-and-white rope. Then he began to unknot it.

13

MAX HAD SPENT THE LAST HOURS FIGHTING TO keep her balance while berating herself for trusting Alexander. Not that she'd have done anything differently. She would still have gone after the Hag and she'd still have been caught, and she could only blame herself for that. Alexander had only stopped her from fighting a suicidal battle. But it still burned like a tall drink of acid. It was one thing to be taken in by a clever con, another to let herself be sweet-talked like a moron. But even that wasn't true. He'd hardly said a word. *I want to stay with you.* Max had believed him. She wanted to believe that his word mattered to him as much as her word mattered to her. Or maybe she'd just been blinded by lust.

She'd been as wrong about him as she'd ever been about Giselle. She'd called him a waste of skin. Maybe she was more a waste than he was.

The door swung suddenly inward and Alexander stepped in. Max's expression hardened. The coppery bitter scent of his Uncanny blood filled the small room. His shirt was soaked through, as was one of his pant legs.

He looked weary and bruised. His eyes were sunken and hollow. He stopped outside her prison, swaying like he was about to fall over.

"I can get the rope off and get you out of the cable ties, but I cannot open the cell," he said hoarsely.

Shock tremored through Max. Was this a trick of some kind? Of course it was. But she didn't have a choice.

"Hurry the fuck up," she said, her throat so dry the words made her bleed. She was almost grateful for the moisture.

He pulled up a chair and sat down. She could do no more than watch him. What was he up to? He sprawled, his gaze fixed above her head. He pressed his hands to the side of his head, his fingers curling so tight his knuckles turned white. A long minute passed. Then another. Alexander began to breathe unevenly. Finally he made a harsh sound and the pressure on Max's neck loosened. She fell like a log, slamming against the floor.

She rolled onto her back, lifting her head to look at him. The fucker was telekinetic. Holy shit. Selange was an extraordinary witch to accomplish that. "Can you get the cable ties?"

He scraped his fingers across his scalp. "Yes."

Max wasn't sure he really could. It looked like it had taken everything for him to untie the rope. "Start with my hands."

He released the riot cuffs after another three or four minutes. Then one by one, he split through the ties binding her arms. Each time took a little longer, and more of the night slipped away. Max didn't let her impatience show.

At last she gained the leverage to push her arms outward and snap the rest of her bonds. In a moment she'd freed her legs. Her body was on fire as blood flowed back to the areas the cable ties had clamped. Her neck throbbed from where the rope had bruised her. Max pushed herself gracelessly to her feet, bracing herself against her knees. Alexander slumped in the chair like a dishrag. He looked gray. His hands trembled and his bruises had darkened.

She coughed and felt her tissues giving way. She stopped by pure force of will before she tore herself apart. "What now?"

He gave a slow shake of his head, never looking up. "Saw how you got through the veil at the Conclave. Hoped you could get yourself out."

Was this the trap? To see what she was capable of? Selange could be watching even now. There were cameras discreetly placed at regular intervals along the wall. Still, Max had little choice.

I want out, she told herself firmly, trying to invoke the locking spell. She held tight to the desire as she put her hand on the catch and flipped it. She pulled on the cell door. Pain curled up her arm in elegant agony, as if an artist carved her with a knife.

It was a ward to keep anyone from even attempting to escape. Max's defenses could not help her. She gasped—a raw, sobbing sound. Her arm felt heavy as lead. She tightened her muscles. It was a pitiful effort. She was ridiculously weak. The magical lock held. Max gritted her teeth, anger flaring. The witch-bitch wasn't going to keep her so easily.

She put her other hand on the door. *I want out!* She

yanked and felt a give as the locking spell curled away. She staggered backward, wrenching her hands free of the bars. She caught herself up, then doubled over as dizziness swept over her. "Fuck me," she muttered.

The pain in her arms faded, but it left behind a poisonous ache. Max underestimated Selange. The witch-bitch was better at torture than Max had thought.

"Are you all right?"

Alexander stood just inside the cell. She straightened, glowering at him. Abruptly she pushed past him, ignoring the tremors in her legs and the collar of throbbing hurt around her neck. She went to the safe where Selange had locked the hailstone. This time there were no guarding wards and no pain, only a sensation like soap suds bursting softly against her skin as the magical lock gave way. The door popped open a crack. Max hooked stiff fingers under the lip and jerked it open.

The compartment was empty.

She stared, then reached inside to feel about as if the box with her pouch inside it could be hiding in the small enclosure. Her fingers brushed the back panel, and again she felt soap suds crackling and it swung open.

The witch-bitch had taken the hailstone out from the other side. Max's expression hardened, her chin jutting like an ax blade. She slammed the door shut and turned on Alexander. He swayed in place. He was gray, his cheeks gaunt. His face was hawkish and proud and his eyes were hot with something she couldn't identify.

"Where can I find Selange?" she rasped. His eyes widened and he frowned. Anger chewed in Max's gut. "Forget it. I'll find her myself. You've done enough."

She strode past him out the door. He caught her arm and she snatched his hand, twisting, feeling his bones bend beneath the pressure. When he didn't resist, she shoved him away.

"This way," he said.

She hesitated and followed him a short distance. Trusting him now was no more dangerous than not. He'd helped her escape. *He'd helped her get caught.* Her jaw tightened. She didn't know what to think of him.

He stopped outside a door. "These are my rooms. There is a stair up into Selange's rooms. But you need food and water first."

She considered him from slitted eyes, trying to figure out the trap. She couldn't see it. "Fine." The truth was, she should be hauling ass out of Selange's covenstead. But she'd be damned if she'd let the witch have the hailstone without at least trying to get it back.

Alexander entered ahead of her and motioned toward a small alcove containing a kitchenette and a small table with two chairs. Max dropped into a seat. She hurt and she was exhausted. These injuries were too much on top of her previous wounds. Her healing spells weren't responding well, and her body was too ravaged to feed them.

She sat up straight, opening herself to the hurt. She embraced it, pulling it close like a lover. She knew the trick to suffering was not to deny it, but to learn to enjoy it, to convince her mind that she craved it. Then she turned the pain to strength.

Alexander opened a tall, two-door pantry. It was crammed full of food and drinks like he'd stocked up for the apocalypse. Maybe he had. He grabbed a box of powerbars and dropped them on the table, followed by a big jar of chunky peanut butter, a canister of roasted almonds, and a container of Nutella. From a drawer he grabbed two spoons, then pulled four quarts of orange Gatorade from the refrigerator. Last he took out two cartons of strawberry ice cream out of the freezer.

"There's more," he said, sitting down opposite Max.

Max had already popped open a Gatorade and was guzzling it down. She felt it soaking into the parched tissues of her throat as it flowed down into her stomach. She finished and drank the second.

They ate quickly, neither speaking. Max tasted nothing. She chewed methodically, one eye always fixed on Alexander. He fetched more Gatorade and a jug of water. She drank it all.

"I don't like liars," she said suddenly.

"I did not lie to you." He was silent a moment. Then, "You take too many risks. Do you wish to die?"

Max felt her lips turn in a bitter smile. "Some days. Do you expect me to believe that this was all your plan? Help your buddies capture me and then break me out?"

"No. I do not expect you to believe anything I say." His eyes narrowed. "They would have slaughtered you in Julian if I had not stepped in."

"Better than ending up on your witch-bitch's altar. Besides, I'm hard to kill."

Alexander grimaced and folded his arms over his chest. "It did not seem so the other night."

He was talking about their escape from the Conclave. Max shrugged. "I'm still breathing, aren't I? So now that you've gotten me out of my cell, what do you plan to do now?"

His expression shuttered. "I will help you get your hailstone and get back to the truck in Julian."

"Will you now? And after that?"

"You are my Prime. You tell me."

For a moment, all Max could do was stare. He was playing the Prime card? Either he was a class A idiot or he thought she was. *Or he means it.* Only time would tell what he was up to. "All right. You need fresh clothes. You stink of blood. Be quick."

If he was surprised, he didn't show it. He only nodded and disappeared. Left alone, Max slumped in her chair, giving in to exhaustion and pain. A minute later she heard the shower start. Her teeth ground together. They didn't have time. She stood and went into the living room. It was sparsely furnished with cabinets along the wall on one side, a set of bookshelves on the far wall, and two stuffed chairs and a floor lamp. On the other side was a door into Alexander's bedroom. She went inside.

His bed was a king-size four-poster with dark blue sheets. It was bracketed with antique nightstands. Opposite it was a wide-screened TV on top of an entertainment center. Max opened a drawer, curious to know more about Alexander and what made him tick. It was full of DVDs. She ran her fingers over the spines. She didn't recognize most of them, but then, she wasn't much of a movie watcher. One caught her attention. She slid it out. *Mad Max.* It had been released the year Giselle had made her a Shadowblade. She'd taken her name from it. It seemed appropriate. Mad Max's character embodied her sense of betrayal and anger, and her hunger for revenge.

The water shut off and Alexander came through the bathroom door. He was fastening a towel around his hips. Droplets of water stippled his tea-colored skin. Max's stomach tightened. The angel had been perfect in his symmetry and carved muscular beauty. Alexander was almost as perfect, with corded muscles over his shoulders that smoothed into flat planes on his chest and rippled hard down his abs. Her fingers itched to trace them. She curled her hands into fists. *He was as poisonous as he was pretty*. Her mouth hardened. She wasn't that hard up. In his chest were three raw puckers where bullets had gone in. The wounds had begun to heal, each surrounded by a mottled halo of purple and blue. He stopped when he saw her.

"Don't mind me," she said, crossing her arms. "Take your time." A dark flush rose in his cheeks. He said nothing, going to his dresser and pulling out clothes. He stalked back to the bathroom, shutting the door firmly.

A minute later he was back. Max had pushed the drawer of movies back in and was investigating a series of Asian paintings on sandpaper that were hung on the wall beside the bed. He had various knickknacks scattered about, and few black-and-white pictures of landscapes. His movie collection was expansive, and like her, his taste was for dark, quiet colors. He wasn't messy and the room was lightly scented with cloves.

When he opened the bathroom door again, she turned, watching him pull a dark green silk shirt from the closet and button it over a black undershirt.

"Do you have weapons?"

He went to the blank wall between the bed and the bathroom and pressed a button beneath the thick carpet with his foot. A panel slid back, revealing racks of weaponry in a broad closet. There were handguns, rifles, compound bows, crossbows, knives, swords, spears, bandoliers of flashbombs, grenades, and shelves of bullets, arrows, and crossbow bolts.

"Are you getting ready for the end of the world?" Max asked, unmoving.

"I have had many years to collect these."

"What about the stash of food?"

He lifted one shoulder. "I prefer not to expose my weaknesses. If I am wounded, I can fortify my healing spells here without being seen. But if you wish to get your hailstone before we leave Aulne Rouge, we must hurry." He lifted his hand toward the array of weapons.

Max didn't budge. She glanced meaningfully at the button on the floor and back up at him. "I don't plan to get locked in a tiny little cell a second time," she said in a level voice.

Alexander's eyes turned to ice and his body went rigid. Abruptly he stepped inside. "Will this satisfy?"

"Fool me once," Max said, and followed. She reached for a Colt .45—standard military issue—and a black-bladed combat knife. She checked the gun. It was loaded. She chambered a bullet and pushed the gun into her waistband and shoved the knife in her back pocket. She grabbed six extra clips and put them in her front pockets, then grabbed a bandolier of flashbombs and grenades and returned to the bedroom while Alexander armed himself. He slid a bulky vest on. It bristled with ammunition. Next he buckled a .45 onto his hip and slid the strap of an Uzi over his shoulder, letting the barrel dangle beneath his arm. He strapped a combat knife to his other thigh before stepping out of the closet and sliding it shut.

"Anything else you want to take with you?" Max asked.

"The night is getting away."

"And yet you're wasting time. You've got two minutes, then we're gone."

She watched while he pulled out a rectangular gym bag from his closet and quietly filled it with clothes. From the top of his dresser he took some things she could not see and put them into the top, then zipped it up.

"That's it?"

"It is enough."

"Not a lot to take away after so many years— Exactly how long have you been with Selange?"

He grimaced. "Now who is wasting time?" He hefted his bag and strode through the living room, opening a door beside the kitchenette that Max had figured was a coat closet. Inside was a spiral stair. Alexander dropped his bag outside the door and lifted his dangling Uzi. "I will go first."

The stair spiraled up the forty-foot shaft. Max followed hard on Alexander's heels, squeezing up on the narrow landing beside him. A heavy wood door bound in iron with no handle confronted them. Max felt Alexander's muscles bunching as if he strained against a great weight. He set his hand against the wood. A minute passed. Then, after a faint click, the door swung noiselessly inward a few inches. He let out a harsh breath. She could hear his heart pounding with his effort. So his telekinesis wasn't that strong. Good to know.

Max wanted to be first in. She wasn't in the habit of leading from behind. But she didn't want Alexander at her back either. He glanced a question at her and she jerked her chin to tell him to go ahead. The quirk of his lips told her he knew what she was thinking.

They entered into a palatial bedroom the size of a basketball court. It was carpeted with a patchwork of deep-piled rugs and smelled thickly of ritual oils and incense. Max wrinkled her nose, the cocktail stench thick in her mouth and throat. It was both caustic and sweet, irritating her raw throat. She could detect frankincense, ambergris, and apricot oil as well as benzoin and wood aloe. She wasn't sure what Selange was up to, except that she'd begun to ready herself to conduct powerful magic. A pall of smoke from the incense and from the angelfires burning to the south filled the room. Skylights showed strips of the black sky above, but Max felt the night slipping away. Dawn was maybe two or three hours off.

Alexander crept silently over the thick carpets, his gun held ready, his head swiveling back and forth. He peered into the next room, then moved past the doorway. He was heading for an archway cut into the rock wall on the west side of the room. Max followed.

On the other side of the arch was a workroom. The walls were lined with shelves and cabinets, and bundles of herbs hung from overhead racks above the workbench running around three-quarters of the room. The circle, star, pentagram, and triangle—the *anneau*—was cut into the stone floor, and at the center of it was a roughly carved altar, about six feet long and three feet wide. On it sat an opaque white box. Every square inch of it was inscribed with symbols. It shimmered as if Max were looking at it through a haze of heat. A circle of something that looked like dirty crumbles of ice surrounded it in a six-inch moat.

"I was afraid of this," Alexander said, lowering the nose of his gun.

"What?"

"The box comes from Babylonia. It destroys anyone who tries to open it without using the proper invocation."

Max glared at the box. "So it's got a lock and I am a walking key. No problem." If her locking spell worked; if it was strong enough. New pain creeped up through her feet and wrapped her bones. Her compulsion spells didn't like her risking herself. They thought Giselle needed her alive. She gasped as pain threaded through to the marrow of her bones. In a few minutes, it would force her to her knees. She started forward.

Alexander's hand on her arm stopped her. She looked down at it and then up, twitching out from beneath his grasp.

"Can you safely open it?"

"I'm about to find out."

His eyes flattened. He was clearly unimpressed with her attitude. "It may kill you."

"It might. But then it might not. I want my hailstone back." Max looked away. He didn't need to know how badly she wanted it.

"Why? What harm if Selange keeps it?"

"Well, if it's any of your business . . . First, it belongs to me, and she doesn't get to torture me *and* keep my stuff. Second, you sound a whole lot like a guy who still serves her."

"Is it worth your life? I have seen that box kill, and it is an ugly death."

"Yeah? Well, shit happens." The pain was getting worse. If she didn't get going, she wasn't going to be able to. "Keep an eye on the door. We don't need interruptions."

He didn't move a moment, then stepped jerkily back. "Your call, my Prime. But for the record—I do not serve Selange anymore. I just have no interest in watching you kill yourself."

Max grinned cheekily. "Then don't look."

The *anneau* wasn't invoked and nothing stopped Max from approaching the altar. Her legs were stiff with increasing pain and tremors shook her body. *Damn Giselle and damn Selange both!* She gripped the edge of the altar to steady herself and studied the circle around the box. It was a mix of salt, herbs, iron shavings, and who knew what else. It was an all-purpose natural ward against the Uncanny and Divine.

She pulled the knife from her back pocket, and hesitated. If it was just a locking ward, she'd be able to break it without a lot of trouble. But if it was mixed up with something like the one on her jail cell—one designed to hurt and deter anyone from even trying—it could really harm her. She licked her lips. She needed that hailstone. Magpie's prophecy played through her mind, and Max knew the only chance she had of saving Horngate from an attack by Guardians was the hailstone, and even that was slim.

Suddenly Alexander was standing next to her. "Let me," he said, putting out his hand for her knife. "You should tackle the box with as much strength as you can." When she hesitated, he stiffened, his lip curling. "You do not have a choice."

He was right. But at least he didn't tell her she was going to die again. "Do it." She handed him the knife and stepped back.

His arm rose and he slashed downward through the circle. With a flash of orange light, the magic exploded. The force picked Max up and threw her backward. She collided with the stone wall, her breath blasting from her chest. She dropped to the floor in a heap. Her mouth gaped as she sought to pull air back into her lungs. She coughed and her stomach backflipped, making her vomit. At last she sucked a breath and then another. She lunged to her feet, swinging around to look for Alexander.

Holy shit. He was still on his feet. The gray had returned to his skin, and blossoms of red decorated the whites of his eyes where blood vessels had popped. He was breathing raggedly and looked like he didn't know up from down, but he was still standing. Max wiped a hand over her lips. Her hand came away with blood on it. *Note to self—don't ever underestimate him or it might be the last thing you do.*

And so might opening the damned box.

Max returned to the altar. Her compulsion spells coiled through her muscles like barbed wire. She let the pain fill her, drawing strength from it with a grim smile. The box was made of some sort of white stone, and the lines of it continued to waver and shift like a desert mirage. There was no sign of a latch or lock. Taking a breath, she reached out with both hands to lift the lid. Her fingers sank through. Magic grabbed her.

Max could not hear; she could not see. Her entire world was white. She could not feel her body. She tried to struggle, but it was like she was bouncing off the inside of a white room made of mist and magic. She tried to scream, but she had no mouth.

Something whispered across her mind. It was like the sound below sound of a plucked harp string. Where it trailed, acid burned. Max struggled. There was no escape. She was trapped in the box.

She floated in the agony. It screwed itself through her. It went deep into places that even Giselle had never touched. Max writhed and screamed—pain did that. It made you lose your mind. She let it go. It was what her body needed—if she still had one. She didn't know. The battle was in her mind, in the white, misty room. She felt sanity rub against her like a paper wall. She was pressing against it. If she ripped through, she'd never come back. She clung to the boundary like a rock in a terrible ocean. Far away she could feel something moving. It was a whisper of sound—a barbed breeze through her brain. She should think of something. She should remember . . .

A lock. A key. She was the key.

I want . . .

What did she want?

Thoughts fragmented and drifted wide apart. Shards

collided and shattered to dust. And still that razor tickle.

I want . . .

She no longer knew who she was, and that knowledge frightened her. It also relieved her.

Somewhere in the white she could feel something taunting her. A knowing, a watching, an enjoying. *Coward.*

Fury roused her. She did not know her name; she did not know why she was here in this place. She gathered the dust of her memories, sifting and searching. She found names she did not recognize, places she did not remember seeing, faces that made her heart hurt and made her stomach clench. If she had a stomach or a heart or a body.

She kept searching. She needed to remember something. It was important. She brushed aside the pain, annoyed. If she had no body, how could she feel? And if she had a body, then she could fight. *Yes.* Fight.

What weapons did she have? What could hurt the one laughing in the milky white?

Then she found a face she remembered. A face and a name, and with the name, answers.

I am Max. I. Want. To. Unlock. The. Box.

With a sudden wrenching sensation, the white was gone. Max stood again beside the altar, the lid of the box clutched in her hands. She sagged against the stone, tears running down her face.

"Are you all right?"

Alexander. He grabbed her around her waist to steady her, his arm like warm iron. She let herself lean on him. How long had she been in the mist? Her body throbbed as the pain receded. Her muscles were clenched tight as rocks.

"Fine," she said, and wondered if it was true.

She hesitated before putting one hand in the box. Inside was her medicine pouch, the hailstone a cold, hard knot inside. She pulled it out and put it in her pocket, then replaced the lid.

"C'mon," she said as she pulled away from Alexander. "There isn't much darkness left."

He handed her back her knife, and they returned to the iron-bound doorway. Max paused at the foot of Selange's bed. She could rig it to blow. Her fingers ran over the knobby edges of the grenades in her bandolier. She looked at Alexander. He waited, the door open, saying nothing. There was no time. She rolled her shoulders to loosen them and followed. They went back down the spiral stairs and through his quarters. In two minutes they were at the outer door. It was closed but not locked.

"Expecting trouble?" she asked Alexander softly. He was jumpy, scouring the corridor up and back, his Uzi held ready. His hands were shaking as if he were close to the edge of collapse.

"Maybe. Something was following me on the way in."

"Something?" Her brows rose.

He only nodded, scowling.

"I take it this wouldn't be one of Selange's usual guard dogs," she said.

"*I* am Selange's usual guard dog," he said. "The rest are out hunting children."

Max's stomach twisted. She'd forgotten. Her lip

curled in a snarl and she started to turn back. "I need to kill that bitch."

Alexander grabbed her arm. "No. You are good, but not that good, and you are not a hundred percent right now. She is a witch and she has the strength of her covenstead around her. We can come back and do it later."

He spoke as if he was still Prime and she one of his Shadowblades. Max bristled even though he was right. "Do you think you can stop me?"

"I will if have to."

"You do remember you're not Prime anymore, don't you?"

"Are you saying that your other Shadowblades would treat you differently?"

Two days ago she'd have said yes. But then they'd dragged her back from the edge of death, and now they had ideas about watching out for her. She repressed a groan. Alexander saw her surrender and a faint smile touched his lips. She wanted to slug him. "My *other* Shadowblades? I'm not all that certain you're one of mine," she retorted.

That wiped the smile off his face. He dropped his hand and stood back stiffly, his expression austere. "Shall we go?" He pointed at the door, his body blocking the passage. He wasn't going to let her go back for Selange.

"Lead on," she said dourly. As soon she could, she was going to give her Blades a lesson in who was boss. She glared at Alexander's back as he drew open the door and peered out. She did not know what to make of him or what he was up to. She shook her head and sighed quietly. She knew Giselle would have cut his throat and been done with him. But if he had done all this to save Max, then she owed him. At the very least he deserved a chance to prove himself.

She rolled her eyes. She was getting soft. Hopefully it wasn't a fatal condition.

14

THEY STEPPED OUT INTO A RIDICULOUS GARDEN. No jungle should have been possible in the desert of San Diego. Max almost expected to hear the screeches of baboons. Instead it was silent. A smoky fog hung thick, lending them cover. She sniffed the air. The wind blew from the southwest, carrying smoke and ash. It made it impossible to smell anything else. Alexander crouched low and dashed to a nearby fig tree. She followed. He bent close so that his lips brushed her ear.

"Go southeast to the wall. There is a gate there and outside is a car for you. I will make sure you are not followed."

Max twisted her head to look at him. He read the suspicion on her face and jerked like she'd slapped him. "We go together or we don't go at all."

He nodded once. "Yes, boss."

He turned and led the way downhill. Max was used to hiking in the thick scrub and forests of Montana and passed like a shadow through the dense jungle foliage. Alexander was louder. She fell back. If their pursuer was tracking them by sound, he'd go after Alexander. When he did, she'd be on him. She drew her knife, holding it ready.

They'd gone perhaps a quarter of a mile when the hunter struck. He dropped out of the trees, a blur of gray fur. He clung to Alexander's back, raking him with deadly curved claws. Alexander flung himself against a tree, crushing the creature into the trunk with a sound of snapping bone. Max had begun running the moment the hunter attacked. She leaped on him, yanking his head back. He screeched and howled. She stabbed her knife through his throat and shoved outward, severing his throat, arteries, veins, and tendons in one stroke. Blood gouted from the wound even as she grabbed his head and snapped his neck. She dropped the body, cleaning her knife on his fur. The scent of the Divine rose thickly from the corpse.

"What is he?" she asked, giving Alexander a hand up.

He frowned. "I do not know."

Then he made a growling noise and pushed Max back. She started to shove back and then looked at the creature again. It was melting. No—it was shifting shape. It blurred into a kind of gray goo, then started to solidify again. Lying at their feet was a beautiful chocolate-skinned man. Flecks of gold danced in the air around him like fireflies, then settled. As she watched, the wound in his throat began zipping itself shut.

"Bastard," Alexander said, and she could hear the cold dislike in his voice.

"What is he?"

"One of Selange's familiars. A Tatane faery. Shapeshifter, obviously, and a vicious bastard. He liked killing." Alexander pulled out his knife and with one blow, drove the blade into the faery's forehead. "It will not kill him. I do not know what will." He turned to look at Max and his legs buckled. He dropped slowly to the ground with a look of startled surprise. He looked down at himself. Once again blood soaked his shirt and vest. Max helped him strip them off, using the shirt to sop up the blood running from the claw wounds slicing deeply across his chest and left shoulder. Max could see bone and muscle.

"Did Selange set him on us?"

He shook his head, pain cutting grooves into his face. "I doubt it. She is preparing to cast a major spell. Likely he took the opportunity to do a little hunting on his own."

"Let's hope so. We've got to go."

She picked up his fallen vest and shoved it inside his pack before slinging it over her shoulder. Next she pulled him to his feet and slung an arm around his waist to help him along.

"Thank you," he said. "You do realize it would have been simpler for you to let me die?"

"Really? How so?" Max said acidly. "I'm all for simple."

"I might be your enemy. You have no way to know. Everything I have done could be a devious plan to gain your trust and get inside Horngate. It would be risky to take me home. But you are not the kind to leave me behind, not if I am truly one of yours. But how can you know one way or the other? If I was dead, you would not have to decide."

Damn, the man was smart. But then he was Prime, or had been. Losing the part in the pageant didn't mean he'd lost everything else that made him qualify for the role.

"Shut up," she said with what she thought was remarkable eloquence.

They found the gate and the Celica. Max flipped the passenger seat forward and pushed Alexander into the backseat. She found a roll of paper towels in the cargo area and used his shirt to bind a wad of them to his shoulder. Then she made a fat pad of the rest. "Press this to your chest. See if you can get it to stop bleeding. There's a med-kit in Akemi's truck and some healing salves that Giselle made up. They should help. If you can survive that long."

He stared up at her. "Why are you bothering? You do not trust me."

Max grimaced. "My guess is it's because I'm dumber than a box of rocks. Shut up, now. We've got to get going."

Max backed out and went around to the driver's side. She connected the wires again and the car started easily. There wasn't much gas, maybe a quarter of a tank. It would have to be enough. With the heavy smoke cover, they might win a couple more minutes against the dawn. They were going to need every second.

She put the car in gear and let go of the clutch.

"I meant what I said before," he said suddenly from behind her. "I belong to you now. You are a Prime worth serving. Do not for a moment think I would choose a paltry witch like Selange over you."

Max slammed in the clutch and the brake. The tires squealed as they skidded to a stop. She gripped the steering wheel so hard that she heard the plastic cracking. She did not look back at Alexander.

"It isn't a choice between me and Selange. You belong to Giselle if you belong to anyone. As for me—" She broke off, the muscles in her jaw knotting. She didn't want his admiration or friendship or whatever it was he was offering. She wanted nothing from him. She didn't even trust him to tell her whether she had food stuck in her teeth. "As for me, I'm just an idiot who ended up a Shadowblade, and I'm still kicking myself. I happen to be good at the job, but mostly because I want to live long enough to kill Giselle. I'm no hero and I'm no saint. Don't think I am."

With that she gunned the engine and popped the clutch. Another screech of the tires and they were racing back to the freeway, back to Julian.

15

WHERE ARE WE?" MAX DEMANDED AS THEY reached the on-ramp for the freeway.

"Granite Hills on Interstate 8. Go east. After about twenty miles, turn north on Highway 79. Follow the signs."

Alexander was breathless and his heart was racing. His wounds burned fiercely. Max let off the clutch and turned onto the freeway. She floored it. The engine whined protest, but soon they were going over ninety miles an hour. The tension rolled off of her and he knew it had more to do with what he had said than the coming of dawn.

"How long have we got?" he asked, then coughed raggedly. His body throbbed. Kev's claws had cut deep, and his body was too depleted to handle it. The bullet wounds Thor had given him had closed, but fire wormed through his flesh where each had passed, and there was still a slug in his thigh that needed to be cut out.

"Sunrise in less than two hours," came Max's terse answer.

She took the turn onto Highway 79 as fast as she

dared, the Celica sliding sideways and fishtailing before straightening out. She was forced to slow down on the winding road. The tires squealed with every curve, and it was all Alexander could do to keep from throwing up.

"Where did you learn to drive? NASCAR?" he asked when they snaked through a series of sharp turns. He braced his arms and legs to keep from flopping around the backseat.

"Once upon a time in the nineties, there were no speed limits in Montana," she said. "Horngate is in the Rockies and I drive Giselle around a lot."

Alexander grinned despite his agony. She had a streak of malevolence running through her that he liked. He wanted to ask her more—to find out more about her and Giselle and Horngate, but he was afraid to. Likely she would think he was spying for Selange.

"Are you okay?" she asked, surprising him again with her concern.

"I will live," he said lightly, then added softly, "I promise you that I have no loyalty to Selange anymore. I only wanted to get you away safely."

She did not respond. Alexander closed his eyes as they swerved around another turn in the road. Neither spoke again.

They reached Julian in just over forty-five minutes from the time they had got on the freeway. Max pulled off on the shoulder of the road and shut off the car. It dieseled, then died. She looked over her shoulder.

"Wait here. I'll get the truck."

She disappeared and Alexander struggled to get out. His body had stiffened and every movement was a triumph. He heard the truck roar to life and half expected

Max to drive away without stopping. Instead she pulled up beside the Celica and hopped out, coming around to help him. She wrapped a blanket around his shoulders before settling him into the passenger seat. He was shaking, he realized. He'd lost a great deal of blood, and the claw wounds were like streaks of acid sinking into his flesh. Realization struck him. The bastard had had poison on his claws.

Max pulled away the makeshift bandage on his shoulder. The poison had festered, turning his flesh a greasy black. Mixed with the blood that continued to leech out was a greenish yellow discharge. It was thick and crusted Alexander's skin all around the wounds. Beneath it ulcerous sores opened. Her expression turned hard. Without a word she opened the rear door of the crew cab and pulled a wood box from beneath the seat. She flipped it open and pulled out a plastic jar. The smell was foul—like rotten onions and animal entrails. The salve itself was white and lumpy. Alexander gagged and held his breath. Max dipped two fingers in it and scooped out a dollop. She stroked it onto the cuts slicing across his shoulders. He jerked and bit back a groan.

"Been a bad couple of days for the two of us," Max said as she leaned across him to apply the salve to his chest. "You should steer clear of me and Giselle. We're bad news for you."

He caught her wrist, snaring her gaze when she looked up. "I made my choice. I do not regret it."

Something flickered in her eyes. She shook her head and pulled free. "You've got a serious problem, Slick. You should be running for cover. Are you stupid? Or a masochist?"

"Trust me, I do not like pain, and I trust I have some intelligence or I would not have made Prime," Alexander said drily.

"Then I think you're a few clowns short of a circus. Should I be fitting you out for a straitjacket? Sending you off to see a shrink?"

"Is it crazy to know when you have found something worth having?" he asked, ignoring her sarcasm.

Her brows went up. "Worth having? Buddy, you need a mirror. 'Cause I don't know what's worth this. Not when you have a get-out-of-jail-free card."

He did not answer. Nothing he said would convince her. But he knew that there was more to Horngate than most covens. There was friendship and loyalty and a sense of doing what was right. He wanted that. Max had it and did not know how valuable it really was.

Max finished applying the salve and straightened, wiping her fingers on her pants and screwing the lid back on the jar. "That should help. One more stop and we can go find cover for the day." She glanced over her shoulder at the orchard behind. Smoke made it hard to see the trees. Her mouth tightened. "In a few hours this place is going to be charcoal."

She slammed his door and got behind the wheel. They reached the driveway to Julian Springs Orchard, and she turned in without slowing down. When they neared the house, she turned off, driving across the lawn to the grotto. The truck bumped over the uneven ground and the debris from the house.

"What are you doing?" Alexander asked.

"We came for the Hag and we're not leaving without her."

"Is there time to search for her?" he asked, sensing a sudden brittleness in Max. She was walking the edge of something and he was not sure what. It felt dangerous. Her mood had shifted in that moment of looking at the smoke, and he had no idea why. Her face had pulled into harsh lines and she had gone inward again. He was beginning to understand that this was a mechanism for protecting herself, and from where he stood, she needed protecting. She was brave and capable and tough. But she also had a habit of flinging herself into danger to protect her own with no consideration for herself.

He snorted softly. Somehow she had decided he was one of hers. Enough that she had defied Giselle and helped fight off Kev and treated his wounds. And she thought he was insane.

She pulled the truck to a sharp stop and jammed it into park, but did not shut off the engine. Ash fell thickly, coating the hood and the windshield. She said nothing as she jumped out. Alexander followed, stumbling. The ointment she had used had eased the pain of his wounds, but he was still as ungainly and weak as a newborn calf.

He followed her around the truck. She had dropped the tailgate and was wrestling with a rock—the same one she had been standing in front of when he had attacked her from behind. Her muscles corded and bunched as she lifted it on end. For its size, it seemed remarkably heavy.

Alexander jogged forward and grappled the stone with her. "A rock?" he asked as he helped her lift it. They staggered toward the rear of the truck.

"The Hag," Max corrected raspily as they set their burden on the tailgate. The rear of the truck sank beneath its weight. "Legends say she usually spends summers as a stone. I don't know how the redcaps lured her out in human form or what she's doing in SoCal, though."

"How can you be sure it is her?"

"Blood ties. I can feel her."

They pushed the stone inside and closed up the rear before clambering back into the truck.

"Hold on tight," she said as she put the truck in gear and turned it sharply around. "I think we can make Escondido. I'd rather not spend the day in the box in back."

The truck did not take the turns as well as the low-slung Celica. But neither did it slow to go up hills. Max drove like a demon, sliding over into the left lane to take the corners faster. Luckily there was no other traffic.

Twenty miles brought them into Ramona. Max did not slow down as she blew through town, passing several hotels. As if sensing Alexander's curiosity, she said, "Too close to the fires here, and Escondido is bigger. If Selange comes looking for us, I'd like to be somewhere less obvious."

Dawn was starting to break when she pulled into a Super 8 in Escondido. She left the truck running and pulled a credit card from a pocket on the visor. "Wait here," she told him, then was gone.

Five minutes later she returned. "Room 126 around back."

She parked and handed Alexander the door key. As she stepped out, despite the covering smoke, blisters rose on her skin from the creeping light.

"Fuck. Hurry."

She tossed him his bag and grabbed two of her own

from the floorboards behind her seat. She followed close on his heels as he let them in. He went to the window and drew the shade closed. Max was unzipping one of her packs. She pulled out two rolls of duct tape and a folded aluminum blanket. She pulled off long strips of tape and hung them from the edge of the desk by the window in readiness. Then she shook out the blanket. It was big enough to cover the wall. She folded it in half and began tacking it down over the window, covering the curtain, too. Alexander grabbed the tape to help. When it was hung, they went over the edges to fill in any gaps. Then Max taped over the cracks in the door.

When she was through, she sat on one of the two queen-size beds with a sigh, scratching her arm. "That was too close."

"*That* was too close?" Alexander asked incredulously. "Not taking on Selange's Shadowblades in Julian? Or getting out of the Conclave alive? Or standing between Giselle and the angel? Or what about getting the hailstone out of that damned box?"

She shrugged, the corner of her mouth moving up in a half smile. "I wouldn't complain about having a boring couple of days," she said wryly.

"May I ask you a question?"

"You can ask," she said with a wary look.

"The moonlight burned you. And outside—you are more susceptible to sunlight than any Shadowblade I have ever met. Why?" Her expression closed like a door shutting. He sighed. He'd crossed the line again and bounced into the wall of thorns she surrounded herself with. But then she surprised him again.

"The honest answer is that I don't know. I'm not even

sure Giselle does. If you figure it out, let me know." With that she stretched and stood. "I'm going to shower. You shouldn't until the salve finishes doing its job on those wounds." She rifled through the bag that had contained the blanket and duct tape. "Here. Eat these." She tossed him a ziplock bag of powerbars.

"I am getting really tired of these," he said with a curled lip.

"Better than nothing. Should have snagged the cooler out of the truck."

She grabbed the other bag and disappeared inside the bathroom. Moments later he heard the toilet flush and the shower start.

He kicked off his shoes and lay on the bed nearest the window and stared up at the popcorn ceiling, slowly chewing one of the bars and listening to the water, thinking of it flowing over her skin, between her breasts— He broke off the thought before he could pursue it. *That is not going to happen. Not in this lifetime.* He rolled on his stomach to hide the sudden swell in his groin. Max had not come out of the bathroom before he fell asleep.

He sat up straight when she shook him awake.

"We've got a half hour before we can head out. You'll want to clean up. Eat some more. You didn't get much this morning."

Alexander swung his legs off the bed and stood. The crusted mess on his chest and shoulders cracked. He looked down at himself. Red stripes remained where Kev had clawed him, and stiff soreness permeated his muscles. He looked at Max. She sat cross-legged on the opposite bed, her elbows resting on her knees. She looked drawn, but the bruises on her neck from the noose had faded to yellow splotches. Her fingers shook and a tremor ran through her. Her jaw was set in a tense line.

A thrill of unease ran up Alexander's spine. "Something wrong?"

"Want me to make a list?"

"I could probably use a scorecard."

"I called Horngate. No one is answering. I can feel my bindings to Giselle—she's alive. But something is very wrong."

Max's voice was flat, but emotion churned in her eyes. A tremor shook her again. It wasn't fear—her compulsion spells were hammering on her to get home and protect her witch. They would not stop attacking her during the day when she could not travel. They could literally cripple her before she could get back.

"Are you okay?" he asked, knowing she was not.

"I'll survive. I always do. Go shower. I want to get on the road as soon as we can."

Alexander hesitated, then did as told. Max did not like sympathy. The last time he had offered it, she had nearly torn his throat out. They had a fragile peace between them at the moment, and the last thing he wanted to do was blow it.

They were on the road by eight. The vestiges of the sunset burned Max's skin as they loaded into the truck. The darkened windows blocked the rays, but it took several minutes before the burn rash subsided.

She drove through a Burger King and they ate while they drove. It wasn't Alexander's usual fare—he did not usually like fast food—but he ate the greasy burgers and fries with gusto.

They drove up through Victorville and Barstow, across into Nevada, through Las Vegas and then up into Utah. Max stopped only when she had to for food, fuel, and bathroom breaks. She did not speak, turning inward so deeply Alexander was not sure she could see the road. Tremors continued to ripple through her, though she never acknowledged the fierce pain she must be feeling. At every stop she tried to reach her coven with no success.

They stopped in St. George just before dawn. There was not enough night left to reach another town. Max got a room at the Holiday Inn, then they went to the Wal-Mart and loaded up with food before returning to the room.

Max paced as she ate. Alexander watched her, leaning against the headboard. He was feeling better, though his body still felt unwieldy and weak. Max continue to look drawn, like she'd lost ten pounds just that night.

"Certainly Horngate must be safe. Giselle is a powerful witch with a full coven. Perhaps there is a phone outage in the area?" he suggested, though it was unlikely.

Max's mouth twisted. She looked at him consideringly, then blew out a slow breath. "Did you hear what the Hag said about a war coming?"

Alexander nodded.

"It's already begun. That's what this business with the angel and the scrolls is about. The Guardians are summoning the witches to war. Seems the big guys are pissed at the way humans have been abusing the earth and the way magic is being strangled. They're planning to exterminate most of humanity in order to bring magic back to the world in a big way. Witches will be their generals and the rest of us their armies. The scroll the angel brought said they'd raze Horngate if Giselle didn't answer the call to serve. My bet is that the scroll Selange got says something similar." She scowled at him. "You don't look all that surprised."

"When Selange took your hailstone, she said that with it she might be able to defy the Guardians. I added it up and figured they sent the angel." His eyes narrowed. "But it does not make sense that they would threaten Horngate. If they need covens to serve, why do that?"

"I don't know. Giselle thinks maybe they destroyed Old Home because Alton wouldn't cooperate. Though if he did get a scroll, he wasn't saying." Max stopped pacing suddenly. "But what if he did? We're assuming they all said the same thing, but the angel said that the fire was a gift, a threat, and a promise. But for who?" She rubbed her mouth with the back of her hand as if to remove a bad taste, then drank from a bottle of milk. Setting it aside, she stared back at Alexander. "He's a weasel and he's up to something. He wanted Giselle to scry before the Conclave—he wanted to weaken her for some reason, or he wanted her to hightail it home. But why? And then, why is Selange resisting? The Guardians could give her a lot of power and she serves them—all witches do."

"Why does Giselle object?" Alexander countered, and was surprised when she answered.

"She apparently had a vision a while back. She decided she is going to save what she can. Horngate will be a sanctuary."

He stared, even more certain he had made the right

choice to stay with Giselle and Max. Then another thought struck him. "Perhaps that is why they are threatening Horngate. If she does not join the war for the Guardians, then she sets a bad example for other witches. She is very strong. She could cause problems."

"Against the Guardians? They'll swat us like a fly."

But something in her expression told Alexander she did not entirely believe it. There was something she was not telling him.

She blew out a breath. "We need to get home."

"How much farther?"

"It's another thousand miles. That's another night and a half. I don't know if they can hold off that long—if they are even under attack. With Sunspears and Shadowblades trading off the driving, Giselle should have made it back to Horngate yesterday, and she'll have strengthened the shield wards. I just don't know how long the Guardians were going to give her to answer before they attack. And what the fuck is Alton up to?" She shook her head. "I need a shower and sleep. Try to eat. I've got a feeling we're going to need all the strength we can muster."

She strode into the bathroom, leaving Alexander to stew over the new information. He knew why Selange was resisting the call of the Guardians. She was a flesh mage. No matter how much power the Guardians gave her, once humanity was destroyed, she would be entirely dependent on them. She'd fight tooth and claw to avoid that.

He was still staring at the ceiling when Max returned and lay on top of her bed. Soon she was asleep. But it was not peaceful. She shook and her body knotted against the pain of her compulsion spells. He watched her for hours, unable to help her. Sweat gleamed on her skin and she tore at her face and arms with her nails. Then finally, in midafternoon, she seemed to conquer the pain. Her breathing steadied and she stopped struggling, her body going still. It was almost like she fell into a coma. He scowled at her. At this rate, she might be dead before they got to Horngate.

He lay down at last. His last thought before fading away was that Max had said *we,* like she had accepted him into her Shadowblades. He hoped it was true.

16

THE NEXT NIGHT ALEXANDER BEGAN A CAMPAIGN of asking Max questions as they drove north through Utah and Idaho. He wanted to pull her out of herself. That inward-looking habit could only agitate her compulsion spells, and he did not know how much more she could take. She looked haggard, and her body had been through so much in such a short time that he feared the straw that might break her. He had to be careful, though. At any moment she might shut him down. He had to avoid walking out onto any of her personal minefields. The trouble was, he had no idea where they might lie.

"Tell me about Montana," he asked after they had eaten their drive-through meal.

He shifted in his seat to watch the play of emotions across her face. She gave him a sidelong glance. Not entirely friendly, but not unfriendly either.

"What do you want to know?"

He shrugged. "Do you like living there?"

"I do. It matches who I am."

"How so?"

"It can be a harsh, unforgiving place. The Rockies are full of sly, secretive valleys and canyons, the peaks thrusting out like knives. What grows there has to be tough. The forests aren't easy things. They aren't lush and green. The trees root into the bones of the mountains, and they don't invite intrusion. The things that live there are hardy and dangerous—mountain lions, wolves, bears, moose, and elk. Each one knows how to kill to survive. The valleys aren't much more inviting, though they've been tamed by ranchers." She paused thoughtfully. "I never thought I'd be happy there. Now I can't imagine being happy anywhere else."

"Where did you come from before that?" Alexander asked tentatively.

"Nosy today, aren't you? All right, if we're going to play the question game, how old are you?"

He let out a silent sigh of relief. She was not shutting him down. "Selange made me in 1904. At that time I was twenty-three years old."

"You look pretty good for an old geezer," Max said. "So how did you end up with her?"

Alexander looked down at his hands. He did not often talk about his past. But if he wanted to know more about Max, he would have to give as much as he got. "I was born in Canada in 1881. My parents were Bohemian. They had emigrated to Kolin in the district of Assiniboia, which today is part of Saskatchewan. They were poor, hardscrabble ranchers. It was a difficult life. My father drank and was sometimes violent. My mother . . . she was tough. She left him when I was ten years old. She never came back. I never saw her again. It made my father bitter. He died five years later in a saloon brawl.

There was a smallpox epidemic a few years after that, and both my brothers died. I left soon after. I worked herding cattle mostly, then trapping up in Washington and BC. Even did a little searching for gold in California.

"I met Selange in San Francisco. Even then she was a powerful witch. She had come from France ten years or so before. She was hungry to establish a coven in America. There was a lot of free territory—it was all just a matter of staking it out. I had just come in off a tramper down from Seattle. I was footloose—I was not sure what I wanted to do or where I wanted to go. Then I saw her."

He smiled at the memory with bittersweet emotion. He had been so damned *young*.

"And?" Max prompted.

"And I was lost. I followed her carriage. I could not help myself. I did not know it then, but she had glamoured me. She had need of Shadowblades in this new land.

"One day she invited me into her carriage and into her bedroom. Then she asked me if I wanted her gifts. I said yes to everything. Anything. A man like me could not hope to touch a woman like that, and there I was in her bed. The bedsheets alone cost more than I was worth. Everything smelled—like a garden. Within a month I was a Shadowblade."

"Well, at least you got laid. Giselle just got me drunk," Max said sourly. "All right. Fair is fair. I grew up in Iowa. Went to college, and my roommate turned out to be a witch. One night we went to a bar and she started asking me all these questions. You know, what if I could never get sick, never grow old . . . I said that would be great. Next thing you know, I woke up on her altar."

"When was that?"

"Nineteen seventy-nine."

Alexander sat up. "But—"

"But what?"

"It is just that you are so strong. I thought you surely must be older than that."

"I'm a fifty-year-old child wonder. If my family could only see me now."

That did it. Her expression went cold and once again she started withdrawing inside herself. Alexander could feel the stillness settling around her like armor. He scrambled for something—anything—to keep her from going away. The only guaranteed route he could think of was to go running straight out into the obvious minefield.

"Where is your family?" he asked. "You are so young—surely they must still be alive."

She twitched and jerked her head to look at him. Her eyes had turned nearly black. They looked like black holes. Alexander stiffened, more than a little expecting her to reach out and try to rip his head off. Her hand on the steering wheel tightened and the other flexed in her lap. His gaze slid to the knives strapped to her forearms beneath her pushed-up sleeves, and he wondered if he should be reaching for his.

"They live near Sacramento."

He was so shocked that she had actually replied that for long moments he had nothing to say. Finally: "Do you see them? Do they know?"

She shook her head. "I just disappeared one night and

they never saw me again. Papers said I'd been taken by a drifter, and a big manhunt ensued, but of course they didn't find me. Couple of years after that I made sure the cops found evidence of my death. I didn't want them to keep hoping. It was killing them. They left Iowa and went to the Sacramento Valley and grew cherries and peaches. They've retired and moved to a place called Del Webb—it's a retirement community. My brother still runs the orchard. My sister owns a bakery."

Her voice was expressionless, as if the words had nothing to do with her. Alexander did not know what to say. He had never known what to say to new Shadowblades who had to give up their families and friends—their entire lives. Selange made the choice easier. She promised that she would kill the families and friends of any Spears or Blades who came into contact with someone from their past—even accidentally. No one doubted that she would follow through.

He was scrabbling for something to keep her talking when she shocked him again.

"So what about you? Did you leave someone special behind in San Diego?"

Alexander thought of Thor. "One. A friend."

"Not saying much for a man of your advanced years. You must be a real ass. Or maybe you just have really bad breath. Which is it?"

He was pleased to hear the humor. She was climbing out of her own personal abyss by sheer strength of will. He had no right, but Alexander was proud of her. "Perhaps I just have discriminating taste," he said drily.

"I'll be the judge of that. Tell me about this friend of yours."

Now it was Alexander's turn to be swallowed by shadows, guilt, and sorrow. He felt himself tensing. He wanted to brush away the question, but if he did, he knew that the deadly silence would return and the delicate bridge building between them would collapse in rubble. If he wanted trust from her, he was going to have to give it. That meant sharing his painful secrets, as she had inexplicably shared hers.

"It is not a pretty story. I did not really know he was my friend until it was too late. Like you, he defied his witch for me." He told her how Thor had helped him escape, how Alexander had shot him, then cut through his spine and left him bound with the others in the van.

"I hope it's worth it," she said when he was done. Blunting the tartness of her words, she reached out and clasped his hand before pulling back.

"It was," he said quietly. He shook off the dark mood that felt a little too much like self-pity. "Besides, it is really only self-preservation. Imagine what Niko, Akemi, and Tyler would do if I let anything happen to you. Not to mention Giselle."

She grimaced. "It isn't your job to look after me."

"I do not see it that way. And neither do the others." He paused. "You risk yourself too much."

"Do I? How much is too much?"

He shook his head. "I do not know. But I worry about you," he added, speaking more honestly than he wanted.

"You and me both," she muttered, then shook her head. "Get over it. I can handle myself just fine, and pain is just pain. It goes away eventually."

"Unless you die first," he pointed out.

She shrugged. "Still goes away." She sighed and ran

her hand through her hair. "I haven't adjusted well to being a Shadowblade. I have some anger issues."

"Really? I am shocked."

She grinned unrepentantly at his sarcasm. "For a long time my goal was to see Giselle dead. I didn't really care what happened to me as long as I got to kill her first."

"And now?"

She sobered. "There's going to be a war, and like it or not, we're in the middle of it. It's time to give up the revenge fantasy and get on with doing my job."

"Somehow I doubt that will make you behave any more carefully," Alexander observed. "Not after you nearly died getting me out of the Conclave. I was a stranger and an enemy. What would you do for your co-venstead?"

Max tapped a finger against her lips, then glanced at him. Her eyes were hot and hard. "The real question is what wouldn't I do. But you're in luck. There's a really good chance you might find out soon."

17

MAX DROVE LIKE A BAT OUT OF HELL THROUGH Idaho and up into Montana. She got a ticket just north of Pocatello, accepting it from the cop without argument and driving sedately away. Ten minutes later she was doing a hundred miles an hour again.

Alexander's persistent conversation had eased her compulsion spells slightly. She knew what he was up to and forced herself to let him help her. All she could think of was the silence at Horngate and Magpie's cryptic warning before the Conclave. The words ran over and over through her mind, prodding at her to hurry faster. *No safety there, not for anyone. Not until you return. Only you can make it safe.*

They spent the day in Dillon, less than two hundred miles from Horngate. There wasn't much open that early but for a local dive that served as both a bar and restaurant for railroad workers. They managed to get a greasy breakfast before they had to hunker down in a hotel, but Max was too wound up to sleep. She paced the room as Alexander watched. At last he stood and guided her to the edge of the bed and pushed her down. Then he knelt behind her and rubbed the tense muscles in her shoulders. It was all Max could do not to flinch away from him.

His hands were warm and soothing. But she didn't want soothing. She needed to hit something, to yell and swear. Her stomach knotted with helplessness. The pain of her compulsion spells throbbed and chewed, and Max was grateful for them. The moment they faded was the moment Giselle died, and probably Horngate, too. Her body seized with fear. She wasn't thinking about revenge anymore; Max was praying to whatever gods were listening that Giselle had made her a strong enough weapon to save Horngate. Because if Magpie was right, then Max was their only hope.

At last Alexander gave up on the shoulder rub and straddled her from behind, pulling her back against his chest and holding her loosely.

"What are you doing?" she asked, starting to lever away.

"You are not alone in this. I am here and I am worth five Shadowblades—I was Prime, after all. You can use me however you need me."

"I don't want to *use* you," Max spat, leaping to her feet and spinning around. "I don't fucking want to *use* anyone."

"But you have to. That is what you are now. You are Shadowblade Prime of Horngate, and you protect your witch and your covenstead. You use the weapons you have at hand, and I am one of them. Or is it that you still do not trust me?"

Max went still. Trust was a leap of faith. She'd made it

once with him when she let him choose to serve Giselle or leave. And then he'd betrayed her. Or not—she still wasn't entirely sure. But if he was acting, he deserved an Oscar. The problem wasn't with him. The last time she'd really trusted anyone had been thirty years ago, and Giselle had shattered that trust. Max wasn't sure she was really capable of it anymore.

And yet she wanted to trust Alexander. Whenever she looked at him, she saw his bone-deep understanding of what it meant to risk her people, to want to guard them, to need to keep their pain to a minimum. And though she'd only known him a few days, he already knew more about her than anyone else except Giselle. Plus she enjoyed his company. Those hours outside the Conclave before the challenge had been so . . . normal. Like real people living lives where they didn't go around getting tortured and cutting throats.

He was waiting for her answer, his gaze heavy, his expression growing harder with each passing second. She opened her mouth but words failed her. Even the smart-ass ones. "I need a shower."

She fled to the bathroom and stayed there until the water ran cold. It was not until she stepped out that she realized she hadn't brought a change of clothes inside with her. "Terrific," she muttered. Being naked that close to Alexander was like waving red meat in front of a starving pit bill—where she was the pit bull. "Down, girl," she told herself, then resolutely opened the door.

He was sitting on the end of the bed flipping through the channels on the television. He looked at her, his expression remote, but his eyes were like coals. His anger filled the room and made it hard to breathe. Shit. Max hesitated, holding the towel tight. His gaze slid downward to her feet and back up slowly until he met her eyes again. She swallowed. The anger had changed into something else. Something far more dangerous and just as hot.

"I need my clothes," she said pointlessly in a strangled voice, grabbing her gym bag and disappearing back into the bathroom. For a moment she contemplated a cold shower. Not that it would work. She yanked on her clothes and scrubbed her hair dry with a towel, combing it with stiff fingers. When she returned, Alexander had not moved.

"Look," she said, her voice husky. She cleared her throat. "Look, I don't know what to think about you. I want to trust you. And maybe eventually I will. But it's not going to happen today."

His expression relaxed fractionally. "And will you give me the chance to prove myself?"

"What do you think you're doing right now?" she asked in exasperation. "We're in a hotel and I'm sleeping in the same room with you. At any time you can stick a knife in my head like you did that faery. The fact that I'm not sitting in the corner with my gun on you all day long must mean I trust you a little, right?"

His smile surprised her. It was that slow, lean smile that made her toes curl and her blood bubble. Oh. Damn. And here she was in a hotel room sleeping no more than five feet away and no way out. "You might just be reckless and suicidal. Remember? That is not the same as trust," he pointed out.

If she looked into those eyes anymore, she was going to do unspeakable things to him. She plopped down on the bed a couple of feet away and stared at the TV. "Could be. Looks like you're in for a wild ride either way. Call me the Roller Coaster of Death. So what do you want to do now? Got a deck of cards?"

They ended up sitting on Alexander's bed and watching an old black-and-white flick called *A Comedy of Terrors*. Though Max wasn't into movies or TV, she had to admit it was funny. She liked that it had nothing to do with anything relating to witches or wars. At some point she fell asleep. When she woke, her head was on his shoulder, one arm resting on his chest. He was inches away, watching her. To her utmost humiliation, she blushed. Then she realized what time it was.

In the blink of an eye she was on her feet. Urgency prodded her. She strapped on her weapons, checking her .45 and leaving the safety off. She went to the sink and rinsed her face and combed her hair. Turning around, she found that Alexander was equally ready to go.

"It's still early," he said. "We've got a good fifteen minutes."

Max didn't know what to do with herself. She began to pace aimlessly, flipping the truck keys around her thumb. Alexander leaned against a wall, watching her.

"Thanks for—" *Sleeping with me. Could we do it again sometime soon? Maybe with fewer clothes and a little more action?* "Thanks," she said finally, the red returning to her cheeks.

"My pleasure."

She eyed him. "One hopes you've had more interesting days with a woman in your bed than that."

"More interesting? Possibly. More pleasurable?" He shook his head. "No."

"You must bring home some real corpses if me falling asleep on you lands at the top of the list."

He smiled. "You underestimate yourself."

"I *snore*."

"Not loudly. And you will be glad to know that you did not drool."

Max shook her head. "You didn't have much of a life, outside of being Prime, did you?"

"Do you?"

She grimaced. "True enough." Curiosity prodded her. "All right, I'll bite. What was so special about last night?"

"And if I say that you made it special?"

Max rolled her eyes. "Then I would say again that you're a couple of clowns short of a circus."

"You do not believe me."

"Yeah, because I was born yesterday and then fell off a turnip truck."

That smile again. Crap. He had to stop doing that. "I can explain, if you are interested."

"Sure," she said. "I'm always up for a good joke and we've got a few minutes left."

He looked serious. "First and most importantly, you did not talk during the film."

"Snoring doesn't count?"

His lips twitched but he held off his smile. "No."

"Well, at least you have standards. What is second? No, wait, let me guess. It had to be a really high hurdle. Maybe . . . the fact that I was in the same room with you?"

He shrugged, a slight flush staining his cheeks as he looked down. He turned unexpectedly serious. "Something like that." His chest lifted and fell as he drew a heavy breath and blew it out. He spoke softly, "The truth is that when I am with a woman, it is not usually in that way."

"You're saying that you usually get laid?" Max was delighting in his discomfort. In this, if nothing else, he was as nervous as an eight-year-old boy. And he blushed. She was glad not to be the only one.

He looked at her, his gaze unflinching. "That is it in a nutshell. My relationships with women consist of either sex or nothing. No friends, no one to lie on a bed with and share my love of movies with. But you know exactly how it is; that is what it means when you are Prime. You cannot afford to be close to anyone. *That* is why last night was so remarkable. Sex is easy. Time with someone who understands—really understands—that is a treasure beyond price."

"Well," Max said, taken aback. The unexpected honesty that had grown between them in the last couple of days was starting to make her feel like her skin had been peeled off and acid poured all over her. It was too much, too soon. Or maybe too much ever. It was like a drug—it made her high and completely sick all at once. She wasn't sure she was ready to lose her safe cage of isolation. "Good thing I didn't drool, then," she said lamely at last. "C'mon. It's time."

She started for the door, but suddenly he was standing in front of her, not quite touching. She looked up warily. His face was set, his eyes thick with emotions she could not read. Max felt the feathery brush of his breath on her cheeks and heard the quick beat of his heart. It sounded loud, as if it were trying to hammer its way out of his chest. Her stomach clenched, though whether it was from anticipation or flat-out fear of what he might say, she couldn't tell.

"Do not get me wrong. If you gave me an invitation, nothing could keep me out of your bed." He paused, then said deliberately, "I would very much like to get an invitation."

Max's eyes widened and her face heated. Her mouth started working before her brain. "Why so shy? Say what you mean, why don't you?" Inside she quailed. *Oh, no no no. Do not tempt me*.

His lips quirked, then the humor leached away as she sobered. "I don't mess around with the men in the coven, especially my Shadowblades," she said with quiet finality. Flirting was one thing, but anything more—it was a mistake of epic proportions.

His eyes narrowed and he gave a slow shake of his head. "That is all right then. Because I want so much more than just to *mess around*."

He slid his hands over her hips, holding her gently. Slowly, his eyes fixed on hers, he bent to kiss her. His lips were butterfly soft as he touched hers experimentally. When Max did not pull away, Alexander slid his hands up, curving them around the back of her head. He leaned back a moment, looking a question at Max. This was such a bad idea. And yet— She licked the taste of him from her lips. It was all he needed. With a guttural sound, he kissed her again. This time his mouth was hungry and demanding. His head slanted and he pulled her closer.

Heat unfurled in lazy curls through Max, and her body flared with desire. Her lips opened. She stroked her tongue delicately over his. He sucked on it gently, then delved past, deepening the kiss. Alexander didn't rush and neither did Max. If she was going to be stupid, she was going to savor every moment. It wasn't like it was ever going to happen again.

He pulled away too soon, still holding her, his fingers rubbing the back of her neck lightly. Max's mouth tingled deliciously. Heavy heat settled low in her stomach. She ran the tip of her tongue over her bottom lip. He followed the slight movement with his eyes and swallowed. He stepped back, the muscles in his jaw flexing.

"We should go."

Max nodded. She didn't know what to say. She didn't know what she *wanted* to say except to beg for more, and that was a road she wasn't willing to walk, even if they had the time. Just at the moment, however, she didn't have the willpower to resist. She wanted to know what the rest of him tasted like. She wanted to be skin on skin with him.

Abruptly she shoved past to the door and yanked it open. She was a moron. Worse—she was the village idiot in a city of idiots. His voice halted her on the threshold.

"Rules are made to be broken. You do it all the time. So do me a favor. Think about it."

"How the fuck do you think I'm going to *stop* thinking about it?" she muttered, and his snort of laughter told her that he had heard.

But forget she did. As soon as she pulled out onto the freeway, everything but Horngate faded from her mind. Her compulsion spells clenched down hard. She didn't stop for food. She doubted she could eat.

They came through Hellgate Canyon and got off

the freeway at Reserve Street. It was like driving back into Julian. A heavy pall of smoke was in the air. Ash drifted lazily in the hot, still air. Max rolled her window down, nearly choking on the scent of Divine magic. She'd never smelled it so strong. With blind fingers, she checked her weapons, her gaze fixed on the road ahead. She chafed at the lights, barely resisting the urge to blow through them. Getting pulled over would delay them far more.

At last she was out of Missoula and going south on Highway 93 heading toward Lolo. She turned west on Lolo Creek Road and roared through the narrow canyons as fast as she dared, the mountains rising steeply on either side. Trees clung to them like barnacles. The smoke was thicker here, and the smell of magic grew nauseating. Alexander gripped the overhead handle and braced his other hand on the console. He said nothing, even when they skidded around a turn, tires screeching.

She stamped the brakes as they came up on the turn to Horngate. An arch of elk antlers curved over the wide entry with a sign dangling down beneath that said HORNGATE GREENHOUSES in letters shaped like leafy tree branches. They snaked up the picturesque road, the evergreen forest marching close on either side. The covenstead was still another ten miles in, just south of Deer Peak on Burdette Creek. Now she could no longer drive fast. The road was too narrow and winding, and the smoke and ash had become so thick that it felt like a scene out of a disaster novel. Still Max hurried as much as she was able.

Her skin prickled with fear. The stench of magic had

become so thick she could almost touch it. It coated the inside of her mouth and nose and filled her throat like tar. Her stomach lurched. She swallowed.

"What is this?"

"I do not know," Alexander said. His voice was hushed and she could hear the tense apprehension in it.

Fire bloomed along the ridge above them. It flared and swept across the dry timber with supernatural speed. Smoke billowed and leaped to the sky. Max bit down on her lower lip, tasting blood. Fucking angel. But it wasn't his fault. He didn't have a choice. He belonged to Hekau. If it was hard to say no to Giselle, Max could imagine what it was like to defy a Guardian.

She drove through the steep folds of the mountains. They were less than a mile from the coven when she came around Deadman's Spur and slammed on the brakes. The tires squealed and the truck slid sideways before coming to a jolting halt. She yanked open the door and vaulted out, staring in shock.

Sweeping across the road was a curtain of opaque gray. It filled the gorge from side to side like a great overturned bowl, rising to cover the ridges that hemmed in the road. Behind it smoke and flames flickered from the serried ridges to the north, west, and south. The barrier shone with a faint pearly light. Jagged streaks of crimson and black flickered wildly across it. She could see nothing on the other side. Cold oozed through her gut. Horngate's shields should be a transparent pearl white, and she should have been able to walk right through them. But something was wrong. She could feel a repellent malevolence pushing out at her. It felt . . . *hungry*.

Alexander caught her arm when she would have gone

closer. "If you want to try to go through it, then send me," he demanded softly.

Max pulled out of his grasp and approached until she was just inches away from it. He went with her. The surface of the barrier rippled like silk in the wind, and something thicker and darker rolled beneath it. If it came down to it, she'd have to be the one to try crossing it, whatever Alexander wanted. He didn't have the lock-spell to open doors for him. She might have a snowball's chance in hell of getting through. He wouldn't.

She touched the lump in her pants pocket. She had the hailstone. It could give her passage. But then she'd have wasted it on something that she might have been able to do for herself. She needed to use it to help Horngate. If only she knew what to *want*. She took another step back. There *was* another way inside—if it hadn't been sealed, too. The problem was it might be just as deadly.

"Let's go," she said to Alexander as she spun around. She didn't get five feet.

"I think not."

Max whipped about, yanking her .45 out of her holster. "Alton— What the hell are you doing here?"

The witch stood just at the edge of the road in the shadow of a tall cedar, smoke smudging the edges of his silhouette. He stepped out onto the pavement like he was a demon rising out of hell. Max's stomach clenched and bile flooded the back of her tongue. In the last few days he'd grown younger still. He now looked to be in his early twenties. His skin glowed with a radiant health and his eyes were a luminescent green, as if he'd drunk radioactive waste.

"Very good to see you, Max. I've been waiting for you," he said in his sickly sweet baritone voice. He ran his hand over the top of the shield, and streamers of red knotted beneath his fingers. He smiled, a greedy, smug expression that made her want to punch him.

"Waiting for me?" she said cautiously. "Why? How did you know I was coming?"

"It was foreseen. I have been sent to collect you. And Giselle of course. If she survives."

"Survives?" Adrenaline surged through Max, and her compulsion spells jerked tight, cutting deeply into her soul. Despite the pain, she held herself tightly in check. She needed answers, and it seemed that Alton had a lot of them. Plus he'd clearly gone from a mediocre witch to a force worth worrying about. She couldn't attack him head-on and win.

"Oh, yes. Shall I tell you what is going on inside?" he asked eagerly. The idiot bastard wanted to gloat.

"By all means. Tell me a bedtime story," she said mockingly. "I'm all ears." She shoved her gun back into her holster and crossed her arms expectantly.

He stiffened at her mockery, shaking himself, his jaw jutting. Good. One thing that hadn't changed was his ego and his need to tell everyone how important he was.

"Do not underestimate me. I am far more powerful than you can imagine," he said haughtily.

Unfortunately Max believed him.

He bent forward, his voice dropping. "If you must know, I tampered with the shield," he said gleefully.

"Tampered? How? What have you done?"

He smiled pompously at her fear. "I've done many things. The Guardians are moving to reclaim the earth and bring back the magic. But they don't wish to ruin the world by overdoing it. Some cataclysm will be necessary, of course. But they must be careful. In cleaning up the human mess, they don't want to kill the land or the creatures that belong here."

He waggled a finger and made a tsking noise. Max barely refrained from rolling her eyes or telling him to hurry the fuck up and get to the point.

"Setting off the Yellowstone volcano, for example, would cause a nuclear winter, and that can't be allowed. Or melting all the glaciers—that would cause too much devastation. So they have called on witches to lead their armies of magical beings to wipe away the human plague." He gave a little shrug as his smile momentarily disappeared. "It requires sacrifices, of course. But I have to serve when called, don't I?"

Max's teeth clenched. "Do you? What sacrifices have you made?"

"Old Home, for one," he said and, there was not even a hint of sorrow in his face. "Sekti had to destroy it so that Giselle would scry before the Conclave. I would have hexed her. Then I would have been able to take you all so much more easily. But the bitch wouldn't do it." His lip curled. "She should have. She was my ally. She broke her promise. Now she'll get everything she deserves."

Max bit her tongue, then spoke through gritted teeth. "What exactly does she deserve?" And who the hell is Sekti? Another Guardian?

"She deserves to see Horngate burned to ash. She deserves to crawl on her knees as my slave for the rest of her life." His mouth hardened, his teeth baring in a snarl. "She will never refuse me again." He fairly spat the words. "Right now, Hekau's fire angels and one of Marduk's angels of the sword are battling within these shields. No one can interfere. Not even you—I've made sure of that." He stroked his hand over the shield. "Even if they want to, they can't drop the shields. Not without me." He smiled triumphantly. "I went to Giselle two days ago. I begged for her help, but she refused." He scowled. "I knew she would. She will pay for that, too." He shook himself and glared at Max. "While I was there, I set a special spell. When the coven invoked the shields, they stepped into my trap. Now they cannot release the shields until they are entirely depleted. And when the coven falls, I will be waiting." He paused, then smiled slyly. "You don't know it, but you and Giselle and Horngate—you are a valuable prize. They all want you very badly."

"Why?" Max's voice echoed like a gunshot, her throat tight like someone was strangling her. "Who wants us?"

A secretive look. "I shouldn't say."

"Why not? What could it hurt? How could I possibly stop you?" Max wheedled. Her body was starting to shake as her compulsion spells pounded at her.

"The Guardians do not agree about how to get rid of the humans, or who will take ascension in the new world. You and Giselle and Horngate—somehow you are at the center of a Junction—a fertile intersection of possibilities. Whoever controls you can control the outcome of those possibilities. So much is tied to you that no one can even see beyond the next hours. But while the others fight over which one of them gets to have you, I will claim you for Sekti. The angels will destroy each other, and then I will have Giselle and Horngate, too." He straightened, raising his jaw and looking down his nose at Max, his face twisting in a mask of greed and pride. "Sekti has given me power beyond anything you can imagine. I can crush you with a thought. Now I want to see you on your knees, bitch. I am your master now and I want to see you grovel."

He stepped forward and raised his hands, green witchlight whipping around them like snakes. But before he could do whatever it was he had in mind, a blond Shadowblade slid out from the smoke and silence behind him and slammed his fist against Alton's head. The witch dropped to the pavement with a wet, guttering sound.

In the same instant, Max sprinted for cover on the other side of the road, yanking her gun out as she ran. Alexander was right behind her. She didn't make four steps before more of Selange's Shadowblades broke from cover. Eleven total, each with raised weapons aimed right at Max and Alexander. They were surrounded. She stopped, turning to look for the witch. How had she found Horngate? She must have flown or used both Sunspear and Shadowblade drivers to get here first.

"Look, Alexander," she said derisively. "More company. Don't they know we have better things to do than entertain their sorry asses?"

"Brave words," Selange said, emerging from the shadowy cleft of a pile of boulders just beyond the circle of her Shadowblades. She was dressed in khaki pants and a sleeveless linen blouse. Her crimson mouth was an angry slash and her body was rigid with fury. Or fear.

Max wasn't sure. She had to have heard everything that Alton had said.

"What do you want?"

"I want the hailstone, and after hearing all that, it appears you might be valuable to me as well."

Max felt Alexander tense. He was standing with his back to hers, his gun trained on the Shadowblades behind.

"What would you do with the hailstone? The Hag gave it to me, remember? Or have you decided to risk using it yourself? That might be fun to watch."

Desperation rippled over Selange's face, then her expression settled into a mask of twisted fury. "That's none of your business. I'm going to teach you a lesson or two about your place before I turn you over to Hekau."

"Better witches than you have tried to show me the light. I'm a slow learner." Max was playing for time, but the fact was, there was no way out of this that didn't end really badly. Magpie's warning echoed through her mind again. *No safety there, not for anyone. Not until you return. Only you can make it safe*. Horngate needed her now. She changed tack.

"Look. You aren't stupid. You heard what's going on. If you wanted to suck up to the Guardians, you wouldn't be here looking for the hailstone. You want a way out. Which means you need to work with me."

Selange laughed. "You're nothing. What can you do?"

"Well, for one, I have the hailstone. And for two, there's a couple of seers who think I might have something up my sleeve." Max didn't know if Magpie counted as a seer, but it sounded good. And Giselle had a touch of her mother's power. For the sake of Horngate, Max hoped the two of them were right. "What have you got to lose?" A lot. If Selange went into Horngate to fight Hekau's angel—and a second angel, if Alton had not lied—she would have a hard time explaining herself to Hekau if it didn't work. This was a point of no return. Still, a flesh mage like her had more to lose if the Guardians wiped out humanity. She would go from being a powerful witch to being a doormat.

The speed of Selange's reply told Max all there was to know about how deep her fear of that possibility was. "What do you have in mind?"

"There's another way inside Horngate. With two witches, your Shadowblades, and the hailstone, we might have the strength to do something."

"That's not much of a plan," Selange said with a sneer.

Max wholeheartedly agreed. "Got a better one?"

Selange's hands curled, the red fingernails like bloody claws. Clearly she wanted nothing more than to pound Max to a bloody pulp. Alexander, too. But she was stuck at the bottom of a big black hole, and the only possible way out was Max. "I have no choice."

"Not if you don't want to lose your flesh magic." But that didn't make sense, Max realized. She went still, her mind racing. Selange couldn't possibly hope to stop the Guardians from destroying humanity. That meant Selange wanted something else. The hailstone? Was it powerful enough to replace the power she would lose when humanity was destroyed? Or was she planning something else? She'd heard every word Alton had said about Max, Giselle, and Horngate being at the Junction of possibilities. What if she'd come for the hailstone but now had her eyes set on capturing that Junction and using them to bargain with Hekau? With both, she might be able to save her ass.

The lead that settled into the pit of Max's stomach told her she was right. But that was something to worry about later, after she'd figured out how to save Horngate.

"Where is this other entrance?" Selange demanded.

"Not far. But we're going to have to climb." Max didn't wait for a reply or for Selange to call off her dogs. She holstered her .45 and opened the back door of the truck. Alexander stayed beside her, his back to the truck, his gun still raised as he kept an eye on his former comrades.

"Do you know what you are doing?" he asked.

"Nope. But we have to get inside. It's this or try walking through that barrier. The odds are slightly better this way."

"You cannot trust Selange."

"Aren't you quick with the obvious, Slick? I know I can't trust her. But for now, the enemy of my enemy is my friend."

"And what if she is not the enemy of your enemy?"

Max had no answer for that.

BEFORE THEY STARTED OUT, THEY TIED ALTON UP, AND Selange wrapped a witch chain around him. It was the witch version of Kryptonite. That she had it handy in her van was telling, and Max promised herself again to keep a close eye on Selange inside Horngate.

The entry was a mile-and-a-half hike northeast over the unforgiving terrain of the Lolo National Forest. The mountains heaped together like the folds of a rucked blanket. The timber was dense, and the hogbacks were made more treacherous by deadfall and rusty stretches where pine-beetle infestations had destroyed the trees.

Well used to the rough terrain, Max easily outpaced her companions, with the exception of Alexander, who clung determinedly to her trail. More than once he saved himself with sheer strength alone as he stumbled and slipped over the knife-sharp ridges and sheer valley walls. Max was repeatedly forced to wait for Selange and the rest of her Shadowblades. The witch was soon limping and breathless. Sweat dripped down her forehead and stained the neckline of her blouse. Her hands and arms were scraped, and there were bruises on her arms.

They were a ridge away from Horngate's back door, and Max's compulsion spells were sawing her to pieces. Her heart was beating so hard she thought it was going to tear out of her chest. She couldn't bear to stop moving. As a panting Selange caught up again, Max turned and bounded up the slope. Footsteps followed. She glanced over her shoulder. Alexander was ten feet behind her. The scruffy, long-haired blond in faded jeans and battered cowboy boots who'd clobbered Alton trailed after. She remembered him. He had been one of the ones in Julian who had captured her.

Fifteen minutes later, she and her two shadows crested Sweetwater Ridge. The rimrock overlooked a verdant, glacier-carved cleft. A creek meandered through the meadow bottom, and aspens and birches marched beside it like silvery sentinels. On the opposite side of the valley, wild flames leaped from crown to crown of the massed evergreens. It caught and leaped again in the still air. Angelfire didn't need wind.

Smoke hung thick and the stench of the Uncanny and Divine was smothering. West of them, the magic gray-and-red-mottled barrier humped up between the mountains. Max crouched, leaning over the edge of her perch to look down.

The path into the pocket valley was nothing more than a series of narrow ledges, jutting footholds, and a tracery of cracks for the fingers. The inaccessibility made it the perfect place to hide Horngate's back door. The fire had not yet reached the entryway. When it did, it would be impossible to get through for hours at least, if not longer.

She stood and walked down the stone shelf. Halfway down, she turned and looked at Alexander. "Trust me?"

His eyes narrowed suspiciously. "Yes."

"Good."

She smiled wickedly at him, then gave a little hop sideways over the edge of the cliff.

18

MAX DROPPED ABOUT TWENTY-FIVE FEET, LANDing on a jut that couldn't be seen from above.

"Max!" Alexander's voice echoed down the valley. He was furious.

"Your turn," she called up. "The ledge isn't all that wide, so don't jump out too far or you'll splat into the valley floor. Stand where I did so you don't miss."

She moved to the far end of the shelf, and seconds later Alexander landed in a crouch near the edge. He thrust to his feet, storming across to her. He caught her arm, jerking close.

"What the hell was that?"

Max smiled, unabashed. "Girl's gotta have fun." She looked over his shoulder at his companion who'd just made the leap. "That's Thor?"

Alexander nodded, stepping back. She nodded at the other man, who looked surprised that she knew his name.

"It gets tricky from here. Follow carefully."

She started down. At one point a twenty-five-foot gap required another lunging jump. The landing shelf was the size of a postage stamp, fitting only one person at a time. Max talked Alexander and Thor through each step of the difficult descent to the bottom. Finally she reached the top of the moraine that skirted the bottom of the valley. She bounded down it at an angle, pebbles tumbling after her in a small avalanche. Moments later, Alexander and Thor stood breathlessly beside her, both looking tattered and bloody.

Max turned and jogged to the creek and jumped across it. She kept going, stopping beside a tumble of granite boulders ground smooth by time and weather. They lumped up forty feet or more.

"What now?" Alexander asked after a few moments.

"This is the part you're really going to hate," Max said. "From here I have to go alone."

"Like hell you are."

Thor made a snickering sound and Alexander gave him a blistering look that shut him up fast. Alexander looked back at Max. She didn't wait for him to argue. When she spoke, her tone was hard and final.

"The passage was designed so that only I can get through it. You would be killed the moment you set foot inside. When I get to the other side, I can shut down the defenses. So you need to sit tight and wait." She looked at Thor again. "I'm not your Prime, but my advice would be to head back up the cliff and show your friends the way down so they don't break their necks. Hopefully I'll have this open before the fire cooks all of you."

Thor nodded and gave her a casual salute. "Safe journey." He turned and loped away.

Max began pulling off her weapons and setting them aside. When she was through, she faced Alexander again. His expression was glacial. She lifted her chin, glaring back at him. Indecision made her hesitate. Did she tell him? She gave an exasperated sigh.

"Under the heading of full disclosure, you should probably know that I've never successfully made it through the passage. The last time I tried, I nearly didn't get out alive."

He gaped. "What?"

"Giselle didn't want to make it too easy—a back door *is* a hole in Horngate's defenses, after all. Theoretically I can get through. Supposedly it was designed just for me."

He stomped over, standing close and staring down at her, his jaw flexing. "Theoretically?" He pushed the word through gritted teeth.

Max licked her lips, more nervous than she wanted to admit. But the locking spell had worked better for her in the last few days than it ever had before. And just at the moment, more than anything else, she wanted to get inside Horngate. She hoped it was enough. "I didn't realize it then, but I think she expected the Guardians to come for her sooner or later, and I don't think even they can get through this gauntlet. She didn't create the spells for this; she called in a favor from someone." *What creature had magic great enough to stop the Guardians?* She hesitated. "The trouble is, it doesn't really want to let anyone in, even me."

He snatched her arms as if he wanted to either shake her or pick her up and throw her to knock some sense into her. "What makes you think you can get through this time?"

"Need," she said simply, then pulled herself away. "We don't have any other choice. I'd better get on it."

She didn't wait for him to say anything else. She turned and walked headfirst into the stand of boulders. With a flickering flash, she was inside a cave. Silence surrounded her like a shroud. Extending before her was a long, straight passage. Milky-blue magic filled it like thick cobwebs. She felt its pulse in her bones. The smell of the Divine was so thick it was hard to breathe.

She reached into her pocket, fingers rubbing over the soft leather of her medicine pouch and the cold lump of the hailstone inside. The last time she'd attempted to get through here, she'd only made it about two hundred feet before crawling back. Her body had been wasted, almost skeletal. Her hand clenched. This time she couldn't afford to turn back.

Slowly she took the pouch out of her pocket and hooked the hailstone out onto her palm. If she didn't make it, she could still help Horngate. All she had to do was swallow it. *Know what you want. You will have it*. She snorted softly. If only it were that easy. But the question was, what to want?

But she'd been thinking about it the entire drive back to Montana. Max had one idea and no time to think of anything better. No time to waste either. Quickly she popped the hailstone in her mouth. Its cold burned her tongue. She concentrated and swallowed, holding on to her wish with all her might.

She felt the cold of the hailstone slide down her throat to her stomach. It sat a moment like a glacial seed. The she felt it *open*. It uncurled like the petals of a frigid rose. The cold shifted suddenly to heat. It flared and rushed out of her on a nuclear wave-front. Max gasped and dropped to her knees, her heart thundering. Then the heat was gone. She drew a breath, her arms and legs shaking. She pushed slowly to her feet and leaned against the wall. She gave herself only a moment's rest.

Time to walk the gauntlet.

She gathered herself, thinking of Horngate and her need to be inside where she could help. "They need me—let me pass," she said aloud, and started into the milky-blue cobwebs.

At first it was like walking through a sticky mist. The filaments of magic clung to her, tearing away from the walls and wrapping her in a layered cocoon. Behind her, more strands grew from the walls.

She made it twenty feet before it became harder. Now it was like leaning into a stiff wind. The web grew more dense, the strands thicker. Max's mouth twisted grimly. This was only the beginning.

Another sixty feet and she was chopping at the magic with her hands. The web was made of thick cords now, and they coiled and knotted around Max like snakes. They sank through her clothing, through her skin and her flesh. She could feel them blindly sucking on her soul—her essence. She was being eaten alive, just like before.

"Let me through!" she yelled, but no one and nothing answered.

Every passing moment weakened her. She thrust forward desperately. She was not turning back this time; it was all or nothing.

At 120 feet, she could hardly raise her arms. Her legs were leaden. She had no sense of time. She forced herself to keep scuffing along. She could feel her flesh shrinking over her bones, her skin loosening like stretched-out rags.

Then finally, she came to the point of no return. She didn't know how she knew, but she did. One more step and she would not have the strength to get back. Brambles of fear wormed through her. How much farther? Could she last? Would she be worth anything if she did?

She swayed. The magic wrapped her head and she could only see shimmering blue-white shadows. She felt parched and brittle. Her tongue was like a stick in her mouth. She couldn't even blink her eyes anymore, and inside, she felt her organs like hard lumps of clay.

Did she go back?

The decision was already made. Giselle had made this entrance just for Max. If she'd foreseen the need, then she also foresaw Max using it.

She shuffled forward. A moment of crystal silence, and in that drop of stillness, the sudden knowledge that *something* was there, waiting for her.

Max didn't have time to think of what to do. She was ripped out of her body. Claws pierced, skewering deep inside her. She was shaken, whipped from side to side like a squirrel in a dog's mouth. Then she was slammed against something. She felt cracks creeping across her mind, across her soul. Bits of herself flaked away. Now something squeezed her, then turned her inside out.

The violation was more than she'd ever suffered at Giselle's hands. She could hide nothing. She screamed without sound. She struggled to fight, to hold herself together.

Then the magic tightened, coiling and crushing. She shattered. She drifted in pieces like petals on a lazy wind. She had no name, no purpose, no hungers, no dreams. She was nothing. The petals curled and faded from blue-white to gray and sifted away into nothingness.

Horngate.

The word stirred something. Where did it come from? What was it?

Need.

A thrust of urgent desperation.

Danger.

Suddenly the dried petals drifted back from the nowhere place beyond reason. They curled and fluttered, condensing around the immutable core that was all that remained of the one who'd sought passage.

Max.

The one had a name.

More bits of herself streamed back, attaching themselves, fitting together like puzzle pieces. Each one brought back a memory, a feeling, a flavor. Slowly she coalesced out of the destruction of herself until she found herself back in the cave. She lay on the ground. She sat up. She felt fine—no pain, no weakness. She rolled to her feet. Behind her was the passage. In front of her was a door.

All around her was that feeling of something or someone waiting, watching.

"Hello?"

You are the one I was told would come. The one whose heart I could not break.

The voice resonated all the way through Max. It was like standing in the middle of a drag-racing track with engines roaring all around her. She staggered and steadied herself against the wall.

"You'll let me through to Horngate?"

Always.

The smugness and warm tenderness in the word made Max tense. "Who are you?"

"I have no name. I was born of Onniont, the horned serpent, and Nihansan, the spinner of webs. I guard. I wait for you. You are my gift."

Max's mouth went dry. "Your gift?" she repeated, hoping she'd heard wrong.

"You alone in all the world can withstand my powers. You alone can walk through my webs and live. You are the one I have waited for. It has been so long."

The yearning in the creature's voice made Max want to weep for its pain, even as fear thrust skeletal fingers around her heart.

"What do you want of me?" she asked carefully. She didn't want to anger it. She didn't know if she could survive another bout with its webs.

"You."

"Me?"

"Yes. You will come to me. You will walk the web roads with me. You will speak to me truth and you will share your fire with me."

Max swallowed. She didn't know what any of that meant. What had Giselle promised this creature? Not that it mattered. At the moment she needed to fetch the others and get into Horngate.

"Sure, Scooter. Whatever blows your dress up," she said, not knowing if she'd just agreed to bear its children. "I have friends I need to bring through. Will you allow them passage?"

"Yes. For you."

A web of magic spun into being before Max. As she

watched, it formed a vaguely human shape. The weaving tightened and grew dense, and the shape became more pronounced. Then suddenly, between one blink and the next, the milky-blue light flared searingly bright. When the brilliance faded, a man stood before Max. He was neither young nor old. His skin was red mahogany, his hair long and blue-black. His features were sharply etched like wind-scoured stone. He was beautiful. And naked. Max let her eyes drift down his well-muscled body. Maybe it wouldn't be so bad having his children.

"You might want to put on some clothes, Scooter," she said, wondering if this was his natural form. She was pretty sure it wasn't.

A moment later he wore a buckskin vest and pants. They were soft and worn. His feet remained bare.

Without another word, Max led the way back to where she'd entered. Her companion padded along softly next to her. His skin radiated heat.

"Do you know what's happening in Horngate?"

He nodded. "There is war. The warriors of Giselle fight. They cannot win."

"I've brought help," Max said, her voice edged in steel.

"It will not matter. You cannot win."

For him it was an observation. Arguing with him would be like arguing with a tree.

"I'm damn well going to try."

"But it is not the solution." Now his voice was admonishing. It sounded ancient. It probably was. She was going to have to look up his parents in her library when all of this was done. If she was still alive.

"Then you tell me, Scooter—just what is the solution?"

"You are."

Max stopped and whirled on him. "Could you be a little less cryptic? I don't have time for puzzles."

He stared at her, his eyes the color of polished onyx. Flecks of milky-blue swirled in their depths. "*You* are the riddle. *You* are the answer that no one expects. *You are the only answer*." He said it like the words weren't actually complete gibberish.

Max growled and speared her hands through her hair, grabbing and pulling it hard. She shook her head. "Fuck this. I don't have time." She stormed away, aware that he stayed right at her side. She didn't slow down when she reached the entrance, but marched through the illusion out into the smoky night.

Outside she was instantly surrounded. She looked for Alexander. He rushed to her side.

"Are you okay?"

His eyes went past her as her mystical new friend emerged. Instantly Alexander reached to push her out of the way. Max waved him off. He held himself still, quivering with restrained ferocity.

"This is—" She broke off. There was no explaining him. She took another tack. "This is Scooter. He's going to walk with us through to Horngate. But first everyone lay down your weapons."

Selange laughed shrilly. "I don't think so. We are not going unarmed into another witch's coven."

"Then stay here and cook." Max glanced pointedly up the ridge. The fire was spreading down into the valley. She started to turn back to the cave.

"Move an inch and my people will drop you in your tracks. Make your choice. We go in armed, or you don't go in at all. I'll take my chances with the hailstone and leave Horngate to deal with its own problems."

"Try it, bitch, and I'll rip your throat out," Max said. It was an empty threat. She was unarmed and Selange's Shadowblades had brought their weapons to bear.

"*My* gift," Scooter whispered, his voice like grinding rocks. His milky-blue magic thrust up from the ground all around the Shadowblades. In seconds their weapons had been torn from their hands. A handful of gunshots rang out, but the bullets were caught in a tightly woven web.

Max bared her teeth at Selange. "Here's the way the game is played. You can go running back to Aulne Rouge with your tail between your legs and wait for the Guardians to come knocking at your door, or you can come inside and make a stand here with us. Decide now. I'm not waiting."

She motioned for Alexander to put down his weapons and follow. Once again Scooter walked at her shoulder. A moment later she heard footsteps and low, vicious swearing. Selange was enraged, but she was coming.

Alexander followed so close on Max that he was nearly trampling her. He didn't like her new buddy. She wondered what he'd think of the bargain she'd struck—not that she knew what the terms really were. She rolled her shoulders to loosen them, dismissing the problem. It only mattered if she survived. No sense worrying about it until then.

In a few minutes Max realized the passage had changed. It was wider and somehow more menacing. It dead-ended in a wide hollow in the rock. There was no sign of the door she'd seen before.

"What's going on?" she demanded. Was this a trap?

Scooter turned to face the others as they filled the small space. His expression was cold. "There are those here who mean harm to Horngate."

As if Max didn't know that already. "Yes. But for now they are allies. They have come to help me fight."

He looked at her. Nothing she or they could do would win the battle. But he did not say it. Instead he turned his attention back to the others. Slowly he paced forward to Alexander, who stood still as if he couldn't move. His jaw flexed and the cords of his neck tented, and Max realized that he had in fact been frozen in place.

"You belong to Horngate," Scooter said after a moment, and went to the next person. It was Selange's Prime. "You are an enemy." He lifted his hand and touched his forefinger lightly to the other man's cheek. In blue magic, he drew a bar with two dots above and another below. Slowly he went to each of Selange's Blades, then to the witch herself. Her eyes bugged with fury and fear, but she was as helpless as all the others. Max grinned at her.

Scooter judged each and made the mark on their cheeks. When he reached Thor, he was slower. Finally he made the mark. It was a squiggly line with four dots below and none above. He said nothing and returned to Max's side.

"What belongs to Horngate belongs to me. Her enemies are my enemies. Know if you hunt here, if you harm those who belong to me, I will flay the skin from your bones and eat your hearts and livers before I cast you into the abyss between worlds."

Max felt the words shudder through her like blows.

She had no doubt that Scooter could do as threatened and more. With a graceful spin that seemed too fluid for anything human—which Scooter definitely was not—he faced the wall. The stone faded to a thick web of blue magic. Then the strands of magic untied themselves, shriveling away until all that remained was the iron-bound door Max had seen before. He looked at her.

"You are the gift and the answer. I will wait for your return, and we will walk the web roads together."

Max nodded with no idea what she was agreeing to. It didn't matter. If she could see Horngate safe, she'd pay whatever price was required. She reached for the door. Time to go to war.

19

ALEXANDER DID NOT KNOW WHO OR WHAT Scooter was, but he knew he did not like the creature, nor did he trust him. He smelled powerfully of the Divine, and when he looked at Max, his gaze was intensely possessive. What had Scooter meant when he said she was the gift and the answer? Foreboding sluiced through Alexander. What had Max promised in exchange for help in getting back into Horngate?

He followed hard on her heels. He wanted to demand answers. But she was Prime and he had no right. Nor was there time. For a fleeting moment he let himself regret the end of their time alone together.

They entered a stone chamber. The walls were glassy smooth with streaks of quartz, copper, and gold running through the black basalt. A shimmering, translucent screen of magic cut the room in half. On the opposite side were ranks of tall steel cabinets. To the left was a doorway, and to the right a flight of steps going up. Max did not slow down, but marched through the screen as if it were not there. Alexander and the rest of her companions trooped in, none daring to try the curtain themselves. The door shut behind them with heavy finality, and there could be no doubt that Scooter was standing guard.

Alexander glanced at Thor. The mark Scooter had rubbed onto his face had faded as if it had never been. The same with the others. Cleo was red with rage and couldn't tear her eyes from Alexander. He ignored her. The others hardly paid any attention to their former Prime at all. Selange's face was a mask of hard-held emotions. He knew it was taking everything she had not to simply explode.

Max slapped a hand against a fractured starburst of quartz. The wall bloomed with brilliant light and the curtain evaporated. She did not look behind her as she sprinted for the stairs. Alexander and Thor were a split second behind. She bounded upward, bursting through a set of double doors when she reached the top some eighty feet up through solid stone.

The room they entered was cavernous. The walls were the same polished basalt as below, with a groined wood ceiling layered in gilt. The walls were hung with a dazzling array of art. Balls of golden witchlight bobbed against the ceiling, casting a light that was as bright as sunshine. In the center was an *anneau* floor. The circle and star were lit, and eighteen of the coven witches stood in position, hands stretched out to each other. They looked weary and wasted, held in place more by magic than by their own will. A handful of others milled in the corner of the eerily silent room, looking both strained and resolute. It took a moment for Alexander to realize that they hovered around Giselle. The witch was slumped on a padded chair. She was gaunt, her eyes sunken and rimmed with black. The bones of her skeleton prodded sharply beneath her skin. Beside her someone plied her with a glass of water. As Max raced down the hall, Giselle slowly raised her head, rubbing a shaking hand over her eyes as if to clear away a mirage.

"Max? Thank the spirits. I knew you were alive, but—" Her lips snapped shut and a wave of something akin to pain rippled across her expression.

Her bindings had told her Max was alive, but not her condition. For all she knew, Max had been captured. Alexander marveled at Giselle's demonstration of feeling, and he wondered at it. Max hated her. Yet Giselle clearly did not feel the same. He had seen it in her concern after the Conclave and again now. For her, Max was far more than merely her Shadowblade Prime.

Max strode forward, dropping to a crouch and gripping the arms of the chair. She wasted no words. "What's going on?"

Giselle straightened in the chair and slowly came to her feet like a broken marionette. Her eyes flattened as she gazed past Max. "You brought company."

Max rose to her feet. "They wanted to see what sort of party you were throwing."

"I see."

Alexander had no doubt that she saw plenty. Giselle was young by witch standards, but she had brains and an iron will. Selange did not cow her in the least. Giselle's gaze shifted back to Max. Before she could say anything, the hall shook and a thundering rumble grated through the silence. Alexander felt a sudden wash of heat and heard a faint crackle—of fire or stone he could not tell. Neither was good.

Giselle scowled, her eyes cold and hard. "Hekau sent Xaphan—the fire angel—to get my answer on her offer. When he didn't like it, he started lighting the forest on fire to give us some incentive. But then another angel showed up. Seems the Guardians are having themselves a pissing contest. They can't agree on the best way to fight this war they've decided to unleash on the world, and they are playing tug-of-war with Horngate as the rope."

Max nodded. "So I heard." Giselle's brows rose in a question. "Alton mentioned it when he tried to attack me. He's the reason the coven can't let go of the shields."

Fury swallowed the witch, and in an instant magic crackled around her in a nimbus of black lightning. Everyone but Max jumped away

"That bastard," Giselle said, and her eyes went coal black and started to glow. "I'll kill him."

Alexander stepped back, feeling the magic of her rage hammer at him. Every hair on his body lifted, and fear dug hard hands into his gut. She was much stronger than he anticipated. He glanced at Selange, who swallowed, her hands locked together, staring at her rival.

"Pretty show, but you're wasting energy and time," Max said. "Mind if we get back to saving Horngate? You can go postal later."

Giselle shuddered and her eyes locked on Max. Slowly the cloud of energy seeped back inside her. But her eyes continued to glow with ebony light.

"Shortly after Xaphan began burning the forest, Tutresiel arrived to challenge Xaphan. We invoked the shield wards to try to protect ourselves against the fires and the fallout of the angels' battle, but we can't shrink them down. I've done everything I can. The circle and star are trapped. Alton's doing, no doubt. Did he say how?"

"Just that when he visited here he set a spell and it would shut off when everyone was depleted."

"We must find it and break it. There's no other way."

Again a shuddering boom shook the cavern. The timbers of the ceiling creaked ominously. Giselle looked up worriedly. "We'd better hurry or there will be no point."

Max rubbed a hand across her mouth. Alexander edged closer. She was starting to get the same feral look she had had in Julian, right before she was about to throw herself into a suicidal battle with Selange's Shadowblades.

"We're not going to withstand much more of this," said the black-haired cook from the kitchen truck. The white stripes in her hair seemed to almost glow. Her gaze was locked on Max. Something in the way she spoke sounded portentous. When the words made Max jerk like she had been struck, Alexander was certain there was more going on here than he knew. He wanted to demand answers, but doing so would more than likely get him locked up somewhere in the bowels of the mountain. As far as Giselle was concerned, he was still the enemy. He bit down hard on the inside of his lip, forcing himself to stay quiet.

"Make your Prime use her hailstone," Selange said into the tense silence. "Have her wish the angels into hell. Better yet, have her wish them into your service."

Giselle stiffened. "Hailstone?"

"Didn't she tell you? But of course not. She wanted

to keep it for herself. You can't trust any Shadowblade or Sunspear. They'll turn on you when you least expect it." Alexander met her searing look with an unrepentant grin and a bow. An ugly flush seeped up her neck into her cheeks. Her hands clenched. She glared at Giselle, her voice turning silky. "She fed the Hag her blood and was given a hailstone for her trouble. Make her give it to you."

Max smiled wickedly at Selange. "Sorry. Used it already. But if you want, I'll let you wait until it drops out of my ass and see what kind of magic you can do with it."

"You used it?" Giselle asked. She thrust herself forward, grabbing Max's arm. "Tell me what you asked for. Tell me now." Despite her demanding words, her tone was breathless and placating. "What did you want, Max?"

For a moment Max didn't speak. She'd gone inward to that cold place of calm. Alexander's hands twitched. She wanted freedom beyond anything else. His stomach tightened and he knew without a doubt what she had wished for.

But then, he had forgotten she didn't leave any of hers behind. And Horngate was hers.

"I wanted—" She paused, her jaw jutting as her eyes locked tight on Giselle. "I *want* the Guardians and their minions to forget Horngate and all who live inside its borders. Forever. I want them to forget Horngate ever existed."

Giselle's hand came up to cover her mouth and she closed her eyes.

"You stupid bitch!" Selange shouted. "What good does

that do us? The angels will destroy us. What kind of stupid fool are you? If you were mine, I'd see your skin flayed away every day for a year. I'd gouge out your eyes and fill the sockets with hot tar. I'd—"

"Want to see what I can do with you?" Max asked softly. "Or are you the kind of witch-bitch who can dish it out like a lunch lady on crack, but your tits shrivel up when you get a taste of your own medicine?"

Alexander bit back his laughter. Like it or not, Horngate needed Selange right now, and she did not take well to ridicule. Especially from him.

"Can't you control your dog?" Selange said coldly to Giselle. "I remind you I am a territory witch with a powerful coven under my rule. You would do well to show me the respect I deserve."

"As I recall, you broke the rules of the challenge, sending your Blades after Max and Alexander. And then what about the right of free passage? You deserve a great many things from me. Respect is not one of them," Giselle shot back.

"You'll choke on those words when you ask for my help," Selange spat.

"Then you might as well leave now, don't you think? Why don't you go out the way you came in?" Max said.

Selange paled and fell silent.

Giselle smiled slowly and looked at Max. "Well done," she said softly.

"She's right, though. Doesn't exactly help with the here and now."

The mountain shuddered again. A sound like the moan of a wraith ran through the room, raising the hair on Alexander's arms. He scanned the ceiling. A heavy beam sagged downward, then dropped free. It smashed against the floor with a sound like a bomb going off. Luckily it was at the far end of the cavern and no one was injured. This time. Splinters of wood sifted down, and there were more creaks and moans as the entire ceiling shifted uneasily.

"The mountain is going to come down if we don't stop them," Max said. "Where are my Blades? And Oz?"

"They went to try to fend the angels off. I haven't heard from them since."

"That will not work," Alexander heard himself say. "They are immune to mortal attacks."

"We had to do something," Giselle said coldly. "I have done what I can. Now I must try to break Alton's spell and pull the shields back where they can do some good for those of us here." She looked at Max, who was looking up at the ceiling, her brow furrowed in thought. "What is it?"

Max lowered her head, rubbing her hand over her mouth, her eyes narrowed as she chased an idea. At last she turned purposefully to Giselle. "If my hailstone wish worked, then the Guardians should be forgetting about us, right?"

Giselle nodded, frowning. "Right."

"Then when do the angels start to forget?"

The witch waved her hand dismissively. "Not until they leave. It will be too late by then. They won't leave until they destroy each other and us with them. Even if we get shields between us and them, we'll give out before they do. A coven at full strength can't stand against even a single angel. Our only real hope is for them to kill each other soon, and that is unlikely. They do not die easily."

A dangerous, reckless smile curved Max's lips, and Alexander felt himself go cold. "No, that's not our only hope. But you'll need to get the shields working—enough to buy me some time. Otherwise there's no point."

"Time? Time for what?"

"I'm going to talk to them."

"Talk? And what will you say?" Selange said derisively. "'Please don't slaughter us'? Are you insane? The only chance we had was to destroy them using the hailstone."

Alexander was equally incredulous. But Max was dead serious. That dark, wild recklessness gleamed in her eyes, and he wanted to knock her down and tie her up until she came to her senses.

She never looked away from Giselle, who looked more thoughtful than dubious. "It's entirely possible that I might be able to convince them to join Horngate," Max said. "If they did, their Guardians would forget them."

"Why would they? Even if they could get around their compulsion spells?"

"Because there's a chance they might one day be free. That's worth more than you know."

Giselle did not have time to answer. Another massive blow struck the mountain. The floor leaped and buckled, and heavy chunks of stone and wood fell, shattering the quiet. The air filled with smoke and dust, and above, a fissure gaped in the rock ceiling. Thunderous crashes exploded throughout the cavern as more chunks of stone and ceiling collapsed. Flaming meteors of burning rock and wood fell through the gash in the mountain above, and where they fell, they spread.

Max had shoved Giselle down by the wall, using the

chair as a shield for the witch. She batted away the falling rubble with her hands. Alexander stood beside her, helping to protect the witch and those who huddled beside her. At last the avalanche slowed to a sift of pattering stones. Above, Alexander could hear the struggle between the angels continue. There was a clang of metal, like dozens of swords clattering together. The smell of sulfur and smoke was thick, and orange flames limned the stone far above.

Alexander coughed and gasped, then froze in place. A mass of timbers and stone filled the *anneau* floor like the rubble from an earthquake. None of the witches could have survived it.

Max eyed the rubble, her jaw shaking, her teeth clamped tight. She turned away and pulled Giselle to her feet. "Will that have broken Alton's spell?" she asked hoarsely.

Giselle nodded. "Probably." Like Max, she did not allow herself the luxury of grief.

"Can you raise a shield?"

"I think so. But I can't hold it long. Not with the magic they are throwing at us."

"They are not trying to hit us," Alexander found himself saying. "When they do, we will be in real trouble."

"Then we had better hurry up," Max retorted. She turned to Selange. "If you don't want to die today, I suggest you help. And you," she said to the Shadowblades who surrounded Selange like a wall. They were bleeding and covered with gray dust, and two were missing. "You're welcome to come help, but if you decide to stay here and protect your witch-bitch, let me give you a little something to think about. If anything happens to Giselle, I will hunt Selange down and kill her. If I can't, then my Blades will, and if they can't, then the Sunspears. Trust me on this—*someone will come*. Remember what Scooter said—you're his enemies. So when you're thinking about protecting your witch-bitch, remember that you'd better be watching out for Giselle, because if you don't, you sign Selange's death warrant."

Max didn't wait for a reply. She thrust past Alexander and he followed. They bounded over the debris. At the far end, they found the door blocked. It took two minutes to clear it. In that time, molten rock began dropping from the crevice above. It landed on the pearl-gray shield that was slowly rising like a bubble. Where it hit, the shield puckered and pitted. The flames died slowly, the light of the shield fluctuating erratically.

Once they'd cleared the door, they entered a lofty, pillared sitting area. Once cozy nooks were scattered all around. Hallways led away like spokes of a wheel. Alexander could tell that much, though here, too, the ceiling had begun to collapse and many pillars had broken, shattering the tile floor. Except for the sounds of the battle above, a suffocating silence flowed through the space.

"Where is everyone?" he asked.

"I hope they are in the greenhouses—those buildings have their own weather wards, and that might protect them from the fire and smoke. But if you're asking why there aren't a lot more people in the hall, then the answer is that we are a small covenstead. There are only about eighty of us altogether." Max waved a hand at the cavernous space. "Giselle built this place expecting a crowd one day. Maybe she should have named us

Noah's Ark instead of Horngate. Let's hope we aren't about to be the *Titanic*."

She led the way down one of the hallways. A dozen yards up, she stopped. To the left was an ornate marble stairway leading upward. Or it had been. It had crumbled to bits. Max didn't say a word. Alexander was not sure he would have heard if she did. The mountain shook again, and the hollow, moaning sound it made was deafening, as if the earth itself screamed agony. The sound went on, the air filling with dust, rocks, and debris raining down. He coughed, sprinting after Max as she turned back the way they'd come. She darted across the open area, hurtling overturned furniture and the squat boles of the fallen pillars as the mountain shook. At the far side she slid into a concealed hallway. It was so narrow that she had to turn sideways to get through. At the end was a vertical shaft with a steel ladder bolted to the wall. Flashes of orange light winked faintly above. Rocks pinged down, clanging against the metal rungs and cracking like bullets against the buckled floor.

"Stay close."

"My own personal Max-umbrella," he said as she started up into the barrage.

She looked down. "Was that a joke? I didn't think you were capable. Did you sprain something?"

"You are a bad influence."

"Not that bad—the joke sucked."

He pushed on her calf. "Get going before you add another rock to the rest in your head."

She climbed rapidly, ducking and weaving back and forth, dodging what she could. Still Alexander heard more than one stone missile hit flesh. She never flinched nor uttered more than a grunt. He kept close, feeling the battle above in the vibrations that ran constantly through the steel beneath his hands and growled softly from the stone chimney enclosing them.

Divine magic filled the air, pulling and twisting like a live thing, raising silver sparks in Alexander's hair and along his skin. He wasn't the only one. The fiery flashes from above were growing stronger, and heat washed down over him, increasing with every rung of the ladder.

Three-quarters of the way up, they reached a point where a spur of granite had fallen and lodged sideways in the chimney. The ladder was crushed and swayed away from its moorings. A gap to one side of the fallen rock was big enough to squirm through, but with precious few handholds, and the stone could give way at any second.

Max did not even slow down. She climbed to the top of the uncertain steel and leaped. Her body bowed and her hands clawed for a hold, and her feet scrabbled against the rock. Then she heaved herself up, disappearing from sight. The monstrous slab of stone scraped and groaned, and he held his breath as he waited for it to break free.

"Alexander?" Max called. She sounded breathless.

"Here."

"Can you follow me? There's a lip there just inside the gap. Grab it and pull up until you can get your feet on it, and then push up. I'll grab you."

Another thundering roar struck the mountain, and magic rushed down the shaft. The stone pipe blurred under the onslaught, momentarily turning to liquid. The magic didn't affect the ladder, but the rivets that held it in place popped free, and the ladder tilted away from the wall. The boulder dropped at the same moment. Alexander relaxed his hands and jumped, sliding down the ladder. A few seconds later as the rock solidified again, he clenched his hands and stopped his fall. The slab of stone had wedged again. Slowly he climbed back up, the ladder creaking protest as it bent back to rest against the opposite wall.

"Alexander?" Max's voice echoed. "Are you there?"

"Yes."

"Can you get up?"

"Give me a minute."

He reached the top of the ladder and scanned the stone. Even as he watched, it grated downward with an ominous groan. There looked to be a narrow crevice on the opposite side. The only way to reach it was to leap across, grappling a handhold on the unstable boulder. He did not let himself consider. He launched himself across the fifteen feet and slammed against the granite, clawing a horizontal crack. He hung there, his heart pounding. Nothing happened. He let go with one hand, spidering his fingers across the rough surface. He found a place to grip and swung over, his legs dangling uselessly. Another handhold. Another. One more. He was across. He looked up into the opening and saw Max above. Behind her, the top of the shaft was a fiery furnace. She smiled fiercely with that wild recklessness that scared the hell out of him.

"Just remember I told you to run when you had the chance. You could have been lounging on a beach somewhere," she called.

"Sounds boring," he said, his arms straining as he scanned for another handhold. The stone slipped a couple of inches. He lost his grip and dangled one-handed. He twisted, his shoulder popping.

"Just above you there's a lip," Max said. "No—to the right. That's it. Hurry."

As if he needed to be told. He hooked his fingers over the inchwide outcropping and pulled himself up until he could reach Max's outstretched hand. He gripped her tightly and kicked up through the gap until he sprawled on the fallen hunk of stone. The heat here was like a blast furnace.

"Boring might be a nice place to be right about now," she said. "Come on. This rock could go at any time. I do not want to be on it."

Her eyes danced and her face was alight. Alexander rolled to his feet beside her. "You are enjoying this."

She grinned. "Aren't you?"

Remarkably, he was. "Perhaps neither of us has enough clowns for a circus."

"Of course we don't. Comes with the job. That's why we're standing here talking nonsense while the world is going to hell all around us. Let's go."

The ladder was entirely destroyed but for a few rivets and scrap. The walls of the shaft were crumbled and fissured from the heat and the magic quakes. Max took off her shoes, tucking her socks inside. She knotted the laces together and slung them around her neck. Alexander eyed her suspiciously before doing the same. He was not a climber, but he recognized that having his toes free would be an advantage.

He glanced up again. Fire rimmed the rectangular opening above, and even as he watched, molten rock dribbled down along the wall.

"How are we going to get past that?"

"With luck. Come on. We don't want to get struck by another magic wave. We won't have anything to hang on to."

Max started up. She climbed easily, moving like a spider. Alexander did his best to follow her path, but soon his fingers and toes were raw and he shook with the ferocity of his concentration.

The closer they came to the opening, the more intense the heat grew. The air rippled and Alexander longed for a drink of water. Still Max did not slow down. Finally, just fifteen feet from the top, she crawled into a steel conduit, then reached down to help him inside.

She leaned back out and looked up, then retreated back to Alexander. She sat down and started pulling on her socks and boots. He followed suit.

"This leads down the hill to Skunk Creek. There's a splice about halfway that goes to the greenhouses. It's not far, maybe a half mile. There's an access shaft at the intersection and hopefully we can get out. If not, we'll go all the way to the creek and hope the angelfire doesn't burn water, too."

"I do not think this is normal angelfire," Alexander said. "The fires south of San Diego were not this hot. The rocks did not melt there. I believe this is Xaphan's battle fire—otherwise it probably would not hurt another angel like Tutresiel."

"What's your point?"

"It may very well burn water."

"Aren't you a bright ray of sunshine?"

Alexander shrugged. "Tell me to walk into the battle fire and I will." He was not sure why he said it. She had not questioned his loyalty since they had arrived at Horngate. But the sharp taste of her doubt lingered, and he wanted to kill it permanently, though he knew trust was earned, not claimed.

She looked at him. Her eyes narrowed. "I know. You don't have to convince me. Now let's go before they turn the mountain into gravel, and hope to hell that this tunnel hasn't collapsed."

They could stand hunched over. Max led the way in a clumsy jog. She'd gone only a hundred feet when she stopped. The pipe sagged pregnantly downward, leaving a gap less than a foot high and not much wider to fit through. Max shook her head and drew a harsh breath. She crouched, bending low to look beneath. She straightened and reached her hands under, pulling upward. Metal creaked. Her muscles bunched and corded, but there was no more give. She let go.

"That will have to do."

She lay on her stomach and started to crawl through. Her shoulders were a tight fit, but she squirmed along with a few choice curses.

Then the mountain shook again with a sound like thunder. A wave of power rushed up the tunnel and slammed Alexander in the back. His head banged against the curve of the steel pipe, and his vision fogged momentarily. Instinct made him grab Max's feet. He lunged backward, dragging her out of the hole. A second later the steel conduit shimmered blue and the bulge in the pipe sank with a groan to seal the tunnel. It started to flatten and the two scrambled backward, hands pressing into the now spongy surface of the corrugated-steel floor.

"Get on your feet," Max said, pulling Alexander up. "Keep your feet moving or you'll end up stuck."

As it was, when the magic wave passed, the sole of his boot was tightly embedded in the steel. It took a hard yank to pull it free, and some of the metal came with it.

"Now what?" he asked.

"I guess we walk into the fire."

"There is no other way?"

"If that stone finished its fall down the shaft, it sealed the hallway below. The only way left open is up."

She pushed past him in the strangled space of the pipe. Alexander caught her arm. She stopped and eyed him narrowly. "You got a problem?"

"Aside from the fact that we are about to die? No. But I want to say thank you before it is too late."

"For?"

"Letting me in. Trusting me. It means a lot. If the tables were turned, I do not think I would have been so generous."

"Some would call me stupid. You would, in fact."

He smiled fleetingly, then sobered. "Try not to get killed."

"Likewise, I'm sure." She started to pull away, then turned back. "Fuck it," she muttered.

She reached up and pulled his head down, kissing him hard. He wrapped his arms tight around her, snatching her close. The kiss was almost brutal in its need. Teeth ground against teeth, and their tongues devoured each other. The taste of her made his gut twist with a violent hunger.

As quickly as it had begun, it was over. Max pushed away and Alexander let her go reluctantly. "I thought you did not mess around with the men in your coven," he rasped, his heart thundering in his chest.

Max touched her fingers to her swollen lips. "Call it . . . a last request. Even condemned prisoners are allowed that much, right? Now—let's go jump into the fire."

He shook his head, following her. "If we get out of this alive, you and I are going to find a quiet room and lock the door for a week or two."

She laughed, and the sound rang down the conduit. He was not sure if it was because he had suggested they might survive, or because she found the idea of being with him amusing.

20

MAX RETURNED TO THE MOUTH OF THE CONDUIT. The heat was hotter now and burled down the shaft in fierce waves. Flames crackled and popped with fierce energy. She looked up quickly, then ducked back inside, her skin ruddy. Her brow furrowed and her mouth pursed, then she shook her head.

"It's too late to go up. We'll be cooked. We have to try going back down and hope we can get through."

She leaned out over the lip of the opening. "The rock fell. Not quite all the way to the bottom. It looks like there might be a gap we can get through. We'll have to hurry. If there's another magic strike, we'll lose our handholds and pancake on the bottom." She started to pull back inside, then stopped. "Wait a second. Look at that."

Alexander came to look past her. A gray-green film covered the bottom of the shaft. It shimmered and rippled like water. Slowly it rose. It was the shield. As they watched, a drop of molten stone dropped down the shaft. It hit the magic screen, and this time the surface did not falter or pucker.

"Selange must be helping Giselle," Max said. "It's handling the heat better than when it started, which means . . . Change of plan," she said with sudden energy.

"We are going up after all," Alexander finished.

"The shield should cool the rock enough to climb. Leave your boots on. We're close enough we should make it easily enough. Get ready."

The thin shell of magic rose higher. It pushed up through the mountain, rising up through the bottom of the conduit. It was cold and it stung as it swept up and over their heads. As soon as it passed, Max climbed out into the shaft.

The shield had cooled the rock considerably, and in just moments the two Shadowblades clambered up out of the shaft and into an apocalyptic wasteland.

They stood on a mountain above the U-shaped river valley that held the greenhouses and a collection of barns and pastures. A hundred yards downslope Alexander could see the fissure gaping like a mouth above the underground hall. The field of bubbled and black rock spread out from beneath their feet, covering an area the size of three football fields. Xaphan's battle fire had melted the stone, and the molten rock had run and pooled like liquid wax. Above it the shield rose some three feet, coming to just above Alexander's knees. Already it was tattering, as if the two witches were struggling to hold it. Acrid smoke drifted lethargically over the ground. All around on the receding ridges, forest fires raged, orange flames leaping from crown to crown. Overhead, lightning flashed as a dry summer storm rolled in. It was like standing in the middle of an active volcano.

A sound like clashing swords drew Alexander's attention. It was the angel of the sword—Tutresiel. His wings were silver, each feather metallic and sharp. Every beat clattered. Like Xaphan, he was albino white with crimson eyes, but his hair was matte black and hung to his shoulders. The blade of the sword he wielded was at least seven feet long and shone with an incandescent white witchlight.

The two angels squared off just thirty yards on the downslope side. The two circled each other in the air. Xaphan's wings blazed with orange and blue flames that trailed through the night like streamers. Max turned, her expression tense.

"Over there," she said, pointing ahead, then sprinted across the hillside.

Her Shadowblades and a group of Sunspears waited in a cluster of towering boulders. A tall, broad-shouldered Spear leaped forward to wrap Max in a hard hug—Giselle's Sunspear Prime. He was soot-stained, and streaks of blood marked his arms and chest. His shirt had been slashed to ribbons. Despite that, he radiated strength and command.

"Max—it's about time you showed up. We thought maybe you took off for Machu Picchu and left us to play with the angels by ourselves." He yanked her to the side as his glance fell on Alexander. His voice dropped into a threatening growl. "Who's this?"

The two stared hard at each other, and Alexander could feel the brutal power of the Sunspear Prime. He bristled, his teeth baring.

"Relax, Oz. He's one of mine. His name is Alexander."

That did not alleviate the other man's suspicion, but

he reluctantly turned his attention back to Max, who had slid out of his grasp.

"How bad is it down below?"

Alexander noticed that the whites of his eyes were turning gray, and black threads embroidered the underside of his skin, stitching up from the collar of his shirt and across his face. He was a Sunspear and the night was poisoning him—all of them. He had another hour at most before he dropped dead. It would worsen much more quickly if he had to draw on any of his spells.

"Part of the hall collapsed. It took the circle and star with it," she said, the words clipped. Even as Alexander watched, she was pulling inward, going deep. It was like watching her strip away a human skin and let the beast inside out. It was beautiful and terrifying, because whatever minuscule sense of personal safety she carried with her disappeared with that vestige of humanity. "Aulne Rouge's witch Selange is down there. She's helping Giselle with the shield. They won't be able to hold it long with the angels going at it the way they are. We need to stop them."

"We've thrown everything we have at them. Guns, RPGs, arrows, even a damned flamethrower. Nothing fazes them," Niko said, looking haggard. "The fuckers don't even notice."

"What about the voodoo artillery?"

Alexander frowned. Voodoo artillery? Practitioners of the craft did not often consort with witches.

"It isn't real voodoo. It's what she calls magic weapons."

He looked down in surprise at Akemi. The small Asian woman was as dirty and bloodstained as everyone else. She met his surprised glance and looked back at Max.

"She trusts you," she said softly. "She wouldn't let you walk behind her if she didn't. Don't even think about screwing her over or I'll stick a knife in your ear."

Akemi stepped away and Alexander did not doubt the threat was real.

"Down!" someone shouted. In one swift movement, they dove beneath the level of the shield. Alexander was slower, and Niko swept his legs from beneath him, dropping him hard.

The two angels had tired of circling and had closed on one another. Xaphan erupted with a burst of fire, more potent than the flames of a jet engine. It blasted like a laser at Tutresiel, who smashed the column with his sword. When he did, the magic exploded like a nuclear bomb. Azure light coruscated away in every direction. It burned like acid, and Alexander's skin was suddenly covered with blisters and weeping sores. A powerful wind scoured the ruined mountainside, scraping his ulcerated skin and filling the air with ash. It was bitter and cold and smelled of sulfur and ozone. Alexander clutched at the ground to keep from being blown away.

The earth trembled and lurched and a high-pitched screech rose from deep inside the mountain. It knifed through Alexander's skull and he slammed his palms to his ears. His companions did the same.

It let up after twenty seconds, and the ground settled with a series of quivering shudders. Alexander stood as the others did, too. His skin was rough and red, the wounds healing quickly. Alexander's stomach clenched.

All that power and the bastards were not even trying to hurt Horngate or its defenders.

"Shield's gone," someone said.

There was no way to tell if it had shattered or contracted below the level of the ground.

"We have to stop them now," Max said. "Or there won't be anything left of Horngate."

"Brilliant idea," mocked Lise, a shotgun propped on her shoulder. "Wish we'd thought of it earlier." She yawned exaggeratedly, the black threads beneath her skin thickening even as Alexander watched. Pain was etched in grooves around her mouth and eyes. "If you've got a plan, let's hear it. It's past time for my nap."

"I need to talk to them."

Dead silence followed, and a rapid exchange of incredulous looks. Alexander sympathized. It sounded like a joke.

Tyler spoke first. "Are we supposed to laugh?"

Max just shook her head. "We're going to divide into two groups and hit them simultaneously." She looked at Alexander. "Can you swipe the sword with that Jedi mind trick of yours?" She accompanied the question with a wiggle of her fingers near her eyes.

Slowly he nodded. "I have to be close—within four feet. And it would help if he was distracted and I was not."

She looked at Oz, who stood with his arms crossed, his jaw jutting. "You're serious. You want to try to talk to them." His voice was even, but a dangerous thread of contempt twined the words. His eyes were hot and hard as he stared at her, and Alexander felt a sudden thrust of jealousy.

"I think I might be able to convince them to stop. And we can't beat them by force."

"You *think* you *might* be able to convince them? You don't inspire a lot of faith. It sounds like a suicide mission."

"It might be," Max agreed. "But it might work, too. Unless you have another idea that has a snowball's chance in hell of working? Because standing around here with our thumbs up our asses looks like it might get us killed, too."

Oz's expression tightened, his eyes narrowing to slits. The muscles in his shoulders bunched as if he was working hard to restrain himself. Alexander could sympathize. Finally Oz gave a slight shake of his head. "No."

"All right, then let's go before you Sunspears drop dead," she said.

Despite her cold words, there was concern in the look she turned on him. He made a wry face of understanding. Something moved between them. It was the silent, charged communication of long familiarity. Alexander resisted a nearly overwhelming urge to step between them. That would not win him any points with Max.

She divided them up, and Alexander found himself on a team with Niko, Akemi, Lise, and Oz. They were joined by five more Shadowblades and three other Sunspears. The rest were to go with Max.

"Do any of our weapons slow them down at all?" she asked Oz.

"Pisses them off mostly. They don't seem to have an aversion to iron, salt, rowan—pretty much anything we have to throw at them. Mistletoe worked a little on Xaphan's fire, but we used it all. None of the voodoo artillery worked worth a damn. We hit them with RPGs and it knocked them ass over teakettle, but they came flying back like nothing happened."

"Do you have any RPGs left?"

"A few."

"Then use them on Tutresiel. Get him on the ground and Alexander close enough to get the sword out of his hand." She swiveled her head to look at Alexander. "I don't suppose you have any idea how to kill an angel?"

He shook his head. "They all have an Achilles' heel somewhere, but each one is different, and as far as I know, all the lore says that only angels can kill angels. Undoubtedly the Guardians can as well, but they are not exactly on our side tonight."

"All right. Then we do what we can. Get his sword away from him and try to tangle him up for a few minutes."

"And Xaphan? How will you get at him?" Alexander asked suspiciously.

Oz gave him a sharp look, then turned expectantly to Max.

She shrugged. "I'm going to get his attention. I think he'll talk to me. After all, I owe him a debt."

"You what?" Oz demanded. "Are you out of your fucking mind? There is no way I'm letting you near him. He'll make a puppet out of you."

"No, he won't," Max said in a cold, metallic voice. It brooked no argument. "You've got sixty seconds to get ready and then we move out."

The gathered Shadowblades and Sunspears jumped as if whipped. They scattered and returned with their weapons. Oz went with them. When he returned, he handed Max a .45 and a belt full of clips. Someone nudged Alexander, and he turned. Akemi held out a Redhawk revolver and a box of shells.

"Thanks," he said as he took it, shoveling the shells into his front pockets.

"I want it back," she said. Then: "Can you really get the sword away from him with your mind?"

"I will do whatever it takes to buy Max the time she needs with Xaphan."

"Would you die for her? For us?"

He glanced down at her. Her suspicion made her belligerent. His lip curled, his eyes narrowing. She flinched from the malevolence that rolled off him. "Wouldn't you?" he asked softly, then he fell in behind Oz as they started down toward the angels' battlefield. As Max and her team split off, he wished for a moment to say something, though if he had been given the moment, he was not sure what it would have been.

"Mondays suck," Niko muttered, and someone laughed.

"Look on the bright side," Lise said. "This might be our last. Never have to deal with another Monday or Mercury in retrograde or someone leaving the cap off the toothpaste."

"Not to mention no more getting Magpie mad and eating charred food for three days straight," Tyler said.

"And no more of Max's workouts," someone else groaned. "She broke my ribs in twelve places last time."

"Don't forget Montana winters. No more endless fucking winters," another voice chimed in.

"I wouldn't miss Britney Spears. Or *American Idol*. Or road construction."

"What about Microsoft Windows?"

"Or the IRS?"

And so it went as they marched into battle against creatures they had no hope of beating. No one mentioned what they would miss. Or whom. But Alexander could not help but think that he had a lot more to lose today than he had a week ago. He was not going to let it go easily.

The two angels were circling each other again. They were eerily silent except for the metallic clash of Tutresiel's wings. Flames fell in droplets from Xaphan's wings, and once again the mountain caught fire. Tutresiel's sword wove through the smoky air as he prepared to strike.

Oz stopped and they clustered together. "We have to get him on the ground. We'll hit him with everything at once. If he drifts low enough, try to pull him down. Watch his wings. They'll chop you to bits. Get into position. I'll signal you to fire." He paused, looking around at each one. "It's been a pleasure knowng you." There were nods and murmurs. "Let's get on with it."

They scattered in a ragged semicircle. Oz and Akemi flanked Alexander on his left and right. The Sunspear Prime wasted no time. When all were in place, he pumped his fist in the air.

The angel was no more than fifty feet in the air. Six RPGs struck and exploded nearly simultaneously. The air shook with the concussion, and heat flashed outward. Tutresiel went careening. Alexander followed at a run. Akemi and Oz clung to his flanks like burrs. She had a crossbow and was firing iron-tipped rowan bolts as fast as she could. Every bolt struck and bounced uselessly away. Now came the rapid popping of gunfire and more explosions.

Tutresiel tumbled, the sword slashing wildly through the air. Alexander narrowed his attention on the angel's hands and the hilt of the incandescent sword. Witch-light shouldn't have bothered his eyes, but looking at it made his eyes hurt and splotches marred his vision. He knew that before long his retinas would burn out and he would not be able to see. Tutresiel floundered, rolling through the air, heading for the ground. At the last moment he seemed to find his bearings, but he couldn't stop his momentum. He slammed into the ground and tumbled head over heels, his wings chopping gouges out of the rock.

A moment later, Tutresiel rolled lightly to his feet. Alexander was right behind him. He rushed forward, ducking under the half-furled wing and slamming against the angel's legs with every ounce of muscle he had. It would have shattered the bones of an ordinary human. Caught unawares, the angel sprawled forward. His wings raked Alexander as he rolled clear, and he felt his flesh part over his shoulders and ribs. Where the feathers sliced deeper, bone split as if cut by a laser. The pain was fierce, and blood ran down Alexander's back in a stream. He leaped to his feet. His left arm was heavy and lacked strength. He jumped onto Tutresiel's back between the roots of his wings and ground his knee into the angel's neck.

Tutresiel's hands were invisible inside the brilliant light of the sword. Already he was rearing up to throw off Alexander. Now others swarmed the angel. Alexander felt his fellow warriors as they flung themselves headlong onto Tutresiel. Oz slammed the angel's head with the butt of his gun.

Alexander took advantage of the moment. He reached out with mental hands and yanked Tutresiel's fingers away from the hilt of the sword. The angel clamped down tightly, defying Alexander's telekinesis. The Shadowblade responded by pressing his palms to the sides of his head and letting go of everything else. He poured all of himself into unlocking Tutresiel's hands.

He did not think he would be able to do it. The angel's strength was greater than he had imagined. He concentrated on the bones of Tutresiel's hands. They were made of some stuff much harder than ordinary bone. Alexander settled on the knuckles and crushed them one by one. He was quick. This sort of thing he had practiced. A moment later the hands had weakened enough that Alexander could tear them away. He used the last of his strength to send the sword skidding a few feet.

Alexander's head reeled and his vision was a gray fog. He thought it was Akemi who leapfrogged over him and ran to get the sword. He wanted to warn her not to touch it. But his voice was nothing better than a croak. She bent to grab it. Blue-white light flared like an exploding sun, blinding Alexander completely. A shrill scream rent the night and cut off suddenly.

He was bucked off the angel. He landed hard on his back, agony chewing at his wounds, and his breath left him in a gust. He lay still, gasping, unable to see. The fighting continued around him. There were screams and grunts, the thud of fists on flesh, the clash of Tutresiel's wings, gunfire and more explosions. Someone stepped on Alexander's thigh and someone else tripped over his stomach. He turned on his side, curling up to make himself smaller.

It was a minute or two before his eyes started to clear. It felt like years. He was helpless to do anything. His returning vision was blurry. He saw moving splotches of color in vague shapes. He shook his head. Every moment sharpened the world around him. He pushed himself to his feet, reeling from side to side. He had lost a lot of blood. His healing spells were trying to close the wounds in his back, but he could feel a *wrongness* there—an infection of prickling, festering magic from Tutresiel's wings. His healing spells were fighting hard, but Alexander did not know if they could win.

He staggered in a circle, assessing the situation. The angel had regained his feet, but not his sword. He crouched on the ground, his wings spread wide. Lumps scattered around him indicated where the Horngate defenders had fallen. Five still stood on their feet, but Alexander could not make out who. He rubbed his eyes and shook his head. Pain rippled down his back and dug thorny fingers through his ribs. But now he was beginning to see details.

The sword lay beyond the ragged wall made by the five remaining defenders. Oz was one of them, and Niko. They were bloody. Oz could barely stand on his half-severed leg. His skin was heavily laced with the black tracery of night poisoning. He did not have much longer to live. Tutresiel was not entirely unscathed. Silvery-white blood trickled from several wounds on his head and chest, and his fingers were crooked from where Alexander had broken them. But even as he watched, they were straightening.

"You fight bravely," the angel said. "But you cannot truly harm me or Xaphan."

Before Oz could retort, Alexander spoke. "We know that."

Tutresiel slowly turned. His crimson eyes narrowed. "You spend yourselves freely on a war you know you will not win."

"We do not need to win."

That caught the angel up short. He remained crouched, his wings lifted as if he would launch straight up into the sky. But he was curious now, and that tethered him as surely as any shackles would have. Alexander had counted on it.

"What do you need?"

Time. He needed time for Max. Alexander examined Tutresiel. How was he going to buy it?

He thought he knew what she was going to say to the angels. But it was not his place to speak for her, and he could be wrong. He settled for the tantalizing bit of truth he did know. "My Prime wants to talk to you. To both of you."

Tutresiel's livid eyes widened. "Talk? What could some puny Shadowblade have to say to me? Begging will do no good."

"She does not beg," Alexander snapped, his jaw jutting. "She has something to offer. If you will wait, I believe it will be worth your while." He bit off each word, his teeth clicking together. "What do you have to lose but a little time?"

"The question is, what do I have to win?" Tutresiel countered as he stood with inhuman grace. "Anything you have I can take."

Alexander shook his head slowly, a deadly smile curving his lips. "Not everything."

The angel stared a long moment, then nodded. "Very well. If Xaphan will stay his hand, I will hear what she has to say. It should be entertaining at least. Where is she?"

Alexander looked across the waste. Max stood in front of Xaphan talking emphatically. He seemed to be listening to her. Then without warning, his wings swept forward and she was engulfed in billowing flames.

An animal sound ripped from Alexander's throat and he started running. He forgot about Tutresiel and Horngate. Every part of him was focused on that column of flame burning like a beacon in the night. But even as he ran, he knew he was too late. Max could not survive Xaphan's battle fire. Alexander's only thought as he skimmed over the ruined mountainside was that he was going to kill the angel. Somehow he was going to kill the bastard. But there was not enough vengeance to fill the sudden ragged hole that opened up in his chest. This was a pain he did not know if he could survive.

21

MAX SPLIT FROM OZ'S TEAM AND HOPED THAT they could stop Tutresiel long enough to let her speak to Xaphan. Now she knew what Scooter had meant when he said she couldn't beat them, but that she was the answer. Now if she could only convince them her plan was a good one.

The angels were circling each other. Xaphan's wings were glorious. They rippled with orange and blue flames. Droplets of fire fell to the blackened stone of the mountain. Where they landed, the rock ignited. Suddenly a loud barrage aimed at Tutresiel began. Max had been waiting for it. Her team shifted and spread out, preparing to fire on Xaphan.

"No," she said. "Leave him alone."

Beside her Tyler raised his brows. He lowered the RPG launcher from his shoulder. "Seems a bit silly carrying all this firepower around if we aren't gonna use it."

"It's a smoke screen. I didn't need the argument," she said.

"Which argument was that?"

"The one that said I'm insane and shouldn't bother trying this. Oz, Niko, and Alexander would've shit heifers and there's no time."

At Alexander's name, Tyler's brows went up again, but he was silent on the subject, saying instead, "You don't think any of the rest of us will argue with whatever it is you have in mind?"

"Nope," Max said. "You'll believe me when I say that this is Horngate's last chance and if I don't do it my way, then it won't work at all. You'll trust that I know what I'm doing, no matter how stupid it looks."

"How stupid is it going to look?" he asked warily.

"Like I'm out to win this year's Darwin award. Maybe next year's while I'm at it."

"And we just stand here and watch."

"No. You go help the others distract Tutresiel."

"Oz will chop my balls off. Niko and Akemi, too."

"The good news is that being that you're a Shadowblade, they'll grow back. If you survive."

A smile flickered and died. His face turned somber. He clearly didn't like this. But he didn't fight her either. "Good luck then. I'm buying the beer when this is over."

Max smiled. "Moose Drool?"

"Whatever the lady desires," he said with an ironic bow. But when he straightened, his expression was somber. "Try to be careful."

"I always try," she said with a little shrug.

"Not fucking well hard enough," he said, scowling.

"Sometimes it pays to go balls to the wall. Like now, for instance."

He glanced up at Xaphan, whose attention was fixed

on the embattled Tutresiel. "All right. Good luck. See you when I see you."

He gave a brash salute and jerked his head at the rest of their team, who followed him reluctantly. They had all heard the exchange and liked leaving Max no more than Tyler did. But Max was Shadowblade Prime, and in the end her word was their law.

She didn't watch them go. Instead she looked up at Xaphan.

"Come down," she called. "I've got something to say to you. That is, if you aren't too busy destroying my covenstead."

His head tilted toward her. His crimson eyes glowed and his skin was fiery with the reflected light of his wings. He dropped to the ground, his flaming black wings extended wide.

"Ah. I wondered where you were," he said. "I thought I would see you sooner. I didn't think you were one to lead from behind."

"I'm afraid I was late to the party." Max glanced over her shoulder. Tutresiel was on the ground. She looked back at Xaphan, raising her brows. "Friend of yours?"

His lip curled, in anger or pain, Max didn't know. "Don't you know?" he said softly. "We are not allowed friends. We exist only to serve."

Max thought of Alexander and the way her Shadowblades had staked a claim on her after the Conclave. Friends she had, whether she wanted them or not. More than that—they were her family. Up until a few days ago, that would have made her want to slash the ties with a rusty machete, but today she found she was strangely pleased to be tethered to them.

"I might be able to help with that," she said, knowing that Tutresiel could return to the battle at any moment. She had to make this quick. And convincing.

He frowned. "Help with what?"

"What if you didn't have to serve Hekau anymore?"

He jerked back, then snarled, his crimson eyes narrowing to slits. His wings stretched high, like he would strike her down with them. Max didn't let herself flinch.

"You're a bitch," he said, his voice guttural with hate and anger. "I will serve her until I die, and I am immortal."

"Yeah, right. I know all that chapter and verse. But humor me; what if you didn't have to? What if you could be bound here to Horngate instead?"

"I can't, and why would I want to put my head in the noose of a weak witch when I serve one of the most powerful Guardians?"

"Giselle won't live as long as Hekau. And you're stronger than she is. You'll gain your freedom eventually."

A longing Xaphan couldn't hide suffused his face. Then his expression twisted with hatred. "Enough games. Is this all you had to say to me?"

Max stepped forward until she was close enough to touch him. "It isn't a game. I can do this for you. And Tutresiel, too. I can break your bindings. But only if you bind yourself to Horngate."

"It is impossible," he said through gritted teeth. Then a wild insanity flashed through his eyes. "I will teach you to lie," he whispered.

Suddenly his wings snapped forward, curving around Max. Flames exploded around them both, billowing upward in a whirlwind of fire. It didn't touch her, but her skin began instantly to blacken. Her hair melted. Her eyes cooked and in moments she was blind. Agony swept her. She could feel her blood boiling. Stabbing pains lanced through her chest. The air was gone. She could not breathe. All she could do was suffer. Escape was impossible.

She'd failed.

But he wasn't done with her. Xaphan pulled her close against his alabaster chest, his mouth close against the hole in her head that marked where her ear had been. Max had thought her pain could get no worse. She was wrong. His touch chewed through her like a chain saw. She screamed, but was incapable of sound.

"Why? Why did you do this? I did not think you could be so cruel. I thought you understood." The words were harsh with a vast anguish that spoke of too many horrors suffered, and too many dreadful deeds committed. Max understood that.

She needed to make words, but could not. The heat had charred her throat and lungs. She was dying. Her heart fluttered. She felt its uneven beat throb through every screaming nerve. It slowed, and gray erased the edges of her mind. She should have felt relief. Instead she fought to stay alive, to speak.

One word. If she could muster just one word and push it out through her ruined mouth.

One word that would make him understand that she had not lied.

Promise.

No one made promises in the world of the Uncanny and Divine. It was bad enough to acknowledge a debt.

But promises went deeper than magic or memory or blood; they were bonds that could never be broken.

Max struggled to form the word. She forced her desiccated tongue to shape the syllables, pushing the word through the charcoal tissues of her throat and beyond her teeth. She could not feel her lips, if she even had them.

It was a mighty effort, but too little, and far too late. Her heart spasmed and she went rigid.

Then coolness seeped through her. Where it touched, the pain leached away. It swallowed her, shielding her from the heat. Slowly she became aware that she was pressed close against Xaphan, his arms wrapped around her, one hand stroking the back of her neck. His forehead was pressed to her shoulder.

As her vision returned, she could see that the conflagration still surrounded them. But she did not feel the heat. She licked her lips—*she licked her lips*. Somehow Xaphan was healing her.

He did not let go of her as he lifted his head. His expression was tortured. "Tell me," he said.

Max babbled, wasting no time. "I let the Hag in Julian feed on my blood. She gave me a hailstone in return. I used it to make the Guardians forget Horngate ever existed. I made them forget everyone who belongs to Horngate. If it worked, and if you were bound to us, then Hekau would forget you. I promise it's the truth."

He gaped, his arms flexing so hard that Max felt her bones creak. She did not fight him. That was the last thing she needed to do right now.

"Do you have proof?" he rasped.

She shook her head. "No." Only actually doing it would say for certain. "What have you got to lose?"

She knew the answer. Nothing. And everything. Hope was a treacherous thing. Letting it grow only to have it ripped up by the roots could do more damage to him than his fire had done to her.

"If it fails, I will still have to destroy Horngate." His jaw was rigid and she could read the pain etching grooves around his eyes and mouth. His compulsion spells were grinding on him.

Max took a sudden breath as an idea struck her. *Could it be so simple?* But of course it was. She had told Giselle so. Words like *promise* and *owe* meant something to creatures like her and Xaphan. They meant more than any spell or compulsion. Those words were carved into their souls because they were offered freely, straight from the heart. No binding could tie anyone tighter.

She pushed back slightly. His arms loosened, but he did not let go. It was as if she were his anchor in a far greater maelstrom than the fire that whirled around them.

"I ask you for your word. Promise me that you will protect and serve Horngate in the best way you know how."

It was like she'd slugged him. His face went slack and every muscle in his body knotted. "What is this?" he whispered. "What are you asking?"

"There is no binding stronger than your word given freely. Promise me to protect and serve Horngate, and that's all I need."

"All *you* need? What about your witch?"

Max smiled slowly. "This isn't about her. She may be the heart of the covenstead, but the rest of us are its blood and its teeth. She'll accept. I promise that, too."

"Can you?"

The fact was that Giselle wouldn't like it one bit. She'd want more guarantees. But she couldn't have them, not today. Besides, if Xaphan broke his promise, he wouldn't be part of Horngate anymore, and then Hekau would come for him. It was powerful motivation.

"All I need—all Giselle needs—is your word," Max said firmly.

He started to speak, then coughed. His body tremored and his neck corded as he struggled against his compulsion spells. "You have it. I promise to protect and serve Horngate to the best of my ability," he rasped as silvery blood flowed down his nose and out his mouth.

As soon as the words were out, a wave of power pulsed through the air. It swept away from them, shredding the wall of flames.

Max grinned, her body going weak with relief. Holy crap. It worked. "Welcome to the family."

"Family?" he repeated dazedly.

There was no time to reply. They were surrounded by Sunspears and Shadowblades. A bristling Alexander was at her left shoulder, his gun aimed at Xaphan's forehead. On the right was Niko, his gun a scant two inches from the angel's eye.

"Let her go," Niko ordered.

Xaphan smiled and let his arms fall. Max stepped back, feeling giddy. Her body throbbed with remembered pain but her heart was racing. She wanted to jump up and down.

"You do realize you can't actually kill him, right?" she asked the two men. "And he can probably burn you to a crisp before you get off more than a couple of shots."

Gently she pushed both of their arms up. "Anyway, it's all right. He's one of us now."

"One of us?" Niko echoed incredulously. He wasn't the only one.

She turned and glanced around the circle, frowning at how few remained. Oz was on his feet, but his skin was mostly black, dappled here and there with patches of healthy-looking flesh. He slumped, leaning hard against Tyler.

"That's right," she said crisply, her jaw jutting. "He belongs to Horngate. Now I want all the Sunspears under cover. Take them around to the Mossy Log entrance." She glanced at Xaphan. "Can you put out your fires?"

He nodded and leaped into the air. He quickly disappeared into the smoke.

"Alexander, Niko, and Tyler stay with me. The rest of you, help the Sunspears inside, then come back for the wounded."

They responded instantly. Oz tried to fight them, but was dragged away. Max turned to eye Tutresiel. He stood thirty feet away, his wings folded, his sword braced against his shoulder. He was waiting for her. How the hell had they managed to get him to do that? Max strode toward him, her mouth dry. Xaphan had been willing to listen because they'd shared a fragile bond from their first meeting. Tutresiel was a stranger.

"Do you know what you're doing?" Niko asked beside her.

"Yes," she said tersely, and hoped it was true.

The angel waited, his legs planted wide. He wore leather biker pants with zippers up the sides of his lower legs and heavy boots. The pants were charred and holed from the

RPGs and bullets. His torso was bare, the scraps of his shirt on the ground beside him. Streaks of silvery blood decorated his skin, mixing with smudges of black char.

He watched Max, his face brooding. "I am told you want to talk to me." He looked up as Xaphan dropped out of the sky to land behind Max. His black brows rose as he lifted his sword from his shoulder. "Are you ready to begin again?"

"It depends on what you decide," the fire angel said.

"Decide? About what?"

"Joining Horngate," Max said. She held up a hand before he could rake her over the coals. "Just hear me out. If you're like Xaphan, you're not any happier serving your Guardian than he is. If that's the case, I want to offer you a deal. You can join Horngate and you will be free of Marduk."

Tutresiel sneered, but he couldn't look away from Xaphan. "That's impossible." He didn't sound all that certain.

"It is possible," Xaphan said with a sort of childlike wonder.

"How?"

"She swallowed a Hag's hailstone and made a wish that the Guardians would forget Horngate and anyone who belongs to the covenstead."

That caught Tutresiel up short. "You believe her." It wasn't really a question.

"It's true. I have bound myself to this coven. I am free of Hekau. You saw the magic of the binding."

"You bound yourself?" Now Tutresiel was surprised.

"I promised to protect and serve Horngate," Xaphan said. "It was enough."

"So now the question is, do you want the chance to join the covenstead?" Max asked.

"And if I don't?"

She gave a tight smile. "We go back to fighting you. And if the covenstead is destroyed in the process, then you and Xaphan go back to running errands for your Guardians, and we become fertilizer."

"And if I agree?"

Max stepped forward until she was a couple of inches away from the sword. She met his crimson gaze, reading the hope that warred with cynicism and hostility. "Then you have to promise to protect and serve Horngate to the best of your ability."

"What if I lie?"

She smiled slowly. "Then the binding won't take and we'll go back to fighting. Thing is, though, Xaphan has a whole lot more motivation to win than he used to." She hesitated. "I'm not saying you get out of jail free, though. You know what's coming. The war is going to get ugly and Giselle doesn't mean to be a pawn in it. We won't sit here behind a curtain of forgetting while the rest of the world goes to hell. She wants to build a sanctuary here, and she'll want you to help. All you're doing is changing masters."

His lip curled. "You might do better luring me with honey rather than salt."

"Salt is the meal. I tell it like I see it. No surprises, no lies. Just plain, unvarnished truth. If you are going to choose us, you do it with full disclosure. I don't want to hear you whining later."

He didn't immediately respond, his gaze settling on Xaphan behind her. Max wondered what was going on in his head. She had little enough sense of him. That he listened at all showed both that he wanted to snap his tether, and that he acted thoughtfully.

Finally he gave a slow nod, and the white fire of his sword faded until the blade appeared to be normal steel. His hands tightened and his body went rigid. He opened his mouth and no sound came out. His face contorted and he staggered back and fell to one knee. His body convulsed and the sword clattered to the ground. He doubled over, catching himself with his hands. A web of blue magic wrapped him, and he flung himself backward with a harsh scream, his wings scraping and chopping wildly. Someone grabbed Max to drag her out of the way, and she shrugged the hands off. She needed to witness this. She stepped closer.

The magic web began to solidify, cocooning him in a solid shell. Tutresiel was swept by a seizure, his arms and legs kicking and twitching, his body bucking wildly. Max hesitated, then did something supremely stupid. She flung herself on top of him. Electricity zapped her like she'd plugged her finger into a transformer. Her hair rose on end and her muscles seized.

"Say it!" she urged, her body spasming, tears streaming down her face. "Say it!"

The words were broken and sounded as if they were cut from his throat with his own sword. "I . . . swear . . . to serve and . . . protect Horngate . . ."

Once again a wave of power rushed away as the binding took. The attacking blue magic vanished, and Max slumped on top of him. "I need a fucking nap," she muttered.

Hands pulled her up. Alexander and Niko held her

between them. Her legs were like jelly. Tutresiel hadn't moved. He looked at her, his expression bemused. "It worked."

"Yeah. Welcome to the nuthouse," she said. A moment later she felt strong enough to push away from Niko and Alexander. She turned to look at the carnage of the battle. There were too many bodies. Her chest ached as a different pain lodged there. It wasn't going away soon, she knew. Who was dead? She could see at least ten bodies. "Let's check for survivors. Take the wounded Sunspears first. They need to get out of the night as soon as possible."

She glanced at Xaphan, her jaw rigid so that she wouldn't scream. "That healing trick of yours—can you help them?" He nodded and went to examine the closest body. She looked at Tutresiel. "What about you?"

He shook his head. "I have no ability to heal. I will help ferry them inside, if you will show me the way."

"Follow me," Niko said. His expression was a mask of grief. He was holding Lise. She was bloody, her skin charcoal gray.

"Give her to me and run," Tutresiel ordered, holding out his arms.

His sword was gone. Max had no idea where it had gone. Niko hesitated, then allowed the angel to take her. He immediately turned and started running. Tutresiel leaped into the air, skimming over the ground right behind, his wings pumping powerfully.

Max drew a breath and tried to make herself go to the cold place inside where she couldn't feel the horror of losing the lives of the people she had sent to die. Family. Dead family.

Alexander was kneeling over someone. He turned him onto his back and checked his pulse. Kamikani. Alexander looked up at Max, sympathetic sorrow coloring his expression. She looked away, feeling the glacial walls inside her starting to crack. She needed that cold strength now. There was still work to do. Selange was inside with all her Shadowblades and Giselle, and the moment the angel battle stopped, she'd have realized that Max succeeded. It wouldn't take her two seconds to decide to snatch Horngate for herself. But to do that, she'd have to kill Giselle.

"Finish this," she ordered over her shoulder as she sprinted across the scorched battlefield as fast as she could go.

22

MAX DIDN'T HEAD FOR THE MOSSY LOG ENtrance. Instead she headed up the mountain on an angle, up past Cougar's Leap, through Miner's Notch to the top of Elk Point. All the trees here had burned to ash and the ground still smoked, though true to his word, Xaphan had put out the fires. She reached the hatch she was looking for. It had been buried beneath a thick layer of leaf meal and huckleberries, but was now carpeted with soft, hot ash. Max brushed it away. The latch was melted and fused. She dug her fingertips into the crack between the door and its jamb and yanked upward. The warm steel stretched and tore. She grabbed the sharp edges and ripped them apart, slicing her hands. The metal groaned and screeched. In seconds she had a hole big enough to pass through.

On the other side was a shaft like the one she and Alexander had climbed up out of. It had been too far away to suffer damage from the magic of Tutresiel's sword blows. Max swung down and gripped the top rung, her feet finding purchase lower. There was no time to climb down. She hooked her boots around the outside of the ladder and grasped the sides. She loosened her fingers and began to slide down.

The skin and flesh of her palms turned raw and then shredded away. The blood only slicked the runners of her slide. Fifteen feet above the bottom she jumped, landing in a crouch and leaving behind a bloody handprint on the floor. She launched to her feet and was running in the same breath.

The underground warren that tunneled beneath Horngate was not laid out in any particular pattern. Rather it was a constellation of clusters of rooms and chambers connected by snaking passages. These circled a hub made up of the massive central hall, the kitchens, and common areas. Max ran through the maze, vaulting down entire flights of stairs. She'd lost the gun Oz had given her and stopped only once, at a weapons locker, jamming two knives into her back pockets and grabbing a shoulder holster and sliding it on. It already held a loaded .45 and four full clips. She chambered a shell and started running again.

The closer to the hall she got, the harder it was to get through. She climbed over rubble and squeezed through tiny crevices. More than once she had to retreat and try a new route. At last she came to the lofty outer chamber of the hall. Much of the timbered roof had collapsed, and with it, massive chunks of rock. Not a single pillar still stood, and the air was thick with dust. It was eerily silent except for a trickle of pebbles tumbling from above, and the crunch of debris beneath her feet.

The exit she and Alexander had used to leave the hall was still clear. Max eased up to it and peered inside.

The devastation was terrible. Smoke and dust choked

the air, though the fires were out. The long fissure gaped in the roof of the mountain, and Xaphan's battle fire had burned mercilessly through the hall. The smell of burned flesh turned Max's stomach. She heard moans and agonized whimpers. She scanned the wreckage. Where was Giselle? The spells that bound them together told Max that the witch was alive, but for how long? Selange would not wait to make her move, and make it she would—she needed the haven that Horngate would give her from the Guardians, and the fact that two angels were now bound to Horngate would only whet Selange's appetite more.

Max riveted on voices from the other end of the hall. She slid inside, creeping over the wreckage with predatory silence. The witches were not where she had left them. They had shifted across the hall and away from the fissure above. Ash stirred around her feet as Max passed. She hunched over, keeping her profile as small as possible.

She dropped down behind a tumbled chunk of granite, peering around it. Her mouth tightened. All she could see of Giselle was a hand and a wrist. Blood trickled between her swollen fingers. They were purpled and twisted, as if someone had crushed them beneath a boot. Max couldn't see the rest of her. She was hidden behind a pile of rubble and the surrounding bodies of Selange's Shadowblades. Max's compulsion spells jerked to a fine tautness. Twitches popped through her body like electrical shorts. She held herself tight. Bursting in wasn't going to help.

Slowly she inched closer, her gun raised and sighted in. She caught a glimpse of Selange between the thicket of her Blades.

"I said kill her," Selange said. "Stop wasting time."

"Didn't you hear her Prime? She'll hunt you down and kill you." It was Thor.

"Then I'll have you kill her, too, and every last member of the coven. I have to take control of the territory's *anneau* quickly, and it will be better if I take it from her as she dies. Marcus—now."

Selange's Prime stepped forward. Max was out of time. She dashed forward on silent feet as he bent down. Max ducked low until she found a clear angle between the enemy Shadowblades and leveled her gun, snapping off a shot. A red hole blossomed on the Prime's forehead. His head jerked back and he flopped onto his back. Instantly the rest of the Blades spun and formed up in a wall between Max and Selange.

None of them had weapons—Scooter had thankfully seen to that. But there were still eight of them and Max had no illusions that she could take them all on.

"Leave now and I'll let you live," she said, playing for time. Niko would bring backup as soon as he could.

"I don't think so," came Selange's cold voice. "I am about to kill your witch and take Horngate for myself. It is you who will die."

There was the thud of a foot hitting flesh. Giselle moaned, a weak, breathless sound. Max's compulsion spells exploded inside her. She *had* to move. She lunged, shooting at the Blades in front of her. She tried for head and heart shots to kill them or take them out of the equation for a few minutes.

But they were moving, too.

A long-haired woman fell, and a spike-haired man. She ran out of bullets before they converged on her, and then she was fighting. She kicked and struck, ducking and sliding between them as if it were a deadly dance. She hardly felt the blows that fell on her. Her compulsion spells had disconnected all sense of pain. Bones cracked. Her shoulder caved in and her arm dangled uselessly. Someone struck her on the back of her calves and she went down on her hip. She rolled and twisted to her feet. But her right leg was leaden.

She bulled ahead. Selange was not far now. Blood dripped down in Max's eyes. She slammed an elbow into the chest of the Shadowblades that lunged at her from the side. Bend, shoulder thrust, lift, flip. Her teeth gritted and she shook her head to clear her eyes. Someone slammed her from the side and she went sprawling onto her back. A hard kick to the ribs. A punch to the chest. Her breath exploded from her lungs and she couldn't get another. She gasped and gagged, tasting bile and blood.

She heard footsteps approach, and a wave of Selange's rich, floral perfume swept over her. Max clenched herself, trying to pull herself up. A heavy foot on her throat held her fast. She felt the brush of air as Selange knelt beside her and stroked a finger gently over Max's swollen, pulped lips.

"Where did Giselle find you? You're a pain in the ass, but I would have paid a steep price to own a Prime such as you. What a shame."

Max laughed, a broken, rattling sound. "Couldn't afford me, bitch," she coughed.

"And I can't afford to let you live." Selange rose and took a step back. "Finish her, Thor. Then her witch."

The foot moved off Max's throat. She waited for the

blow. It surprised her that now that death had finally come to get her, she didn't want it. She tried to roll to the side, but her body was too battered to obey.

Thor's hands slid gently around her jaw. "I'd rather not have to do this," he murmured so that only she could hear. "If you've got any tricks up your sleeve, now's the time."

"No sleeves."

"Then I've got no choice." He paused. "Alexander was right about you."

Was he? Max wondered hazily. *What was he right about?*

"They'll hunt you down. Selange will not survive the month," she whispered

Thor's hands tightened. In a moment he would snap her neck. Max twisted and kicked, but her heels only slid across the floor without finding purchase.

"Thor! Get on with it." Selange's voice was sharp with fear and eagerness.

But another voice cut across hers, implacable and cold as space. "Get your hands off her now."

Max stiffened. Tutresiel. She blinked, trying to see. She felt a caress of wind, and the dust and ash around her stirred, even as the clang of his feathers rang overhead.

"He's talking to you, asshole," Niko said from somewhere beyond her feet.

Thor's fingers relaxed fractionally. There were the sounds of scuffling.

"I'll slit Selange's throat if you don't step back now," Alexander said, his voice so full of rage that it sent goose bumps popping all over Max.

Thor let go, his thumbs sliding gently over Max's cheeks in something like an apology. He stood up. Instantly Niko was beside her. He pulled her to her feet, holding her upright. She could not stand on her own. Alexander had an arm around Selange's neck and a knife against her throat. As his gaze ran over Max, his arm tightened and the point of his blade dug into the witch's neck. She yelped. Thor tensed, and several of her remaining Shadowblades edged toward her.

Hands settled on Max's shoulders. She flinched and started to jerk away, but then felt a cooling flow of healing magic spreading through her. As good as it felt, Giselle was more important. She twisted out of Xaphan's grip. She could stand now, though her legs seemed made out of Silly Putty.

"See to Giselle. Please."

She motioned for the angel to go, then followed, leaning heavily on Niko. The witch lay on her back, one bloody arm flung over her head. Her skin was papery and clung to a body that seemed hardly more than a skeleton. Bruises mottled her arms and one eye, and there were scorches on her legs and chest. Xaphan crouched beside her, his wings lifted and lightly spread. He frowned as he laid one hand over her heart. He looked up at Max.

"She's very weak."

Max felt like she'd been kicked, and she didn't dare think about why. "Is she going to die?"

"No, but even with my help it will take her some time to recover. I cannot rebuild the flesh she lost to magic, nor can I renew endurance. She will need to be careful."

"Do what you can."

Max turned and started to fall. Niko caught her. She let him hold her as she looked at Selange. The witch was dusty, with a few cuts and bruises, but she was healthy enough. Max would have liked nothing more than to kill the bitch, but it wasn't her call.

"Put her on ice until Giselle can deal with her," she said to Niko. "The spell cages are probably short-circuited, and the same with the witch chains. Dose her with drugs and bind her. Keep her under so she can't draw on her magic, and put a witch circle around her in case she wakes up and tries to break free."

"And her Blades?"

Max eyed them. Most were wounded and healing slowly. "Bind them and lock them up. Make sure they get something to eat. When you're done with that, start searching this mess. Find out who's alive. Check the greenhouses."

"Right away." Niko looked at her, his brow furrowed. "What about you?"

"When Xaphan is done with Giselle, I'll have him do what he can for me and then I'll find her a bed and some food. That's another thing. Make sure all of you eat something and move all of our Sunspear and Shadowblade survivors inside." She rubbed a hand over her head. So much had to be done, and with the fissure in the roof, her Blades couldn't be in here once daylight hit.

"When will the Sunspears be ready to work?"

Xaphan answered. "I have given them healing, but they need food and rest. For the moment they are still weak. The sun will give them more strength."

"So sometime tomorrow?"

"Perhaps."

"What will you do with me?" Tutresiel landed beside her, his wings folding. His sword had disappeared again.

"Will you help look for survivors?"

"Do I have a choice?" The bitter anger had crept back into his voice.

"Not if you want to keep your oath," Max said, exhaustion and pain making her sway. She tensed her shaking legs. "It's up to you. Go back to your Guardian for all I care."

"One master isn't much different from another," he said scornfully.

"Look," Max said, impatience making her snap. "Stay or go. I don't care. The one thing Horngate can offer you is freedom from Marduk and no more compulsion spells. It's a home, if you want it. You made the oath and you are bound to Horngate and we need help. So get on it before I have to kick your ass."

She paused. The heavy feeling in her chest was more than exhaustion or the grief she'd been holding back at the deaths of so many. She was finding it hard to breathe. She panted shallowly, hearing a bubbling, liquid sound in her lungs. Darkness pressed against her brain. Her legs turned to liquid, and Niko's arm clamped around her. He shouted her name. She didn't answer. Instead she slid into sweet oblivion.

MAX WOKE WITH A JOLT. SHE FLUNG HERSELF UPRIGHT, braced to fight. Her hand tangled an IV pole and she barely caught it before it crashed to the floor.

"You are safe."

She jerked around. Xaphan was perched on the back

of a chair in the middle of the room, his wings folded, the flames flickering along the edges of the black feathers. He looked slightly drawn, his cheeks hollowed. His elbows rested on his bent knees with his hands linked loosely.

A quick scan of the room told Max that they were in Giselle's suite. The floor and walls were buckled and the furniture had been tumbled wildly. One wall had a spiderweb of cracks across it. She was standing on a mattress that had been dragged into the middle of the room, wearing nothing but underwear and a tee shirt. A tube ran from the IV pole to her hand. Beside her, Giselle lay on a gurney attached to two IVs. Her bruises had faded, but she was so pale her lips looked blue.

"How is she?"

"She'll live. You will, too, though you do seem to have something of a suicidal habit."

Max grinned. "You've been talking to Niko."

"I've been talking to everyone."

That caught her attention. "Everyone? Who? How many survived?"

He nodded. "Many took refuge in the greenhouses. They thought the hot springs would protect them from my fires. There were several injuries, but none will die."

Tears threatened Max again. She gritted her teeth. She was really getting soft. "Thank you."

He shrugged. "There must be something special about this coven. I've never seen any Sunspears or Shadowblades willingly fight so hard and suffer so much. It seems worth protecting. And I did make an oath."

"You and I both know that you can get around a lot with a few mental gymnastics," Max pointed out.

"Perhaps I think there might be something special here also," he said with a level look.

"Yeah, right," Max muttered. "How long have I been out?" She frowned. "What are you doing here with us?"

"You have slept for forty-two hours. It is now ten at night and the last of the sunlight is gone."

"What? You should have woken me!"

He shook his head. "You were hurt far more than you know. I healed you, but my healing is different from what your witch does for you. It takes longer and it is easy to pull it apart until it is done. You needed the sleep. And Horngate did not face any threats."

Max's stomach growled loudly. She ignored it. "Why are *you* watching us?" And not somebody more trust-worthy. She didn't say it.

He gave a little shrug, an odd look rippling across his expression. "They asked me to. They thought I could protect you best, and they do not trust Tutresiel."

"But they trust you?"

Again that odd look, a mix of uncertainty, incredulity, and exasperation. "You told them I was one of you. Apparently they need nothing else." He shook his head. "The loyalty they have for you is astonishing."

She flushed. "I need to go check on things. Are you all right here?" She paused. "How long has it been since you had a break?"

He smiled. "I am an angel. I don't need a break."

"Bullshit. But if you can hold on awhile, I'll send someone to spell you."

Her stomach growled again. She found a pile of clothing waiting beside the bed. It included her gun and holster and a pair of combat knives. She grabbed them all up and went into the wrecked bedroom to change. Surprisingly, the toilet in the bathroom worked. She eyed the shower wishfully, but contented herself with washing her face and hands, then found a brush and pulled it through her hair. The mirror had broken and the pieces had been swept up by someone. Just as well. She probably didn't want to see what she looked like.

She returned to the main room and went to stand beside Giselle.

"How long before she wakes up?"

"She's been in and out. She should not get up for another few days, and then she should take it easy."

"She will," Max said. "If I have to chain her down."

"Try it," Giselle said, and began to cough.

Max gave her a sip of water from a cup on a small side table. She was surprised at the relief she felt to hear Giselle's voice. She frowned. None of this changed what had happened between them. Yet it changed everything. She might not be ready to forgive, but Max thought she could agree to a truce. "You know what happened?"

Giselled nodded wanly. "You saved us."

"Yeah, well, I had a lot of help. Selange and her Blades are here and we have to do something with them. It's up to you."

"Send Selange home."

"Are you sure? She's going to be trouble. She's not a Guardian; she won't forget us. She's the type that will hold a grudge."

"There's been enough death, and her coven needs her."

Max nodded. "All right."

Just then the door cracked open. Max tensed, but it was only Magpie with a tray. She stopped inside the door, then strode in.

"About time you woke up," she said to Max as she set the tray on a hospital table and slid it over Giselle's bed. She punched the button to raise the back of the bed. "The kitchen is running. Get some food."

Max's stomach growled again and she nodded. "On my way. Just as soon as I deal with a couple of things."

That earned her a scowl from both Magpie and Giselle, but Max ignored them and headed for the door. She wanted Selange out of Horngate and Montana as soon as possible. There wasn't much night for them to use, so she'd better get them started right away.

Outside, the corridor was empty. She turned toward the hub. Her muscles felt a little like tapioca and she was light-headed. The sound of voices reached her, and she followed them toward the kitchen and dining commons on the north side of the great hall.

In forty-two hours, much of the debris from the magical quakes had been cleared away, though the damage could not so quickly be erased. Max wondered how stable the undermountain complex was.

The scent of cooking food wound around her in tantalizing coils. She drew in a deep breath, her mouth watering. She stepped inside the dining commons. The long rectangle had kitchen and cafeteria-style counters at one end and a scattering of tables. The place was deserted except for Oz and Lise and two other Sunspears. When she walked in, Oz thrust to his feet and wrapped his arms around her, pulling her tight against him and lifting her off her feet. Lise gave a catcall as Max returned the hug. Oz smelled of sweat and smoke and sunlight.

"Dammit, Max," he muttered, his forehead resting against hers. "I thought I told you not to do anything stupid."

"It worked," she pointed out.

"Yeah, and a lot of us are still alive, thanks to you." He straightened. "Are you going to join us?" He gestured at the table.

"In a while." She nodded a greeting to the other three. "I've got to go take care of Selange. Have you seen Niko or Tyler?"

"They are on guard duty. How's Giselle?"

"She's good. What about Tutresiel?"

"The angel?" His mouth tightened. "The bastard is around somewhere. He doesn't sit still long. I've got Derek keeping an eye on him."

Max nodded, not wanting to ask. She forced the question out. "How many did we lose?"

Pain carved deep grooves in his face. "Four of mine. So far. Liam could still go either way."

Tears burned her eyes. "And my Blades?"

He ran his hands up to her shoulders, sympathy and sorrow softening his gaze.

She looked away. "How many?"

He drew in a breath and slowly let it out. "Six. Giselle and Magpie are the only witches left of the *anneau*."

Slowly Max ran her fingers through her hair. An ache filled her, sharp and wild and more painful than she knew how to bear. So many dead. She couldn't bear to ask for names, not yet. She pulled away from Oz; she needed to be alone. "I've got to go. I'll see you later."

She backed away and strode back the way she'd come. Tears ran down her cheeks and she didn't wipe them away. She turned a corner and stopped, leaning back against the wall, her arms tight around her stomach.

"You survived," Tutresiel observed sardonically.

She scowled, turning her head to look at him. He stood a dozen feet away in the mouth of another corridor. She faced him, brushing away her tears roughly.

"I've been looking for you," she said.

"Have you?" he asked, his brows arching. His sharp cheekbones and crimson eyes made him look demonic.

"I need your help."

"Do you now? What for?"

"Come on."

She walked away and he fell in beside her. His wings made soft, metallic rubbing sounds as they walked. Max said nothing. She was searching for that cold, quiet place inside where pain gave her strength. It was elusive, and the ragged, aching hole inside her gaped wider.

Niko and Tyler were in the corridor outside the holding rooms. They grinned at Max as she approached.

"Good to see you upright," Niko said, his obvious relief belying his sardonic tone. His gaze shifted to Tutresiel and his expression turned cold.

"Giselle wants Selange and her Blades out of here now."

"She's going to just let them go?" Tyler asked.

"Except for Thor. He's mine. Let's do it."

They went inside. The circular room had steel doors running three-quarters of the way around. Niko yanked the levers free on one of the doors and yanked it open. Inside was a big cell. Selange's Shadowblades were laid out on the floor like cordwood. Just as Max and Alexander had been bound in Aulne Rouge, they'd been cocooned in wire-wrap straps. Tyler and Niko went in and sliced their legs free so they could walk. The six of them were filthy. They stood slowly, staggering and swaying as they eyed Max. All but Thor, who remained on the floor. He watched Max from lidded eyes.

"Out now, all of you," she ordered. "Get Selange," she told Niko.

"What are you going to do with Thor?" Alexander asked. He had come to the doorway of the prison room, two more of her Shadowblades on his heels. His expression was tight and closed, his dark eyes churning with emotions she didn't want to read.

"He and I have a score to settle," Max said. "I owe him."

"He was only following orders. You know he could not refuse."

"I know what he was doing," she said, then turned to Niko as he emerged from Selange's cell with the witch draped over his shoulder. She had been sedated and hung like a sack of potatoes. Like her Blades, she was still covered in ash and dust. Her bruises and cuts had not been healed, and dried blood still streaked her skin.

"Get the bitch out of here now." Max paused and her mask slipped. Her lips trembled. She firmed them, speaking with quiet implacability. "Akemi's truck is down on the road. You'll need to pick it up. Alton, too. Giselle will want to talk to him. Tutresiel, I want you to follow Selange and make sure she leaves Montana. No stragglers. Now get moving. They need all the night they have left."

She ignored Alexander's taut, searching look as he helped herd the Shadowblades out. He hesitated as he passed, but her expression was forbidding. He gave a jerky nod, his mouth pulling tight, and left. Niko lingered, looking like he wanted to say something, then he followed Alexander. Finally it was just Tutresiel and Max. She glared at him.

"Well? Got something you want to say?"

"You are not going to tell me to kill them? It's stupid to leave them alive. Sooner or later they will be back—probably sooner."

She shook her head, sighing heavily. Hunger was making her start to shake. "Just make sure they don't double back."

He gave a mocking bow. "As you wish."

With that he left. Max took a breath. One last thing to do, then she could grab some food and go find a hole to crawl into and lick her wounds in peace.

She went to a cabinet on the wall and withdrew a vial, syringe, and plastic case with ZOLL BIPHASIC RBW in block letters on the front. So armed, she went to kneel beside Thor in the big corral cell.

"Good to see you made it," he said, his voice raw and cracked.

"Thanks to you taking your time."

He made a movement that might have been a shrug, then gave a pained grin. "Why I am still here?"

"Because I owe you." She reached out and rubbed her thumb over his cheek where Scooter had marked him. It had told her that Thor didn't belong to Selange, not really. At least not willingly.

"How would you like to join my Shadowblades?"

His eyes widened, then he sucked in a gasping breath, his chest arching off the floor. "I can't," he rasped. Pain twisted his expression.

"I know. But I think I can help with that. And unless you flat out tell me no right now, I'm going to do it. For what I owe you, and because Horngate can use you." She silently counted out ten seconds. His head knocked hard against the floor. The tendons of his neck corded and his teeth clenched as his compulsion spells tortured him, trying to force him to say no.

"All right then. So you don't want to say no. Time for you to die." With her one hand, she flipped the top of the vial open, then hesitated. "I've been thinking about this a lot, and I think it will work. Your compulsion spells are tied to your life. When you die, they should let go. The only problem is that once your heart stops, the odds of me waking you up are close to zero. If this was a reliable way to break bindings, everyone would be doing it."

She looked at him, silently asking the question. He squeezed his eyes shut and gave the faintest nod. It was all she needed. She poured a droplet of the brown, viscous liquid out of the vial onto his forehead. It sank in and disappeared like rain on parched earth. Thor's body spasmed and shuddered, then shook with convulsive tremors. A moment later his eyes rolled back into his head and he slumped dead.

Max counted the seconds as she drew a knife and began cutting away the wire ties. She tore his shirt open, exposing his muscled chest sprinkled with curly blond hair. Thirty seconds. She waited. At last she saw the bindings unravel. The neon blue tendrils curled away, shriveling up until they disappeared. Quickly Max unlatched the defibrillator case and flipped it open. She grabbed the bottle of gel and tore it open with her teeth, spitting out the lid and squirting gel onto the paddles and rubbing them together. She toggled the machine on and set it to three hundred joules. Only higher settings worked for Shadowblades and Sunspears, if defibrillation worked at all. She pressed the paddles to his chest and pushed the button with her knee. The jolt lifted him off the floor. Next she snatched the syringe and ripped away its wrapping. The needle was a good eight inches long. She jammed it into his heart and thumbed down the plunger, flooding his heart with adrenaline, then hit him again with the defribrillator. She began compressions on his chest while the machine recharged.

"Come on, dammit," she muttered.

She hit him again with a jolt of electricity and pumped his chest some more. Ten compressions and then she bent and opened his mouth, pinching his nose shut. She drew a breath and blew into his lungs carefully. Too hard and she'd rupture them. Another breath. She sat up and grabbed the paddles again as the machine beeped its readiness at her. She set the paddles against his chest again and moved to press the button.

"Don't," he groaned, and coughed, turning onto his side. His muscles clenched and he threw up. A thin spattering of clear liquid was all that came out. Max cut the rest of the cable ties and waited. He stayed that way for about five minutes, before he recovered enough to sit up, rubbing at the welts on his arms.

"Now let me ask you again, do you want to join Horngate? You don't have to. You can walk away free as a bird."

He frowned at her. "I'm bound to Selange." Then he sat up straighter, his eyes widening. "Wait a minute. I feel . . ." He surged to his feet, his hands running through his long hair as if searching. He locked his fingers behind his neck and folded his elbows to his head. "I can't fucking believe it. I really am free, aren't I?"

"Dead will get you that way," Max said, packing the defibrillator back up. She picked up the poison vial and carefully snapped the lid back on. "So what do you want to do?"

"Eat," he said instantly. "I'm so hungry I could eat a bear, hide and all."

"I'll feed you," she said with a tired grin. She couldn't believe it worked. For years she'd daydreamed about finding someone to kill her and bring her back, but she didn't trust anyone enough, and she didn't want to risk dying before she could pay Giselle back. "But I need to know if I've got to walk with a gun at your back or not."

He dropped his arms and cocked his head to the side. "You're serious. You took Alexander and you'll take me, too. Why?"

"Lately I've been told I'm stupid. And just a little bit insane."

He grinned at her. "Alexander said you were a Prime worth serving."

She made a rude gesture. "No one serves me."

"Wanna bet? All right. I don't have anyplace else I want to be. I'll stay."

"Then make an oath. Right now. Promise me you'll protect and serve Horngate to the best of your ability."

His brows rose. "That's it?"

"As far as I'm concerned. Giselle will probably demand more."

He rubbed his hand across his stubbled jaw. He nodded. "I promise that I'll protect and serve Horngate to the best of my ability. Until I die."

A shimmer wash of pale yellow magic swirled around him and was gone. Max shook her head. "You shouldn't have put a time limit on it. If you want to leave here, I'll have to kill you again and you almost didn't wake up this time."

He smiled, hooking his thumbs in his belt loops. "See, the truth is, I'm not actually as dumb as I look. I know a good thing when it runs a cattle prod through my chest. Alexander was right about you, and now that you let me in the door, I don't mean to get away easily."

"You're both dumber than a box of rocks," Max muttered as she went to put the defibrillator away. Thor was waiting behind her when she turned around. She sighed. "Come on. Let's get some food."

23

ALEXANDER RETURNED TO THE COVENSTEAD WITH a leaden stomach. It was Max's right to have her revenge on Thor—he had tried to kill her, and he was the next likely choice for Selange's Prime. It made sense both strategically and personally to kill him. But Alexander should have tried harder to stop her. He owed Thor. He should have fought for him.

Niko parked the truck near the massive greenhouses. They still stood with little damage. A miracle of magic. The plants inside had not fared so well. They had dried to tinder.

"What the hell do we do with this rock?" Tyler asked as they climbed out.

"It's not just a rock. It's the Hag," Alexander said, rubbing the back of his neck.

"Seriously?"

"Yes." he said.

"Let's leave it—her—here for now," Niko said. "Giselle or Max will tell us what they want to do with it."

They walked back to the entrance to the underground compound. No one spoke to Alexander, though their silence did not seem angry or resentful. It was more somber and mystified. Too much had happened, and Alexander was hardly important in the scope of it all.

Inside they stayed together as they wandered down to the kitchen. He hoped Max would be there. He wondered if they all felt the same way. They needed to be around her. They needed the comfort of her strength, and they needed to reassure themselves that she was still alive. He was no different from any of them.

She was not there. Instead when he walked in, he found Thor sitting at a table with Lise. She was watching him shovel enchiladas into his mouth with a cynical smile. She looked up and her smile widened. Thor lifted his head and set his fork down.

"I suppose you're another one of us, too," Niko said sourly, crossing his arms.

Thor stood slowly. "I guess I am."

"How?" Alexander demanded.

Thor shrugged. "Let's say I've been born again. Hallelujah, praise the Lord, and pass the whiskey."

"She killed you?" Tyler asked.

Thor nodded. "And then I made her a promise." He put a hand in his pocket and pulled out a sheet of paper. "Are you Niko?" he asked, holding the paper out to the blocky, dark-haired man.

Niko took the paper and read it. "Tyler, you're with me. We're going to give Xaphan a break. The rest of you go help the coven with cleanup."

Niko turned and pushed back out, and they fell in behind him. Thor walked next to Alexander.

"Why did she do it?" Alexander asked softly. "I thought she was going to put a bullet in your head."

"Me, too. Turns out she believed me when I told her I didn't want to have to kill her."

"You stalled until we got there?"

Thor nodded. "You were almost too late."

A spasm flickered across Alexander's face. The memory of Thor's hands on Max's throat kept playing in his mind's eye—a few more seconds and she would have been dead. He was appalled at how much the idea of that hurt. "Thank you."

A hard look settled over Thor's face. "Don't. I knew you wouldn't let me live if I killed her. I was ready for that. Selange wasn't going to send me hunting children ever again."

IT WAS CLOSE TO DAWN AND MAX STILL HAD NOT TURNED up. Alexander was getting worried. He had hardly seen her in the last four nights. He had begun to think she was avoiding him, which, if true, offered him some hope that he bothered her as much as she bothered him. Tyler had told him that she had gone for a run in the mountains hours before, and she still wasn't back.

He finished dumping a load of rubble on the heap outside, then stood just inside the entrance of the mountain. The minutes ticked by. He paced back and forth. A bare scrape of sound alerted him, and he turned just as she came around a jut of rock.

She stopped, her brows raised, then walked past him. He swung the door shut and latched it before following. She went twenty feet and stopped. She did not look at him. "Is there something you want?"

So much. He did not say it. "Thank you for Thor."

Her shoulders shifted. "I didn't do it for you. I owed him. And Horngate can use him."

"Yes, it can. But that is not why you did it." He put his hands on her shoulders because he could not resist touching her. He gently turned her around to face him. "You scared years out of me. I thought Xaphan was going to burn you alive. And then to see Thor with his hands on your neck—" He grimaced. "More people than just you owe him for not killing you."

"I'm not sure I did him any big favors."

Alexander frowned, his thumbs rubbing her neck lightly. "You are angry. Why?"

She shook her head. "Not angry. I'm just . . ."

"Just?"

She pulled out of his grasp. "I just need sleep. There's a lot of work to do to rebuild Horngate. And to get ready for this war."

Not until that moment did he realize she was deep into that inner place where he could not follow. He resisted the urge to grab her and shake her out of it. But he could not let her walk away either. He had to hold her there and bring her back out of herself. He ran his tongue over the edge of his teeth. Alexander was struck by the notion that she was fragile. Just like steel, under the right conditions she could shatter.

"You have not eaten in some time. Come join me. You can sleep on a full stomach."

She hesitated, then nodded grudgingly. "I could eat." She narrowed her eyes at him. "But that's all."

"I know. You do not mess with the men of your coven. Unless it is a last request for the condemned prisoner, is that right?"

"You remember that, huh?"

He rubbed his lips with his thumb. "How could I forget?"

"Work on it," she said shortly. "It won't be happening again."

With that she stalked away. Alexander smiled and followed. It would happen again. Sooner or later. He would make sure of it.

24

THOUGH SHE WAS AWARE OF ALEXANDER TRAILING behind her, Max was no longer thinking of him. Her chest ached with a churning mixture of rage, grief, and hatred. She'd spent most of the last four nights scouring what was left of Horngate. There were no trees left for several miles. Nothing green grew, and much of the mountain above had been turned to slag. The greenhouses still stood, but the plants within had died. All that was left of the coven's twenty-two witches were Giselle and Magpie. Max had eight Shadowblades left, counting herself, Thor, and Alexander. Another had died of his injuries since that night. There were seven Sunspears and forty-two humans—the families of the witches who'd died. The shields were down, and Giselle was in no shape to do anything about them. Horngate was pitifully crippled. Having Xaphan and Tutresiel meant that Selange would think twice about attacking right away, but eventually she would come.

Horngate needed to rebuild.

And that meant Max was going to have to do things she'd sworn she would never willingly do. Like find victims for Giselle to turn into Sunspears and Shadowblades. It meant working with Giselle—helping her.

Max didn't notice when Alexander fell behind. She strode through the fortress to Giselle's apartment and thrust through the door without knocking. The gurney had disappeared and the furniture had been situated back in the room. Giselle was swaddled in blankets as she lay on a couch staring up at the ceiling. She was alone.

She sat up as Max barged in. She was barely more than a skeleton wrapped in a skin suit. Her hair was crisp like straw, and her hands shook uncontrollably. She eyed Max with resigned wariness. Max glared back with a spurt of hot anger and began prowling restlessly. She didn't know what she wanted to say. The idea of saying she wanted a truce actually *hurt*, like jagged glass wedged in her chest.

Finally she flung herself into a chair opposite the couch, slouching low. "All right. I'll help."

Giselle didn't need any explanation. She sat up, her eyes widening, her cheeks flushing. With relief? Triumph? Max ground her teeth together.

"You won't fight me anymore?" Giselle's voice quavered, though whether from weakness or from emotion, there was no telling.

Max smiled a cold smile. "It all depends."

"On what? I won't release your bindings. I told you that before."

"I remember, and I'm not asking for that. But if you want my full cooperation, then you don't fuck me over anymore. And I get a say in how things are done. You have to stop keeping secrets, too. I want to know what's going on. If you do that, then you can have me. All of me. Balls to the wall. Take it or leave it."

"I still get the final say on decisions," Giselle warned. "And you have to trust that everything I do is for Horngate."

Max nodded, her lip curling, feeling like she'd been chewing on rancid meat. She always knew that everything the witch did was for Horngate. It wasn't until the last few days that she'd realized she was no different—there wasn't much she wouldn't do to protect the place—her home, her people. That didn't mean she and Giselle were going to start having slumber parties and braiding each other's hair. Abruptly Max stood. "So we're agreed?"

"Yes."

"Fine."

Max turned and started for the door, then stopped. She swung back around.

"For the record, just what did you promise Scooter? He—it—said I was his gift."

"Scooter?" Giselle frowned.

Max sighed gustily. "Your little friend in the basement—the one who's been guarding our back door. Just what is he expecting from me?"

Giselle smiled faintly. "Oh." She shook her head. "I honestly don't know. My visions told me that you were the one he was looking for. I don't know why. But I know we need him here."

Max tipped her head. "For what?"

"I don't know that either. But try not to—" She waved a hand meaningfully.

"What?"

"Piss him off. Send him screaming into another dimension. Just play nice."

Max shook her head. "I just hope his idea of playing doesn't leave me in a coma." She paused. "There's another thing."

"What?" Giselle was wary again.

"My family—I want to bring them here. And everyone else who has family should fetch them, too. Before the Guardians let loose on the world."

For a moment the witch said nothing, then slowly she nodded. "Do it. And, Max, we need to rebuild, and fast. I have some ideas, but you're not going to like them. As soon as I'm on my feet again, we're going to get started."

And just like that everything changed. Enemies were friends, and friends were enemies. Max smiled. It was thin but without hate or bitterness. "I'll be ready."